Praise for Jack Bow...

The Saracen Incident

"The story rips along, the characters are well defined, the technical aspects captivate without overwhelming, and in the background there is a loving view of the Eastern corridor."
—J. Craig Wheeler, Author

"A modern detective story successfully intertwining tech, political ambition and murder."
—Amazon Reader

"Action, meet tech! . . . Bowie blends in rich detail about the book's locations up and down the East Coast and unexpected plot twists to create a book just right for the beach or a long evening in front of the fireplace."
—Amazon Reader

The
LIBERTY
Covenant

An Adam Braxton Thriller

Jack Bowie

To my wife Sharon, and daughters Lisa and Jennifer,
with all my love.

Prologue

HE STOOD TO the side, alone; shivering in the freezing rain and tensing for the next explosion. Each eruption from the seven M15 rifles shook him to his core. The solemn salutes gave him no solace, no sense of closure. They were only a burning reminder of the loss of what was, in fact, a part of him. No other human being had ever been so close; had shared the successes and failures, the secrets and desires.

And *they* had killed him. Had filled his head with their appeals of duty and promises of glory, then sent him into the poisonous desert storm.

Even as his brother had withered away before his eyes they had still denied him. Denied him the comfort of knowing it was not just "in his head"; it was not his fault!

Endless lines of white marble markers stretched in all directions, disappearing into the early morning Potomac fog. Monuments not to the bravery of warriors but to the hubris of politicians and generals. His brother would be lost in a soulless geometric plane of green and white.

He winced as the next salvo echoed over the Virginia hills. Only once more and their feigned remorse would be over. They would go back to their limestone fortresses and their manicured estates, and pretend that everything was the same.

But it would never be the same, and he would make them pay! Only once more.

PART ONE

The Watcher

Chapter 1

IT WAS TENNESSEE and he was Terry.

The ten men knelt in a clearing of the dense Appalachian woods. Wind whistled above their heads, a reverent chorus to their silent prayers. They were in a circle, with hands joined and heads bent; a confusing mix of dirty jeans, stained T-shirts, and well-worn camo fatigues. Each had his revolver of choice holstered on his belt. They already knew their own parts of the mission, there would be no need for further instruction or explanation.

Terry watched the ritual from beside a battered old oak tree, about twenty yards from the group. It would have been inappropriate to join, even though it had been his command that set the night's operation in motion. The temperature had fallen to the forties, still comfortable for physical activity but with just enough bite to keep everyone alert. Moonlight filtered through wispy cirrus clouds; enough light to provide guidance but not identification. God was smiling on them tonight.

He would have to commend Shepard for the use of the circle. For centuries, no millennia, the shape had been a symbol of supernatural power. The Druids had discovered its magic in the forests of primeval Britain and integrated it into their rituals and constructions. Their greatest achievement was Stonehenge, the mystical ring of stones that still rose majestically on the Salisbury Plain. He had once stood there, alone in a biting English winter night, to immerse himself in its strength. What uncountable secrets remained hidden within its circumference?

The shape had subsequently appeared everywhere: King Arthur and his Round Table, Yin and Yang, the Circle of Changes. He had even used it, sparingly of course, in the blistering sands of the Middle East to bind his men to their duty.

What would be his civilization's legacy three millennia hence? Rap music? The liberal rhetoric of equality for misfits and sodomizers? Tonight would mark the beginning of a new course for his country. A return to the values on which their civilization had been based.

After over two minutes of silence, one man broke the chain. Pete Shepard was just past forty, short and stocky, with silver-gray hair shaved close to his scalp. He had lived in this part of Tennessee his whole life. A faded red bandana encircled his neck, and a pearl-handled Colt M1911 hung prominently at his side. Terry couldn't help but smile at the selection of weapon. The old .45 was archaic compared to modern automatics, but its combat mystique alone was enough to command the respect of the gathering. Despite the fact that this particular one was purchased at a derelict pawn shop in Nashville.

Shepard rose to face the group. His voice cut through the cold air.

"We ask you, Lord, to be with us tonight, as we do your work. To protect us, our families, and the Covenant. Amen."

The circle echoed the blessing. Their leader gave a nod and the men disappeared into the night.

"Nicely done," Terry said as he approached Shepard.

"Thanks, Terry. The boys'll get in line when you lay it out square."

"They'll follow through all the way?"

"It was tough. They've got families too. But yes. They will."

"You've always known how to lead, Pete. That's why we came to you."

"I'm mighty proud. You'll tell 'em that?" Terry nodded understandingly. "Don't know what happened with Will. He always was a little slow, but never did nothin' to hurt anyone. I figure his wife put him up to it."

"That's probably it. But he talked to that reporter. Talked about *us*." Terry turned away and looked into the darkness. "You're sure everyone is in there?"

"Yup. Kappy's been watchin' all day. They're all there. You figure we have to do 'em all?"

"You have to send a message, Pete. For all of us. We can't have anyone breaking the Covenant." He put his hand on Shepard's shoulder. "Von Clausewitz said that 'Out of a thousand men who are remarkable, . . . perhaps not one will combine in himself all those qualities which are required to raise a man above mediocrity in the career of a general.' I know how tough it is to be a leader. You can become that general. You know what's at stake."

"Yessir. I do. We been waitin' for this all our lives."

"I know, Pete. We're gonna change this country. Beginning tonight."

A soft tapping broke the stillness of the night and the men's eyes moved down to an invisible log cabin nestled at the edge of the woods. There was nothing to see yet, just the sound of wooden wedges being driven into jambs.

"Have you started on those plans yet?" Terry asked.

"Yup. Got the boys goin' on 'em yesterday. We should have the molds in a week or so. What do ya want with those things, Terry?"

"That's great, Pete. Really great."

At first it was just small bursts of light, like window candles welcoming a tired traveler. The traitor had built the home himself. It had taken him three years to construct it for his family. The inferno reduced it to ashes in less than three hours.

The screams from inside had only lasted a few minutes.

* * *

Back in his motel room, Terry hunched over the small Formica-topped desk and slowly pecked the message into his cell phone. His joints ached from standing in the cold, damp evening, but he shrugged the pain away. His employer demanded prompt updates.

When he punched "Send," the custom iPhone app encrypted the message with AES and sent it into the Cloud.

The Advanced Encryption Standard was the latest cryptographic magic used to keep Uncle Sam's top secret messages safe. Ironic that the Commander was using the same technology to protect his own communications.

Sanction completed. Tennessee is secure.

ALPHA teams in place. Coordinated action possible.

Operation HALFTIME initiated.

Chapter 2

THE AFTERNOON SUN was slowly disappearing over Providence Ridge filling the Georgia sky with broad brush strokes of sparkling crimson. FBI Special Agent Charlie Thomas squinted in the light, then collapsed his secure cell phone and settled back into the makeshift blind he had constructed in a depression on the hillside. He grimaced as another scrub pine needle jabbed into his backside. The damn needles had left permanent puncture marks in the most uncomfortable of places. It would make for interesting discussions with Laurie if he ever got back home.

When were they going to let him off this goddamned mountain with its prickly pears, voracious fire ants, and carnivorous flies, to do some real investigation work?

It seemed like all he had done on this assignment was wait. He had spent the last week camped on the side of the ridge, watching the activities in the valley below. The object of his attention was a nondescript Georgia farm, which, according to one of the Bureau's informants, had become a center of local militia activity.

Thomas's initial research had been intriguing. Halfway between Atlanta and Columbus, the property was convenient to both cities, yet remote enough to assure privacy. Four hundred acres of pristine Georgia farmland, about half cleared, the other half in heavy pine woods. Seemingly perfect for farming, yet apparently unused for years. And its ownership was a lawyer's delight, a nexus of interlocking corporations that, so far, even the Bureau's investigators couldn't untangle. These results had prompted his supervisors to give him the go-ahead for the next stage—surveillance. Unfortunately, in the Georgia countryside, you couldn't very well just sit in an air-conditioned rental and take pretty pictures.

So here he was, legs aching from fatigue, sitting on the hillside, huddled under camouflage netting and broken branches, taking his notes. He had cataloged visitors to the farm—there didn't seem to be any permanent residents—and mapped the movement of people and materiel among the old farm structures. There was no question the informant had been correct: there was a local militia cell using the property as a base of operations. He had watched as lines of pickup trucks brought fatigue-dressed males to late night meetings and crack-of-dawn exercises.

Binoculars in one hand, pen in the other, he had recorded the movements of people he knew only by their physical appearance: Gimpy, an old veteran with a bad right leg, Beau Brummel, with a swagger and perpetually ironed fatigues, Baldy, whose head reflected the sun like a mirror, and Walrus, the overweight apparent leader of the group. They had become his distant friends, these faceless creatures: his only contact with the rest of the world.

He prayed for the call that would let him escape from his woodsy prison, meet his adversaries face-to-face and find out what was really going on. Before the goddamn chiggers ate him alive.

*   *   *

"How was your weekend, Mr. President?"

Joseph Matthews looked up from the State Department's latest Mid-East advisory and saw Chad Dawson, his Chief of Staff, taking his seat in one of the Oval Office's plush, easy chairs. Dawson had requested the late afternoon meeting only a few hours before.

"Excellent, Chad. Excellent." Matthews closed the files, rose from his desk, and walked toward the sitting area. "Having the kids come down from school was wonderful, but they drove Margaret and me crazy. Maybe being President of the United States isn't the toughest job in the world."

Dawson began to respond but Matthews raised his hand as he sat across from his Chief of Staff. "Let's hold off for a minute. I've asked Steven to join us. I'd like to get his opinion on the results. I trust that isn't a problem?"

"Uh, of course not, Mr. President," Dawson replied flatly. "I have an extra copy of the report here."

Matthews smiled at his aide's obvious discomfort. Dawson was the ultimate facilitator and detail man. He had no time for the brusque, sweeping pronouncements of General Steven Carlson, the Director of National Intelligence. Still, the conversation affected them both. They could manage to put up with each other for a few minutes.

Carlson appeared at the famous "invisible door" and marched into the room. His uniform had changed from dress blues to custom-made silk suits, but the ex-Marine looked just as prepared for battle as he had been at the height of his military career.

Matthews had known Carlson since their days at Annapolis. They had both come from Mountain states and found they shared many of the same goals and values. They had toughed-out plebe initiation by drawing strength from each other, then sailed through the next three years finishing first and second in their class—Carlson had gotten the final nod based on his unequaled physical prowess.

After their initial tours, Matthews had jumped and returned to the family ranch in Wyoming where he executed well-funded campaigns for State Rep, then Governor. The clear-speaking, good-looking veteran then attracted the attention of the Republican National Committee and continued his ascension first to the Senate and now the Presidency.

Carlson had stayed in the Marines, advancing to a four-star, before retiring to a comfortable position at a Fairfax beltway bandit—at least until his newly-elected friend had nominated him for Director of National Intelligence.

Over the years, they had shared their lives: loves gained and lost, enemies engaged and vanquished, positions offered and accepted. Matthews relied on Carlson's counsel for nearly everything. The Marine was his sounding board, his advisor, and his confessor. But most importantly, he was the monitor of Matthew's political health.

The DNI strode across the tufted Presidential Seal to the sitting area. Even at sixty, he looked like he could play tight end for the Redskins. His five foot ten inch frame was straight as a spear, his gray hair still military-short, and his neck and shoulders thick with muscle. His face was as craggy as the Rockies, and the jagged scar along his jawline only gave it that much more character. He had gained a bit of girth, but Carlson still pitied any man that got in the General's way.

"Good afternoon, Mr. President," Carlson said cheerfully, pulling over another of the chairs. "You too, Chad."

"Good afternoon, General," Dawson replied without looking up from his papers. "Here are the results from J.T.'s latest poll. He just sent them over." Dawson handed a folder to Matthews, then one to Carlson.

Matthews thumbed through the results. J.T. Wells was the administration's political analyst. In reality, their head pollster. Matthews' existence was dictated by polls: What did the populace think about his legislative agenda? About his trip to Mexico? What he had for dinner? It was a never-ending game of chasing their own tails.

And now it would get even worse. Just two weeks ago, at a noisy, obscenely-expensive New York City national convention, he had been named as the party's candidate for the upcoming election. The selection had been a foregone conclusion, so he had been spared the pain of primary battles, but now the cold, hard political winter would start. Ironically just as D.C.'s sultry August rolled in.

God, he hated the battles that he knew were ahead. The negative publicity, the begging for more and more money, the backroom deals and equivocations. Three and a half years of debilitating work reduced to three months of sound bites, sore hands and empty smiles. But he had no choice, there was still so much he needed to do. And he knew *he* was the one to do it.

The two men before him were here to make sure it happened that way.

"Mr. President," Dawson began once Matthews' eyes had lifted from the papers, "These results show you are in a very strong position entering the general election. Approval ratings on trade and the global environment are all well over seventy-five percent. The public is pleased with your handling of the Turkey intrusion and foreign terrorism concerns have abated." He paused and managed a nod to the DNI. "Fiscally, as long as Jamison keeps the Fed in line, we should have no problem in this area as well. Finally, the signing of the intelligence exchange agreement with NATO in a few weeks will be an outstanding PR event. All in all, a very rosy report."

Dawson stopped and all eyes turned to Matthews. It sounded like an enviable position, but Matthews hadn't gotten to the Oval Office by believing everything his staff told him.

"Thank you, Chad. That does sound quite positive. Steven, any comments?"

"Actually, yes, Mr. President," Carlson replied, stretching even taller in the sofa. "Chad has summarized the positive findings very well. But I believe there must be some negatives. Politics are never this rosy. Is there a 'however' we should be aware of, Chad?"

"Chad, is there more?" Matthews asked.

Heads now turned to the Chief of Staff.

"Yes, Mr. President," Dawson answered. "There is one area that requires some attention. I believe it has ramifications for the re-election campaign. The polls suggest you are vulnerable on domestic policy."

"How can that be?" Matthews responded. "We've nearly balanced the budget and still kept taxes flat."

"Ah, that's *fiscal* policy, Mr. President." Dawson's voice exhibited a well-developed deference. "It's the quality of life that seems to be the problem. With the threat of foreign terrorism reduced, the population begins to worry about more mundane issues like employment and public safety. Your continuing education plan was soundly defeated in the House, the crime rate has started up again, and Henneberry is crowing about the drug problem. These are not positive trends."

Senator Mitchell Henneberry was a decorated veteran and Chairman of the Senate Judiciary Committee. He had been a constant thorn in the side of the Republicans ever since the Democrats regained majority in the senior chamber.

"It seems to me that Morgan has been handling things quite well," Matthews said.

"Mr. President," Carlson interrupted, ignoring Dawson and turning to Matthews. "As much as I respect the man's experience and contributions, A.G. Kahler is a wet fish. He has the charisma of a telephone pole. The American people want a dynamic, energetic individual as the nation's top cop. Someone who represents our best and brightest."

"That's not a particularly positive phrase, do you think?" Dawson asked. "It didn't work very well for McNamara."

"Thank you for the history lesson, Chad." Carlson scowled at the Chief of Staff. Bulging veins and tendons strained against his starched collar. He turned his attention back to Matthews.

"Nonetheless, Mr. President, the latest results show a significantly lower acceptability rating on the domestic side. Approval in our target constituencies has dropped ten points since the last poll. Fifteen points in the conservative Democrats. This could become a rallying point. There's no question Henneberry could very effectively stake out this territory."

Dawson rapidly shuffled through the pollster's report. "General, where did you get those figures? They're not here."

"Oh, sorry," Carlson replied. "J.T. faxed me a copy earlier this morning. I reviewed the details with him an hour ago."

Matthews let the animosity cool before responding. "Even if I accept your premise, Steven, what would you have us do? I will not replace Morgan."

"Of course not, Mr. President. That would be a definite sign of weakness. I am only suggesting that we incorporate these findings into the campaign strategy for the next three months. Wherever possible, we should look to minimize any negative domestic publicity and highlight foreign policy successes. And make sure we place our best people on any issues when they arise."

"That is an excellent suggestion, General," the Chief of Staff replied. The edge on his voice was unmistakable. "We will make every effort to see that we don't put stupid people in prominent positions." He turned back to his boss. "But really, Mr. President, we *should* thank J.T. for the poll. Your domestic approval is nearly fifty percent. Combined you have an unbeatable position. Your record is exceptional and the people realize it. I don't think we need to go around worrying that the sky is falling."

Matthews waited for Carlson's retort, but the DNI refused to take the bait.

"Thank J.T. for a very thorough analysis," Matthews finally said to Dawson. "I'll review the results in detail tonight. I don't think any immediate changes in policy are called for. Let's talk again in a few days."

"Yes, Mr. President," Dawson said with a nod. "We really must prepare for the Congressional Caucus meeting now."

"I'll leave you two for that," Carlson said, abruptly rising from his chair. "I've got to get ready for tonight's call with the Australian security Ministers. Thank you for the review, Chad. Mr. President."

Matthews watched as his friend headed back over the Seal. When he had first taken office, Matthews had carefully stepped around that circular section of carpet. He had felt guilty putting a foot on it. Now, he and his staff trod across it regularly, just as thousands of others routinely trampled across all the other trappings of his office. It was metaphor he tried not to dwell upon.

Carlson was a man that commanded attention, from friends and foes alike. His thoughts on defensive responses might be very enlightening. "Oh, Steven?" Matthews called.

Carlson spun back to face the voice. "Yes, Mr. President?"

"If you have any specific suggestions in these domestic areas, I'd be very interested in reviewing them with you."

"Certainly, sir. Thank you."

Carlson disappeared through the door and Matthews waited for the inevitable analysis.

"I'm sorry, sir," Dawson began as Matthews knew he would, "I know General Carlson is your friend, but sometimes he just gives me the creeps. I never know if he means what he's saying."

Matthews had to tread carefully. His friendship with Carlson was well-known and had compromised his relationship with other members of his staff on more than one occasion. It was a difficult line to walk but one he would not sidestep.

"You're not alone there, Chad. However, Steven is a valuable resource for all of us. I value his counsel."

"Yes, sir. I know. But he's so . . . well, *private*. I never see him relax. Does he have any family?"

"No one close. He never married. His first family was the military. Now I think he's adopted us."

"Do you really trust him? Some of the things he says, . . . well they don't sound like he's your ideological soul-mate."

Matthews couldn't hold back the grin. His Chief of Staff didn't miss a thing. "He is a self-possessed professional, Chad. Just like the rest of us. Do I agree with everything he says? No. Do I respect his opinions and ideas? Absolutely. Sometimes I need someone who can say things that I can't. Think of Steven as our lightning rod. Just be careful you don't get too close.

"Look at it this way, would you rather have him working for the opposition?"

"I don't know, Mr. President. Can we be sure he isn't?"

Chapter 3

IT WAS GEORGIA, and Gary leaned into the corner of the room, disappearing behind the shadows. It was time to see whether this cell was up to its task.

"Not a bad place, Macon, but you gotta get some better beer. I can barely drink this shit." A tall, lanky man dressed in a flannel shirt and jeans popped the top of a beer can, leaned back in his chair and dropped his feet, clad in a pair of ornately carved leather cowboy boots, onto the table. Mud fell from the boots and piled on the oak tabletop like tiny anthills.

"Well it sure hasn't stopped you from swillin' it, Tommy," said a heavy, gray-haired man. "And Jesus, keep your goddamn feet off the table."

Macon Holly swiped at the boots with a huge hand and knocked them to the floor. Tommy Wicks had to grab at the table to keep from falling over.

Gary shared Holly's opinion of the redneck. Wicks was a real pain-in-the-ass. It had been hard enough to convince Holly to take over as leader of the cell without Wick's taunting him at every turn. If they didn't need the supplies from Wick's father's store so badly, Gary would have thrown him out.

"Did you talk to Bobby Joe?" Holly asked Wicks.

"Yup," replied Wicks. "The old man ain't ready to join up yet, too scared of the Patrol, but he said we could use his access."

"He'll come around," Holly said. "He's under a lot of pressure on that loan for his farm. Pretty soon he'll figure out that those kike bankers ain't no friends."

Tonight, Holly had called his "staff" to a meeting in their new command center, a recently renovated farmhouse. The house's great room was the only location where they could gather comfortably. The conspirators sat around a rough-hewn trestle table in front of a huge stone fireplace. Light from a roaring fire cast their faces in alternating ruddy glow and ominous darkness. Shadows played on the ceiling, cast from the antlers of a majestic twelve-point buck leaping through the rock above the fireplace's mantle. The room reeked of sweat and fertilizer. It was the second home for men that worked for a living.

"Sure was nice of them to give us the farm, Macon," said a scrawny man at the end of the table. Cal Napes raised his beer in a mock salute and exposed a mouthful of black, rotting teeth.

"They did not *give* us this spread, Cal. I told you before, we're just the caretakers. But we're damn lucky to have a place like this, 'stead of traipsin' all over the county for a place to meet in private. We got a nice piece of land with barns, sheds and this farmhouse. All for the Covenant. But if we don't take care of it," he glared at Wicks, "they'll take it away and give it to somebody else."

"Except there ain't nobody else to give it to, Macon," responded Wicks. "We're the only cell of the Citizens for Liberty in this part of Georgia. So quit with your whining and let's get down to business." He turned to his right. "Sean, I heard the shipment came in. When can we get some of your new toys?"

Sean O'Grady was a ruddy-faced Irishman who ran the local hardware store. Middle age had grayed a head covered with curly red locks, but it had not dampened his enthusiasm for the hunt. During the day he sharpened knives, cut keys, and dispensed general wisdom to his customers. At night he focused on a more serious avocation.

"Two boxes arrived today," Grady replied. "Goddamn Uzis. Don't know how the hell he got 'em." He almost turned around to look at Gary, but a glare from Holly held him back. "They look brand new. It'll take a day or so to check 'em out, but they'll be ready. Just gotta do a little . . ."

"Good," Holly interrupted. "We need all of 'em for the Gathering. But everybody here's gotta be trained on 'em by next week."

"Why the rush, Macon?" Napes asked.

"Cause we need to!" Holly yelled. "You got something better to do?"

"Shit, Macon," Napes replied. "Take it easy. I'll be here. What's with you?"

"Just trying to look good for the visitor," Wicks said in Napes' direction. "But Macon knows he can count on us, right Macon?"

"Sure, Tommy. Sure. I always know where you stand." Holly held his gaze at Wicks, then looked back to the group. "One last thing. With the Gathering comin' and all, there'll be a lot of folks from other cells spending some time with us. Get 'em what they want but stay out of their way. We got the best damn camp in Georgia and we're gonna share it with 'em." Holly turned to Napes. "Cal, you're head of security. Your job is to make sure there ain't no Feds hanging around."

"No problem, Macon. I can smell a cop a mile away."

And they can certainly smell you too, Gary thought. He made a mental note to double-check Napes' preparations.

"We need more than that, Cal," Holly countered. "We gotta make sure everyone is who they say they are. We can't have any FBI or ATF boys sneaking in. We're part of something bigger now and we've got to be careful."

"Whadda I got to do?"

Holly shook his head. Gary could see the frustration in his eyes. Would this group really be able to execute their plans?

"You talk to everyone that comes in," Holly explained. "Ask who sent them; what cell they're with. And who's their captain. Then check out what they tell you."

"How am I supposed to know all that?"

"I'll get you the names. All you'll have to do is look them up. If anyone doesn't check out, you tell me. We'll take care of it from there."

Napes stared at the ceiling as if it offered divine guidance to Holly's instructions. "Okay, Macon," he finally replied. "I guess I can do that. But things sure are getting complicated."

"That's what happens when you start working together, Cal. But now we're really gonna start changing things."

"You sure got everything worked out, Macon," Wicks said with a sneer. "But with all this *sharing* going on, are we gonna have the supplies? What about ammo? We got enough, Sean?"

"The damn Uzis can burn six hundred rounds a minute," O'Grady replied. "We'll need at least ten more crates for all this training."

"Sounds like a hole in the master plan, Macon," Wicks offered.

"I'll get the ammo, Sean," Holly snapped back. "But lock up half of the boxes. These trigger-happy boys'll burn through our whole stash if we let 'em. That should leave enough for the training."

Holly walked across the room and stood over Wicks. "Good enough for you, Tommy?"

Wicks bobbed his head.

Holly turned back to O'Grady. "Oh, Sean. Make sure Ricky gets enough time on the range. He's a part of the team too."

"Sure Macon. You got it," O'Grady replied.

"Where *is* Ricky?" asked Napes.

"Back at his place," replied Wicks. "Tryin' to make sure that new monkey bartender doesn't steal the night's take. You'd think he'd learn."

"Alright, that's enough," Holly said. "You got a problem with Ricky, you take it up with him. For now, get the hell outta here, all of you. I've got other things to do tonight."

As they got up from the table, Wicks whispered in an overly-loud voice, "Time to suck up to the boss, eh, Macon?"

Wicks turned and Holly returned his icy stare. Gary just shook his head. One day that asshole was going to open his mouth once too often.

The rest of the cell gathered up their belongings and slowly filed out of the room, passing within a few feet of Gary's position in the corner. No one would speak to him, of course. It was well known that the Commander's representatives were off limits to all but the cell's leader.

Gary heard the truck engines start, their rusty mufflers sending out noisy spits and growls, then fade into the distance. After five minutes they were gone; only the sounds of tree frogs and crickets breaking the pastoral quiet of the Georgia evening.

He finally stepped from the shadows in the back of the room and slowly walked toward the table. Holly's fatigues were drenched in sweat despite the cool evening, and they clung like wet towels from his shoulders.

"Sit down, Macon," he said. "The meeting went well."

Holly grabbed one of the chairs and squatted down.

"Yeah. Thanks, Gary. The mission'll come off real good. You'll see."

"I'm sure it will. You're doing a great job, Macon. Everyone knows that."

"What happens next, Gary? I mean after Alpha?"

"What comes after Alpha, Macon?"

"After Alpha? I guess Bravo. Then Charlie, and Delta, and . . ."

Gary held up his hand and Holly stopped the recitation. "Now you understand the plan, Macon. That's all there is to it. With each mission more patriots will join the Covenant; and we'll grow stronger with each one.

"But you're the key, Macon. Right here in Tyler. No one is as important as you."

But you have no idea why.

Chapter 4

National Security Agency, Fort Meade, Maryland
Monday, 8:30 a.m.

GARRETT ROBINSON SAT patiently in his chair waiting for the knock on his door. It wasn't that he didn't have enough to do; he was managing seven different projects, any of which could dissolve into worthlessness at a moment's notice. It was his job to keep the teams of prima-donnas focused on their targets and out of cerebral cesspools.

The National Security Agency arguably employed the most brilliant team of mathematicians on the planet since Bletchley Park. The Puzzle Palace, as it was affectionately known, was the United States center for SIGINT: Signals Intelligence. Whether information flowed through the air, along a metal wire, or in a glass fiber, the NSA's job was to capture it, classify it and turn it into intelligence on behalf of America's citizens. And to see that the messages of those same citizens were protected from the eyes and ears of other, less friendly, elements.

They were in a never-ending game of cat-and-mouse with similar groups all over the world; some organized around traditional national boundaries, some not.

Within an organization of over forty-thousand employees, of course, specialization was required. The actual structure of the Agency was fluid and designed for obfuscation, but Robinson led a special projects group focused on cryptanalysis: the decoding of secure messages. Other groups worked the opposite side of the coin: cryptology, the creation of code and ciphers to encode messages. Power ebbed and flowed. For a few years the cryptologists would have the edge with an "unbreakable" code. Then there would be a breakthrough, the code would be broken, and the cryptanalysts would have their day. So it went, back and forth. It had been this way for millennia. What had Robinson on edge was that his most brilliant employee felt the need for a face-to-face meeting. Kam Yang was a Chinese-born, American-bred and American-educated cryptanalyst. To many, Robinson included, Yang was the brightest star in the Agency's crypto-constellation. But he was a singularly private individual. He worked alone, communicated primarily by secure email, and never participated in the "my IQ is bigger than your IQ" arguments of his colleagues in the cafeteria.

Yang had recently made a discovery, worthy of notice by the Director, that promised the latest breakthrough to the cryptanalysts. He had found a computational solution to the nation's most advanced cypher: the Advanced Encryption Standard, or AES. At least theoretically. Even Robinson had been bewildered by the mathematics in Yang's preliminary paper.

Robinson had charged him with sampling some of the Agency's "cold stack": the backlog of daily messages that they couldn't decrypt by known methods. This would be the test of his theory.

Was the meeting request to report a success? Or a failure?

A sharp rap at his door broke his reverie.

"Come in." he called.

Yang entered the office, a stack of manila folders under his arm. He was five foot eight, slim with short black hair and hazel eyes that burned with a dark fire. He wore standard NSA summer attire, freshly-pressed chinos and a blue oxford shirt. Just under thirty, Garret gauged he still had another decade of mathematical brilliance remaining.

"Now still okay, Garrett?" Yang asked without a trace of accent.

"Certainly, Kam." Robinson motioned to a chair next to his desk. "What is it?"

Yang sat down and handled a file across the desk. "I was going through the backlog and was able to complete a decoding. I thought you would want to see it right away."

Robinson hesitated. "Is it commercial?" he asked. Agency policy required that any intercepted commercial messages be immediately logged and archived. Access was extremely limited to avoid any insider trading scandals. It wouldn't do to have too many millionaires popping up at the NSA.

"No, sir."

"Okay, let's take a look." Robinson reached for the file and brought it down to his lap. As his eyes scanned the purloined transmission his expression never changed but he began to rock slowly forward and back in his chair. Yang had done it.

"Interesting. Is there anything more?"

"Not yet, but I've put the routings on the priority list. I'll get anything else that takes the same path."

"Good. Start a file. Call it," he glanced down at the page, "QUARTERBACK. Eyes only. Let's see what shows up next."

"Yes, sir." Yang rose and headed toward the door.

"And Kam . . ."

"Yes?" he turned back.

"Congratulations. I'll let the Director know of your success."

"Thank you, Garrett."

Robinson watched as Yang closed the door behind him. He was caught. This was a major breakthrough. It needed to be reported. But to who?

* * *

Roger Slattery fidgeted uncomfortably in the back of the assault-proof Escalade wondering where he was about to be taken next. His boss, the Deputy Director for Intelligence at the CIA, had called an hour earlier and requested his presence in the parking garage "for a meeting." It hadn't been that unusual, he had had any number of similar requests in his past, but he doubted this time he was about to be whisked off to some godforsaken place on the other side of the planet to save the free world. Been there, done that, and his advanced age made such a request quite unlikely.

More probable was that his boss had gotten entangled in yet another political tar-pit and was looking for some off-the-book suggestions on saving his hide. Slattery had known the man for over twenty years and every request from the DDI had caused some upheaval in Slattery's life. At least it was now not likely to involve implements of physical torture.

The passenger door opened and Peter Markovsky slid in. As soon as the door closed, the driver—Slattery only knew him as Glen—started them out of the underground garage. Markovsky was a small, owlish man, with short white hair and penetrating eyes hidden behind a pair of thick wire-rimmed eyeglasses. He was career-CIA, having seen extensive field duty in Europe and the Middle East. In addition to being a recognized expert in expressionist art, he was one of the most cold-blooded agents in the history of the Agency.

"Sorry to be late, Roger," he began with a friendly tone that made Slattery even more uncomfortable. "Had a call with the Director that went long."

"No problem, Peter. Where are we going?"

Markovsky smiled like a cat eyeing a canary. "Come on, Roger. Can't we just go for a pleasant ride in the countryside?"

The car emerged from the garage into a torrential Washington rainstorm. The wipers were barely able to clear the sheets of water from the windshield.

Slattery stared out the side window at the deluge then turned back to his boss with a frown.

"Okay, so it isn't a pleasure trip," Markovsky conceded. "We've been summoned to the NCTC by Carlson."

The National Counterterrorism Center, or the NCTC, as it was commonly-known, was a pristine new addition to the country's visible commitment in the fight against terrorism. Located in McLean, Virginia, it was just a few minutes ride from Langley. NCTC employees, under the guidance of the Director of National Intelligence and including members of the constituent intelligence organizations, planned, gathered, analyzed, and reported on information related to terrorist activities.

"A new threat?" Slattery asked.

Markovsky shook his head. "Not that I know of. The DNI called this morning and asked that I bring my best counter-terrorism expert to today's meeting. You drew the short straw. I need to give you some background on this one, however. It gets a bit touchy."

Slattery shuddered. This sounded like a *deep* tar-pit.

"Steven Carlson had all the right credentials," Markovsky explained, "Marine General, operational responsibility for Middle East counter-terrorism and a stint as Director of the Defense Intelligence Agency. And after he was approved as DNI, he did all the expected things: he formed committees, commissioned analyses, and generated reports. All with the anticipated results—nothing changed."

Slattery remembered when George W. Bush signed the bill creating the Director of National Intelligence position in 2004. The 9/11 Commission had described the suspicion, distrust, and even animosity among the members of the US intelligence community. It had been a complex, overburdened amalgamation of sixteen primary agencies and a varying number of other civilian and military groups. The DNI position, and NCTC, were created to eliminate the duplication and competition, and to provide a single source of validated, integrated information on America's enemies.

At least that was the theory. The problem was that no one could organize away decades of deeply-ingrained behaviors. The spooks only talked to other spooks, the military only to other soldiers, and no one talked to Justice.

It was stupid. Slattery knew that our enemies talked to each other more than we did. But at least as far as he was concerned, the vote was still out as to whether Carlson could change any of it.

"After a couple of years of frustration," Markovsky continued, "his covert training apparently took over—he went black. He formed a small group of trusted representatives from across the community to help him direct the intelligence effort. He calls us his 'advisory group.' We're off the record and have no operational responsibilities. That's still the purview of the individual agencies."

"Does it work?" Slattery asked with only a bit of trepidation.

Markovsky stared into his lap then turned back to Slattery. "I'll let you decide. I think we're here."

Ten minutes later, Markovsky and Slattery were settled in one of the innumerable Sensitive Compartmented Information Facilities, or SCIFs, in the NCTC. It had been six months since Slattery had last visited the building. He could have been in this SCIF or any other. They were all the same: stale, recirculated air, bland, yellow walls, and the requisite pictures of the reigning President and DNI. Just the place for Carlson to hold court.

Markovsky was seated in an upholstered leather chair near the end of the long conference table while Slattery fidgeted in a hard plastic seat against the wall behind him.

The DDI stuck his head into a pile of papers he pulled from his briefcase, leaving Slattery to watch the posturing and strutting of the attendees. There were only six chairs at the table. He recognized the three that were occupied. In addition to Markovsky, there was

Jerome Garcia from Homeland Security, David Scott from the State Department and Admiral Georges Delacroix from the J3 Operations Directorate of the Joint Chief's office. Delacroix was a huge Louisiana Creole who towered over the other attendees, even seated. Markovsky said he spoke for all the intelligence groups of the military including the DIA.

So far, Slattery had to give Carlson the benefit of the doubt—he had picked an excellent team. His selections were not the agency directors: those figureheads cared more about their appointments and the political climate than substantive issues. They avoided taking sides and making real commitments. These were the rogues, the outspoken employees that knew their agencies' strengths and weaknesses; knew how to work the system to their advantage, and knew that the only thing that counts is results.

Claude Stroller, Markovsky's counterpart from the National Security Agency arrived, and took a seat next to Slattery's boss. He whispered something in Markovsky's ear, then turned back to speak with an associate sitting behind him. They had a short exchange, Slattery couldn't catch any of it, and Stroller returned to his own paper work.

General Steven Carlson marched in next, trailed by a single staffer, not the brood of gofers that normally accompanied him. The DNI looked older than Slattery had remembered. How long ago had it been since he had visited Langley? He still had the ramrod carriage of a Marine drill sergeant, but bags of skin hung limply under his eyes, and his skin showed a yellow pallor; too many days protecting the nation's secrets.

Carlson scanned the room, stopping at the remaining empty chair at the table.

"We'll wait until our final representative arrives," the DNI announced, showing only a slight irritation at the delay.

As they waited, Slattery returned to the unfamiliar man sitting behind Stroller. He was dressed casually: blue blazer, khaki pants, starched oxford shirt and a striped rep tie. A look out of place in the sea of dark pin-stripes. As if he sensed the attention, the man turned toward the CIA agent. He gave a quick look, then went immediately back to his papers. Apparently Slattery wasn't important enough to warrant continued attention.

All heads turned at the sound of the electronic latch and the last member of the advisory group entered.

Slattery couldn't help but join the rest of the attendees as they stared at the figure striding toward the table. Mary Ellen Flynn, Special Assistant to the Director, Federal Bureau of Investigation, was built like an Olympic swimmer. Five feet ten, with broad shoulders and narrow hips, she was a poster-child for FBI recruitment. Her fiery red hair was pulled back from her face and tied in a neat bun; a concession to the conservative nature of her colleagues. Dressed in a trim light-blue double-breasted suit, cut to highlight her tiny waist, and tight-necked white silk blouse, she walked confidently into the room, completely aware that all the other eyes were focused on her entrance.

Flynn's specialty was counterterrorism and she had been on assignment to the FBI's Counterterrorism Division since Slattery had met her three years ago. She took her seat and spoke directly to Carlson.

"I'm sorry for being late, General. I wanted to get the latest status from our agents in the field."

"That's perfectly alright, Mary Ellen," Carlson replied. "We had just gotten settled ourselves." Carlson adjusted the papers on the table in front of him and took a deep breath.

"Before I begin, I wanted to explain the new participants in the room today. You all know that there is an election coming up and the potential for significant changes in this group's membership as a result. I have asked each of you to bring a trusted associate as a first step in mediating any succession disruptions.

"I will not bother with introductions for the sake of time. Given your chosen professions, I'm sure you will remedy this omission expeditiously.

"Admiral Delacroix, if you could summarize the Joint Chief's recent report on chemical warfare threats?"

Chapter 5

Tyler, Georgia
Monday, 11:30 a.m.

HOLLY PULLED HIS Ford pickup into the graveled parking area and collapsed across the steering wheel. Things were moving too fast. He had always felt he could hold the pieces of his life together: his family, the store, and his commitments to his friends. But the last three months had pushed him to the edge of collapse.

First his family, then his business went to hell-in-a-handbasket. Then all the shit with Charlie and Gary. When would it end?

He needed something to eat. Maybe a sandwich and beer would help his mood.

Holly walked out of the blinding Georgia sunlight and into the cave-like darkness of Ricky's, a crumbling brick and stucco greasy spoon three miles outside of Tyler. The familiar smells of frying oil and tobacco smoke immediately calmed him. His eyes hadn't yet accustomed to the dim fluorescent illumination, but he navigated automatically across the beer-soaked sawdust floor to a barstool, oblivious of the other patrons. It was his first mistake of the day.

"Well, if it's not the local revolutionary," came a voice next to him.

Holly turned and saw to his disgust that the voice came from George Brown: owner, editor, and chief reporter of the town's only newspaper. Brown was a transplanted Yankee who, Holly was convinced, had come to Tyler simply to make everyone's life miserable.

"Why don't you just shut the hell up, George?"

"Jesus, Macon. Having a bad day already? You must have been up all night plotting the destruction of the IRS."

"Hey!" A short, bald gnome popped up from under the bar. Ricky Dalton's head had been hairless for as long as Holly could remember. And that was a helluva long time.

"You two cut the shit," Dalton continued. "It's too early in the day." Brown nodded and went back to his lunch plate. "What'll it be, Macon?"

"Gimme a barbecue and a draft, Ricky."

"Comin' up." Dalton grabbed a mug from the drain pad, filled it with an unlabeled amber fluid, and slid it down the bar to his friend. He then disappeared through a door behind the bar marked "Employee's Only."

Holly raised the glass, emptied it in a single swallow, and slid the mug back down the bar. Dalton would get the hint.

Holly had just started to relax when his barmate tossed another grenade.

"Saw Charlie last week."

Holly spun on the stool toward the reporter. "Charlie? What the hell are you doing talking to him?" Charlie Kearns had been Holly's predecessor as the head of Citizens for Liberty.

"I thought I might do a story on the wages of crime. I went down to Jesup to talk to him."

"I'm surprised he talked to you. After the way you reported the trial."

"He doesn't have anybody *else* to talk to. He said he hadn't seen you in over a year."

Brown was right. Holly hadn't visited his ex-best friend since just after the sentencing. He wanted to remember Kearns as the vital, bull of a man he was before they broke him. What was he going to say anyway?

"And I just reported what I heard, Macon," Brown continued. "It wasn't that complicated."

"You heard what you wanted to hear, you bastard. Charlie never meant to do nobody no harm. Those ATF bastards broke into his place, trashed it, then arrested him for possession of explosives. For a couple of stupid sticks of dynamite. He'd been cleaning his fields that way for years. Never did try him for that though. Did they?"

"No. He just tried to kill some cops. Guess that's not important."

Holly slammed both fists on the bar top. "Jesus, George. After the Feds confiscated all his savings he couldn't pay his mortgage. Then the damn city bankers came to steal his land. He told 'em to stuff their goddamn papers. So they came back with the Patrol and Charlie tried to scare 'em off. That's all he did, just try to scare 'em off."

"You gotta obey the law, Macon. You can't go shooting at people just 'cause you don't like what they're doing."

"You can if what they're doin' ain't right. You've got a right to protect yourself. That's what the Constitution says, George. You ought to read it sometime."

"I've read it, Macon. And you're way off base. You're living in the past. You and all your crazy friends. The sooner you realize it, the better off we'll all be."

"One of these days somebody'll come after you, newspaper man." He poked his finger at Brown's face. "Then you'll think different."

Holly turned and saw Dalton reappear from the kitchen with his sandwich. There was no way he was going to put up with anymore of this crap.

"Wrap that up for me, Ricky," he yelled. "I'm leaving. The air in here's making me sick."

* * *

"What was all that about?" asked a man sitting next to Brown.

"That, Mr. Luckett, was Holly Macon, keeper of the flame of liberty and head redneck of Tyler, Georgia."

"Oh. Your favorite foil. You've done quite a few pieces on him as I remember. I'm surprised he didn't rip your face off."

Brown shook his head. "I'm not. Actually Macon's not all that bad. He might be a decent guy if he wasn't mixed up with all this militia shit. And he's got bigger problems than me to deal with lately."

Brown took another bite of his Ricky's Special, southern spit-grilled pork barbecue with the hottest sauce Brown had ever tasted. It was probably just as well the sauce was so pungent, the meat would have been inedible without it. He looked over at his friend's order and noticed the sandwich was barely half eaten. It floated in a pool of dark orange grease on the paper plate.

"What's the matter, Taylor? Not hungry?"

"It's a little too, eh, spicy for me, George."

"Bullshit. You're just getting soft up there in the big city." Brown chugged the remaining half of his beer and slammed the glass mug on the bar. "Another round for me and my friend, Ricky," he called.

"Not for me," Luckett replied waving his hand over the draft. "It's a little early in the day."

"Jesus," Brown muttered, "you used to be a real reporter. Must be getting soft hanging around with all those politicians."

"Maybe just a bit smarter, George. You don't have to attack everything head on to get something done."

Dalton brought another beer and had almost escaped when Brown lit into him. "Hey Ricky," he began. "Did I introduce you to my friend here?"

"No, George. You didn't."

"This is Mr. Taylor Luckett. He's a big shot reporter up north." Brown chugged another half mug. "Washington, Dee Cee. If you ask him real nice, he'll make you famous."

"Don't think I need that, George," Dalton replied with a smile. "What brings y'all down to Tyler, Mr. Luckett?"

"Just a little vacation, Mr. Dalton. George and I worked together in Baltimore and he keeps telling me what a wonderful place Tyler is. I had some free time so I came down for a visit."

"Well, I hope you enjoy your stay." A couple called from a booth and Dalton nodded in reply. "Got work to do. Nice meetin' you, Mr. Luckett. And don't go believing everything George here says about us. We're just a bunch of simple country folk tryin' to get by."

"He owns this place?" Luckett asked after Dalton had left to tend to his other customers.

"Does now," Brown replied. "Ricky's father built this place over forty years ago. It's the local redneck hangout. Ricky took over when his dad died. Still refuses to serve anybody in a coat and tie."

"Sounds like a real institution."

"Yeah, except it ends here," Brown said softly.

"What do you mean?"

"Ricky's never been successful in love. He's the last of the Daltons." Brown grabbed his mug and downed half of the heavy liquid for emphasis.

"Don't you think you should take it easy, George?"

"Hell, no, Taylor. I'm just getting started. How come you didn't tell Ricky you were down here checking out the militia?"

"Somehow it didn't seem polite," Luckett replied.

"Well, shit. Now where was I? Oh, yeah, Macon Holly. He's had a shitload of trouble lately. First, his daughter got herself pregnant. She'd been a terror for years. Staying out all night, runnin' away from home. I heard they even locked her in her room for a week once, but it didn't help. Anyway, she got knocked up by some stupid sonuvabitch, not much more than one of the migrant laborers, and Macon made the jerk marry her. Big mistake if you ask me. He had to give the louse a job and now he's got another mouth to feed."

"Doesn't Holly own the feed store? He can't be doing that badly."

"Not all that well these days," Brown said shaking his head. "When the subsidies got cut, a lot of the cash dried up. I don't know how much credit he's sitting on, but all the farmers are having a hard time paying their bills. The banks are buying a lot of land out here."

Dalton passed by and dropped another mug in front of Brown.

"The militia must not be having any trouble recruiting then," Luckett commented.

"Nope. Folks 'round here read about the boom in the Sun Belt, the growth in Atlanta, but all they see here is tough times. You can't blame 'em for listening to that bullshit."

Luckett started to reach for his sandwich, then stopped and went for a sip of beer instead. "What about this property you told me about last month?"

"Holly's farm? Don't know much. Just been hearing about this big place west of here where Holly and his buddies, the Citizens for Liberty, they call themselves, hang out."

"How did Holly ever buy it? You said he was broke."

"I didn't say he *bought* it. Just that he uses it. I checked out the records at the courthouse and the only name I could find was some Atlanta law firm. Don't know who owns it, but Macon and his crew seem to be running it now."

"Then he's got one helluva benefactor," Luckett replied. He tapped the soggy sandwich with his fork and it slid slowly across his plate. "So what does he do out there? He can't be farming it."

"Hell, no. Just planning his revolution." The reporter grinned and finished off the new mug. "Typical militia shit. Target practice, runnin' through the woods playing soldier. What do any of these stinkin' groups do? You're the expert. Mostly I think they just swill beer and blame their problems on the Trilateral Commission. Or was that what they did in the nineties?"

"Come on, George. You really ought to take these folks seriously. Look at Waco, the Montana Freemen, and McVeigh in Oklahoma. Aren't you worried about what they might do?"

"Macon and his crowd? Hell, no. They don't have the balls to do anything serious. You want another?" Brown asked lifting his glass.

"Nope. I have to be at Hartsfield by six and I still want to look at those files of yours. Let's head out."

"Okay. Whatever you want. Hey, Ricky," Brown waved to the proprietor. "Just put this on my bill."

Chapter 6

"MARY ELLEN, DO you have any updates on your militia monitoring activities?" Carlson asked as the formal agenda seemed to be coming to an end.

So far, Slattery was feeling pretty good about the meeting. He was glad Markovsky had brought him along. Real information was being shared and the participants around the table had kept their egos mostly in check. He wondered how long that could last.

"Actually, General, I do have an update the group may find interesting." She opened a leather folio, straightened in her chair, and leaned forward over the table. Slattery recognized a ritual she used when she thought she had something important to say. "As you remember, at the last meeting we discussed the Bureau's activities in regards to domestic militia. We have an active program of observation, and, where deemed appropriate, intervention. One cell in particular has recently caught our attention."

"Where is the cell?" asked Garcia from Homeland Security. This had been his first comment at the meeting. Rotund, with short curly hair, Garcia looked suspiciously like his late musician namesake.

"The cell is in Georgia," Flynn replied sharply. "There is a summary in your briefing folder."

Garcia flipped through some papers and then nodded reluctantly.

"We now have some new information from the cell," Flynn continued. "Our agent has identified the major players and we are running backgrounds, but most are coming up empty. They appear to be simple locals caught up in the militia movement. We have not identified any overt action or organized demonstrations."

"Why bring this to the group, Mary Ellen?" It was the representative from the Joint Chiefs, Georges Delacroix. "It sounds pretty routine."

"A couple of reasons, Admiral," Flynn responded. "First, there *are* a few contacts from outside the community. We're trying to get a handle on their identities. It's quite unusual for strangers to be brought into one of these cells."

"Mary Ellen?" interrupted Scott. Unlike his Homeland counterpart, the State Department representative had an insatiable appetite for detail. "Excuse me, but your file says the cell's camp is fairly large, over four hundred acres. Who is the owner?"

"That's point number two, David. We have been unable to identify ownership. But it doesn't appear to be any of the militiamen we have identified so far."

"Isn't that rather unusual?" Scott continued.

"Yes." Flynn referred back to her notes. "In addition, there have been recent enhancements to the property: new buildings, a renovated farmhouse, heavy construction equipment."

"So who's paying for it?" asked Delacroix.

"We don't know, Admiral. It is possible the cell has access to some hidden assets."

"But that doesn't fit with your description of a bunch of simple Southern honkies," said Garcia.

Heads dropped at the colorful description. Even Slattery had a hard time holding back a smile.

"These inconsistencies are the immediate objectives for our agent, Jerry. I'm sure we'll have an answer by next week's meeting." Flynn closed her folder and sat back in her seat. "That's all I have for now, General."

"Thank you, Mary Ellen," replied Carlson. "We appreciate your update and will place a follow-up on the agenda. Peter, you said the CIA had some new information for us before we adjourn?"

Slattery's head popped up. *What new information?*

"Yes, General." Markovsky opened a folder, adjusted his spectacles, and began addressing the group. "Interestingly, we have recently received information from an asset that concerns our last topic. The asset believes there is an effort to coordinate the activities of a number of independent militia cells. We do not have any further details at this time, other than that the coordination appears to be focused in the south."

Flynn glared at Markovsky, a red flush rising like a thermometer on her face, then turned the scowl onto an assistant sitting behind her right shoulder.

Finally the FBI Special Assistant turned back to the DDI. "What may I ask," she spit back, "is the CIA doing running domestic agents? Last time I looked that was illegal, Peter."

"Of course you are correct, Mary Ellen," Markovsky replied calmly. "Our information came from an informant outside the U.S."

"Who is this informant?" asked Scott.

"That's not important at this time, David," answered Markovsky.

"I think it is," challenged Flynn. "Is there some reason you are unwilling to name the source? You do *have* a source don't you?"

Markovsky hesitated and looked around the room, seemingly to find some support for his position. Then he reached up, removed his glasses and squeezed the bridge of his nose. Slattery, at the least, recognized it as the spook's affectation when he needed time to think. And that was an interpretation that left him very concerned. His chair became more uncomfortable.

"If you insist, Mary Ellen," Markovsky finally replied with a nod, "the asset's code name is, . . . IMAGER."

"Then *where* is he, Peter?" Delacroix pushed.

"That is not relevant," Markovsky replied. "IMAGER received the information indirectly. So far as IMAGER is aware, the plan to bring the cells together is completely domestic."

"I'm glad *he* is satisfied, Peter," Flynn said with continued hostility, "but I'm not. If someone is going to organize the efforts of these radicals, we'd better the hell know who it is. These assholes have been enough trouble acting alone. If they started to coordinate their efforts, it could be real trouble."

"I agree, Mary Ellen," Carlson interjected, apparently trying to blunt the edge of the conversation. "Peter, what additional information can we get from your asset?"

"That is not clear at this time, General. Since the original disclosure was accidental, I don't know what continuing intelligence we will be able to deliver."

"In other words you don't know jack-shit," added Garcia. All heads turned to the Homeland representative.

"Please," said a surprised Carlson.

"I assume, however, you will contact this IMAGER and *request* that he investigate?" continued Flynn. "And share the resulting intelligence with us?"

"Of course, Mary Ellen," the DDI replied calmly. "We have already sent the instructions by courier. But again, I cannot guarantee that further information will be available. I only bring this unsubstantiated information to the group because of its potential importance."

"Yes, thank you, Peter." Carlson replied, a little too quickly in Slattery's opinion. "All of us appreciate your contribution. I will expect an update at coming meetings." Markovsky nodded politely.

"Then if there's nothing else, we're adjourned." Carlson threw a final glare at the DDI, then marched out of the room.

The room slowly emptied amid a background of murmurs and whispers. Stroller and Markovsky hung back as the others left.

"Charlie's waiting for you with the car," Markovsky said to Slattery. "You go ahead."

"You're staying?"

"For a while. I have some things to discuss with Claude. Glen can take you back and then come back for me."

"Ah, yes sir. I would like to talk later."

"Of course, Roger. Of course." Markovsky flashed one of his well-practiced Capitol Hill smiles and turned back to the NSA Assistant Director.

What the hell was his boss doing? Slattery had never heard of an asset named IMAGER. Sure, he didn't know everything that went on at the CIA, but something in Markovsky's demeanor was off. Plus he had pissed off everyone in the room.

This assignment was going downhill very fast.

* * *

George Brown strode gingerly down the dusty macadam Main Street of Tyler, Georgia. He placed each step carefully; the dim lights from second floor apartments in the old brick and clapboard buildings provided little useful illumination. It wouldn't do for the town's leading publisher to stumble and collapse in the road.

It had been a tough afternoon. After reviewing his files with Luckett, he had driven him to Hartsfield, only to be caught in one of Atlanta's famous traffic jams for two hours. That had made him late for his dinner date. *Much* too late according to his on-again, off-again girlfriend Crystal. She had tacked a crude sketch on her door and apparently left for the evening. At least there had been no answer when he had knocked.

He had stopped at Ricky's for a nightcap then convinced himself he had to get back to the office to write up the story. He hated to work at night but he had an edition to get out the next day and couldn't afford to put off finishing his lead. His brain felt like a cobweb-filled attic, so he had parked in one of the open areas at the end of town, hoping the walk down Main Street to his office would clear his head enough that he could compose a coherent story.

Main Street? Not quite the name he conjured up as he looked around. What the hell was he doing here? Tyler was a rural Confederate crossroads barely hanging onto life in the twenty-first century. A walk down this road was all it took to feel the failing heartbeat of the town. Stu and Mary Upton still ran the corner drugstore on his left, although they had closed the soda fountain a few years before in the face of the McDonald's and Taco Bell up in Jefferson City. The prescription business was hurting; hardly anyone had enough money to go to the doctor, so the Uptons made most of their money selling patent medicines to the senior citizens, hunting magazines to the adults, and contraceptives to the ever-decreasing number of teenagers.

He passed the Post Office where it had stood for fifty years, right in the middle of "downtown," but its neighbor Woolworth's had pulled out in the mid-eighties. The boarded-up windows and cracked pavement were all that remained of that American landmark.

Far ahead, beyond where the scattered window lights could reach, stood the only attraction left: Macon Holly's agricultural supply store. The county wasn't completely deserted, and there were still a few farmers left needing fertilizer, feed, and associated paraphernalia. Holly kept a pair of rocking chairs on the loading dock, and on hot summer afternoons the local old-timers would gather to reminisce on better times and bemoan the decline of Tyler's younger generation, most of whom had fled the area for the bright lights of 'lanta.

Coming up was the most anachronistic establishment along Main Street: the *Tyler Guardian*. Left dormant after the death of its previous owner, the *Guardian* had been resurrected by Brown, a northern transplant who had set himself up as the voice of truth in the poor southern region. Raised on Ralph Nader and Woodward and Bernstein, he had seen himself as a crusader, bringing enlightenment to the region. What was surprising was that he actually had a readership. Brown had learned to temper his editorial outbursts with newsy features on local history and 4H doings, enough to assure a regular, but meager, circulation. He supported the local Baptist Church and every Christmas held a special party for the town's children.

To be fair, most of the time Brown actually did enjoy his small portion of celebrity. When he wasn't off researching some governmental impropriety he could be found socializing along Main Street, or arguing politics at Ricky's. He had become a town fixture over the past ten years, his involvement making up for his Yankee background and leftward leanings. Most of the town liked him, although there were those whose business he had scalded, who had other feelings.

Brown walked up the rickety stairs to his building's porch, unlocked the door and stepped into his office.

Chapter 7

TOMMY WICKS WAS already at the equipment shack when Holly arrived.

"Evenin' Macon," Wicks said as Holly approached the shack.

"Tommy," Holly replied with a nod. What had Wicks been doing before he had arrived? "Been here long?"

"Just a few minutes. Thought we'd better be sure everything was ready. What's the matter? Afraid I'm sabotaging the mission?"

"Hope you didn't work too hard," Holly replied ignoring the barb. "Gary's not gonna be here, you know. Or did I forget to mention that?"

Wicks glared at his leader then turned back to his truck.

They went about the rest of their preparations silently, neither having anything further to say to the other. Holly always watched his back when Wicks was around. He knew the younger man was ambitious, he had been playing up to Gary ever since the stranger had approached them. Holly didn't think Wicks would cause him any physical harm, but he remembered what Charlie Kearns had told him: "Ain't nothing wrong with being paranoid. Some of them folks really are out to get you." And Charlie had been right.

Napes and Ricky Dalton arrived next in Napes' decrepit pickup. It clattered and boomed all the way down the muddy access trail. Holly had been right to refuse to let Napes use the vehicle tonight. It would wake up the whole town.

O'Grady finally drove up around 11:30 with his special packages. He and Holly passed out the Uzi's while Dalton transferred some of the gasoline cans that Wicks had filled at his depot to O'Grady's van.

Holly had dictated the required clothing at their rehearsal the night before: leather combat boots, camouflage fatigues, and well-stocked ammunition vests. Standard dress for 80% of the males in Placer County. Most of the team had followed his instructions. Napes' outfit differed only in the unlaced construction boots and a red Caterpillar cap. Holly could only shake his head.

No one bothered with masks or face paint. There wasn't any need to conceal their identity. Holly didn't intend to let anyone see them and if anyone did, they'd be crazy to report it. He'd see to that personally.

"When we goin'?" Napes asked.

"Eleven fifty," Holly replied. "That's what I said isn't it?"

"Yeah. But what's the big deal when we go?"

"Gary said he wants it on time. At midnight." A breeze blew Napes' b.o. in Holly's direction. It was almost enough to make a man gag. He couldn't understand how the man's wife stood it.

"And we sure don't want to do anything different do we, Macon?" Wicks was sitting in the back of Holly's pickup checking out his new possession. The smirk on his face make Holly sick.

"Give it a rest, Tommy," O'Grady said. "If you want out, we'll do it ourselves."

"Screw you, Sean," Wicks yelled back. "What's the matter? You scared?"

O'Grady jumped into the pickup and grabbed Wick's jacket. "Look you little bastard. I've seen more . . ."

Wicks fell to the bed of the truck and raised his Uzi, pointing it at O'Grady's chest. The Irishman froze.

"*Stop it!*" Holly screamed. "We don't have time for this shit! Tommy, put the goddamn gun down. Sean, get back to the van."

O'Grady scowled at Wicks and hopped onto the ground. Wicks went back to fondling his Uzi.

Scared? Yeah, they were all scared. Wicks was just too crazy to know it. They had talked about a mission like this for years. Something to show the government they were serious. But they had never gotten up the guts to pull it off; not until Gary came. Their new partner had provided the motivation and the resources. Now they *had* to do it or face the consequences.

They had been training for over two months now, following Gary's plan step by step. It *was* time to make a statement. They had sat back too long, letting the Feds take away their freedoms. Charlie hadn't put up with it. But he had been alone. Now they were together, with the Covenant. He hoped his team was up to the challenge. As long as he stayed close to Napes, they could pull it off. Holly checked his watch one last time. "Let's go." He headed to his pickup with Dalton, and O'Grady went to his van. Napes jumped in the back with Wicks. They headed down the trail and out to the highway.

* * *

Brown slumped over the monitor of his ancient PC, giving his aching hands a much-needed rest. The editorial was coming out his head slowly, sort of like molasses on a winter day. It was a solid story, why was he having so much trouble?

On Saturday he had tracked down his Georgia Representative for background on the article, but the man had been too busy cowing up to a room-full of tobacco lobbyists to give him an interview. He had, however, gotten what he *really* wanted: a quotable denial of any wrongdoing in the highway contract investigation. It would look wonderful next to copies of financial records that showed regular, substantial deposits into his private account from a certain local construction company. It was going to be a great lead, although he was sure it would anger some of his fellow townsfolk. They screamed about the crooks in Washington, but defended the ones that lived next door.

Most of the folks in Tyler were nice enough, even to this Yankee from Pennsylvania. He had graduated from UPenn in journalism and taken a job with the *Baltimore Sun*. Bouncing from assignment to assignment, covering charity bazaars to human interest, he never felt he was getting the experience he wanted. He knew he was good, others had told him so, but it would take years to climb through the arcane maze of the *Sun*. He wanted to call the shots: pick the stories, do the investigative work.

Then he had read a small want ad: local newspaper office for sale, no offer refused. The previous owner had died with nothing to leave his family except the legacy of his paper. Without considering its location, he had immediately called the widow and struck a deal. Cashing out what little was left of his own inheritance, George Brown had packed a trunk and moved to Tyler.

It was probably just as well that he had missed the date with

Crystal. He inevitably would have gotten into a fight with her over something. They always did. She was great in bed, but a real drag otherwise. He longed for a real friendship, a companion. Taylor Luckett's visit had been pleasant but a bittersweet reminder of the intellectual excitement of his younger days. So far Tyler had offered no such relationship. Maybe it was time to give up trying to be the next Horace Greeley. He needed to get out of this town and get a real job.

Brown glanced down at the screen and all he saw were fuzzy blotches. The sharp white characters of his story were gone. Frustrated, he set down his glasses and rubbed his eyes.

Probably shouldn't have had that last beer. I'll take a break and finish up later.

Brown clicked off the table light and laid his head down on the desk.

*   *   *

Holly felt the rush of adrenaline as they hit Georgia 318. The two vehicles followed the highway toward Tyler, turning off about a mile from town onto a dirt access road. Tyler had few real inhabitants to worry about. Most of the shop owners had homes in the surrounding farmland. There were a few laborers and displaced youngsters that lived in apartments above the businesses. The rents brought a little more money into the town, and provided facilities for the migrant laborers imported during harvest season. Holly expected they would all be sound asleep by now, but he didn't want to take any chances by driving down the middle of Main Street like a conquering army.

The weather was cooperating. It had turned cool during the day, so most windows would be closed. A few wispy clouds shone against the filtered light of a half-moon. It was enough for them to navigate by, but wouldn't provide enough for any identification.

O'Grady and Dalton had driven around to the north side of town; they would take care of the back of the building. Holly, with Wicks and Napes in the back, pulled up in the gravel lot behind the Post Office.

His two riders slung their sub-machine guns over their shoulders, grabbed the red plastic containers from the bed of the pick-up, and followed Holly around the building to an alley that ran between the Post Office and the bricked-over facade of the now-defunct *Placer Savings and Loan*. When they reached the front of the buildings, Holly stuck his head around the corner and looked out onto a deserted street. There was not a light on in any of the windows. He waved his arm and Wicks and Napes dashed across the street to the opposite row of buildings, disappearing into the shadows of the second story overhang.

Holly could visualize the next actions but only an occasional squeak of floorboards provided confirmation. Thirty seconds later it was again silent.

He checked his watch. It was 11:58. The tension was building in every muscle. Blood pounded in his ears. "Do it!" he whispered.

He saw a flash of light from across the street. 12:01. Two figures emerged from the shadows and raced back to the alley.

"That's it, Macon," Wicks panted. "Let's get outta here." The arms and neck of his shirt showed dark stains of sweat. He started back down the alley.

"In a minute," Holly replied. "We gotta make sure it catches."

The small flicker spread horizontally across the porch and began climbing upward. The evening's breeze brought the pungent fumes of the burning siding across the street. The trio watched the flames rise up the walls, licking at the windows and searching for a way into the structure.

Holly stood silently, mesmerized by the sight. That should take care of any more of the bastard's lies. The flames reminded him of Klan cross burnings from his youth. Gary had been right, this was their real initiation. His cell needed the reality of the event to secure their commitment. They had bought into the Covenant tonight whether they realized it or not. Now they were together 'til the end.

12:04. They only had a few more minutes before the light and sound would raise someone's attention.

"Now. Let's go," he whispered and turned down the alley.

"*Ahhhhh.*"

They had gotten about ten feet when the scream froze them in place. Thinking they had been spotted, Holly drew his pistol and spun to his rear. Nothing. The only sound was the increasingly loud crackle of the fire across the street.

He didn't have time to investigate. Their safety margin was nearly gone.

"*Ahhhhhhh.*" Another scream.

It was coming from across the street. Could someone have seen them? If so, he had to find out who. They couldn't leave any witnesses.

Holly waved his men to the sides of the alley and stalked back toward the street. He had just poked his head around the corner when a flame shot through the front door of the newspaper building.

But it couldn't be a flame. It was moving!

* * *

George Brown ran screaming through the door, trying desperately to escape the conflagration inside. He couldn't see. The smoke that had awakened him from his stupor had teared his eyes to the point of blindness, but he had managed to find the door. Flames still swept around him. But he should be outside! The air around him was so hot! What was happening?

* * *

"Shit!" Holly yelled. The figure was racing across the street, right toward the alley. It was only ten yards away.

Holly raised his pistol to drop the apparition when the world exploded next to him. A spray of bullets leapt from the alley, chipping the asphalt street and creating a cloud of projectiles even more deadly than the Uzi's parabellum slugs.

He turned and saw Napes quivering in the alley, his spent weapon hanging loosely at his side.

"I got him, Macon. I got him good, didn't I?"

"Shit, Cal," Holly whispered. "Why the hell did you have to do that?" He grabbed the automatic from Napes. "You probably woke the whole goddamn town."

"He was like some kinda ghost, Macon. He was comin' after us."

"Jesus Christ, Cal. We'll talk about it later."

"I thought there wasn't supposed to be anybody around, Macon," Wicks accused.

"There wasn't supposed to be. How the hell was I supposed to know somebody would be in there?"

"You figure it was Brown?"

"Doesn't matter much now does it? We've gotta get out of here."

Wicks was the first to turn down the alley. Holly grabbed Napes by his vest and shoved him ahead, pushing him behind Wick's lead. As they ran down the alley, long shadows stretched out before them, cast by the still burning mass in the street.

* * *

The Tennessee cell had had none of the complications encountered by their confederates in Georgia. The offices of the *Tennessee Populist* were in a refurbished barn on the outskirts of Chattanooga. Nestled in a small clearing among stately oaks and elms, it was hard to believe the structure was a bastion of left-wing rhetoric. The publisher and owner, Carleton Graves, was a senile old Tennessean who wanted nothing more than to use his paper as a soapbox from which to spout his bleeding-heart liberal views. A life-long atheist, he had ranked the demise of school prayer as the most important story of the twentieth century. In recent years his favorite targets had become Shepard's friends in the Christian Right. Exposés of their extravagant lifestyles and extensive contributions were getting a little too much public attention. It was long past time to silence the old coot.

Shepard had picked three of his top lieutenants to execute the strike. They circled the building just past midnight, first dousing the old barn board with gasoline, then breaking in and sprinkling just enough thermite over the old printing press to assure it would never again spout its blasphemous accusations.

The team retreated to the edge of the woods and watched as Shepard lit a Molotov cocktail and arced it gracefully over the split-rail fence surrounding the structure. The side of the barn burst like a firecracker on impact; Shepard had to use his arm to shield his eyes from the inferno. Satisfied they were successful in the mission, he gave a quick thumbs up to the team then waved them into the woods.

Two hours later there was nothing left in the clearing but charred timbers and a pile of useless molten metal.

* * *

Gary stuffed the dirty fatigues in his duffel and made one final pass through the motel room. Everything had gone well. The targets had been efficiently dispatched.

They were minor missions, but they would build confidence. Soon the pattern would be clear even to the blind agencies and their ineffective leaders. But they would not be able to stop it. And the Commander would have his revenge.

Nothing had been left behind. As his last task, he typed another update into his phone.

```
ALPHA completed successfully.

BRAVO plans proceeding.

HALFTIME on schedule.
```

Chapter 8

Tyler, Georgia.
Tuesday, 9:30 a.m.

DEREK THOMAS FLIPPED a cigarette stub through the open pickup window and slammed his hands on the steering wheel.

Eight days on that goddamn mountain! For what? They go out one night, torch a building, murder the owner, and he's asleep in a stinking motel room.

Well, the damn bureaucrats finally released him from his constraints. When he had checked in last night, Atlanta had told him infiltration had been approved. Now it was going to be different. Today he would find out what these goddamn weasels are doing.

So far, things had been pretty easy. There had been little problem getting into the property. His cover had been carefully constructed, and security at the farm surprising lax, just a few superficial questions from a filthy militiaman. The last two days had been spent talking with the militiamen and taking part in the day's activities. He had joined in some exercises, fired off a few magazines, and openly shared his hatred of blacks, Arabs, Feds, homosexuals, and any other inferior species he could think of.

There hadn't been one mention of arson, however. Could he have missed something? Some slip that would have saved the publisher?

What he *had* been able to do was identify his suspects. He had learned that Gimpy was Sean O'Grady, a vociferous IRA supporter with a penchant for automatic weapons. Beau Brummel was Tommy Wicks, a smart-ass young businessman who had inherited his father's string of very profitable farm equipment stores. Baldy was Frisco, a short, muscular loner with an incongruous New York accent, and Walrus was Macon Holly, the apparent leader of the cell. Thomas had so far been unable to get very close to Holly, he always seemed to be running from one meeting to the next, but he would come later. Thomas had already selected today's target.

Baldy—he still thought of his new friends by their handles—moved through the cell wordlessly, as if he had no interest in their activities. The other cell members, for their part, left him alone and even went out of their way to avoid his presence. Baldy's primary duty seemed to be as courier. He would appear in a shiny Toyota rental, always carrying a black nylon bag, disappear to somewhere on the farm—it had numerous barns, houses, and other outbuildings—and reappear a few minutes later. He did this twice a day, once in the morning when he arrived, and again about 4:00 in the afternoon just before he left for the day. Between these times he simply hung out. Thomas had never seen him actually have a conversation with anyone. The few times he had dared to speak to the man, he had received only a few perfunctory words—in that odd accent.

Thomas had finally been able to determine Baldy's destination: a small storage shed behind the main farmhouse. The farmhouse was the activity center of the cell. The major gatherings were held there as were smaller meetings of the militia's elite, usually run by Walrus/Holly. Behind the farmhouse was a freshly cultivated field, growing more weeds than vegetables, and a small building that looked like a tool shed. The oddity was that some militiamen would enter and not come out for hours. Baldy, on the other hand, usually only stayed a few minutes. Something was going on inside that shed and Thomas was going to find out what.

It was only mid-morning, but the Georgia sun already burned high in the sky. The few militiamen tending to the chores of the property had returned to the farmhouse porch for shade and a cool drink.

It was time to break the back of this goddamn cell. Thomas wasn't going to let them murder anybody else.

He hopped out of the pickup and grabbed a rusty rake and shovel from the back of the truck, implements confiscated on a previous scouting mission into the backwoods of the farm. If he was going to wander around like a laborer at least he would look the part. Hefting the tools onto his shoulder, he headed for the rear of the farmhouse.

* * *

"We had no idea Brown was in the office, Gary. It was dark and quiet." Holly slapped his hand on the table. "Shit!"

Holly was back in the old farmhouse, trying to make sense out of the prior evening. Gary had called him at the feed store and suggested they meet at the farm. Somehow Gary's suggestions always felt like orders.

So Holly had driven out and found an unfamiliar rental car parked by the front porch. He had no idea how long his benefactor had been there. After checking downstairs, he had finally found Gary in one of the upstairs bedrooms. Walking into the room, the smell of Hoppe's No. 9 cut at his nostrils. Gary was sitting at a small dressing table, calmly cleaning his SIG P226 automatic. The pieces were spread neatly across the tabletop.

"There's nothing to worry about, Macon." Gary turned his face to Holly, while his hands continued to reassemble the weapon. "It was an unfortunate coincidence, but he *was* the enemy wasn't he? We're in a war now, you and I. We have to stick together. And there will be casualties. We both understand that. Right?"

Holly nodded, then looked directly at his benefactor. In most ways, Gary looked very ordinary. He was a little shorter than Holly, maybe five foot ten, and slim with short brown hair and an unremarkable face. Except for his eyes. They were stark white disks dotted only with tiny ebony pupils. He had never seen anyone with no color in his eyes. 'Albino eyes' he had heard someone call them. Eyes from hell, if anyone asked him.

"Sure, Gary. I was in Afghanistan, I understand." But that was in somebody else's country. They all knew Brown was a jerk. He didn't understand what they were fighting for. He had been blinded by all the propaganda. Hell, he had been part of it. But had he deserved to die?

"Have you heard about the other missions?" Gary asked.

"I haven't heard nothin'. All the news has been on Brown and the *Guardian.*"

"That's not a surprise. They were all successful, Macon. Everything we wanted. The Feds'll try to deny us as long as they can. They don't want anyone to understand how far we've come. But we'll show 'em, won't we, Macon? Soon they'll see how strong we are. Then the rest of the country will join us."

"You really think so, Gary? Sometimes I wonder if anyone else cares." He had been worried about this a lot lately. Some of his friends had come into the store that morning and acted, well, different. They talked to him as usual but there was a look in their eyes. Something that cut right through him. Did they know he had killed Brown? Did they understand why?

"Sure they do, Macon. I talk with a lot of people. So does the Commander. We know what the people really want. They want liberty, and freedom. They want the Feds to get out of their farms and out of their homes. Let them live the way they want to. No, don't you worry, we'll have *everyone* on our side very soon. You'll see. And then we'll start changing things." Gary punctuated the final statement by thrusting a full clip into the butt of the newly assembled weapon.

"I hope so. I really do."

"I know you do, Macon. And you've done really well here so far. Got the boys clickin'. They feelin' okay?"

"Yeah. Everybody was a little, well you know, spooked last night. But they calmed down real quick."

Gary turned back to the SIG giving it a final polish. Without looking up he said, "Who shot the filthy propagandist, Macon?"

Shot! How did he find that out! There had been nothing on the news about that. Holly had wanted to keep it a secret; just inside the cell. "Ah, it was Cal. Brown surprised us runnin' out of the office and all."

"That's understandable, Macon." Gary finished his cleaning and slipped the automatic under his jacket. Then he looked up and stared hard into Holly's eyes. "Napes can handle it can't he? Not go blurting it out everywhere?"

Holly was driven back into his chair from the gaze. What could he say? "He'll be fine, Gary, just fine. He's a good soldier."

"That's great, Macon. I know you can handle whatever comes up. Now tell me about the Gathering. Preparations going okay?"

"Sure, Gary. Absolutely. We've got everything under control. Following your plans to the . . ."

Holly heard a scream from outside. Gary jumped from his seat, stormed down the stairs and through the back door. Holly tried his best to keep up with the man.

"What the hell is going on?" Gary yelled.

"Boss!" cried Frisco running up to the farmhouse. He was out of breath and barely able to get the words out. "It's the shed!

* * *

Thomas walked to the shed door and knocked his shovel against the jamb. No one approached him and his noisy ploy garnered no response. He lifted the latch and walked in.

The door opened into a dark, musty storeroom. He stepped in, closed the door behind him, and looked around. Nothing seemed out of the ordinary: sacks of fertilizer tossed on the ground, rusty farm tools hanging on the walls, and a well-worn 1967 John Deere pin-up calendar dangling from a rafter. He was checking the sacks when he saw a thin strip of light between two wall panels. It could just be from the bright sun outside, but he went over to investigate anyway.

He ran his hands along the rough boards. They seemed to be solid, but he wedged his fingernails into the slot and gave a yank. The wall suddenly came loose and swung back, nearly knocking him over.

On the other side of the wall was a stark white concrete staircase descending into the earth. As he peered down all he could see was a flickering light at the foot of the steps. He pulled a Glock 9mm from the crook of his back and cross-stepped down the stairs, hugging the cold, damp sidewall. There shouldn't be anyone around, but he wasn't going to take anything for granted with this crowd.

At the foot of the staircase was another door, this one metal with heavy hinges and extensive rubber weather-stripping. The door was open, light from the area beyond providing his original clue. A cool breeze from the room brushed his face and flowed up to ventilation ducts in the ceiling of the landing. The air had an odd smell, like a doctor's office. He paused, waiting for a telltale sound or movement, but all he heard was the dull drone from the exhaust fan above his head. Satisfied there was no one else around, he stepped over the raised threshold and into another world.

All around him were shiny metal tables replete with test tubes, beakers, centrifuges and electronic equipment he didn't recognize. The walls were covered with shelves holding a huge assortment of jars and beakers.

Thomas finally recognized the odor. The pungent smell of acetone permeated the windowless space. He hadn't seen a laboratory this extensive since the last time he was in Quantico. Whoever built it wanted nothing but the best.

It was too complex for an explosives operation. You could make a bomb with a bucket and a stirring rod. It had to be drugs. That's how they were supporting the operation. No one would have guessed from the bucolic rural scene above.

Thomas walked over to an odd apparatus sitting on one of the tables. It was a tray with dozens of tiny receptacles, like miniature Petri dishes. He was reaching for the tray when he heard a noise and spun around.

He never saw what caused the sound.

Chapter 9

"How was the dentist, Megan?"

Wonderful," Connelly replied as she rushed past her assistant's desk. "I've got to get a fifth molar pulled." She had just endured forty minutes of poking, scraping, and filing on her teeth only to find there was still more work to be done. Now it was ten o'clock and she had three hours of work to make up.

Not a promising way to start the day.

"Five wisdom teeth! Cool! My mother says that's a sign of good luck."

"Your mother thinks everything is a sign of good luck, Cathie." Cathie Petrie was a young, ambitious farm girl from the Napa Valley, who had come to the city to find her fame and fortune. Reality struck early, however, and she had accepted a job as an underpaid assistant in a struggling Bay area start-up. Brighter than her background would have suggested, Petrie had developed as rapidly as her boss, and the two now shared a close friendship as well as a business relationship. Petrie's greatest asset had been her ability to keep her hyper-active boss relatively organized through the chaos at Vision One.

"What have we got this morning?"

Petrie followed Connelly into the office and recited the plan for the day. "Robin called and cancelled the con-call on the advertising plan. She said the agency guy, I think it was Mendelsohn, wants to make some last minutes changes to the proposal. Your staff meeting is at 11:00, and the new product review is still on for 4:00. Paul called and said he would check back later. Your tickets for D.C. are on your desk. Out Thursday morning, back Saturday afternoon."

Damn. She'd forgotten about that trip. Three days gone for one lousy day of meetings with government clients and prospects. That meant even more work she had to get done this week.

"Are you going to see Adam?" Petrie added.

Connelly froze. Adam Braxton, her ex, now lived in Northern Virginia. He was a computer security consultant and had recently gained national attention, or maybe notoriety, on the rumored discovery of an Internet mole. Their relationship had remained cordial, at least as long as they lived on different coasts, but she wasn't sure she was ready to see him in person.

"Maybe," Connelly replied without much enthusiasm. "But I'll have to recheck the schedule."

Petrie paused then offered, "Okay. Just wanted to ask. You keep mentioning seeing him sometime."

Connelly shook off the anxiety and started unpacking her briefcase, carefully laying the file folders across her desk while planning the day's agenda in her head.

"Did Paul say what he wanted?" She asked. Paul Venton was Vision One's CEO. It wouldn't do to put him off.

"He said he just wanted to discuss the advertising budget. Nothing urgent."

"Okay, it sounds like I've got some work to do. Hold any messages 'til I get caught up."

Connelly sat down behind the pile of papers, took a deep breath, and started reading.

* * *

Connelly couldn't sit and push papers any longer. She had to get away from these four walls. Ever since her promotion to Chief Marketing Officer, her life had turned into one flood of paperwork after another. She felt farther and farther away from the business.

There was only one sure-fire remedy for these blues.

She left her office and took the elevator to the basement. There she walked down a dim corridor toward a pair of huge unmarked swinging doors. Pushing them open, she stepped into a surreal world of flashing monitors, rainbow-colored cables, and more computing hardware than NASA needed for a shuttle launch. It was Vision One's subterranean research laboratory. Buried in the basement of the corporate offices, the laboratory was the home of the company's sharpest minds, and their competitive advantage.

"What's up, guys?" Connelly called into the maze.

Looking around she was disappointed to see only two researchers. A glance at her watch explained it. It was 2:15. Lunch time for the techies who lived on a slightly shifted schedule from the business world upstairs.

A short, curly-haired woman spun away from her workstation. "Hi, Megan. What brings a bigwig like you down to the trenches?"

Bonnie Jefferson was a graphics software expert Vision One had stolen from Google. She had led the team that produced the first commercial release of their product. Now she was back doing what she really liked, advanced research on new graphical interfaces.

"It got lonely upstairs," Connelly replied. "Besides, I have to make sure you're working your fingers to the bone. That's my job isn't it?"

"You know, the last time a manager came down here we made him disappear," said a deep voice from the corner.

"Give me break, Tony. There are enough people disappearing as it is." Connelly turned toward Dr. Anthony Caravino, a world-class geophysicist and one of Vision One's top researchers. He was a critical interface to the company's oil and gas customers.

Vision One had once been a small, close-knit family. A tight group of entrepreneurs struggling to keep their start-up alive. Now they were growing up, and the children were leaving the nest. She couldn't help but feel a certain loss. It was good to still have a few of her old friends around.

"Yeah," Caravino replied, finally turning in her direction. "I know what you mean. We miss Ben a lot. I hope he gets back soon."

"Me too." *How did Tony know who I meant?*

Connelly began wandering around the lab, more to break the direction of the conversation than to examine all the new equipment, then came over behind Caravino.

"So, what's new down here?" she asked.

"Show Megan the proto, Tony," Jefferson replied.

"We're just finishing up on the force-feedback joystick," Caravino explained. "Want to try it out?"

Vision One had been working on the new interface for nearly a year. If they pulled it off, it would be another coup for the company. "Sure," Connelly replied. "If I can use it, anybody can."

Caravino jumped up from his seat. "Then let's give it a try."

He led the pair to the back of the room. There, standing out from the corner, was Vision One's breakthrough product: the HoloCube, or 'The Cube' for short. It looked like a struggling artist's attempt at minimalist sculpture. Sitting on the floor was a shining cube of stainless steel, one meter on each side. Hanging from the ceiling was an identical cube, exactly one meter above its partner. Four small square tubes ran from the corners of the upper cube to their corresponding points on the lower.

The Cube always reminded Connelly of the box kite her father had tried to teach her to fly on vacations at the Cape. Only a lot more expensive.

"Here we go," Caravino said, typing at another workstation.

Connelly watched as the top surface of the lower cube began to shimmer with an unearthly glow. Then there was a soft *whoosh* and the space between the cubes filled with a translucent three-dimensional holographic image. It looked like a multi-layer cake: layers of browns and grays below a wide layer of blue.

"I always get shivers when it starts up," Connelly commented with a grin. "What am I looking at?"

"This is a geologic cross-section of the newly-discovered oil reservoir under the Great Salt Lake. Who would have thought we have as much oil in Utah as the Saudi's do in their peninsula?"

Caravino pointed to the top of the image. "That's the sky at the top. We've color coded the various soil and rock textures; darker shades correspond to denser strata. Light brown is the surface sand, gray is shale and black is bedrock. The oil reservoir is the red blob on the lower right of the image.

"The black line running down from the top is the current location of the main drill shaft. The blinking point at the end of the line is Exxon's new remotely-controlled drill-head. You need to get the pipe into the reservoir."

Jefferson rolled a steel pedestal next to Connelly. Sitting on the top of the pedestal was a mass of wires and two joysticks that looked like a control for a toy drone. "Here you go," she said with a grin. "The stick on the left controls vertical motion and the one on the right horizontal. Can you get the drill-head to the oil?"

Connelly raised her eyebrows and stood in front of the device. *How difficult could it be?*

She grasped the left handle and tried to push it forward, but it wouldn't move.

"Something's wrong, Tony. It won't work."

The researcher flashed a friendly smile. "That's 'cause you're trying to push down through mantle rock. The program computes the effort needed to drill on the proposed path and pushes back on the joystick proportionally. The head can't bore into the mantle so you can't move the stick. Try going left."

Connelly tipped the right handle to the left and the dot slid along the boundary. A bright green line followed her path. A row of numbers along the bottom of the hologram spun crazily.

"Okay, what am I doing?"

"The green line is a flexible extrusion recovery line tied to the electronic drill head. You want to get the line to the pool of oil." He pointed to the red blob in the image. "We could compute a trajectory, but the best way is to 'feel' your way with the joystick."

"What are the numbers?"

Jefferson moved over and stood behind the executive. "Those are the spatial coordinates of the head, the length of the drill shaft, and torsion metrics. Try it again. Think of it as a very expensive video game."

"I'll try *not* to think of that," Connelly replied. She tightened her hand around the joysticks and took a deep breath. Staring into the hologram, she slowly guided the glowing dot down the field. The green line snaked toward the blob.

"I'm stuck. I can't get it any farther."

"Just retrace your path," Caravino said. "That's the beauty of a simulation. It doesn't cost anything to do it on the computer. Better now than in Utah."

She moved the "drill" back up the screen, the green line changing to white. About halfway up, she tilted the joystick down and the dot responded. It moved closer to the red blob.

"I think I've got it!"

This time, she managed to keep the drill on course. When the dot reached the pool, red "oil" flowed up the drill shaft and erupted into a fountain of color at the top of the screen.

"Bonnie! What's this?"

"Oh, sorry, Megan," Jefferson said sheepishly. "You weren't supposed to see that. We added a little something to the simulation. It's only for debugging, really."

Connelly shook her head but couldn't help but smile. The scientists had found their own way to deal with the constant pressure. She was still looking for hers. "Not a problem. Just so Exxon doesn't think all we do here is play games."

"Not a chance," Caravino replied. "The VPs that were here last week seemed pretty impressed."

"They couldn't stop talking about all the money they'd save," Jefferson added. "You know, Megan, I could make it even faster with one of the new IBM parallel servers."

"Okay, you two," Connelly raised her hands in surrender. "That's enough. I can tell when I'm outnumbered. Thanks for the demo, though. It's really good stuff." She turned and started for the door.

"Our pleasure, Megan," Caravino answered with a grin. Then his face turned starkly serious. "But really, thanks for stopping by. It's nice to know somebody upstairs cares."

Connelly said goodbye and started toward the doors, but stopped and turned back into the lab. "Tony, have you heard anything from Ben?"

"Got an email last week. Sounded like things were going fine. The systems had passed acceptance and he was getting the software transferred and loaded."

"No problems then?"

"None he told me about."

"Great. That's what I thought."

She walked back down the hall to the elevator tower. So things *were* okay in Utrecht. But then what did his letter mean?

Chapter 10

"HERE'S THE LATEST message, Garrett. It looks like things are heating up." Kam Yang walked around to the side of his boss's desk and dropped the striped folder on an empty corner.

Garrett Robinson scanned the file then set it back down. Yang *had* been able to continue the decryptions. "So it seems. This should be very interesting reading for the policy folks."

"What do you think they're going to do? I haven't heard a thing. The Director *has* seen the reports hasn't he?"

Robinson gave the scientist a sour look. "Of course he has. I've briefed Director Stroller on every one of your dispatches. There's a lot going on, Kam. The world doesn't just revolve around you."

"Yes, sir." Yang's emotionless countenance didn't fool Robinson. He could feel the mathematician's anger heating the room.

In some ways Robinson didn't blame him; like any large bureaucracy, individual advancement in the NSA was built on results and visibility. No matter how good you were, if the brass didn't know it, you languished in obscurity.

"I just hope they see the importance. We're losing valuable time. Maybe if I went to see him."

"No!" Robinson slammed his fist on the desk. "These messages have major policy implications. You know that." He paused and his voice softened. "Look, Kam. Nothing ever moves as quickly as we would like. We're all doing our part. I'm sure I can count on you to do the same?"

Robinson reached for his phone. "If that's all, I've got a call to make."

"Sure, Garrett. I'm done." Yang walked out without closing the door behind him.

* * *

Connelly threw the binder across her desk, where it fell to the floor, broke open and spilled individual sheets of product specifications all over the carpet.

Why can't I make any sense of all this?

When she looked up to check her aim, she saw Petrie standing in the doorway, just waiting there.

"What is it Cathy?" Connelly barked. "I thought I told you no interruptions?"

"Yes, I know, Megan. It's just, well, . . ."

Connelly could hardly hear her assistant. Why was she being so obtuse? And she looked like she had just seen a ghost. "Well, what?"

"It's an email message. It just came in." Petrie cautiously approached her boss's desk and held out a single piece of printer paper. "It's about Ben."

"What do you mean 'about Ben'?" Petrie was frightening her. She grabbed the sheet out of her assistant's hand and scanned the text.

From: Paul Venton

To:Vision One Senior Staff

Subject: Benjamin Lawson

It is with great personal and professional sadness that I must report that Benjamin Lawson died last night of injuries sustained in an automobile accident. Ironically, Ben was on the way to Schiphol airport to return to Vision One headquarters in California at the time of the accident.

Ben was one of Vision One's founders. A Yale and Stanford-trained computer scientist, he was a brilliant researcher, an insightful colleague, and a valued friend. Much of our recent success was due in no small part to his dedication and diligence.

Most recently, Ben has been on a special assignment in Utrecht, setting up our new European subsidiary headquarters.

Our utmost sympathies go to Ben's family.
Information on funeral arrangements will be
forwarded as they are available.

Please cascade this memo to your staffs as
appropriate.

Paul

"Cathie!" Connelly called, looking for her assistant. "When did
you get this?"

But the room was empty. She was alone.

Oh God. Not Ben. Why him? Why now?

She had known him for years, of course. Ever since she had
started at Vision One. But over the last nine months something had
changed. They had been working together on the IPO: building a
new business plan, producing unending reports, resolving issues
with potential investors. It required long hours and tight deadlines.
Enough to bring out the best and worst in a colleague.

At first he had been distant. Difficult to understand. But he was
as committed as she, and soon they had found a pattern of working
that, well, worked. The tasks were energizing and they became
seduced by the activity.

She had seen it before. Two people working under stress, relying
on each other. Perhaps more than they had ever relied on anyone. It
was a formula for disaster. Office romances burned bright in the
intensity of deadlines, but turned painfully cold in the monotony of
day-to-day routines. She had been determined not to let that
happen.

She had failed.

It had not been a blazing affair. More a smoldering expectation.
It had started with a few lingering glances. Some quiet dinners. And
then a brief good-night kiss.

She had marveled at the things they had in common. Parents
who had died too early. A failed marriage and long line of unfulfilled
relationships. An intense compulsion to succeed. He had opened a
door she had long tried to keep shut.

They had gone to dinner at a quiet French restaurant in Palo
Alto, but he had been distant, preoccupied, all evening. She had
feared another rejection.

Then he had reached over and taken her hand. His warmth had rushed through her body, displacing all the doubt. She had never been happier.

"I have to go to Europe," he had said. "To set up the new facility. I know it's bad timing, but it will just be a short assignment. A few months. I promise."

She had stared back into his dark eyes, wanting him more than she had ever wanted anyone. But there would be time; it was just a temporary assignment. He had promised.

Now this. *How could it have happened?*

* * *

Connelly pulled her head up from her desk. Standing in her doorway was Paul Venton looking even worse than she felt.

"Paul! What are you doing here? I thought you were in Europe." After reading the message about Ben, Connelly had forgotten about Venton's morning visit, cancelled all her meetings and locked herself in her office to hide. She smoothed her hair back from her forehead and tried to wipe the tears from her eyes, but knew the redness was visible to anyone.

"I hope you haven't been waiting long" she said as nonchalantly as she could.

"No, it's just been a moment," Venton replied softly. He pulled a chair alongside her desk and sat down. "I'm truly sorry about Ben, Megan. I know how closely you two had worked together the past year. It's a great loss for all of us."

Connelly searched her boss's eyes for recognition of something more than a reference to her professional well-being, but found nothing. Then again, she had never been able to see into Venton's thoughts.

Paul Venton was an enigma. He had personally recruited her for Vision One. Recruited her hard; harder than was necessary in fact. She had accepted because she had needed to escape. Escape from Boston. Escape from her marriage. Had he known that all along?

Not unattractive, Venton had a husky, outdoorsman look with tousled brown hair and only a slight middle-aged paunch, but she had never known him to have a steady companion. For what it was worth, he had never even attempted a friendly flirtation with her, certainly a first for Connelly. He seemed to stand apart from the rest of the world, as if he was watching his creations act out the roles he had written for them. So far he had seemed to be directing quite effectively, but Connelly wondered how he was dealing with this latest twist.

"How are *you* doing, Paul? You knew Ben longer than any of us."

"Oh, I'm fine," he replied, but Connelly heard an unusual weariness in his voice. "It was certainly a shock. Ben was, eh, a very good friend."

"What happened?"

"He was on his way to Schiphol. We had finally opened the new facility and he was anxious to get home. There was some kind of accident and his gas tank exploded. He didn't have time to get out. It was awful."

Connelly shivered at the thought of Ben trapped in a burning automobile. What a terrible way to die.

The last time she had seen him, he was sitting across from her at this very desk. His face filled her mind.

I've got to think about something else.

"Since you're here, I have those marketing numbers we talked about last week," she said weakly. "We can go over those and . . ."

"I don't think we need to do that now, Megan." Venton reached over and put a fatherly hand on her shoulder. "I tried to catch you earlier, before the message went out."

"Oh, I was at the dentist. I . . ."

"It's okay, Megan. I only want to say how sorry I am. We can talk about work later."

He gave her shoulder a tender squeeze and got up to leave.

"Paul?" Another image, this one of a letter, flashed in her mind.

"Yes?" Venton turned back to Connelly's desk.

"Ben didn't seem, well, different, the past couple weeks did he?"

"Why do you ask?"

"Oh, I don't know. He just seemed distracted the last few times I talked to him. Almost like he was worried about something."

"Did he mention anything specifically?"

His tone was sharp, accusatory. Why was he grilling her?

"No. It was just a feeling I got talking to him."

Venton seemed to relax, but his voice turned low, almost conspiratorial.

"I wasn't going to mention it, but Ben had been acting strangely."

There was something wrong! Why didn't he say so in the first place?

"I *was* afraid he had been working too hard," Venton confessed. "His projects were slipping and frankly, his work wasn't up to his usual standards. I asked him to take some time off. That's why he was on his way home." He shook his head slowly. "God, in some ways I blame myself for his accident."

Connelly was speechless. How could he be saying this?

"I know you won't let this go any farther, Megan. There's no point in tarnishing Ben's memory now."

"Ah, no. Of course not, Paul."

"Thank you. We'll talk tomorrow, okay?"

"Sure."

Venton turned and disappeared into the reception area, closing the door as he left.

Why would he say that about Ben? They were friends.

Something *had* been wrong. Lawson's mood had changed over the past few weeks. The daily telephone calls had stopped. So had his emails. She had received a letter, a real one, *handwritten*, last week. It had seemed forced, as if he needed to be careful about what he said.

She had to look at the letter again.

And she had to talk to someone about it. Someone outside of Vision One. But who?

$$* \quad * \quad *$$

The insistent buzz of the cordless phone stirred Robinson out of a sound sleep. Who would be calling him this late?

"Hello," he said sleepily.

"What the hell are you doing!" came an angry voice.

Robinson shook his head to clear out the cobwebs. "What are you doing calling me at this time of the night? Some people try to sleep."

"And some of us can't! Not when their supposed allies are off spilling their guts to our enemies."

"What are you talking about?"

"IMAGER! That's what I'm talking about. Who thought up this stupid little plan? You said you could keep Yang quiet."

Robinson had never heard the man so angry. Was he worried about exposure? "It's compartmentalized. We're completely protected."

"I'm not worried about protection! I'm worried about divulging the existence of the algorithm. We can't afford that. Find a way to bury this."

"Yes, sir. I'll cut off IMAGER."

"Damn right you will. If you can't, I will."

A dial tone had never sounded so ominous.

Chapter 11

SLATTERY WAS REVIEWING the latest Homeland Security alerts when his private phone rang.

"Slattery."

"Roger. It's Peter. Can I borrow you for a couple hours?"

The hairs raised on the back of Slattery's neck. His boss had been completely unavailable for the past two days and now the DDI wants to see him. What did Markovsky want now? Whatever it was, Slattery doubted it would answer the questions he had from Carlson's meeting.

"Sure. What's up?"

"Something new. There'll be a car waiting downstairs in fifteen."

His anxiety level jumped up a step. "An off-site meeting? Do I need to ask where?"

"Probably not. We're going back to McLean."

* * *

Glen and the Escalade had been waiting in the underground garage when Slattery stepped out of the elevator. Traffic was light, so the trip to the NCTC was thankfully brief. Entering the SCIF, Slattery saw that most of the previous meeting's attendees were already present. He pulled up a chair behind Markovsky.

"Nice of you to invite me along again, Peter. I hardly get out of Langley at all anymore."

"Okay, Roger. I know we've been riding you pretty hard lately. I promise I'll get you back before dinner. Is Beth still putting up with all your complaints?"

"As well as ever. She's started taking some classes at George Mason. Wants to be a psychologist. Just when I'm ready to retire, she wants to go sticking her nose into other people's heads. Doesn't make any sense to me."

"Well," Markovsky said with a smile, "maybe she doesn't cherish the thought of having you around the house all the time."

Slattery scowled at his boss, then relaxed back in the plastic seat and returned the grin. Markovsky probably wasn't that far from the truth.

"So why the call?" he asked. "I thought the advisory meetings were on Mondays."

"The DNI called an emergency meeting. I don't know the details but his office said it was urgent. It's almost like he thinks something terrible is about to happen."

"I thought *we* were the ones that were supposed to know that first."

Carlson hadn't arrived yet, so Slattery decided to do some pushing. It wasn't the best time, but Markovsky had been avoiding him for days. It was time to find out what his boss was hiding. "What's the story on this IMAGER agent, Peter? Who the hell is he?"

The door opened and Carlson strode through. The room went silent.

"Guess we'll find out about that emergency now," Markovsky whispered and turned back to the table.

"Good afternoon," Carlson began. "I appreciate your prompt response to my request. There has been a development in our monitoring of the militia groups that Mary Ellen has convinced me should be discussed. Copies of the briefing are on the table. Mary Ellen?"

The DNI nodded to his right and Flynn stood, moved fluidly around the table and took a position at the front of the room.

Slattery had a grudging respect for the Special Assistant despite her abrasive demeanor. She had had to work twice as hard as any other agent to break the Bureau's glass ceiling, but still managed to look like something off the cover of Vogue. She too was wearing a pinstriped power suit, but it looked a helluva lot better on her than the other bureaucrats. Slattery hoped she had the courage to stay a real cop and not get pulled into the muddy gutters of Washington politics.

"Two nights ago," Flynn began, "fires were set at the offices of three small, independent newspapers, the *Guardian* of Tyler,

Georgia, the *Tennessee Populist* of Chattanooga, Tennessee, and the *Free Citizen*, of Leavenworth, Kansas."

As Flynn spoke the names, a map of the United States appeared on a screen behind her and three red spots glowed in unison with her narrative.

"In all cases the fires completely destroyed the buildings. We have determined that the fires were intentionally set."

"This is all very interesting, Mary Ellen," Delacroix interrupted, "but why is the FBI involved in these events? Shouldn't they be investigated by the local authorities?"

"They were initially, Admiral. But by mid-day yesterday our tracking systems had identified a pattern that sent an alert to the serial crime team. As you know, we developed the RIPPER computer program to search for common patterns in criminal events. We have found this enables us to gain a critical time advantage in the identification of serial crimes."

"But you said these fires all occurred at about the same time," Garcia interrupted. Slattery had known Homeland wouldn't give the FBI free rein on this one. "In three different states. They couldn't have been set by the same person."

"You're absolutely right, Jerry. But the program was developed to identify common patterns, not people. And these three registered with a ninety-three percent positive correlation. All the arson targets were newspapers; decidedly *liberal* newspapers. And as best as we can determine the fires were all started at exactly the same time. Midnight in Tennessee and Georgia, 11:00 p.m. in Kansas. The MOs of the arsonists were very similar."

"There must be *some* differences, Mary Ellen," Delacroix asked.

"Yes, Admiral. There was one. In Georgia, the arsonist was also a murderer. The editor of the newspaper, a George Brown, was killed. We don't know if Brown's death was accidental or planned. As a result of these developments, we have activated the Serial Crimes Unit."

"Isn't that a bit of a reach, Mary Ellen?" Garcia asked. "All you have is three small fires."

"Certainly you must agree that the similarities are way beyond coincidental. Look at the facts, Jerry!" Flynn's voice ratcheted higher. "These were premeditated, coordinated events."

"Okay, Mary Ellen," Delacroix said. "Let's say you're correct. But this is still just three arson cases."

"And a murder," Flynn added.

"And a murder," Delacroix repeated. "But even given that the FBI is now involved, why was it necessary to call all of us in?"

Slattery had been busy watching the body language around the table, the action "away from the ball" as his son would have said, rather than the formal exchanges. Markovsky and Stroller had been surprisingly relaxed compared to their usual state of impatient agitation. Normally they would have jumped at the chance to take a swipe at their FBI colleague. He got an uneasy feeling in his stomach. It didn't take long before his concern was justified.

"After RIPPER identified the events," Flynn continued, "we sent local teams to investigate. The initial correlation was completely correct."

"I must again ask, Mary Ellen," Delacroix pressed, "how do these events affect *us*?"

"I believe, Admiral, that these arsons are simply the first step in an escalating militia agenda. An agenda that will require an integrated response by this group."

The room erupted into an explosion of questions. Subordinates frantically shuffled through the briefing to feed information to their bosses. Delacroix, Garcia, and Scott peppered Flynn with demands. Stroller and Carlson, on the other hand, were uncharacteristically silent. And Markovsky also sat quietly, but bowed his head during the questioning and intently rubbed his nose between his forefingers.

"Please, gentlemen," Carlson finally called above the din. "Let Mary Ellen complete her presentation before further discussion."

Flynn held her position at the front of the table and waited for the attention of the room to return. "Certainly you all remember that just such a coordinated militia effort was suggested by Peter's IMAGER intelligence. I must congratulate him on his asset. I believe she has been completely accurate." Flynn smiled toward Markovsky like a starving lion over a fresh kill. It was an expression that made even Slattery shudder.

"Mr. Chairman?" Markovsky asked. All eyes turned to the DDI.

"Yes, Peter?" Carlson replied.

"To be honest, I had hoped that the IMAGER asset would prove to be false. The implications of such coordination are indeed severe. Unfortunately we have received additional information that would support Mary Ellen's analysis. IMAGER believes that these events are a result of covert cooperation, and are the first in a series of such operations. We do not know the identity of the person, or persons, involved, how many operations are planned, or what the eventual goal may be. These are questions that we must still answer."

"So you have made contact with IMAGER?" Flynn asked.

"IMAGER has reported this additional information," corrected Markovsky. "As I explained, this is very indirect intelligence. We cannot put the IMAGER asset in jeopardy."

"Dammit, Peter!" Flynn exclaimed. "Isn't that a decision that must be balanced against the potential danger of the militia threat?"

"Mary Ellen, IMAGER is *our* asset. We will do everything possible to assist your investigation, but I cannot . . ."

"*My* investigation? Look Mr. Deputy Director of Intelligence, if this should turn into another Oklahoma City, I hope you will have an appropriate explanation for the American people."

Carlson stood from his chair and held out his hand for calm. "Gentlemen, Mary Ellen. Please. Despite the FBI's very imaginative presentation, I for one am not convinced of the need to take extraordinary action at this time. I believe we need to . . ."

"What about *your* investigation, Mary Ellen?" Stroller interrupted. "Isn't the cell you have under surveillance in Tyler, Georgia? Didn't your agent have any idea this was going to happen?"

Flynn glared in the direction of the NSA Deputy Director. "The cell is *near* Tyler but we have no proven connection between the arson and this group. These issues are all part of our ongoing investigation."

"Jesus, Mary Ellen. How many militia groups could there be around this damn town?" Garcia asked.

"Just because the cell is local, Jerry, doesn't prove it was involved in the arson. I don't imagine you want us to rush over and storm the cell do you?" Flynn's tone was sharp as a razor.

"I certainly do not recommend any premature action, Mary Ellen, but . . ."

"Mary Ellen," Stroller continued, "what exactly *has* your agent been able to uncover?"

"He has made preliminary identification of the cell's leader and is inside the cell. We are following up on his leads."

"You reported most of that at the last meeting," Stroller persisted. "What has he given you *recently*? Why didn't he know about the attack?"

Flynn shifted her body and began slowly, as if to postpone the inevitable. "The agent who went undercover into the cell hasn't reported in for the past thirty-six hours." Her voice dropped. "We have no explanation of the silence."

The room turned mute. Everyone knew what Flynn was implying.

"Any chance he's just keeping cover?" Carlson finally asked.

"There's always that hope, General. But realistically, I'm afraid his cover has been blown. We don't know what might have happened to him."

A poorly muffled "shit" came from the Homeland representative. Flynn shot him a withering glare.

"So what will you do now?" asked Delacroix.

"We're checking our local sources, Admiral," Flynn replied. "We'll see what we get back, but I'm not putting any more agents in the field until we have more background." She turned to the DDI. "We simply must get more information out of IMAGER."

"I've given you everything we know, Mary Ellen," Markovsky responded.

"And that's nothing she didn't already report," Flynn shot back. "I'd have a lot more faith in this asset if you could give us some more details. Where is she located? How does she get her information?"

"We've been through this before, Mary Ellen," Markovsky replied, ignoring her use of the feminine pronoun. "We are unwilling to divulge any identifying data on the IMAGER asset. We will not jeopardize his cover. I would assume you now appreciate that."

Flynn's face went scarlet. She looked like she was going to leap across the table at the spook.

"*Enough,*" Carlson shouted. "We must respect the CIA's position. For the moment, this investigation remains with the FBI." He turned to the head of the table. "Mary Ellen, is that acceptable?"

"Yes, General," Flynn replied flatly. "I have prepared a detailed report with all our current information." Flynn nodded to her right and a young, square-jawed agent rose and passed a stack of documents around the table.

"I would like each of your organizations to review these materials and check the names and locations against your files. Hopefully," Flynn again glanced toward Markovsky, "IMAGER will be able to fill in some of the holes, but until then, we should use all of the resources at our disposal. My office will act as clearinghouse for the information. If that is alright, General." She turned back to the DNI.

"Certainly, Mary Ellen. I'm sure everyone will afford you whatever support they can."

Slattery had to give Flynn credit for mostly keeping her cool during the inquisition. She had pressed her case, but it was clear Carlson and the rest of the advisory group did not support her analysis. He didn't know how she had managed to coerce Carlson into calling the emergency meeting, but now she was standing at the end of a very long plank. If her theory didn't hold up, her credibility, and possibly her career, was gone.

Carlson nodded and Flynn returned to her seat. He paused for a moment then rose to address the members. "When Mary Ellen approached me this morning with her preliminary results, I initially hesitated calling this meeting, but coupled with Peter's IMAGER intelligence I felt it was my duty to update all of you as soon as possible. This concludes the meeting. Mary Ellen, I would like an update on these matters on my desk in forty-eight hours. Peter, you will inform me of any additional information from this agent of yours. I will evaluate the results and determine if any further action is called for. Thank you."

As the others were gathering up their papers, Markovsky turned to Slattery and handed him the FBI's updated package. "This is for you, Roger. Check it out and give me your assessment tomorrow."

Slattery started to say something, but Markovsky suddenly stood and strode deliberately to the door. All Slattery could do was watch his boss disappear from the room, all his questions remaining unanswered.

What the hell is going on?

Chapter 12

Cerberus Consulting, Tysons Corner, Virginia
Wednesday, 3:30 p.m.

A RUDDY ORANGE sun hovered high above the mountains of western Virginia as Adam Braxton, Founder, President, and Technical Staff of Cerberus Consulting sat hunched over a PC in his Tysons Tower office, desperately trying to complete his report for Systems and Methods, Incorporated. The picturesque scene outside his window did nothing to alleviate the pressure of the deadline.

Cerberus was a character from Greek and Roman mythology; a monstrous three-headed dog with a mane of snakes, the claws of a lion, and the tail of a serpent. It was supposedly the sentry that guarded the entrance to Hades to prevent the dead from escaping and the living from entering. When Braxton had started his information security consulting company, he had decided that this was just the personification of network security he wanted to portray.

Sometimes he wondered whether the monster was trying to devour him rather than his customer's information.

He had gone on that damn trip to Chicago to sign up a new client. It had been completely worthless. The stupid software company hadn't had a clue about internal security. They had wanted a simple magic formula that would solve all their problems. And, of course, one that didn't cost anything.

Now he was even farther behind on the SMI proposal. He had promised the report by end-of-business yesterday. He had to finish it today. Hopefully the delay wouldn't blow his chance for the contract.

His fingers returned to the keyboard.

```
Our review of SMI's information security plan
showed a satisfactory understanding of the external
threats to your IT assets, but did not recognize
the significant additional dangers from internal
sources. While we are sure your personnel
background checks for new employees are quite
thorough, this does not prevent . . .
```

"Adam?"

```
    . . . internal malicious behavior due either to
employee discontent or bribery. One of our
recommendations, therefore, is that SMI initiate a
regular review of key personnel with a focus on the
identification of potential security problems.
Cerberus Consulting would be pleased to work with
SMI on the development of such a program.
Additionally, we would recommend . . .
```

"*Adam!*"

The shout finally broke through his concentration and he glanced up to see his secretary, Karen Chu, standing in front of his desk, her face a portrait of impatience.

"Yes?" he barked.

"Adam, I've only been standing here five minutes. You're more self-absorbed than my husband."

Braxton looked into her smiling face and his anger washed away. "Yes, that has been mentioned to me more than once. But I've got to get this report finished."

"Why don't you let me type it? You are the fastest two-fingered typist I've ever seen, but I do this kind of thing for a living you know."

"It's okay. Really. I have to make a few changes and add the section on biometric identification equipment. It's just easier if I do it myself."

Chu shook her head. "You are impossible. I may be out of line, Adam, but you've got to give yourself a break. The business is going great. Take some time to enjoy your success."

"When I finish the report, I promise I'll go home, lie down on the couch, and watch TV."

"Sure. And it'll probably be CNBC." She turned and headed back to her desk in the reception area of their suite. Then she stopped and added, "You could try to get out sometimes. Maybe even get a date?"

"Karen!"

"Okay, okay. But I'm here if you need any help."

"I know. Thanks. But I've got this. I'll be done in two hours. Oh, can you give FedEx a heads up?"

"Will do, boss."

Chu was a miracle worker. He had brought her on when the logistics of his consulting contracts had been too much for even him to handle. She had jumped into the mess he had created, organized every client engagement, and put him on a strict need-to-know basis.

Chu had burned out teaching math in the Fairfax County school system and had wanted to apply her considerable analytic abilities to a new profession. Over the past year she had learned more about the federal contracting system than any senior executive Braxton had ever known. She had been invaluable in stabilizing his nascent security consulting business. He really did need to tell her how much he appreciated her work.

And she probably was right about getting out. He wasn't unattractive: just under six feet tall with a full head of short sandy-brown hair and clear green eyes. Regular exercise at the gym downstairs kept him reasonably fit, although he did miss the rock-climbing excursions with his Boston friends. Left behind, along with more painful memories, when he had moved to the D.C. area.

Since relocating, there just hadn't been time for relationships. He had been out of work, and worse, once in his career and he never intended to let that happen again. He would never again rely on anyone else to step up and help him.

Enough psychoanalysis for one afternoon, I've got work to do.

```
    . . . that you implement more restrictive, and
secure, access-control devices in critical
information areas such as the capabilities and
contracts vault and main research server areas. I
have included data-sheets on a number of new
Biometric Identification devices that will
provide . . .
```

* * *

This time it was the buzz from his telephone that broke his concentration. Shit! Who would be calling him now?

He grabbed the phone and barked a curt, "Braxton."

"Adam? Is that you? It's Megan."

The soft voice of his ex-wife put Braxton's head in a spin. What could she want? He hadn't heard from her since the conclusion of his Incident investigation. Was something wrong?

"Megan? What's the matter? Are you okay?"

"Yes, Adam," she replied calmly. "I'm fine. Does it have to be an emergency to call you?"

Now he felt like an idiot. *Why does she always do this to me?*

"No. Of course not. It's just been so long since we talked."

"I know. Actually, that's why I called. I'm going to be in D.C. for some meetings later this week. I wondered if you'd like to get together for dinner."

"Ah, sure. I guess. When?"

"How about tomorrow night? If you're busy . . ."

"No. Tomorrow's fine."

"Okay. Can you pick me up at the Sheraton at seven?"

"Got it. Seven o'clock. You're sure everything's okay?"

"I'm fine, Adam. I just want to talk a bit. It's probably about time. Bye."

Braxton couldn't decide if he was more shocked, flattered, or frightened. But he knew he heard a tension in her voice. Was something wrong?

* * *

Virginia State Trooper Gary Alesi set out more road flares and watched patiently as the Great Falls Emergency Rescue Team cut through the mangled metal and plastic. A five-ton GM pickup had broadsided a much smaller sedan, driving it off the road. The car was now nearly wrapped in half around a very old, and very sturdy, Virginia Black Oak.

He had kept in the background while the rescue crew spent thirty minutes separating the vehicles and another fifteen minutes with the Jaws of Life to get to the driver of the sedan. Unfortunately, it had only taken a few minutes for the Reston Medical Ambulance team to complete their work. When they laid their patient out on the plastic bag, it was time for Alesi to step in.

"You guys finished?" he asked the taller of the two EMTs.

"Just about," the paramedic responded. "White male, young, probably about twenty-five or thirty. Dressed in a tux. Anything else is hard to tell. The collision cracked the side impact bars. His air bags trapped the poor bastard and the bars sliced right through him."

Alesi shuddered. He had never been able to inure himself to the violence of a "simple" traffic accident.

"I hope to hell you find the driver of that truck," said the other EMT looking over to the pile of smashed metal by the road.

"Not very likely," Alesi replied. "I ran the plates. It was reported stolen in Arlington yesterday. Looks like the driver took off into the woods after the accident. Probably without a scratch. You guys come up with any identification?"

"Nothin' we found, but you can take a look. Then we'll wrap him up."

He patted the man's pockets and came up empty.

"Nothing here. You can take him. I'll check the car."

Alesi walked back to the crash site and noticed the heavy scars on the trunk of the oak. This had not been the tree's first encounter with human carelessness.

He stuck his head into the car and was hit by the sickening odor of blood and death. There was no way he would ever get used to that smell. He pulled out, took a short breath and looked in again. Lying on the passenger seat was a tuxedo coat. He grabbed for the coat and stepped back from the wreckage.

"Find anything?" the first paramedic asked as he finished zipping up the bag.

Alesi checked the pockets and produced a thin wallet. "Something here." He yanked out a card, took a quick look, then tossed the jacket back in the car. "Shit!"

"What's the matter?" the shorter EMT asked.

"I may as well go home. There won't be any follow-up on this one."

"What do you mean? What's wrong?"

Alesi held up the card. It was an official-looking government ID. Across the top in bold, dark letters was "National Security Agency."

Chapter 13

Sʟᴀᴛᴛᴇʀʏ ᴛᴏssᴇᴅ ᴛʜᴇ last of the library books into the growing pile on the floor of his Langley office. Nothing but bullshit! Markovsky had really dropped a load on him this time.

What the hell was he doing trying to make sense out of the complex of unsubstantiated facts, rumors, and guesses laid out in Flynn's report?

Other agents were hard at work doing important jobs: processing field reports, performing political analysis, producing policy statements. He could see them through the glass partitions of his office scampering back and forth among the cubicles. The drones of the intelligence hive were hard at work.

Slattery had trained and mentored a lot of these employees over the years. Most were very capable and some honestly exceptional. He glanced up just in time to see one of his favorites walk through the open door.

"Jesus, Roger. What are you doing? Planning a book burning?"

"Might as well be for all the good they are. Come on in, Manny. I need the company."

The visitor was Manuel Ikedo, a young analyst specializing in European affairs. The offspring of Spanish and Japanese parents, his unique mixed heritage gave him a most un-American view of political and cultural thinking. This was exactly why Slattery considered him one of the best analysts in the Agency.

Ikedo made a quick scan of the senior agent's office. "You must be on one hell of an assignment."

"The impressive library you see around you," Slattery waved his arm above the jumble of documents scattered on his desk, "is the net result of the best information the FBI, NSA, Homeland and ATF have on militia activity."

"What are you doing messing around in domestic militia business?"

Slattery had to tread lightly here. Markovsky had made it clear that the advisory group's topics were strictly need-to-know. But he really could use some fresh thinking. "Peter must have owed somebody a big favor. I'm trying to see if there's any recent changes in tactics."

Ikedo's brow wrinkled and his head tilted awkwardly. "Find anything?"

"I found out how little we really know about these guys. It's downright scary. This internal shit frustrated me so much I went out to Tysons last night and bought everything I could find on the militia movement: *The Gathering Storm, A Force Upon the Plain, Harvest of Rage.* Everything." He pointed to the mound on the floor.

"That wasn't any better, huh?" Ikedo replied.

"Not really. Most of it is more propaganda than fact. There's enough crap in those for a thousand conspiracy novels: the New World Order, Third Continental Congress, Posse Comitatus. Some of the history's okay, stuff on the Montana Freemen and Michigan Militia, but nothing recent."

"How about checking open sources? Research is getting pretty good at it these days."

The intelligence agencies had frequently been criticized for relying too much on their own classified data and not exploiting so-called "open sources," information accessible through public channels. With the explosion of information on the Internet, this was now one of the richest sources available.

"Sure why not? Let's give 'em a try." Slattery reached for the phone and dialed a familiar number. "Rachael? . . . How are you? . . . Got a favor to ask. I need all you can find out on the militia movement. . . . Of course, it's important. I wouldn't come to the expert otherwise. . . . Great. I'll be right down." He set down the phone and turned back to Ikedo. "Want to go for a walk?"

Fifteen minutes later Slattery and Ikedo were two levels underground, staring at six inches of computer printout, complete with pictures, maps, and diagrams. They were seated at a small conference table inside the Research area. Hardly looking like a library, it was filled with cubicles and oversized LED monitors. Perfect for the computer-age spook. Which mostly left Slattery out in the cold.

"This all you can give me?" Slattery called with a smile to a young Indian woman with long black hair sitting at one of the workstations in a nearby aisle.

"Give me a few more minutes and I'll fill up the rest of your day," Rachel Bhan replied. "That's just the top level stuff. Mostly home pages, archives and newsgroups. I'm still tracing the secondary cross-references and a couple of dark web sites.

"I knew you liked paper so I did the printouts, Roger, but I'll email you the Intelink folder. I hear paper-cuts can be really dangerous."

Intelink was the intelligence community's ultra-secure intranet. It had been designed to improve sharing across the multiple agencies. To Slattery, the technology was usually just another sign of his obsolescence, but today it was also a beacon of his paranoia.

Slattery walked over to Bahn's desk. "About that, Rachael," he whispered. "Can we keep this one between us?"

Bahn furled her normally glass-smooth forehead. She hesitated, then gave the spook a smile. "Okay, Roger, but only for you."

"I owe you, Rachel," Slattery replied.

He returned to the table and continued his study of the documents.

After a couple of minutes, Ikedo looked up from the papers. "You do that often, Roger?" he said.

"Do what?" Slattery replied as calmly as he could. "Come down to Research?"

"No, Roger. Kill the Intelink file." The analyst's voice turned cold. "That isn't exactly Agency policy. What's really going on?"

Slattery tried to look surprised, then realized he couldn't keep lying to Ikedo. His cover story was slipping away fast. "It's complicated, Manny. But important. I can't talk about it here. Later. I promise. Will that do for now?"

Ikedo dropped his head and started wringing his hands. Slattery hoped he hadn't gone too far already.

"Okay," Ikedo finally replied. Then his face lightened and Slattery noticed a sly grin. "But if this is hot, I want in."

Slattery nodded. Nobody liked secrets better than spooks. "Be careful what you ask for, Manny. Deal."

They had been working through the documents for about thirty minutes when Ikedo sighed and leaned back in the chair.

"So when did you get this assignment, Roger?" he asked.

"Peter dropped it on me yesterday," Slattery answered quickly. The analyst knew something unusual was going on. He had to change the subject of this inquisition quickly. "By the way, how's Kit? You still refusing to marry that beautiful lady?" Kit Tomika was an analyst in the Far East section. She and Ikedo had been a "number" for years.

Ikedo's smile disappeared and he stared intently at the ceiling. "Crashed and burned, Roger. She met some hotshot lawyer from State. Said he had more to talk about than spook work."

"Sorry, Manny. Maybe next time."

"Roger!" The call came from across the room. "You ought to come and take a look at these."

Slattery and Ikedo joined the researcher at her station.

"Thought you might like to look at some of the sites," she said. On the screen was a bright, colorful web page with multiple animations of waving flags, men in combat, and military statistics. "This is the homepage of the Utah State Militia. Not bad, huh?"

"Jesus. This beats the tail off anything I've seen out of Washington. How'd these guys get so sophisticated?"

"It's not all that hard these days," she replied. "Any high school kid with spare time on his hands can put up something like this. I can think of worse things they could be doing."

"Yeah, except this kid's getting an education in a lot of other stuff as well. What else is out there?"

The researcher surfed through a few more sites, giving Slattery a brief look at the state-of-the-art in militia information. He usually ignored the reactionary scare tactics on the TV news, but he couldn't argue with this. There was a helluva lot of military and counter-political information on the Internet. Enough to feed any kind of militia conspiracy. And who knows what was going on behind the scenes.

They spent another half-hour in Research and collected at least three inches more of printouts and images. Then it was back to Slattery's office for the analysis. Ikedo scanned through some of the Agency's intelligence data while the older agent reviewed the new material.

"I didn't think we had this much on domestic militia," Ikedo commented looking up from one of the files.

"Theoretically, we shouldn't. By charter we can't work domestic issues. But occasionally some piece of intel will have a domestic connection. So we send the analysis off to the FBI. But it wouldn't do to just throw the background away, now would it?" Slattery grinned at the young agent's naiveté. Had he ever been that green?

"It would still be easier to review on the screen," Ikedo suggested.

"Maybe for you, Manny, but I'm still a paper and ink kinda guy. If I can't touch and feel it, it isn't real."

"So what makes you think someone is trying to coordinate militia activity?"

Slattery was good at hiding surprise. One of the best, he had been told, ever since the interrogation training at the Farm. But he knew he had lost the battle with Ikedo's off-hand remark. His hesitation was an eternity too long.

"Why would you ask that?" Slattery tried to ask flatly.

"Okay, Roger," Ikedo replied with a smile. "The topic never came up. Of course, one of the things *I* would be looking at if *I* were investigating militia would be the possibility that an external group was trying to direct militia activity."

"Why would you look for that?"

"Because of the high risk potential. Individually these groups can be dangerous. Look at what McVeigh did in Oklahoma. But once they reveal themselves they can't escape an investigation by the FBI and ATF. If the activities were coordinated however, they can back each other up: present multiple alibis, commit copycat crimes. Anything that could confuse the authorities. Then there's the Nazi scenario."

"The what? How does Germany figure into this?"

"What did they teach you in school, Roger? The fanaticism didn't start with Hitler. There were over forty organized parties and hundreds of splinter groups in Germany after the First World War. Most of them running around being pains in the ass to the new democratic government but never getting any real support. What Hitler and his band of brown shirts did was give them a vision, a political legitimacy. When the groups started communicating, and acting in concert, that's when the real trouble began."

"What would someone look for if they suspected some type of coordination was going on? Theoretically, of course."

Ikedo thought for a moment before continuing. "Theoretically, first of all they'd forget about big public groups like the Michigan Militia." He dropped the listings of web pages on top of the pyre of library books. "They're too large and too well-known. They're more interested in spreading propaganda than causing real damage. Plus they're probably littered with ATF informants that would turn in their brothers for a trip to Las Vegas. They could never keep an operation secret.

"Then I'd, sorry, these theoretical analysts, would look for the small cells. The ones with a handful of close knit members, often tied together by family. They're usually motivated by a single, very personal, event and keep their focus by fueling the hatred. That's where the conspiracy will start."

Slattery had learned more in the last two minutes with Ikedo than he had from all of the files combined. This was a resource he needed.

"Something wrong, Roger?"

"Yeah. All this shit around me. We've got to get you some more visibility. You want a real job?"

"With counterterrorism? I don't know. Would I have to wear a suit?"

Slattery doubted it would be any trouble convincing Markovsky to reassign Ikedo. He didn't need to divulge anything about the IMAGER background now, but he did need some help isolating the militia targets. And he had just found it.

The phone rang and Slattery picked it up.

"Slattery. . . . Sure, Rachael. Thanks. Send it over."

"What's up?" Ikedo asked.

"Rachael found some new stuff on a couple of the sites. Said we ought to take a look." He stared down at the keyboard. "Uh, I want to check a few other things, Manny. Can you pull it up for me?"

"Sure, Roger."

Ikedo moved around to the back of the desk and confidently typed a few commands. A collage of web pages flashed on the monitor. The headlines exploded Slattery's usual calm:

Movement Strikes at Government Propagandists

Fires Silence History of Lies

Missions for Truth

Revolution Begins!

Chapter 14

"WHAT'S UP, PETER?" Slattery asked after they had passed out of earshot of the lobby guard. "You sounded a little uptight when you called. 'Get your ass over to Fort Meade' I believe were your words. I thought you wanted to go over the FBI report?"

The two men were walking down a non-descript gray corridor in NSA headquarters at Fort Meade. Door after door was closed tight, each with an electronic access lock.

"Sorry about that, Roger," the DDI replied. "Events are moving rather quickly. I got a frantic call from Claude just after noon about the militia incident and IMAGER."

The NSA Deputy Director was another lifelong spook and nearly as uptight as Markovsky. They were both long-time friends and agency adversaries. "I have a hard time picturing Claude as frantic, but what does NSA have to do with our asset?"

"That's the problem. There is no asset. There is no IMAGER. They're all a story Claude and I concocted."

Slattery stopped short and gaped wide-eyed at his boss. "Concocted? What the hell do you mean? You've been giving fake intel to the Director of National Intelligence? They'll send your ass to Leavenworth for that."

"Calm down, Roger," Markovsky replied as he eased Slattery back into their walk. "I doubt it will go *that* far. Actually, the intel is real. Claude got it from a top security SIGINT project. We didn't want to jeopardize the project so we made up IMAGER."

Slattery shook his head. "Sounds like something the Puzzle Palace boys would think up. How'd they talk you into it?"

Markovsky's blank expression told Slattery he wasn't getting an answer to that question.

"Okay, I don't like it," Slattery finally replied, "but I've done worse. So what's the problem? Just keep up the front."

"The project was led by a hot-shot NSA cryptologist, Kam Yang. He developed a decryption algorithm for AES. A real breakthrough. But only he could do the decryption. And last night, he was killed in a traffic accident."

"Shit. That's a game-changer. Who's in charge of the project now?"

"One of Claude's golden boys, Garrett Robinson. That's who we're going to see. He's been baby-sitting Yang since he made the discovery."

"Didn't do a very good job, did he?"

"Nobody's perfect, Roger. Even you."

Slattery didn't want to take the conversation down that road. Markovsky knew too many of his skeletons.

"So what's Robinson's plan? Does he have another way to get the decryption done?"

"I don't think so. From what I heard, Yang kept the algorithm secret. Wouldn't let the agency know the details."

Slattery eyes popped. "Secret? I'm surprised they didn't keep him under house arrest."

"I'm sure they tried. But the guy was uncontrollable. A real screwball. But a genius screwball."

"There's a lot of those around here. He must have fit right in. Who is this Robinson anyway?"

"He's NSA's top troubleshooter. Background is Georgetown, Army and DIA. The org charts show him as a mid-level special projects manager, but he takes his orders from Claude. Ever since Yang discovered the algorithm, Robinson has had the job to keep the lid on it."

"I never heard of him."

"He's always been behind the scenes. He was the guy that came up with the Clipper Gambit."

"The Clipper Chip? Shit, Peter. That was a disaster. We spent millions on it, let go of some real intel, then the damn lobbyists still got it deep-sixed."

Slattery viewed the Clipper Chip as a classic case of federal paranoia gone amok. Even though it had been publicly backed by his agency, Slattery had thought that it was at best ill-conceived, and at worst incompetent.

By the late eighties, electronic communication had been exploding. Cellular phones, the nascent Internet, land-based telecommunications all were carrying an ever-increasing load of data as well as voice. And the data was significant: business negotiations, stock trades, product designs, government contract evaluations. Things that were too sensitive to be broadcast freely over relatively public media. The private sector had decided that it needed to protect itself and invested in any number of proprietary encoding schemes that would protect its transmissions from prying eyes, and sometimes prying wiretaps. Among the most enthusiastic users of this new technology was that part of the private sector known as organized crime.

Needless to say, the eavesdroppers of the country, the FBI, NSA, and all their friends, were beside themselves. They couldn't let private citizens communicate in ways that prohibited their listening in. So they declared data encryption a "national security issue." Laws were passed prohibiting export, researchers had their projects declared "Top Secret" which prevented them from releasing results, even writing scientific papers, and the black agencies set about to invent a "better answer."

That answer turned out to be the Clipper Chip. Introduced in 1993 and broadly endorsed by most government groups, the Clipper Chip was a semiconductor device that was to be placed in every telephone, every computer, and every communication device in the land. It would encode outgoing messages into an unintelligible form, and decode incoming messages so that they could be understood. Outside the device, in the "free," the messages would be gibberish, they couldn't be understood. Or at least not understood by anyone without a football field of supercomputers buried in their basement. The same basement Slattery and Markovsky were now walking over.

The proposal was supported by volumes of complex mathematics, fancy new words like private-key escrow and trap-door algorithms, but most of the country saw it for what it was: a ploy to let Uncle Sam continue to stick his nose in their private business.

How great could Robinson be if he was behind all this? From the beginning, Slattery had had questions about Clipper. As a counter-terrorist he knew the importance of intelligence data on your enemies. Internal communications were a big part of that intelligence. He couldn't do his job without it.

On the other hand, he didn't trust most of his colleagues any more than did the average citizen. Probably even less; he had worked with many of them. The way Clipper had been bludgeoned onto the country, he couldn't help but feel a little uneasy.

In the end, the Clinton administration just couldn't pull it off. Opposition was everywhere; from the American Civil Liberties Union to privacy groups like the Electronic Frontier Foundation and even the European Commission. So in 1996 VP Al Gore was sent out to announce that Clipper was dead and the country would have to live with the result. There had been stillborn efforts at Clipper II and Clipper III, but none ever had a chance of being adopted. The SIGINT spooks went back in their hole. Or so he had thought.

A broad smile filled the DDI's normally somber face. "Not the Chip, Roger. The Gambit. What was the most advanced encryption technique in the early nineties?"

"The RSA stuff I guess."

"Right. Well, NSA found a backdoor to break RSA, and eventually its follow-on, IDEA. So what did NSA have to do?"

"Keep it secret I guess."

"Sure, but what else? This was a time of extensive work on coding and security. Every university and private research lab was working on algorithms. NSA couldn't let something stronger get discovered."

Surprise flashed on the agent's face. "Jesus! You're telling me Clipper was a decoy? Something to keep the security community busy while NSA kept snooping around?"

"Glad to see you're not slipping in your advanced age, Roger. Robinson positioned Clipper as a way to direct security research toward a common enemy, the government. Everybody jumped on the bandwagon. Everybody started analyzing Clipper. That left RSA as the alternate encryption technique of choice. And something NSA could break. Most of the agency didn't even know the truth until the project was closed. Not a bad return for a few millions of dollars investment. Sorry we didn't think of it."

Slattery shook his head. How much longer could he put up with these games?

"Then this should be a very interesting meeting."

The pair stopped in front of a door marked only as "131." Markovsky knocked and the door opened onto a small, crowded office. Standing inside was a very trim man, early-to-mid-fifties, dressed casually in dark pants and a light blue polo shirt. His brown hair was slicked back and he assessed his visitors through deep green eyes. Slattery recognized him as Stroller's subordinate at the advisory group meeting.

"Peter, good to see you," Robinson said as he extended his hand. "I was hoping you would come along when Claude arranged the meeting."

"Good to see you too. Garrett, this is Roger Slattery. Roger's one of our counterterrorism specialists."

"I've heard about your work, Roger. It's a pleasure to meet you."

"Mr. Robinson," Slattery said as he took the agent's hand.

"Garrett, please. Thank you for coming." He gestured to a small table and chairs in the corner of the room and the trio sat down.

"I've briefed Roger about IMAGER, Garrett. How can we help?"

Robinson's *bonhomie* disappeared, replaced by an oppressive gravity. "The traffic accident was very unfortunate. Kam Yang discovered the decryption algorithm and, for reasons known only to him, he chose to keep its details secret from the rest of the Agency. Normally, this would be unacceptable and met with, well, certain sanctions, but the discovery was quite important, as you can imagine. We tolerated his eccentricity on the belief we would eventually be able to understand the algorithm. He had been exposing some parts over the past few months but never enough to let us implement it completely."

Robinson paused and folded his hands on the tabletop. It seemed like he was still considering how much to tell his new colleagues.

"You must understand that this is still not a real-time operation," he continued. "The decryption process can take hours for a single message. Yang had been testing the algorithm on a random sample of messages from the inbound stream and we stumbled across the militia transmission."

Slattery knew that Robinson's "inbound stream" was nothing less than all the signals intelligence, or SIGINT, available to NSA.

And that was a good portion of all the electronic information in the world: military satellite signals, cellular telephone, packet radio, messages on the Internet, and electronic graffiti secretly collected by hundreds of covert intelligence operations. They had caverns of computers collecting, sorting and analyzing that information. Or at least as much of it as they could decode. An increasing percentage of these signals were being encrypted by any of a number of powerful techniques.

"We called the militia file QUARTERBACK, and Yang's focus went to keeping the decryption pipeline filled with its feed. We were getting close to understanding the level of the threat when Yang died."

"Why not just tell the advisory group what happened?" Slattery asked.

"That would have been rather difficult, don't you think?" Robinson replied. "We had already told them IMAGER was HUMINT, human intelligence. Revealing the truth would have compromised Yang's discovery. Something that we are unwilling to do."

And would have exposed your little deceit, Slattery thought.

"How can we help, Garrett?" Markovsky asked.

"We have to discover the rest of the algorithm. Yang has a brother in China, another cryptologist. Kam may have shared the secret with him. We have to contact him and try to get the missing pieces. NSA doesn't have the infrastructure to reach him. You do." The agent fidgeted in his chair before continuing. "We need your help."

The last words were obviously difficult for Robinson. He wasn't used to asking for assistance. Markovsky, of course, took his time responding, enjoying the discomfort of his colleague.

"I brought Roger because of his background in terrorist groups. He's also run a number of covert ops. What do you think, Roger?"

"China is a difficult place. It would be easier to approach him on neutral territory. How receptive will he be?"

"We're not sure," Robinson answered. "Yang's family requested his body be sent back to China. We haven't had any contact with the brother."

"Then why do you even think he knows the algorithm?" Slattery asked.

"We've monitored Yang's personal email back to China. It's encrypted. We can't break it."

Robinson got up and walked back to his desk. He opened a drawer, pulled out a heavy folder, and dropped it in front of the DDI. A thick black stripe ran diagonally across the cover. Printed neatly on a label was "Top Secret – Eyes Only – QUARTERBACK."

"Here's Yang's file. It's everything we have." Robinson's voice dropped; its edge fell away. "We *have* to get that algorithm."

Markovsky calmly picked up the file and dropped it unopened into his briefcase. He glanced over to Slattery, nodded, and got up from his chair.

"We'll review this and get back to you with an analysis. I can't make any recommendations without clearing it with the Director."

"Of course," Robinson replied. "But it's got to be done quietly, Peter. The FBI will have our hides if this is revealed."

"Understood, Garrett." Markovsky turned for the door. "You'll clear our exit?"

"Already done. Good to meet you, Roger."

The pair of CIA agents headed back down the hall to the checkpoint.

"You really want me to help him, Peter?" Slattery asked.

"I don't know. I'm not excited about saving NSA's ass, but I believe the militia threat is real. Which means IMAGER is important. And now we're tied to the charade. By the way, did you make any progress on Flynn's file?"

Slattery saw the opening and jumped through.

"Not much. She's on real thin ice. I'll give you my preliminary evaluation when we get back to Langley. If you want any real analysis I'll need some help. I'd like Ikedo from European Ops."

"Why him?"

"He's got the best background to psych out these groups. Trust me."

"Okay," Markovsky said, "but *only* for the militia analysis. Keep him out of this Yang thing."

"Done. Thanks. So what do you want me to do about Robinson?"

Markovsky reached into his briefcase, pulled out the file and handed it to Slattery. "All yours. Review it and see what you can come up with. Get back to me tomorrow. I'm not taking this anywhere else for now."

Chapter 15

THIS WEEK SLATTERY made it out of the Giant Supermarket in Falls Church with only a single bag. Between his overtime in Langley, and Beth's class schedule at George Mason, there hadn't been much time for home cooked meals. He would be on his own again tonight, so he had picked a few frozen dinners and a half-gallon of Rocky Road ice cream.

Without a few small pleasures what was life worth?

He popped the locks on his Chevy Blazer and was reaching for the door handle when he heard the voice.

"Excuse me, Mr. Slattery."

A statement, not a question, from an unrecognized voice. Slattery dropped the plastic grocery sack to the ground and spun to face the voice. His hands went automatically to guard.

"Oh, I'm sorry," said the voice. It came from a small, emaciated-looking, man. Perhaps ten years Slattery's junior, he was dressed in khakis and a windbreaker. "I didn't mean to startle you."

The agent stood his ground.

"My name is Taylor Luckett," the man continued. "I'm a reporter for the *Washington Post*. I wanted to talk with you about the militia incident at Tyler, Georgia."

Slattery went on full alert. "I'm sorry, mister . . . Luckett was it? I really don't know what you're talking about. Perhaps you're confusing me with someone else."

"No, Mr. Slattery, I'm not confused. Roger Edward Slattery, counter-terrorism, Central Intelligence Agency, on assignment to Peter Markovsky. Currently investigating militia activity for DNI Carlson's own private advisory group; probably circumventing most every statute of the Office of the Director of National Intelligence. Did I miss anything?"

Slattery remembered the name Luckett from a couple news stories he had read. Why the hell would the reporter accost him on the street? If this really was Luckett. "I still don't know what you're talking about. Why don't you just go . . . "

"Goddammit, Slattery. Those bastards killed my best friend, George Brown. I don't have time for your too-cool spook routine. I have information on the Tyler cell. Can we compare notes?"

"I don't think we have *anything* to discuss, Mr. Luckett. I suggest you get out of my way, before I call the police."

"Screw you, Slattery!" The man turned and stomped back toward the grocery store.

Jesus Christ, thought Slattery. *What else is going to happen on this assignment?*

* * *

"Did you make a killing on the IPO?" he asked.

The tiramisu had just arrived and Braxton decided he would try to chip away at a bit more of the nearly impenetrable wall that still separated them. So far, the dinner with his ex-wife had been a stiff and uncomfortable experience. He had taken her to a small Italian restaurant in Georgetown. They had always loved trying new places when they were married. He had hoped the atmosphere at Venetti's—the aromas of garlic and oil, the romantic Italian accents, the colorful tablecloths and decorations—would make for easier conversation.

It hadn't.

He had been surprised at her call, and honestly shocked when she asked him to dinner. To be fair, they had not parted amicably. After he had been laid off he had wallowed in self-pity for months, alienating friends and family alike. Megan had tried her best to help him, but he had fought her off at every attempt. She had finally given up, moved to the other end of the country, and taken a job at a Silicon Valley start-up. From what he had read about their recent Initial Public Offering, it had been a very profitable decision.

"Adam, it's not polite to discuss money." Connelly gave him a solemn stare. "But if you must know . . ." Now she managed a slight smile with that crazy crooked turn of her mouth. It brought back memories of happier times. "We were all really surprised. Going public had always been our dream, of course. I took a big salary hit in exchange for equity. We didn't think we were big enough yet, but Paul Venton, our CEO, just kept pushing. The valuation was a dream come true. I didn't do as well as the Founders, of course, but let's just say it did pay off."

"That's great. I have to confess I followed the negotiations on the Net. I was hoping you had done well."

From what Braxton had read, Vision One had developed the first true 3D holographic display. Holograms had been standard fare in TV programs and movies for years, but Vision One had figured out how to make it real. The technology was revolutionary and enabled deep-pocket customers to "see" information that otherwise was just a list of numbers or flat pictures on a monitor. Meteorologists used it to plot pressures and winds in the atmosphere. Aircraft engineers could see stresses and airflows. Their potential market was huge.

"You're sweet," Connelly replied. "Thank you. But look at you: suit and tie, your own company, and you read the business news. What do your research friends think?"

"They all want me to consult for them, at reduced rates of course. I guess I've been pretty lucky too." He returned the smile.

"Lucky is right. You nearly got yourself killed!" Braxton's eyebrows jumped. "Okay, don't look at me like that. My turn to confess. I tried to find out more about you and that Incident. I didn't have very much luck; mostly just rumors. How did you ever get so involved with those people?"

He shrugged. "It just kinda happened. The more I looked into the problem, the deeper I got. Then when Paul, my friend, was killed, . . . well, I just couldn't let go."

"And how is Ms. Goddard? Are you still seeing her?"

He felt his face flush. "Susan? How do you know about her?" All he received was a wry grin in return. "She's fine. She took a PR job for the new Virginia Senator and I've been trying to build the consulting business. We got too busy. I still haven't figured out this relationship thing."

"I'm sorry, Adam. But you do seem to be happier. I'm glad."

Her voice turned soft and the smile disappeared. She looked tired, gray arcs hanging deeply under her beautiful blue eyes. Had work been that difficult?

"So what's life like working for Vision One these days? Any calmer?"

"Oh, not all that different. Now we just have to keep all the industry analysts happy. We go from one quarter to the next trying to meet their expectations. But we have doubled our installed base in the past six months."

"Super. I did hear you opened a new office in Europe. Are you going to stay in Palo Alto?"

"I guess for now. I actually don't know that much about the European operation. Our CEO has been building that himself." She started to twist the hair behind her ear with her fingers. It had always meant something was bothering her.

"What's going on over there?"

"Just getting the new office set up. European distributors and partnerships. The usual stuff."

"Have there been many personnel changes?"

"Well, some of our key people are being called onto special projects. Getting sent to Holland. It's really disruptive, but there's not much we can do."

He couldn't help but feel she was holding something back. He didn't want to pry, but she had asked him out hadn't she?

"Is anything wrong, Megan? You look really stressed."

"Thanks."

"I didn't mean . . ."

"I know. It's okay. Everybody says I've been kinda uptight lately. I'm probably just being silly."

"Tell me about it. I promise not to repeat any corporate secrets."

She returned his smile. "Oh, it's nothing like that. It's just, well . . . I had a friend. Ben Lawson. He was one of our Founders and our best researcher. We started dating. A few months ago he was pulled over to help set up the Utrecht office."

"That doesn't sound so unusual."

"No, but then last week I got a strange letter from him. Not email; handwritten. He said he had a funny feeling about the project. He didn't explain, but said he'd tell me when he came back."

"When is he due back?"

Her head fell. "He won't be coming back. He was killed in a traffic accident."

Her eyes turned red and teary, despite an obvious attempt to hold back the emotion.

"I'm sorry, Megan. Is there anything I can do?"

"Oh, no. Thank you. Vision One is taking care of everything. I just couldn't help but wonder. Could his death have anything to do with the note I received?"

"That's all you have? Just his letter?"

"Yes."

"Then I don't think you should let it worry you. He was probably working too hard, and got depressed. It happens to a lot of us."

"But Ben was always so grounded; so analytic. It wasn't like him to imagine things."

"I think you're the one letting your imagination go. There's nothing you can do. It was just an unfortunate coincidence."

"You don't think I should try to find out more?"

He didn't want to be too hard on her, but he knew what happened when you began to see conspiracies around every corner. He couldn't stand to see that happen to her.

He reached out and took her hand.

"Megan. It was an accident. You obviously cared about him a lot. But don't let that cloud your judgment. Accidents happen. There's nothing more you can do."

She started to say something then stopped. A look of resignation came over her face.

"You're right. I'm sorry I bothered you." She blotted her tears with the napkin, then set it on the table. "I must look a mess. I'll be right back."

He watched as she walked through the maze of tables. Petite, with short dark hair, a beautiful face and striking figure, heads still turned when she passed.

How could he have treated her so badly? And what could he do to help her now?

Chapter 16

"YOU LOOK LIKE crap, Roger. Bad night?"

"Thanks, Peter. Yeah, you could say that. Had a little trouble sleeping."

The sun streamed through the windows in Markovsky's office forcing Slattery to face the reality of the morning. He fidgeted in the too-soft easy chair. Somehow his body just didn't fit with his boss's definition of style. But then maybe that was the idea.

"Beth okay?" Markovsky asked.

"Sure thing. She said to say hello."

"Great lady Beth. She wasn't mad at my keeping you busy the last few days was she?"

"Oh, she's gotten used to it by now," Slattery replied halfheartedly. In fact, he had spent most of Wednesday evening apologizing, trying to make up for his virtual absence *that* night. Then, after the visit to Robinson, he had been worse company, staying up until 2:00 a.m. last night crystallizing his plan. A late request to Ikedo had gotten him the last piece.

"What's your take on Yang?"

"Well, he certainly was a helluva cryptologist, as well as an incredible pain in NSA's ass according to the file. It's a wonder Robinson put up with him."

"Knowing Garrett, I'm sure it drove him crazy, but he could hardly ignore the intel opportunity. Breaking AES was a dream come true."

"From Robinson's notes they were making some progress on getting Yang's secret, but not fast enough. Now they're dead in the water and they're stuck with IMAGER as well."

"*We're* stuck," Markovsky corrected.

"Okay. But how *did* they pull you into this mess?"

"It's a long story, Roger. I owed Claude a favor. Now what's your recommendation?"

Slattery recognized when his boss had passed the point of pleasantries. He hoped the plan he had concocted in the quiet darkness a few hours before still made sense in the light of day.

"We can't approach Yang's brother directly. It would be suicide professionally and politically. And could get the brother killed. The Chinese state police don't bother with polite questions. We need a middle-man. Someone who can make contact without raising alarms."

"How do we do that? Beijing isn't exactly the most open environment."

"Agreed. But I did some checking last night. There's an international mathematical cryptology conference in Amsterdam next week. Yang's brother is registered. I believe if we could place an asset at the conference, he could make the contact."

"He's bound to be watched constantly by the Chinese security. We can't just drop anyone in. It would be too dangerous."

"But if we found a bona fide scientist, with all the right credentials, who wasn't connected to us . . ."

"And would do what we tell him to . . ." Markovsky added.

"We might have a chance."

Markovsky paused and squeezed the bridge of his nose. "I suppose you have a name to put with this superman?"

"Actually I do. Someone I, ah, worked with, a while ago."

"You can talk this someone into this escapade? He could get himself arrested you know. Or worse."

Slattery looked off into the lush green Virginia countryside. "I know. But with the right motivation . . ."

* * *

George Tracomb didn't know what he was doing here. Why was he making useless telephone calls to people he didn't even know?

It was all that new CEO Dennis Phillips' fault. Ever since he had arrived at the National Culture Collection, all he had done was disrupt their well-practiced protocols. His latest fad was Quality, with a capital Q. He wanted to change NCC, make it a Quality organization. No one knew why he wanted to change, just that it was oh so necessary. Nothing but MBA bullshit.

It was not as if they were failing. The NCC was a world-renowned clinical laboratory. They stocked, catalogued, cultured, and distributed pure biological specimens to scientists around the world. From *aabomyceticus Sieno* to *Zymophilis raffinosivora* they had the definitive cultures. Over 90,000 of them. For diagnosis and therapy development. Everyone knew they were the best. At least everyone except Phillips.

He said it was all about Quality. Well, Tracomb knew about quality. He was a Ph.D. in Biochemistry. He knew everything about monoclonal antibodies, recombinant DNA probes, Elisa assays. That was all he needed to know.

But that wasn't good enough for Phillips. He had decreed that every employee would serve on one of the uncountable Quality Teams— "QT"s Phillips called them—that had been created to improve NCC. Tracomb had been assigned to the Customer Satisfaction QT. He had gone to the first meeting and discovered this meant he would sit in a cramped, sweltering, converted closet for two hours every Friday morning and call NCC's customers. Ask them if their sample arrived, was it what they had ordered, had they had any problems?

Who did Phillips think their customers were, homemakers looking for a new soap? They were scientists, researchers, some with Nobel Prizes. If anything had gone wrong, Phillips would have heard about it long before Tracomb ever made his call.

But here he was, losing valuable laboratory time, going down a stupid list of orders. He had tried appealing to his boss, but she had only shaken her head. Her QT was calling NCC's suppliers asking what his company could do to help *them*. Insanity.

Tracomb ran his finger down the list and stopped after the last margin notation. He moved across to the column with the telephone number and dialed.

* * *

Her red hair tossed in the air like a burning match caught in a whirlwind. One final flare flashed before his eyes then she was quiet. With a satisfied sigh she relaxed, lowered herself to the bed, and wrapped her long body over his.

Robinson finally released the tension in his own muscles, relieved the performance was complete. He had never known such a driven woman; either at work or in bed. There could be little time to rest; at any moment she could spring from the lover's nest and attack her next target.

It had started as simply another of his many valuable contacts. Two aggressive federal executives sharing experiences and trying to squeeze some bauble of insider information from each other. He had sensed a mutual physical attraction and choreographed a careful seduction that had ended two months before here in her bed.

But to be honest, he was never sure who had seduced whom.

Neither held any simplistic romantic notions. They were much too devoted to themselves to harbor dreams of blissful happiness or white picket fences. Still, the relationship had its value; they achieved no small amount of sexual gratification with a high degree of safety—neither could afford to reveal they were sleeping with the enemy.

He heard a satisfied sigh and rolled onto his side, stretching his arm across her china-white chest.

"You continue to surprise me, Garrett," she whispered. "Such emotion coming from a closet sociopath."

"And I love you too, Mary Ellen. Anyone ever tell you you can be a bit blunt?"

She laughed and tossed her long hair to the side of the pillow. "Everyone. Most of the time. But I get the job done."

He kissed her on the ear. "Can't argue with that."

She shot him one of her characteristic scowls and shoved him onto his back.

"Don't get too pleased with yourself. I really am mad at you, you know. I could have used some support at that advisory group meeting."

"You mean about that militia stuff? What was I supposed to do?"

"It was bad enough having to put up with that shit Markovsky, but I didn't need to get nailed by your boss."

"Okay, so Claude got a little carried away. I'll talk to him. You know I'm on your side." He rolled over and started to nibble on her ear.

"My side!" She pushed up and stared down at him. "Apparently not all the time. I saw you and Markovsky scheming after the meeting."

Shit! He had to be more careful.

"I was just trying to find out if he really did have anything new on IMAGER. Don't be so paranoid."

"Wasn't it J. Edgar who said 'only the paranoid survive'?"

"Actually," Robinson countered, "I think it was Andy Grove of Intel. But who's keeping track?"

Flynn stared across the bed and out her Watergate apartment window. "Garrett?"

"Yes?"

"You don't think Markovsky could be making it all up do you?"

"What! Uh, I mean making what up?"

"All that IMAGER stuff. Sometimes I get the feeling there's something phony going on in Langley. I'm sure he's hiding something."

Robinson attempted a carefree laugh. "You've thought the Agency was phony ever since you came to Washington, Mary Ellen. Markovsky may be a bit odd for your taste, but he's a good intelligence officer. I'm sure he's doing everything he can."

"He damn well better be. If I catch him leading us on a wild goose-chase I'll have his ass."

"And I thought that was what I was for."

Flynn paused for just a moment, then caught the barb and pounced onto her lover. She wasn't finished with him yet.

* * *

Tracomb slammed the phone down in disgust. He had been talking with a whining post-doc at the University of Michigan who didn't like the way his order had been packaged! The incompetent student had treated him like some mail clerk. What control did Tracomb have over the post office?

He put his initial by the entry in the log. Nothing worth reporting here.

* * *

Flynn hopped from the bed like a jackrabbit.

"Got meetings at the NCTC this afternoon," she said, striding unabashedly naked toward the bathroom. "Trying to work out this militia problem."

"How's your report for Carlson going?" Robinson asked.

"Screw the report," she called back over the running shower.

"I've got an investigation to run. The hell with Killer Carlson and his damn advisory group."

Robinson smiled at the sobriquet. It was a left-over from his Marine take-no-prisoners attitude. And something that was *never* said to his face—that would definitely be career-ending.

His partner seemed in a good mood. Time to see what she might let slip. "What are you working on?" he called as casually as he could.

"Oh, checking out all the cells around the arson sites. Some of them must be involved." The shower turned off and she reappeared wrapped in a towel. "By the way, you know a CIA agent named Slattery?"

Slattery! What is she doing with him?

"Doesn't sound familiar," Robinson replied. "What does he do?"

"Counter-terrorism under Markovsky. The Director wants me to work with him on the militia strategy. I wondered if you had heard of him."

"I may have heard the name from Claude. Don't know anything about him, though. Sorry."

"Just thought I'd ask. I'll try to be polite. But he damn well better not get in my way."

Shit. He just gave Slattery the whole IMAGER background. If the agent let anything slip, Flynn will have his head. Or some other indispensable bodily part.

"Another working lunch later this week?" she teased while wriggling into a skin-tight blue silk skirt.

"Sounds good to me."

Robinson stretched out across the huge king-size bed, surveying the state of his soon-to-be middle-aged body. He sat up and six puffs of muscle appeared on his abdomen. Well, the assignation had at least one positive result: he was in better shape than he had been in years.

* * *

There were only ten minutes left on Tracomb's shift. He might make it yet.

The closet smelled like a locker room. He had to get out of this assignment.

"Centers for Disease Control and Prevention," the voice said with a slight southern accent. "Could you please hold?"

"No!" Tracomb screamed but the country-western background music had already started.

The voice returned after two full choruses of some twangy love song. "How may I help you?"

"This is George Tracomb from National Culture," he began mechanically. "I would like to speak to . . ." he went back to the listing to check the contact column, "Dr. Weaver."

"Just a moment."

Tracomb waited, rapidly tapping the end of his pencil on the desk. At least she didn't put him on hold.

"I'm sorry, I have no listing for a Dr. Weaver. Do you have a department name?"

"No." There was no other affiliation on the printout.

"Then I'm afraid I can't help you."

"Just a minute." Tracomb went back to the listing and read across. "Dr. Randolph Weaver, one vial biologicals, DZ252M." Nothing unusual, standard laboratory fair. He was surprised the CDC didn't have enough of their own.

"I'm sorry, sir. But we have no Dr. Randolph Weaver."

"Okay. Thanks. I guess I've got a bad name."

"Sorry we couldn't help, sir."

"Yeah, good bye."

Tracomb shook his head. Another screw-up on the list. Probably the damn computers. He scribbled a question mark in the margin and moved down to the next entry.

Only five minutes left.

Chapter 17

"MR. SMITH IS here to see you, Adam."

Karen Chu's mellow voice came over the intercom. Braxton remembered her message from earlier in the day. A Mr. J. Smith from MITRE had called requesting a meeting. He was very insistent, impolite was Karen's word, and she had set up an appointment for 11:30. Just barely time before he had to leave for a client visit in Crystal City.

MITRE Corporation was a major government contractor with projects reaching into nearly every federal agency. Their DoD work was based in Bedford, Massachusetts, outside of Boston, while the civilian efforts were led from down the street in McLean. Braxton didn't know who had gotten him the meeting, but an entry into MITRE could be a gold mine.

"Show him in, Karen," he responded into the box.

DoD, Braxton concluded as the man marched into his office. Smith strode in head high and shoulders back with a leather briefcase hanging at his side like it was glued to his arm. He was heavyset but not fat, with short gray hair and gold-rimmed aviator glasses. He looked like a retired general in a business suit, which was probably close. MITRE was a popular landing strip for military retirees.

"Mr. Braxton," the visitor said as he offered his hand.

"Good morning, Mr. Smith," Braxton motioned to the chair placed at the corner of his desk. "How can I help you?"

His visitor took the offered chair, sat down, and immediately opened his briefcase. He fumbled with its contents for a minute or so, then, without ever withdrawing anything, closed it and set the case on the floor at his side. He seemed to relax after this ritual and smiled broadly.

"I'm afraid I'm not from MITRE, Mr. Braxton," Smith began. "That was a bit of a fabrication to get an appointment without causing too much attention. Actually, I'm with the Central Intelligence Agency. We would like to ask for your help."

Flares exploded in Braxton's head. The CIA! What the hell did they want? Did Mr. Smith—Braxton was sure that wasn't his real name—know anything about his role in the Incident?

"I can't imagine how I could be of any help to the CIA, Mr. Smith," Braxton replied as directly as he could.

"You're aware of the International Cryptography Meeting in Amsterdam next week?"

"Yes. I remember the announcement."

"Are you planning on attending?"

"I'm afraid not. I've got a lot of business to complete and I don't have the time this year. Why?"

"Nothing nefarious, you can be sure." The mechanical smile grew even wider making Braxton even more uneasy. "As I'm sure you're aware, we frequently talk with scientists and business people attending international meetings. Their insights are extremely valuable as we develop intelligence assessments. A simple hallway conversation, a chance meeting with a colleague, all these may be unimportant to you, but could be a critical piece of a larger puzzle.

"Our job is to collect these pieces and construct the mosaic. These conversations are, of course, kept in strictest confidence. For some we can provide a small remuneration, but honestly most simply do it as a way to give something back to their country."

Braxton was sure the motives were hardly so patriotic. He had once thought about such encounters as exciting and romantic, but he now had enough cloak-and-dagger for a lifetime.

"I'm sorry, Mr. Smith. But as I said, I'm not planning to attend. And to be honest, I'm not really interested in working for the CIA."

"You wouldn't be working *for* us. We would never ask you to do anything you wouldn't normally do. Think of it as simply a patriotic contribution. We are quite anxious to get your opinion on some of the recent cryptographic developments, especially in China."

China? They never speak publically about their cryptography programs. How could I have an opinion?

"I hardly think I would be able to help you, Mr. Smith," Braxton continued. "Cryptography isn't my area of expertise."

"Come now, Mr. Braxton. You are very well-known in the community." Smith paused, then said, "One might say even a celebrity after the Incident."

Braxton's heart skipped a beat. So he did know! He tried to read through the pleasant facade on the agent's face, but it was impenetrable. How involved had Smith been in the efforts to trace the Internet mole? How much did he really know?

This man was making him very uncomfortable. Braxton's hands were clammy and his heart pounded all the way to his toes. He had to end this meeting.

"That's history, Mr. Smith, or whatever your real name is. As I said, I really can't help you. Actually, I don't *want* to help you. Now, if you don't mind . . ." Braxton stood up and moved around the desk.

"Of course, Mr. Braxton." Smith rose and reached in his pocket. Braxton froze in mid-step before seeing the hand reappear with a business card. "Please do think about my offer. You would be doing a great service to your country. Here's my card. Feel free to call me at any time."

Braxton gingerly took the card. It was plain white, holding only the name 'John Smith' and a 703 area code telephone number. He turned it over looking for some kind of affiliation.

"That's all you need to get me," Smith commented.

Braxton reluctantly shook the agent's hand and walked him to the door. Smith reached for the handle, then paused, and turned back to face the consultant. The mechanical smile had disappeared.

"In case you have any concerns over the validity of this request, Mr. Braxton, give Sam a call. He can vouch for me."

"Sam?"

The smile returned on Smith's face. This time it almost appeared genuine. "I think you know who I mean. Tell him he still owes me that *Dos Equis.*"

Braxton watched as Smith left the office and turned down the hall. What had he gotten into now?

"That was a short meeting," Chu said as her boss walked by. "No luck?"

"I'm not really sure," Braxton replied. "Give Sam Fowler a call. I've got some questions for him."

*   *   *

"Ladies and gentlemen," President Matthews began solemnly. He was addressing the Press Corp in the James S. Brady Press Briefing room, an idea Dawson must have had over a bout of severe indigestion. Why external events continued to conspire against him, he would never know.

"I believe many of you have read with alarm the recent Report on World Terrorism released by the NATO Counter-Terrorism Analysis Group. Despite concerted efforts by the international community, certain factions, and nations, continue to believe that terrorist acts will help them slow the inevitable progress of peoples to seek freedom and democracy. The United States of America will never accept or condone such acts, and will apply all of its resources to assure that those responsible are brought to justice.

"Because of this documented threat to the sovereignty of our great nation, I have asked the Director of National Intelligence to prepare a detailed analysis of our readiness to identify, prevent, and if necessary, respond, to terrorist activity on our soil. He will complete this report in the next ninety days. Along with his analysis, I have asked for specific recommendations, organizational and operational, which will better enable us to meet this threat.

"I know you all must have a number of concerns on this effort, so I have asked General Carlson to join me in answering your questions. Before we begin, however, I want to assure you and the American public that this effort is purely cautionary. We have no evidence of any existing terrorist plans. But let those in the international terrorist community be alerted that we will not tolerate their heinous actions here or anywhere in the world."

"General Carlson and I will now take a few of your questions. Mr. Harrison." Matthews nodded into the crowd toward CNN's White House Correspondent. Donald Harrison had been a favorite ever since his positive coverage of the Turkey conflict.

"Thank you, Mr. President," the reporter replied. "Will you or the Director be making any changes in the structure of the intelligence community as a result of this request?"

Matthews stepped back as if on cue and Carlson stepped to the podium.

"As you know, Mr. Harrison, the National Counterterrorism Center has been tracking and responding to terrorism threats for some time now. Today we have representatives from the CIA, NSA, FBI, DoE, DEA, State and all branches of the Department of Defense. This is by far the most knowledgeable and capable group of individuals to address the President's request. We will, of course, solicit additional expertise from across the government, but I do not envision any major membership or structural changes at this time."

Hands were again raised and Carlson pointed into a crowd on the right. A tall, slim woman pushed up through the others.

"General Carlson." It was Caroline Guthrie from the *New York Times*. "Is this increased focus a reaction to the upcoming intelligence sharing agreement signing? Have any specific threats been made?"

"Security is always a concern at any major event such as the signing, Miss Guthrie. But the Secret Service and the FBI have extensive plans for the safety of all of our guests. We are aware of no particular threats and anticipate no security problems. This event is *not* a focus for the NCTC."

Carlson shifted his attention and pointed to the left. This time it was a man who broke through.

"Taylor Luckett from the *Washington Post*, General. You seem to have focused on the threat of *foreign* terrorism at the signing. What about the threat from inside the country? From the so-called militia movement, for example."

Matthews saw Carlson's jaw tighten. What was bothering Steven?

"Mr. Luckett," Carlson replied. "We are certainly aware of your personal interest in this particular topic, but we believe the real threat lies in the extensive network of international terrorism described in the NATO report, not in the farms and communities of law-abiding Americans. Miss Guthrie?"

"Excuse me, sir," Luckett interrupted, "but what about the three arson attacks . . ."

"That's quite *enough*, Mr. Luckett," Carlson commanded. He turned back to his left. "Mr. Grant?"

Leave it to Carlson to shoot someone in the head for asking a question, Matthews thought. Luckett was a bit off the mainstream, but he was a good reporter. Ever since Oklahoma City, no one in their right mind ignored domestic para-military activity.

Carlson took three more questions before the President brought
the press conference to a close. There had been no more questions
about domestic terrorism.

Matthews and his entourage filed out of the briefing room in
neat pecking order. Why hadn't he heard about the militia attacks?
He made a mental note to find out.

Chapter 18

"WELCOME TO OUR little corner of the NCTC, Roger. Good to see you again. It's been a long time."

Slattery had requested a meeting with the Special Assistant earlier in the day. It was all part of his strategy to test the militia analysis Ikedo had developed, without alerting Carlson.

He had been escorted up to the third floor of the NCTC where he had been personally greeted by the Special Assistant. The FBI's Counterterrorism Division occupied most of the floor. Flynn had dressed down today, foregoing the staid business suit for a knit top and tailored silk skirt. The outfit made her almost look normal.

"Mary Ellen," he said, extending his hand. "I really appreciate your taking the time to meet with me today. I'm not sure how much I can contribute to your investigation, but perhaps by comparing notes we can come up with some new ideas. It has certainly been an eventful week."

She seemed surprised at his deferential approach and her voice lost some of its usual edge.

"Very much so, Roger. And we can use all the ideas we can get."

She led him into a large, comfortable office. It was decorated in classic Washington Bureaucrat: heavy in oak and leather, with numerous smiling group photographs and the requisite portrait of the reigning Director, Franklin Squires. What was missing was any artifact that would suggest the Special Assistant had a life outside the Bureau.

Flynn directed him to a small conference table across from her desk.

"Would it be too much to expect any new information from your asset?"

Well, she does get right to the point.

"I'm afraid so, Mary Ellen. There's been nothing new since Peter's report at the meeting. I went through what little we had on militia activity, but it left more questions than answers."

"And we don't have a whole lot more," Flynn replied. "We've infiltrated most of the large groups, but they don't seem to be involved in this latest activity."

It was time to play some of Ikedo's insights. "That would be expected. Whoever is organizing this is going to keep it low key. Use the smaller groups. Security is better and there's less chance of running into informers." Slattery noticed Flynn was actually paying attention to his analysis. Maybe there was some value to this meeting after all. "You did hit on the Tyler cell pretty accurately. Where did you get the lead?"

Their eyes met, and Flynn hesitated, apparently evaluating the request. A moment later she responded.

"The Atlanta field office received an anonymous tip. They checked it out and it looked interesting. Special Agent Derek Thomas went on surveillance, then we sent him in."

The tension in Flynn's voice betrayed the effect the agent's loss still held over her. He decided to drop the topic for the moment but wanted to know more about that anonymous tip.

"Anything on Tennessee or Kansas?"

"Some possibilities. The local field offices are preparing briefs with the assistance of the Serial Crimes Teams. Unfortunately, we didn't have much militia focus in either state. I doubt there'll be too many easy answers."

"I understand. These will be very tough groups to identify. How many folks do you have in the field?"

"We assigned a Serial Crime Team to each site and they're backed up with five local agents. We're okay on coverage now, but if this multiplies . . ."

"Not a scenario any of us want to think about, Mary Ellen. I would like to look over those reports when they come in. If that's all right."

Another pause. All investigators were jealous of their data; Slattery had been in the same position enough times to know. But if he was going to pull this out for Markovsky, he had to get Flynn's support.

Flynn finally stared back into Slattery's eyes. "Of course, Roger. I'll have Dawn forward them to you."

So far so good.

"Thanks. We've got some experience profiling the operations of small cells like these." Flynn's eyebrows jumped. "Internationally, of course," he quickly added. "Maybe we can find some common factors to bring into play."

"Understood." Flynn sat back and laid her hands in her lap. "So tell me, Roger, why did Peter put you on this one? Trying to check up on us?"

"Absolutely not, Mary Ellen. Honestly, I think he's worried. He's been uncharacteristically uptight lately. He's bothered by the lack of IMAGER response, and seriously concerned about the ramifications of coordinated action. History paints a pretty bleak picture."

"We must be reading the same books at night. I haven't slept very well either. Tell Peter we do appreciate the help. We believe this is very important, Roger. Even if the DNI seems to disagree."

Slattery nodded. "I agree, but I'm sure Carlson is just being cautious. That's why we need to get some more proof of the coordination." He hated to bring up the next subject, but it needed to be asked. "Still no word from your agent?"

"No. I'm afraid we've lost him." Flynn paused and he saw she was having trouble dealing with the disappearance. Losing a colleague was a wrenching experience for any law enforcement office. No matter how experienced.

"The best proof would be more militia activity," she continued. "Something we definitely don't want. I'm between a rock and hard place, Roger."

An awkward silence told Slattery it was time to quit while he was ahead. Before she started pushing any harder on IMAGER.

"Then we'll have to help you come up with something, Mary Ellen. But I think I've taken up enough of your time already."

Before he could get up, Flynn stopped him. "One more thing, Roger. The Tyler cell is still under surveillance, and it looks like our friends are getting ready for something. There has been a lot of activity at the farm. Supplies have been arriving for days. Now it could just be a great big happy family party," Flynn didn't even try to hide her sarcasm, "but I'm betting it's something more."

Why was she describing this now? What was she afraid of earlier?

"What can you do?"

"Nothing. We have one new agent on surveillance. And there's no way I'm sending *him* inside alone. We have no proof of any criminal activity. Even if they start popping off some handguns and rifles, that's not a crime. Certainly not in Georgia. So we'll sit it out and take pictures. It'll be a day or so before I get the report, but it should be interesting reading."

Slattery was about to open his mouth when Flynn added: "I'll flash you the report as soon as I get it."

He nodded in reply. Time to sneak one in. "Did your informant have any additional information?"

"Informant?"

"Yes. The one who originally alerted you to Tyler."

"Oh. No. We don't know who he was. One thing though. The original call came from DC not from Atlanta. Our informant's a local boy."

A D.C. resident? Maybe things were starting to click.

"Well, look on the bright side. Maybe these exercises will keep them out of trouble for a while."

"We can hope."

Now it *was* time to go. They got up from the table and walked back to the door.

"Thanks again for the time, Mary Ellen. I wish we could have gotten reacquainted under less stressful situations. If you need anything just give me a call."

"I think you know what I want from the Agency, Roger. And for us, they're always stressful situations."

* * *

Matthews relaxed in the Oval Office sofa and watched his friend sitting across the coffee table. It was the end of a very long day for both men and they were enjoying the moment by sharing some of the President's favorite sour mash.

"So explain these militia attacks to me, Steven," Matthews asked. "I didn't see anything about them in the Daily Brief."

"Yes, sir. I didn't feel they were of sufficient concern. These events are a subject of some disagreement among my advisory group."

"Indulge me. Just the basics."

"Last Thursday there were three militia attacks; the ones Mr. Luckett mentioned," Carlson began. "Fires were set at small independent newspapers in Georgia, Tennessee and Kansas. There was one fatality, we do not know whether it was intentional or not. The FBI believes this could be the start of an escalation by these groups. "

"Do you agree with the FBI's assessment of the threat, Steven?"

"I'm not sure, Mr. President. I have asked for comprehensive reports from all the agencies. The FBI's RIPPER program did identify a number of points of commonality, but the sample is so small it's impossible to draw any hard conclusions."

Matthews nodded. "RIPPER has been quite successful. We should not ignore its findings."

"I agree, Mr. President, but we should not rush to any premature conclusions either. I believe our most prudent course is to let the FBI continue their investigation. These could still be simply random events."

"What about this IMAGER agent?" Matthews asked. "Didn't he confirm the coordination hypothesis?" Matthews watched his DNI's reaction as he named the source. It had taken all afternoon to pry the background from the CIA.

Carlson hesitated, then continued unfazed. "That is one interpretation. This is at least third hand information, however. This agent, or whatever he is, has provided no more than a few unsubstantiated allegations. I'm sorry to say this, but Peter refuses to reveal any details on IMAGER. Without additional background there is no way to gauge the information's veracity."

"I appreciate your position, Steven," said Matthews. "You know you have my complete support. I trust you to do the right thing. I only want to point out the sensitivity of our current position."

"I understand, Mr. President. As Chad pointed out, we have to be very careful in our handling of domestic affairs before the election. The Democrats would certainly take advantage of any negative publicity. We don't want to raise unnecessary alarms that might jeopardize the campaign."

"Surely you are not suggesting we ignore criminal activity? A man was murdered!"

"No, of course not, Mr. President," Carlson replied quickly.

"The FBI and local authorities will perform thorough investigations. I am simply not convinced that these events raise to the level of a *national* threat."

"Thank you, Steven," replied Matthews.

The President glanced over to his desk. The desk on which Truman had kept "The Buck Stops Here" prominently displayed. Most saw it as a statement of strength and power. Matthews knew it for what it really was: an oppressive curse.

He reached for his glass. "I know you will give these activities a fair evaluation. But if there is any further escalation, I expect to be notified and an appropriate response taken." He emphasized the point with a careful narrowing of his eyes. It was a look that was never ignored.

"Yes, Mr. President."

Carlson took his glass and tipped it toward the President. They each took a long swallow.

"Now, when can Margaret and I expect to see you for a dinner?" Matthews asked.

Chapter 19

Tyler, Georgia
Saturday, 9:00 a.m.

"THE GATHERING STARTS tonight," Holly began. "I want to go over everything one more time. We gotta get this right."

Gary sat quietly in a dark corner of the great room watching the proceedings around the hewn-wood table. The old farmhouse had become a familiar location since he had completed the purchase nearly a year ago, when they were just forming the plan. The farm had been on the auctioneer's block and the bank was only too happy to take his money. They hadn't cared where the proceeds came from and there would be no traceable connections.

The property was close to both Atlanta and Columbus, yet could give them the privacy they needed. And now the numerous barns, houses, and ancillary structures would support their diverse needs. Holly's cell had agreed to act as the farm's overseers, even with their benefactor's strange conditions.

This meeting was Gary's last chance to make sure things were on track for the training. The next step in their journey.

"The other cells will start arriving this afternoon," Holly continued. "We need to give 'em a place to stay and store their equipment. Ricky, how are the arrangements going?"

"Okay so far, Macon," Dalton replied. "I'm lookin' at seven cells from Montgomery, Atlanta, and Pensacola. Probably about sixty guys. Here's a list of who we expect and where they can set up." He passed a stack of handwritten papers around the table. "I tried to spread 'em out as much as I could. Less chance anybody'll get in pissin' contests before we get started."

Holly quickly scanned the sheets. "Looks good, Ricky," he said.

"Cal, have you gone over this to make sure we know who's comin' and how to check 'em out?"

"Sure, Macon." Napes squinted down at the paper. "Sure."

"Good. We'll all give you a hand."

"Yeah," Wicks added. "Just give me a call the *next time* a Fed comes in."

The others froze and waited for Holly's response. How would the old man handle it?

"Didn't see *you* helpin' out on that one, Tommy," Holly replied. "It only shows how careful we need to be."

Weak response. Something else he needs to learn.

Gary watched the discussions with a well-practiced detachment: evaluating each exchange, noting each response, and analyzing the reactions around the room. It was what he had been trained to do—a life spent in the background.

All through school he had sat in the back of the classrooms, always watching the other students, hardly ever the teacher. The assignments were so easy; it was the other students that fascinated him. How they reacted, how they worked, or didn't work, together. Even college hadn't been that different, although his subjects were more interesting by then: flirtatious coeds, propeller-headed nerds, brain-challenged athletes. He had occasionally picked up some useful bits of information, and turned them into some extra income, but this aspect of his personality hardly had seemed a marketable skill. Not until he had met Professor Bullock.

"What *did* happen with the Fed, Macon?" O'Grady asked.

Holly walked over to the huge hearth, then turned back to the table. "Gary's people took him. That's all anyone needs to know. Let's get back on the schedule. We've got specialists comin' in for the weapons and hand-to-hand training, so we've got to keep up. Tommy, what about arrangements for 'em?"

"No sweat, Macon. I'm meeting the pros when they come in. They'll stay here in the house with us. As long as Sean comes up with the weapons, we'll be fine."

"What do you mean, you . . ." O'Grady blurted out.

"Calm down, Sean. Tommy was just kidding. Right, Tommy?" Wicks gave a condescending nod. "Since you seem to be doing all the house arrangements, Tommy. What about food? We got enough?"

"Food? I thought Ricky was handling that. He's got all the connections."

"You said *you* were taking care of everything with the guests," Dalton accused. "I'm damn tired of your complaining, Tommy. So's everybody else around here."

"I can't friggin' do everything you little . . ."

"*Shut the hell up!*" Holly finally yelled.

The tension was getting to all of them now. It was time to find out who had the staying power. "Staying power"—the phrase had been one of Bullock's favorites.

Edwin Bullock, Earnhardt Professor of Political Science at Princeton University, was an enigma. Was he the gruff, crusty old teacher that berated his students in class? Or the kind, thoughtful mentor to those who sought him out? Or the hard, war-weary veteran telling tales of excitement and danger? Gary had never been able to decide.

The professor had seemed to take a liking to the quiet student. He had taken him under his wing, shown him how to hone his "gift." He had taught him to see things differently. The young man had thought he had known so much, but Bullock had shown him a whole new world of knowledge. Things that others avoided, or simply ignored. A world of secrets and intrigue.

After graduation, he had continued to take Bullock's direction. He couldn't really remember when he had made the commitment, but soon he was sharpening his skills at the Farm, and applying them in the back alleys of Beirut and the deserts of the Middle East. As the years passed, Bullock faded into the shadows; the teacher had others to lead. So he again had been alone, but now he had accepted his fate.

Others had tried to use him, even his trainers; but they had always failed. Now he was his own man, serving the highest bidder, doing the only thing he knew how to do. Observe and react.

"We got too much to do for you assholes to argue all the time," Holly continued. "Ricky, work with Tommy to make sure we got enough supplies for *everybody*. Call in some scores if you have to. Give me a yell if the suppliers give you any shit. We'll find a way to move 'em along."

"I'll get it done, Macon," Dalton said.

Wicks sat back silently, sulking.

"Okay, Sean. I guess that leaves you with our materiel. Everything ready?"

"Will be. I've got all the conversion kits and most everything is fixed. Had a problem with the 12 gauges but that's resolved. I'll have everything ready in time. Got the delivery of the ammo boxes last night. I saved half, like you said. We'll keep the rest down in the bunker beside the equipment house."

"Will they be safe there?" Dalton asked.

"Yeah. It's away from all the exercises, but I'll make sure nobody gets near it."

Holly looked down at his scribbled notes. "Okay. That looks like it. You know what you need to do. Get to it. I'll be here all day with Cal if you need anything. Everybody else is here by dinnertime. Now, y'all get out."

The members broke from the room and made their way back to their vehicles. Holly stood frozen at the end of the table. The old soldier knew what was about to come. The question was how he would take it.

Gary waited until the roars of the engines faded into the distance, then rose and approached the table.

"Relax, Macon," he said. "Your boys are getting it together."

Holly collapsed into the seat by his side.

"We'll have everything ready, Gary. Sure will."

"I know, Macon. I know you will." He held the moment before continuing. "It was a mistake letting the Fed in, though."

"We took care of that! Just like you said! He never told nobody."

"But he could have. This reflects on the whole cell, Macon. And your leadership. I wouldn't want anyone to get the wrong impression. Especially the Commander."

He could see the fear swell behind Holly's eyes. It was eating at his insides like the borers in the corn stalks outside. The old man was in over his head, and didn't have a clue as to what to do about it.

"I can fix it, Gary. Show 'em. Tell me what we need to do."

"I think you already know, Macon. You've got to show them you're in charge, that you can enforce the rules."

"Take charge. Yeah. Someone has to pay."

So far so good. "That's good, Macon. That would show everyone how serious you are."

"But who, Gary?"

"It was a security issue, right?"

"Yeah, I guess. You mean Cal?" Holly's eyes pleaded for a reprieve, but there was no retreat. "Okay. He is security. I'll bounce him down. Take away his authority."

"I don't think that's enough, Macon. This is serious. That Fed could have hurt all of us. Badly. Hurt the Covenant. You've got to send a message they can't ignore. That Macon Holly is committed to the Covenant. With his life."

Holly's face went ashen. "You want me to kill him?"

"It's your decision. You remember Tennessee?"

"The Volunteer Cell? Shepard killed that man's family! Every single one of them!"

"No one questions *his* commitment now. He's a legend."

"I can't do that. Cal's married to my daughter. He's my son-in-law!" Holly's whole body was shaking. He dug his fingernails into the soft wood of the table to keep his hands steady.

What was wrong with this stupid old man? Can't he hear?

Gary could feel the squeezing at his temples. He tried to push it back, but it wouldn't yield. Growing, tightening. Suddenly he jumped to his feet and drove his face at Holly.

"What do you think this is?" he screamed. "We're not running a nursery school! This is a revolution, you whimpering faggot. If you can't handle this I'll get somebody who can. Do you understand me?"

Holly was twice Gary's size but cowered in his chair before the assault. "Okay, Gary. I understand. I'll take care of it."

That was better. Gary pulled back from across the table and let the tension wash away like a receding tide.

"Good," Gary said softly. "I knew you were the right man for us, Macon. But I wouldn't wait too long. People are watching."

Gary walked to the other side of the table and put his arm around the broken man. He raised him up and led him to the door.

"I'll talk to you tomorrow," Macon said as he walked into the darkness.

"I'm afraid not. I'm leaving tonight." The panic showed clearly on Holly's face even in the moonlight.

"But . . ."

"Don't worry, Macon. I know you'll do the right thing."

"Uh, thanks, Gary."

He watched as Holly limped down the stairs, crawled into his dirty red pickup, and drove slowly down the gravel access road. Another man returning to his family, pushing the night's terrors into the shadows of his normal life. All except him, for this *was* his life, to sit just beyond the light and pull the strings that would change the face of the world.

He really did hope Holly could pull it off. It was too late to change the plan.

Chapter 20

Cerberus Consulting, Tysons Corner, Virginia
Saturday, 11:00 a.m.

BRAXTON HAD LEARNED early on in his new career that the only thing special about Saturdays was that he got to sleep in before starting work. His Friday meeting with Takagawa Communications had dragged on all afternoon and then they had invited him to a marathon dinner at an elegant Japanese restaurant. He hadn't gotten home until 11:00, only slightly inebriated from the endless river of sake that had been proffered.

The meeting itself had gone well. He had given the executives a briefing on Internet security with special emphasis on the reliability and security of their existing infrastructure. Security seemed to be the most important concern. Could an adolescent hacker break through the firewall between the public and private networks and wreak havoc in their critical databases? Could a competitor secretly steal pricing policies, marketing plans, or vehicle designs without their knowledge? Could an investigative journalist find a trail of incriminating memos discussing a previously-unknown product flaw? These were the questions the executives had paid Braxton to answer.

When he gave his presentation, they had nodded appropriately at his security review and analysis of current technology. His recommendations had been clear and concise, including a periodic security audit that would be performed by Cerberus. Maybe he *was* getting the hang of this consulting thing; they had bought the package hook, line, and inflated price tag.

Still, the effort had wiped him out. He had collapsed in his bed and had had to drag himself back to the office to prepare the report and new proposal.

He tossed his black nylon bag on the old sofa and flopped in his desk chair. On top of a tall pile of mail was a prominent yellow sticky that read:

Hope Takagawa went well.

Sam called, said he'd leave a message.

Karen

Braxton considered checking the mail, but the sake still pounded in his head and he couldn't bring himself to plough through the words. As he pushed the pile to the side of his desk, the flashing message light on his telephone caught his attention. He hesitated, but his curiosity got the better of him. Grabbing the handset, he pushed the button labeled "Virna."

VIRNA stood for Voice Interactive Response something-or-other. It was a stupid name but easier to say than "my voice mail system."

He punched in his access codes and listened to the summary. Two messages, not too bad.

One last push and he waited for the recorded voice. The first was a comfortable, friendly one.

"Hey, Adam. It's Sam. How the hell are you? Heard you had a visitor today. From Karen's description it could be Roger. Give me a call."

Roger? Oh yeah, Roger Slattery, Fowler's CIA friend. That would explain how he knew about the Incident. At least now he had a name to put to the face. He saw John Smith's card sitting on the desktop and scribbled "Roger Slattery" on the back. But that still didn't explain what the CIA wanted with him.

He waited for the next message. This voice was equally recognizable, but brought shivers down his back.

"Adam, it's Megan. I'm at Logan and figured you'd be at work. Sorry to call you so early, but . . . well, I need to talk to someone."

Her voice shook.

"I've been looking into the European operation. Something's wrong. Something about Ben. I don't know who to talk to. Can you call me? Please? Oh, and Adam? I love you."

Silence.

He replayed the message twice. It still didn't make any more sense.

Ben? Who was Ben? Oh, yes. Ben Lawson. Her friend who had died in Europe. What about him?

What had she said at dinner? Something about the staff at Vision One.

And her goodbye. It tore at him, bringing back memories of other places and other times. Things he dared not hope for.

He checked his watch. It was 11:10. She would still be on the plane to SFO. He scrolled to her home number and hit "Call." It rang three times and a much calmer voice came on the line.

"This is 555-5953. I can't come to the phone right now, but leave a message and I'll get right back to you."

"Megan. It's Adam. I'm sorry I didn't get back earlier. I got in to work late. I'll be here or at home all day. Call me as soon as you get in. Anytime." He didn't know whether he had the courage to say the words. But then they just flowed out so easily. "And I love you too."

He put down the phone feeling very unsettled. He still couldn't understand her tone. What was it?

A chill of fear ran down his spine as he realized he knew. She had sounded scared.

*   *   *

His room was dark as a cave and had a matching dank, subterranean smell. Apparently the concept of fresh air hadn't occurred to the proprietors of the Providence View Motel.

Gary was hunched over the cardboard desk trying to maintain a cell connection long enough to send his message. This decrepit motel was the closest one to the farm that had a serviceable cell signal. And that was giving it a lot of credit. Real life in the field wasn't ever like they showed it in the spy movies.

He pecked out the message and sent it off.

The pain in his stomach had been getting worse ever since the trip from Tennessee. Shepard's first mold had been a piece of crap. He had gone over the design for three hours to fix the details.

Then Holly's incompetence. He had had to blow up at the redneck to get the man to do his job.

Why can't people just do what they are told?

Damned if he was going to have any more doctors check him out. The Percodans took the edge off, and that was all a real soldier needed.

So far the Commander's plan was proceeding well. It required a little more hand-holding than he would have liked, but these were hardly the professionals he was used to dealing with. Really just a bunch of farmers. But then it was probably better this way. He might have felt some trepidation if they had been real soldiers. Civilians always did have trouble seeing the big picture.

A knife of pain sliced across his abdomen and he doubled over in the chair. He would have laid down on the bed, but he was more afraid of that piece of furniture than he was of the demon eating inside him. His legs still burned from his last night on that infested rack.

He went into the bathroom, popped two of the dark brown pills and stuck his mouth under the faucet. He returned to the desk chair, closed his eyes, and softly repeated the mantra he had learned from his *sensei* at the Farm. His body immediately responded, reacting automatically as it had for over twenty years. His heart rate slowed, fatigued muscles relaxed, and unwanted sensory disturbances were silenced. More than once, this meditative state had saved the man's life: giving him a rejuvenation from his job's physical punishments. Tonight, all he needed was a few moments of relaxation before the numbing narcotic would enable him to continue his assignment.

Slowly his face lost its tension, bathed in the glow of the cell's last message:

```
Georgia sanction initiated.

BRAVO on schedule.

Preparations continue for HALFTIME.
```

* * *

Beep.

Braxton bolted up in his bed at the electronic disturbance. He glanced over at his alarm clock. 1:00 a.m. Much too early for his alarm.

Beep.

The phone. Where's the goddamn phone? He groped for the handset and pulled it to his ear.

"Hello?"

"Mr. Adam Braxton?"

"Yes. Who is this?" he barked.

"Lt. Richard Cassidy, sir. From the San Francisco Police Department. There's been an accident. It's your ex-wife."

"An accident? Megan? What happened?"

"It was a mugging, sir."

The room turned ice cold. He could barely voice the question. "How is she?"

"I'm sorry to have to tell you this way, Mr. Braxton. She's dead."

Chapter 21

HOLLY HAD TOSSED and turned all night, finally getting up at 5:00 a.m. The evening exercises had kept his mind distracted, but once he had settled into the small upstairs bedroom of the farmhouse, the previous morning's conversation with Gary ate away at him.

What the hell am I supposed to do? Kill my own son-in-law?

He had paced the floor until his legs had cried in pain, then headed downstairs. It had still been dark, a condition that had matched his mood, and he had sat on the porch, watching the sun come up over the fields and praying for some kind of revelation that would free him from his pact with the devil.

It wasn't supposed to be this way.

Ever since he had been a kid the militia had been a part of his life. Like a second family. His father had been the Materiel Officer and would take him down to the old mill off Robert's Creek where they hid their guns. He had learned all their names, and by the time he was fifteen, could take each one apart and reassemble it blindfolded.

That was when they had initiated him. Taken him out in the woods and set him loose. He had to get back on his own and kill five animals along the way. It hadn't been all that hard. He had hunted with his father since he was twelve. He had come back with two squirrels, an armadillo, a mangy stray dog, and a young deer. His father had said he was damned proud. Then they had all got drunk, told war stories, and complained about the state of the Union. It had been great fun.

It wasn't fun anymore.

After they had come back from the war, they thought things

would be the same. They all had brought stuff back with them—fixing what was broken and improving what wasn't.

Nobody had bothered them back then. They went out, shot some targets, did some hunting. They never hurt no one. Then the Feds started showing up. Asking about their guns. Where did they get them? Who fixed 'em up?

Nobody had ever cared what Sean O'Grady did in the back room. They had a right to own guns didn't they? It said so in the Constitution. Who cares what they did to 'em?

They had heard about the attacks on militia groups in Michigan and Montana. But it had never come home until Charlie Kearns got in trouble. Why did they want to hurt him?

Hurt him? They had ruined his goddamn life.

Holly hadn't thought of himself as a revolutionary. He hadn't known what to do. Then he started hearing about this Commander. He was organizing people, pulling them together. They were all gonna be a part of the Covenant.

Holly had thought that maybe this Commander could protect 'em. Maybe he could teach them how to protect themselves. So he had asked a couple of his contacts up north. Did they know anything about the Commander?

Then Gary had appeared.

He had helped them organize. Gotten them some new equipment. Shit, he had bought the farm for their training.

But then the outsiders had started coming in. With piles of fancy equipment. New rules and lots of secrecy.

Now Feds sneaking in. And it's all *our* fault.

How could he do what Gary wanted? What would his daughter think if she ever found out?

There has to be another way.

* * *

Braxton shuffled aimlessly through the apartment, fighting off the images that flashed inside his head. Just over a year ago he had made the same journey through another apartment. His best friend had died, and he had been asked by his family to help clean out their son's personal belongings. But Paul Terrell had been killed, in Braxton's own apartment unbelievably, and he had felt a deep responsibility for the result.

Megan's death had been accidental, on the other hand, but no less wrenching. Seeing her only a few days before made it all the worse. That encounter had rekindled his love, but now just as quickly it had been extinguished, forever.

Braxton had taken the first flight out that morning to San Francisco. It was the longest six hours he had ever spent.

His first stop had been to police headquarters to talk to Lieutenant Cassidy. The officer had described the fatal mugging, just a few blocks away from her apartment, and offered his condolences. A robbery gone awry, he had said. She had tried to fight off the assailant, but had been stabbed twice in the chest. As luck would have it, the wounds had sliced into her heart.

Cassidy had had little encouragement on catching the murderer. At least he was honest about it.

The cop had taken him down to the Morgue, where he had confirmed her identity. She had looked so calm, so different from when he had last seen her. She was white and cold, like a limestone statue. Where was the sparkle in her eyes, the flush of her cheeks when she argued with him? He had quickly turned away and left.

Why was he called for this responsibility?

The answer was that her parents were dead and her brother was in the military; Braxton thought she had said now stationed in the Far East. She had named him as her emergency contact. Had she meant what she had said in the phone message?

There were few physical things in the apartment to remind him of her. All of her furniture was new, she had left Cambridge with just two suitcases and three boxes of books. But it still *felt* like her: the precise arrangement of her knick-knacks on the bookcases, the carefully-stacked business and technology magazines on the coffee table. Even the cardboard boxes that she never had the time to completely empty were stacked neatly in a corner of the extra bedroom's closet. The room was set up as a home office, much as theirs had been. She had been able to buy a much more upscale oak desk, upon which sat a high-end PC, multifunction FAX/scanner/printer, and bound sets of manuals and reports.

He walked into her bedroom, all flowers and pastels. Next to the bed was a picture of a smiling couple standing by the waterfront. Megan and who? The Ben Lawson she had spoken about? The scent of her perfume was strongest here and he quickly left, unwilling to subject himself to the memories.

The living room was filled with impressionists, a large print of Monet's *Water Lilies* hanging prominently on one wall. Below it was an open secretary, unpaid bills and discarded correspondence scattered across its top, surrounding a familiar picture of her mother and father.

He walked through the dining area and into the small kitchen. The only item on the counters was her answering machine. The lack of clutter was due as much to Megan's culinary ineptitude as it was to her fastidiousness. They had been frequent guests at many of greater Boston's restaurants, preferring the cost of prepared meals to the frustration and heartburn of home cooking.

He returned to the balcony and looked out onto the Palo Alto hills. Lush green rolling hills supported a canopy of early afternoon fog. Commuters rushed between chrome and brick office complexes. It was a very different view from the congestion of Harvard Square. She had come here to begin a new life. Why had it had to end so quickly?

A crippling fatigue embraced him and he trudged back into the living room, collapsing on her sofa to rest. There was so much he needed to do. What was he waiting for?

He had to do something! Grabbing the first thing he saw, he threw a copy of *Technology Review* across the room. It sailed over the dining room table and skidded across the open kitchen counter, knocking the small answering machine to the floor.

Cursing his bad aim, he shuffled over and picked up the appliance. Setting it back on the counter, he noticed the unlit message light. That couldn't be right. Cassidy had told him that Megan had gone shopping on the way back from the airport. She had been killed at a mall near her apartment around 4:00 p.m. She had never gotten home. Why didn't the machine show his message?

Maybe the light was broken. He pressed "Play." Nothing happened. There were no messages.

Something really *was* wrong.

What else have I missed?

His eyes scanned the apartment. The spartan counters in the kitchen, the rich cherry table and chairs in the dining area, the precisely placed furniture in the living room. His gaze stopped suddenly at the secretary. Megan had never let anything in their apartment become that cluttered. She was disorganized, yes. But the disorganization was always in neat piles.

He sat down at the secretary and went through the envelopes. They had all been opened, torn at the ends rather than across the top as Megan had always done. There was nothing significant, mostly announcements for local arts events and offers for yet another credit card. A telephone and electric bill were overdue.

He checked the drawers and found them stuffed with more papers and receipts. Megan's records had never been kept like this. What could have gotten into her?

He set the bills aside and went back in the kitchen. Everything looked normal. The sink was clean, the counter top was clear. Hesitantly, he pulled open one of the drawers. Silverware was scattered everywhere. Spoons were in every divider, table and salad forks immorally intermingled. Cardinal sins in a Connelly kitchen.

He tried to stay calm despite the insistent pounding in his chest. It's not significant. She had a bad day. Her housekeeper did it.

He checked the upper cabinets. What little stock she had was pushed to the sides of the shelves. As if someone had searched through them without caring to put things back.

It isn't possible, is it?

Chapter 22

Braxton had checked the whole apartment. Each room had been the same: superficially everything was in place, but behind the cabinet doors, and inside the drawers, Megan's belongings were in complete disarray.

He had left the bedroom for last. It would be the ultimate test; his most difficult task. Megan's bedroom had been her most private place. It was where the aggressive, tough businesswoman became a tender, caring wife and lover.

He forced himself to step into the room and walk toward the bureau. Gingerly he pulled open the top drawer. Lace underwear was strewn through the box-like space. He could see someone dumping the contents on her bed, searching through them, then gathering the garments and dropping them back inside.

He replaced the drawer and checked the next. Nothing new. The rest of the chest yielded no additional information.

Walking over to the nightstand he picked up the picture of Megan and Lawson. She looked so happy, so free.

Someone had searched Megan's apartment and it certainly wasn't the police. They weren't this neat.

A loud buzzer startled him and he dropped the picture on his foot. The noise echoed through the apartment like a siren in an empty warehouse. It buzzed again and he recognized it as a door sounder. He shook fragments of glass off his shoe and limped toward the door.

Who would be bothering him now?

Peering through the security eyeglass, he saw a woman's face move back and forth in front of the lens. As the face came closer, he pulled the door back against the security chain.

"Yes?" he asked.

"Oh!" She obviously wasn't expecting to see a man answer. "Hello. Is Megan home?"

The woman was tall, with shoulder-length blond hair, full lips and round dark eyes so large they seemed to fill her face. A trim wool business suit highlighted an appealing figure. She swung a thin leather briefcase impatiently at her side.

"No, I'm sorry. She, uh, stepped out."

"I hate to bother you, but I'm in a bit of a fix. My name is Sydney Marino. I work with Megan. I just got back from a trip and locked myself out of my apartment." The woman spoke so fast Braxton could barely understand her.

A hand flew in front of his face and pointed down the hall. "It's down there." He looked past her and saw a small Rollaboard sitting about halfway down the hallway. "Megan keeps a set of keys for me. Could you please look for them? I'm beat."

Marino flashed a smile that exposed a set of perfectly straight, sparkling white teeth. Braxton had no doubt the well-practiced smile had opened a lot of doors for the attractive woman. She hardly looked like a dangerous intruder, so he unhooked the security chain and opened the door a little wider.

"Uh, sure. Do you know where they are?"

"I think she keeps them in the top right-hand drawer of the desk. There." Marino curled a long, manicured finger through the opening, and pointed to the secretary.

Braxton went to the drawer and fished through the contents. About half-way back he found two keys on a simple metal ring. A tag tied to the ring said "Sydney."

"How about these?" he asked, holding them up.

"That's them!"

He walked back and handed the keys to Marino.

"Thanks a bunch. You're a lifesaver. Tell Megan to give me a call when she gets in. Bye."

"Are you a friend of Megan's?" He asked before she turned away.

"Well, yes." Her smile disappeared, replaced by what Braxton took as a look of concern. "Excuse me, but who are you?"

"I'm sorry. My name is Adam Braxton."

"Adam Braxton? You're Megan's ex. What are you doing here?" She stepped back from the door and her voice took an accusatory tone.

"I'm afraid I have some bad news." He pulled the door farther open. "Why don't you come in?

"I'm not going anywhere until you tell me what you're doing here! Where is Megan?"

Marino was not going to budge without an explanation and Braxton didn't want to get into a shouting match in the hallway. He had to tell her the truth.

"She was in an accident," he began softly. "I'm sorry, there's no easy way to say this. She died. I'm trying to sort through her things."

Marino's face went from anger, to shock, to tears. She dropped her briefcase and her hands covered her face. "No! Not Megan."

Braxton waited uncomfortably in the doorway, then finally picked up the case. "Please come in. We can talk inside."

She reluctantly followed his lead and entered the apartment, walking familiarly to the living room and taking a seat on the sofa. Braxton pulled over a chair from the dining area.

Marino wiped the tears from her eyes with her hands. "What happened?"

"The police believe it was a mugging. She was stabbed."

"Oh God! How awful." Her hands leapt to her mouth.

"When did you see her last?"

Marino took a moment to compose herself before continuing. "I've been gone about a week," she said. "I talked to her just before I left. We were going out tomorrow night."

"How long had you known her?" Braxton pressed.

"We met a few months ago, right after I joined Vision One. She was really great. Always helping out when I got in trouble, like with the keys. Is there anything I can do?"

"No, thank you. I was the closest relative the police could find. They called me last night and I came in this morning from D.C. I'll take care of as much as I can until her brother gets here."

"Oh yes, he's in Korea isn't he?"

"I believe so. The police are trying to locate him." It was nice to be able to talk to someone about Megan. He had felt so alone ever since the call from the police. There couldn't be anything wrong with talking to her a bit longer could there? "What do you do for Vision One?"

"I'm a public relations consultant. Vision One hired me to handle their expansion into Europe."

Braxton wrinkled his forehead at the response. *Why would they hire an American?*

It didn't take long for her to sense his concern.

"You're wondering why they hired an American. I specialize in working with companies starting international expansion. I get them going using my contacts, then they take it from there. It's actually pretty interesting work."

"I guess that would be exciting. I hope you like to travel."

"Oh, absolutely. That's the one good part of the job. I've been spending a lot of time in Amsterdam lately." Marino glanced around the apartment and Braxton noticed another tear welled in the corner of her eye. He offered her a handkerchief which she silently accepted. "I'm sorry. I didn't mean to interrupt. I'd better get going."

"That's okay. Don't worry. If there's anything here of yours . . ."

She shook her head. "No. I was the one that was always borrowing things. I'll see if I have anything back in my apartment." She picked up her briefcase and started for the door. "It's just so terrible."

"I know." He escorted her to the door. "Miss Marino?"

"Yes? And please, call me Sydney."

"Okay, Sydney. Megan didn't seem upset about anything when you talked to her did she? Worried about anything?"

"Megan? No. Well, she did seem tired, but I figured that was just all the work. Why?"

"Oh, nothing. I worry too much." He considered asking about Lawson but decided against it. Anything he said could get back to Vision One. "I'm sorry we had to meet under such difficult circumstances."

"Me too. And I'm sorry I snapped at you earlier."

"No problem. I understand."

"If you need anything, please just come by. Apartment 704. Really." She flashed that killer smile again.

"Thank you," he replied.

Braxton watched her walk down the hall, unlock her door, and disappear into the apartment.

He had never really thought much about Megan's friends. Would she have mentioned anything to them about her suspicions? If she had, would Marino have told him?

As he closed the door, he remembered about Megan's things. Someone *had* broken in and gone through the apartment. When? After she had died? Or before? And what had they been looking for?

*   *   *

Braxton located a broom and dustpan in a kitchen cabinet and went back to the bedroom to clean up the mess he had made. He swept up the glass fragments and reached down for the frame. As he did, the frame's backing broke loose, exposing what looked like a corner of white paper between the folds of the cardboard.

He dropped cross-legged to the carpet and carefully pulled out the sheet. It was a handwritten letter, dated a week before. He hesitated, not wanting to invade her privacy, then read the contents.

Dear Megan,

I'm sorry I have sounded so preoccupied the past few weeks. The atmosphere here has been very intense and I'm afraid I have let it affect me. Everything is finally coming together and I feel good about what I have accomplished.

Please forgive me for scaring you. Just put it out of your mind.

I miss you very much but will see you soon.

Love,

Ben

What had Lawson been worried about? What had he told Megan?

None of this made any sense. Why had Megan sounded scared? What could she have been afraid of?

And then there was the way she had died. Megan hated physical violence. There was no way she would have tried to fight off a stranger. Why had she been stabbed?

First Lawson. Now Megan. There were so many questions.

But he knew he had to find the answers.

*   *   *

"Hello?" came a deep growl through the phone.

"Hi, Sam. It's Adam Braxton."

"Adam! Karen told me what happened. I'm really sorry."

"Thanks, Sam. I appreciate it. I still can't believe she's gone."

"Where are you? Is there anything I can do?"

"I'm still out in California, but there *is* something I'd like you to look into."

"Sure, Adam. Anything. But you're really okay?"

"Pretty much. But something's not right out here. I need you to check out someone." He waited for the inevitable complaint.

"Wait a minute, Adam. Do *not* get yourself involved. Leave the investigating to the police for once."

"It's not like that, Sam. It's not about Megan's murder. At least not directly. Take down a name."

"Oh, shit. Alright, let me get a pad."

Braxton waited while his friend located something to write on. He had done everything he could in San Francisco. Megan's brother would be in this afternoon and then he would be on a red-eye to D.C. It was time to get some answers.

Sam Fowler was a crusty ex-D.C. detective to whom Braxton had already trusted his life more than once. Since retiring, Fowler augmented his pension with gigs as a private investigator. He had more contacts than anyone Braxton knew. And Braxton needed the information. Even if it only cleared his suspicions.

"Got it." Fowler was back.

"Okay, name is Sydney Marino. Sydney with a wye. Lives in Megan's building, apartment 704."

"What's he done?"

"Not he. She. She's some kind of PR consultant that worked with Megan at Vision One. Just see if she's legit."

"I'll give it a shot, but my contacts out there are a little rusty. It could take a few days."

"That's fine. Do whatever you can."

"Uh, did you get my message about your visitor?" Fowler asked hesitantly.

"Yeah, thanks. The guy called himself John Smith. Stocky, about six feet tall. Buzz cut and glasses. Said he was with the CIA. And mentioned your name. Something about owing him a *Dos Equis*."

The line went silent for about a minute. When Fowler's voice came back on the line, it was oddly emotionless.

"That's about what Karen said. Sounds like Slattery. What did he want?"

"He wants me to go to an Internet security conference in Amsterdam. See what I can pick up on Chinese cryptographic work."

"The CIA does debrief scientists coming back from international meetings. Pretty common, so I hear. Odd he approached you directly about going, though. Roger's an expert in counterterrorism not an analyst."

"Can I trust him?" Braxton asked.

Fowler hesitated again before continuing. "Trust is a difficult word with Roger. He's a real pro. Dedicated to his job and his country.

"Bottom line, he's a spook, Adam. You can only believe about half of what he tells you. If that much. But if he actually came to see you, and made that request, I have to believe it's important."

Braxton weighed his friend's words. He certainly didn't trust Slattery, but he did trust Fowler. And the opportunity was too good to pass up.

"Thanks, Sam. That helps. And don't kill yourself on the Marino background check. Just leave the information with Karen."

"Why don't I call you?"

"That could be expensive. I'll be out of the country for a few days."

"Don't tell me Adam Braxton's taking some time off. People will talk."

"Sorry, Sam. No such luck. I've got some business to do. In Amsterdam."

Chapter 23

HOLLY SAT ON the steps of the equipment house. In the dusty clearing in front of the house, one of Gary's experts was conducting a hand-to-hand combat exercise. Nine militiamen from Montgomery were being alternately tossed into the dirt by the commando. Holly winced sympathetically every time one of the men hit the hard Georgia clay.

Holly's cell had taken their turn earlier in the day. Everyone had come through without any permanent damage, but he had taken one particularly bad fall on his right side. Now his knee was throbbing through his pants leg and every breath felt like someone was sticking a hot poker in his chest. Hopefully it wasn't a busted rib.

He had told Napes to meet him here at five o'clock. The Gathering was winding down and his short absence wouldn't be noticed.

It was time to handle his "problem." There was one possibility; one way he could get through this and keep his family together. But would his son-in-law agree?

He heard the roar of Napes' pickup and took one last swig from the flask filled with Bubba Olson's finest. At least it took the edge off the pain. He stuffed the flask in his back pocket, locked up the equipment house, and gathered his courage.

"Afternoon, Macon," came the call from his son-in-law. Napes had dressed for the day's duties: his fatigues looked relatively clean, his boots were tied, and he had pulled his oily hair back into a stubby ponytail. "Wha'cha want?"

Holly met him outside the house. "Got some things to talk

about, Cal. Let's go for a walk." He motioned toward the woods.

"Everything okay?"

"So far," Holly replied. "Sounds like everybody's goin' at it." The woods echoed with the pops of automatic fire and an occasional explosive burst. It might bother the neighbors but no one was going to complain.

"Ain't none of them around here is there?"

"Nah, we're safe. Didn't want any of the exercises around the ammo stash."

"Oh, yeah. Now I remember." Napes smiled widely, his mouth showing more empty spaces than solid teeth.

Holly limped down a path, leading Napes around the equipment house and into the woods behind.

"Like a drink?" Holly asked drawing the flask from his pocket.

"Sure, Macon. Thanks." Napes grabbed the flask and took a long draw. "Got everybody in alright, didn't we? Nobody sneakin' in this time."

"You're right, Cal. Looks like this was just fine. But there's still lotsa' folks upset by that Fed."

"Yeah, I know. The boys've been talkin'. Got what he deserved though, stickin' his nose into our business like that."

"Our friends are real upset. They want to know what happened."

"You mean that Yankee been hangin' around?"

"His name's Gary. He's a part of the big organization, Cal. The one that's getting us together."

"Well it's about time somebody did somethin'. Get rid of all the goddamn foreigners and homos, that's what I say. And we don't need no stinkin' Feds tellin' us what to do, neither. Look what they did to Charlie."

"We're gonna change all that, Cal. But Gary's got powerful friends. They paid for this farm, gave us all the equipment. How *did* the Fed get in?"

"I don't know. He came in one day. Said he was from 'lanta."

"You're head of security. Didn't you talk to him?"

"Sure, Macon. Had kinda a funny accent, but he knew folks up north."

"Did you ever check with them?"

"I was gonna. Sure, I was. What's the big deal?"

Holly looked around. They had come about a half mile into the heavy timber. Another quarter mile to go. The sounds of the exercises were all around them.

"They think it's your fault, Cal. That the Fed got in."

"My fault! What was I supposed to do?"

"Check him out. See if he *was* from up north. Talk to your friends."

"Shit. I ain't got time to check out everybody. I got real work to do. We caught him didn't we?"

"Frisco saw him go into the shed," Holly explained. "Then Gary took over. He could have hurt all of us, Cal. Got us arrested. Or worse."

Napes shut up and Holly saw deep creases in his forehead. He was trying to think through the situation. Maybe it wasn't too late.

"Okay. I'll be more careful next time. You tell 'em that, Macon. I'll be careful."

"That's not enough, Cal. The Commander wants someone punished."

"Have him punish Frisco. How'd the damn Fed get in the shed?"

"I don't know. But Frisco's one of Gary's people. You're the one that let him in the compound."

"Who is this damn Commander, Macon? I ain't never seen him. Who's he to tell us what to do?"

"No one knows who he is. But he's a real warrior. With money and power to help us. He's having us work together for the Covenant. I wouldn't want him comin' after *me*."

"So what they gonna do, Macon? Kill me?"

Napes' leer made Holly sick. But it didn't last long after Holly just stood silently next to him.

"Macon? You're kiddin', right?" Holly stood unresponsive. "SHIT! They can't do that!"

"These are very dangerous people, Cal. If we don't do something, they might hurt Annie and Little Betsy. Like in Tennessee."

Napes started rubbing his hands together. His whole body was shaking. "You gotta *do* something, Macon. You gotta get me outta here."

Me. Only "me."

"Maybe there is something I can do, Cal. I can help you get away, disappear somewhere. I doubt they'll come looking."

"Sure, Macon, sure." Napes was stuttering through the words. "I'll just grab a bag from the trailer. I'll be ready to go."

"I can set you up in Phenix City. My brother Griffin's there."

"Thanks, Macon. I can do that." He paused and the confused expression reappeared. "I'll need some money, of course. Just a loan for my ticket and somethin' to get me started. I really do appreciate it, Macon. Sure do."

"My ticket?" What about your family, you bastard?

"You're not taking Annie and Little Betsy?"

"Shit, Macon. I can't be draggin' them all over. I got to hide out. Hell, ain't nothin' gonna happen to them. Annie and the kid can take care of themselves. She's got a *whole* lot of friends. You understand."

"Yeah, Cal." Holly shook his head. "I finally do understand."

Holly led them deeper into the woods.

How had he let it get this far? He had only wanted to protect his daughter.

He remembered when she was just a little girl, bouncing on his knee in a well-worn calico dress, asking to go for a ride in the store's big red delivery truck. She had the same sleepy hazel eyes and thick pouty lips as her mother, and even then had known how to use them to her advantage. They had tried to slow her down, but it had been fruitless. Their awkward lectures on family values could not compete with the slick television shows and flashy movies that had taught their fourteen-year-old child more about life than Holly had ever known.

When she had gotten herself pregnant, Holly had forced the marriage. He hadn't wanted any daughter of his to be labeled a tramp. But maybe there were worse things.

"Jesus, Macon. Nobody told me it'd get like this."

They had reached the edge of the embankment. The pond was just over the rise. Holly put his arm around Napes and gave him a gentle nudge.

"You just have to go, Cal. Until things cool down. It's safer for you this way. And I'll take care of Annie and Little Betsy."

"Yeah, I'll go. I'll pack up my stuff tonight."

"It's the right thing. You'll see."

"Thanks, Macon. I'm glad it's you doin' this. Now about that little loan . . ."

Holly slowed and fell behind as Napes walked up the embankment. When his son-in-law reached the crest, Holly drew a Colt 9mm automatic and fired two rounds into the back of Napes' head. The body lurched, then rolled down the slope and splashed face-down into the algae-covered pond.

Holly stared down at his now-departed relative, feet stuck in the soft mud, the rest of his body floating in the reddish-green slime.

Serves you right, you goddamn sonuvabitch.

He turned and hobbled back into the woods.

Okay, so how do I get rid of the pickup?

Chapter 24

"GODDAMN ASSHOLES!" HOLLY yelled as he dragged himself through the doors of Ricky's. "So here you are. Hope you bastards didn't hurt yourselves helping lock up the farm." He limped over to the table where Wicks and O'Grady were sharing a pitcher of draft.

"Shit, Macon," O'Grady replied. "We were dead tired. And we knew you could handle it. You didn't have any trouble finding us." Chevrons of red, muddy sweat still decorated the Irishman's face. He waved a mug of beer in Holly's direction.

"Just followed my nose, Sean. You boys stunk up Route 58 all the way up here."

"Christ," O'Grady continued, "I never thought that guy would quit. I'm gonna be nothing but bruises in the morning."

"Well if he hadn't had that flight out of Columbus tonight, he probably never would have left," Wicks replied.

"Yeah, but at least you got through it," Holly added. "Those pussies from Pensacola bailed out after lunch. Y'all did good. Gary'll be real pleased."

"Damn well oughta be," Wicks said. "All the work we did."

"I think you should talk to Gary about that, Tommy," Holly replied. "I sure do. I bet he'd be real interested in your ideas."

Wicks glared back at the older man then changed the subject.

"What happened to Ricky? Didn't see him at all."

"Somethin' came up this morning," Holly said. "Had to go back into town."

"He sure did miss the fun part," said O'Grady. "Everybody get out okay, Macon?"

"Yeah. They all were ready to go. Took a helluva beating today. I got 'em out and locked up. No help from you assholes, by the way. I'm goin' to get me a drink."

"You buyin', Macon?" O'Grady called as Holly turned for the bar.

"Not for you, you drunken Irishman," Holly yelled back with a smile.

Holly was too tired to put up with his colleagues' banter. He barely had enough energy to make it to the bar. He slid onto a stool, dropped his elbows, and collapsed his head in his hands. Every muscle in his body was either bruised or cramped. His ribs were feeling a little better but his knee still hurt like hell.

A sudden slap on his back shot a new spasm of pain across his chest. He didn't even have to turn around to know who it was.

"What's the matter, Macon? You're not tired are you?" Wicks dragged a stool over and sat down next to him.

"I guess we're not all as spry as you, Tommy," Holly replied, the sarcasm thick in his drawl.

"Hey, I didn't mean nothin'. I gotta' say, that was one helluva workout. Alexander—that was his name wasn't it—he's one tough sonuvabitch. Wouldn't want to meet him on a dark night."

"Alexander's supposed to be the best," Holly continued. "He wrote a lot of the training guides we've got."

"Jesus," Wicks exclaimed. "Why'd he come down to help *us*?"

"Gary asked him. They're old pals or somethin'. He said it'd help us get in shape." Holly twisted in the stool to relieve the pain in his side. "But you're right. It was one tough time."

Dalton came out of the back room and dropped a frothy mug in front of Holly.

"You two look like hell," he said. "Rough day?"

"Damn right, Ricky," Wicks said. "Where were you? Macon needed someone he could beat up on."

Holly shook his head as a warning, but Dalton didn't catch it.

"Caught some kind a bug. Macon sent me to Doc Flaherty but all he did was give me a handful of pills. I oughta go complain. Don't worry, I'll be back beatin' your butt soon enough."

"Bet you will, Ricky," Wicks replied. "Bet you will."

Dalton suddenly grabbed the edge of the counter and bent down. A coarse, dry hacking cough filled the bar. When the proprietor straightened up, his face was a flush of purple.

"You okay, Ricky?" Holly asked.

Dalton stepped back and coughed again. The bark sounded worse than this morning when he had come out to the farm. Yesterday, Alexander had led them on a night exercise. Unfortunately, the weather had been shitty, cold with heavy rain and wind. Who could blame Dalton?

"Sure, Macon. Throat's just a little sore."

"Gotta take care of yourself," Wicks added. "Ain't nobody else gonna do it for ya'."

"You got that right," Dalton replied as he sent another beer down the counter.

Wicks looked back at Holly with a strange, crooked smile. Holly had told Dalton to keep his mouth shut about going to the doctor. Now Wicks knew. Shit!

Dalton coughed again and the hollow sound made Holly's chest hurt.

"Hey, where's Cal?"

Holly turned to the voice and saw O'Grady striding over to join them. He had wondered how long it would be before the subject of his son-in-law came up. "Not like him to pass up an excuse for a beer."

"Yeah, haven't seen him since this morning," Wicks responded.

"Ain't gonna see him at all," Holly said flatly.

"What's up, Macon?" asked Wicks.

Holly looked blankly across the bar. "The bastard ran out on us. I caught him stealing from the stash in the farmhouse. Said he was sick of taking all the blame for everything. Cursed Gary, Annie, me in spades, and took off in that damn pickup."

Holly downed his beer and slammed the glass on the bartop. He'd made up the story on the way back to the farmhouse. They all knew Napes. It wouldn't surprise anyone. "Screw him, I say. He's been nothin' but trouble ever since he came."

Holly's friends stood mute, looking back and forth at each other, trying to understand what had just happened. After a minute, O'Grady spoke up. "Hey, we're all real sorry for Annie, Macon. But you're right. She'll be better off this way. And I'll feel a helluva lot safer. I never did trust ol' Cal at my back."

His colleagues shook their heads in agreement.

"This does leave a hole in the squad," Holly continued.

"Tommy, I want you to take over security. We need a real hard ass to keep things in line. And you sure as hell fit that bill."

"Shit, Macon. Thanks. I'll get right on it." Wicks seemed genuinely pleased. This could turn out better than Holly expected.

"Give you a chance to get closer to Gary, too," Holly added. *And whatever he gives you'll serve you right.*

"Hey, Ricky," Holly called to the back, "pour us all another round. We'll drop one for Cal, the lousy sonovabitch."

They went through two more rounds sharing stories of the Gathering. Holly kept hoping they would all leave soon. He still had to figure out how to tell Annie about Napes.

"What's with the two guys in back, Ricky?" O'Grady asked, nodding his head at a table in the far corner. The two men seated there were the only others in the place.

"Came in about an hour ago, all dressed up like that. Been nursing two lousy beers ever since. I don't like 'em."

"Sitting a little too close for my good," said Wicks.

"Maybe we oughta have some fun," O'Grady added. "What 'ya say?"

"Do whatever you want," Holly replied as he downed the remainder of his beer. "Just don't do it in here. Ricky and I ain't gonna fix up your messes."

"Whatever you say, Macon," Wicks said. "You're the boss, right?"

Right, Tommy. I'm the boss. And don't you ever forget it.

Chapter 25

THE CALL FROM Gary had come at nine thirty that evening. Holly was still exhausted from the training, and slightly hung over from their celebration at Ricky's, but he was sober enough to know not to argue with his benefactor. He had had barely enough time to call his team, get out to the farm, and gather the equipment before it was time to leave. There were only four of them now—Holly, Wicks, O'Grady, and Dalton—so they all piled into O'Grady's van and waited for their orders.

"What the hell does he think he's doing?" Wicks began. "I can barely see much less run an op. I was all ready to get it on with Lou Ann."

"Then stick your damn head out the window and take a deep breath, Tommy," Holly spit back. "'Cause it's goin' down with or without you."

"What's goin' down, Macon? Where *are* we going?" O'Grady asked.

"Up to the county courthouse," Holly replied. "We're gonna simplify a lot of folk's lives. Everything in the back, Ricky?"

"Just like you wanted, Macon. But what do we do when we get there?"

"We play it the same as the assault exercise. That was our rehearsal."

The Gathering's night exercise had been a mock search and destroy mission on an "enemy position," which in that case was an aged barn in the back of the farm. Holly had thought at the time that the exercise had gone pretty well. He had serious questions whether they could repeat the performance tonight.

"Shit, Macon. We had Alexander leading us then," Dalton said.

"Well now you got me," Holly replied. "Christ, it was only yesterday. Quick in, quick out. Y'all just watch out for civilians. We can't afford another screw-up like the *Guardian*."

"Yeah, well we ain't got the asshole with us tonight either," O'Grady added.

The loss of Napes apparently hadn't had a big effect on his confederates.

Holly checked his watch. 11:10. Time to go.

"Let's get going, Sean."

* * *

The Middleton County Courthouse was an antebellum mansion whose history dated back to before the Civil War. Built by General Redford Travers, its centerpiece was four huge sculptured columns that graced the front entrance, inviting lucky guests into what was once the center of culture and hospitality for most of southeastern Georgia. The property had stayed in the Travers family until 1929 when the Great Crash had finally brought the dynasty to an end. The estate had bounced from bank to bank until 1940 when the county's previous courthouse had been hit by lightning and burned to the ground. The County Commissioners decided the Travers Mansion would make a wonderful replacement and had taken the property by eminent domain. They had sold most of the surrounding land for a tidy profit, and renovated the home into a functional, if overly ostentatious, municipal building.

They arrived at 11:50 and O'Grady pulled the van into a dark corner of the parking lot adjacent to the Courthouse.

"Any guards around?" Dalton asked.

"No guards," Holly replied. "Gary said there could be a janitor cleaning up. If he's there, Tommy and Sean, you take care of him. Nothin' more than necessary. Just get him out of the way."

"Got it, Macon," Sean replied. "Come on, Tommy. Try to hold your lunch a little while longer."

"Screw you," Wicks muttered while running across the front lawn after his partner.

Holly watched as they disappeared behind the shadows of the pillars.

"You okay, Ricky?" he finally asked.

"Yeah. Feeling lots better, Macon. Maybe those pills Doc gave me really do work."

"That would be great, Ricky. I wouldn't have called you except . . ."

"I know Macon. We're short-handed as it is. I can pull my weight."

"Hope so, Ricky. Let's get this shit out of the van."

They unloaded eight canisters and laid them out carefully by the side of the vehicle.

"You take the left side," Macon waved at the near end of the mansion. "I'll handle the right. Set 'em for ten minutes from now."

"Right, Macon. You got it."

Each man grabbed two canisters and headed into the darkness.

When Holly returned to the van five minutes later, Dalton's second pair of canisters was gone. He looked around quickly for his friend but saw nothing but the black shadow of the courthouse.

No point in waiting. He disappeared with his last load.

Twenty yards from the van Holly heard a sound behind him. He slid to the ground, rolled the canisters away from his body, and grabbed his Colt. Slowly spinning on his stomach he scanned the area. Nothing.

Then it came again. From the direction of their van. In the dim moonlight he saw a figure hunch over and grab the side of the vehicle. It was Dalton having another coughing spell. Shit! Maybe it had been a mistake to bring him along. They were running out of time.

He glanced at his watch, 11:56. Only four minutes left!

He gathered up the canisters from the lawn and took off for the back of the property.

* * *

"Where's Macon?" Wicks called as he and O'Grady ran up the van.

"Don't know," Dalton replied. "We took off together. I got back a couple minutes ago and his canisters were gone. He was doin' the far end."

"Shit. What if he doesn't get back? He'll get us all caught."

"I'll go look for him," Dalton said, turning toward the mansion. "We can't leave him."

O'Grady grabbed at his colleague. "Nobody's leavin' now, Ricky.

And nobody's gettin' caught. Macon'll be back just fine. Now, get your asses in the van. When Macon comes, we gotta get outta here fast."

"But what if he . . ."

"In the van, Ricky," O'Grady yelled. "Now!"

They piled in the vehicle and waited anxiously, scanning the property for any sign of their leader.

"What's that on the front of the house?" Dalton asked.

"What ya mean, Ricky?" Wicks asked.

"You know damn well what I mean, Tommy. There's somethin' on one of them pillars. What is it?"

Wicks and O'Grady swapped glances. Finally O'Grady spoke. "There was this old black guy cleaning the floors. We were gonna just tie him up and throw him on the lawn. For sure. Then he goes and calls me a friggin' Irish drunk! Said we were nothing but goddamn Nazis. What the hell does that asshole know about patriotism? My family was fightin' for freedom when he was runnin' around naked in Africa. I tied him to the goddamn pillar. Let him see for himself what we're fighting for."

"Jesus, Sean. I thought you weren't gonna . . ."

An explosion rocked the van and all eyes leaped to the Mansion. The canister charges had two purposes: first, a shaped high explosive breached the integrity of the structure, then a second blasted napalm into the exposed voids. The incendiary flashed white, instantly turning the building into a pyre. While the explosive's report still echoed in the cool night, the mansion was engulfed in flames.

"We gotta get out of here, Sean," Wicks cried. "They'll be coming soon."

"We ain't leavin' without Macon," O'Grady commanded.

Suddenly the rear doors of the van flew open and Holly jumped in the back. "Get us out of here, Sean," Macon ordered between gasps.

The van spit gravel and dirt as it escaped toward the highway.

"What happened, Macon?" Dalton asked once they had gotten underway. "We were startin' to worry."

"I knew I wasn't gonna be able to get back before the explosives blew. I was afraid to head straight across the lawn so I circled back behind. Good thing too. Shit that fire was hot! Anybody inside?"

O'Grady gave a dark stare in Dalton's direction. "Just the janitor. The old guy was clear when we left him. Feisty old fart though. Kept screaming about *his* courthouse."

Holly turned and looked back at the old courthouse through the rear windows. There was nothing more to say. Nothing that could be undone. The records of two hundred years of human sweat, tears, and pain were reduced to ashes in a matter of minutes.

"What the hell good was this anyway, Macon?" Wicks asked as they pulled onto State 805. "The Feds have got copies of all this stuff don't they?"

"Sure they do. Somewhere. But this'll set 'em back years. Time for some folks to get on with their lives and back on their feet. And remember it ain't just this courthouse. We're sendin' a message to all those damn cowards. Ain't nobody gonna take away our rights without a fight."

As the van headed back toward Tyler, the glow of the Travers Mansion disappeared like a setting sun below the horizon. It reminded Holly of the scene from *Gone with the Wind*. The flames, the smoke, the terror. Only this time *he* was the invader. Would the others really understand?

* * *

Gary leaned back in his chair and reviewed the message. All of his cells had reported in. There had been a small glitch in Oregon. He should have realized it was too early on the West Coast, but the body would never be found and the militiaman's family would be well compensated. Synchronicity was critical to the desired effect.

He hit "Send" and the encrypted message flashed into the ether. He didn't know the actual location of the Commander. Only that the address he had been given would be mapped to another, and then to another. Finally arriving at its proper location.

The plan was going well. If they only knew what was coming.

```
Operation BRAVO completed. All units report
success.

CHARLIE preparations progressing.

Mold successful. HALFTIME on schedule.
```

Chapter 26

"GENTLEMEN. AND LADY." Garcia gave a condescending nod in Flynn's direction which the Special Assistant completely ignored. The advisory group meeting had started with Carlson requesting an analysis of militia activity from the Homeland Security representative.

"As you are aware, DHS has had a focused intelligence program on the para-military movement since 2003. It has grown significantly over this period, our best estimates now recognizing almost eighty thousand members associated with greater than four hundred so-called 'militia' organizations." He pressed a button on the laser pointer, and a map of the United States appeared on the display at the front of the conference room. It was blotched with small red circles, prominent areas showing in the Northwest and Southeast. "As you can see, geographically we have the heaviest concentrations in Montana and Idaho, but over forty States have identified militia cells. We continue to treat the movement as a serious threat to national security."

Slattery sat back in his chair behind Markovsky watching the spectacle proceed. Why Garcia was giving the briefing he would never know. The FBI and Homeland had been feuding ever since the younger organization had been formed in 2002, but everyone knew Flynn was the more knowledgeable, and rational, representative at the table. Carlson may have picked Garcia just to piss her off. For her part, the Special Assistant seemed unfazed, silently scribbling on a pad of paper while her colleague presented his report.

"Until now, however, criminal activity on the part of the movement has been local and relatively minor."

"Excuse me, Jerry," Scott interrupted, "but I would hardly call Oklahoma minor."

"Certainly, David. I did not mean to diminish the tragedy in Oklahoma City, but that has never been shown to be associated with direct militia influence. It was simply the unconscionable act of a small number of individuals. Likewise, while they attracted much media attention, the incidents in Waco and Idaho were also localized. They have not, up to now, had significant impact on the overall security of the nation.

"This moderate result is primarily due to the lack of organization within the movement. Most cells operate completely independently, having little or no contact with members from other locations. Even where some larger structure is present, such as the Montana Militia, common activities are more ideological than operational. The primary use of Montana's Web page is for recruitment and spreading of propaganda."

"I presume this evaluation is based on something more than cursory Web surfing?" Stroller asked.

"Of course," Garcia replied. "We have been monitoring their overall Internet traffic and our analysis confirms this evaluation. But you bring up an important point. You must understand that we have only limited resources available to track this activity. To use an analogy, we are sampling the movement rather than studying it directly.

"The results of the past few weeks, however, represent a significant escalation of activity. Seven days ago militia incidents were reported in Georgia, Tennessee, and Kansas." The map behind Garcia cleared and three spots appeared. "Analysis by the FBI, supported by intelligence from Peter, suggested this was a coordinated effort by unknown parties. We have dispatched National Response Teams to the three sites, but subsequent investigations have not clarified the source of this threat.

"Last night, another set of incidents occurred. Six attacks, all at midnight, on county courthouses from Oregon to Maine. The buildings were bombed and burned, destroying all of their documents: land deeds, court proceedings, and criminal records." Six new circles appeared on the maps.

"Copies of these documents must exist somewhere," said Stroller.

"Of course. Most of the data is stored in any number of electronic databases from law enforcement organizations to banks. But all of this will take time to reconstruct. This was not a debilitating strike, but yet another warning. This is a war, gentlemen. Someone is escalating a confrontation with the government. The question is, what will be our response?"

"Thank you, Jerome," Carlson replied from the end of the table. "While I do not agree with your use of the word 'war', I believe we now have sufficient evidence that someone is testing our resolve and reaction capability. That is why I asked Jerome and his team at Homeland to prepare this overview. It is clear to me that some individual, or group of individuals, is using the local militia movement as a front for their own agenda."

"You're saying the problem isn't with the militia?" Stroller asked.

"Exactly, Claude. We must avoid a confrontation with an ill-defined, diffuse movement, and focus on the specific threat."

Slattery couldn't help but smile at Carlson's skills in political bullshit. He couldn't ignore the threat but was doing his best to deflect the advisory group's focus away from his paramilitary buddies and toward some shadowy conspiracy. It would have been comic except for the fact that the IMAGER intelligence backed him up.

"Peter," Carlson continued, "is there any new data from your informant that would help us locate the source of this coordination?"

"We are continuing to try to make contact, General," Markovsky replied. "We are hopeful that the agent will have additional information, but there is always the possibility that . . ."

"I take that as a no, Peter," Carlson snapped. "Mary Ellen, could you give us some details on the attacks? I presume the FBI has started its investigations?"

Slattery glanced over at Flynn and caught her showing an unusual smile. She tore the top sheet of paper from her pad, folded it carefully, and placed it in the pocket of her jacket.

"Mary Ellen?" Carlson, repeated.

"Yes, General." Flynn rose to face the group. "As Jerry described, the six sites were spread throughout the country. All of our teams have not reported, but from the five for which we have preliminary reports, we can draw some very strong conclusions.

"All the attacks occurred at exactly midnight, Eastern daylight time. This is the same as the time of the first set of attacks. There have been five casualties reported; four maintenance staff and one terrorist. It appears that attempts were made to clear any occupants from the courthouses, but these staff were killed none-the-less. We cannot tell at this time if their deaths were intentional, the result of poor execution, or due to overly aggressive attempts at self-defense.

"In Oregon City, a fight erupted between the terrorists and two janitors. Both janitors were injured and we believe one terrorist may have died. No body has yet been found.

"We have also determined the mechanism of the attacks. They were not ammonium nitrate-based, as was the Oklahoma bombing, but a combination of a high explosive, probably Semtex, coupled with an aggressive incendiary. These are not standard militia tactics, and again point to involvement of a much more sophisticated organization.

"The bottom line, gentlemen, is that these attacks are a significant threat to our country. They are severely stressing the FBI's, and I believe all other law enforcement agencies', investigative capabilities. Should another escalation occur in the next few weeks, for example ten or even fifteen incidents, we would be unable to field sufficient forensic and investigatory teams. I recommend that we immediately initiate an aggressive response before additional lives are lost."

Flynn's conclusion caused a stir in the room, and surprised even Slattery. What kind of a response was she suggesting? Carlson had the same reaction.

"And to whom would that response be directed, Mary Ellen?" the DNI asked.

"We have been able to associate certain cells with a number of the attacks. Those in Georgia and Tennessee in particular."

"One of these is the original Georgia cell?" Scott asked.

"Yes, David."

"You have proof of this involvement?" Stroller continued.

"Nothing direct, Claude, but our observer in Georgia did report what could best be described as a training exercise this past weekend. Over sixty individuals converged on the Tyler farm. There appeared to be both hand-to-hand, weapons and explosive training. Everything was border-line legal, but according to our agent, it looked like a terrorist boot camp. It could have been preparation for the later attacks."

"Can you at least place any of the participants at the attacks?" Scott asked.

"Unfortunately no, David. But again, RIPPER has reported a high correlation of . . ."

"Mary Ellen," Carlson interrupted, "your statistical guesswork is hardly sufficient to go invading private property and conducting criminal searches. I, and I believe most of us in the room, cannot condone unsupported assaults on our citizens. I suggest you get back to your teams and tell them to do their jobs and come up with some real evidence. Find out who is behind these attacks. *Then* we'll discuss next steps." He laid his hands on the table and scanned the representatives around the table, ending back to Flynn. "Am I clear on this?"

Flynn had turned scarlet. Her eyes searched the room, pleading for support, but everyone avoided her stare. They all had their own skeletons they could ill-afford to have surfaced. Carlson was too powerful to buck.

"Yes, General," Flynn spat. "Your position is abundantly clear."

Slattery knew all too well Flynn's feelings. He had been there before. Was there any way he could help her?

Chapter 27

ON THE TRIP back to Langley, Slattery had thought of one other connection he could try. He didn't like it, but they were all running out of options. Back in his office, he pulled out a file and dialed the number.

"Taylor Luckett."

"Mr. Luckett. It really wasn't very smart to approach me like that. You could have gotten yourself in a lot of trouble."

"Oh. I was wondering if you'd call back. Look, Sla . . . ."

"Let's not get too personal right now," the agent interrupted. "I'll give you some advice. If you have any information you'd like to share, I'm sure the FBI would be more than happy to listen to you."

"I've tried that before, er, Mr. Brown. Never felt like anyone there was interested. You see, I don't really trust the judgment of the FBI or Homeland Security when it comes to this particular problem. I thought you might be different. I guess I was wrong."

Slattery knew he should just hang up the phone. He was going way out on a limb just making this call.

The trouble was, he sympathized with the reporter. Everything he had read in the dossier said the guy played it straight. And whatever Luckett knew, it had to be better than the junk sitting on his desk. May as well stick his neck out a little farther.

"Tomorrow. Same time, same place, as before, Luckett. You better have something good."

"See you then, . . . Mr. Brown." The reporter hung up.

* * *

Dr. Patrick Flaherty picked up the next medical record in the basket and glanced at the cover. *Richard Dalton.* What was Ricky doing back here? Hadn't he seen him just last week?

"Well, Ricky, how's the business of overthrowing our government?" Flaherty asked as he entered the examining room.

"Shit, doc. Don't give me that crap. You ain't no lover of the IRS either as I remember."

"Okay. Got me there. What's the matter today?"

"It's this damn bug, Doc. I ain't gettin' no better. You gotta do something for me. I'm dying, I tell 'ya." Dalton sat half-naked in the examining room, shivering from the cold.

Flaherty leaned over the table and placed the ice-cold bell of his stethoscope against Dalton's back.

"Shit!" the patient yelled.

"Take it easy Ricky. I ain't done nothin' to you. Yet."

"How come you keep this room so damn cold?"

"So you can have something to bitch about every time you come in. I've never known such a complainer. Now shut up and let me listen."

Flaherty took five additional soundings and slowly hung the instrument back around his neck. Until now, Dalton had been one of the healthiest men in Tyler. A little heavy on the booze at times, but everybody needed something to pass the time. What could have happened?

"Put your shirt back on, Ricky. I don't want you dyin' here in my office."

Flaherty watched as Dalton took a pained breath and slid down off the table to get his clothes. He glanced down at his nurse's notes. Why would his temperature and BP both still be up? And the rales in Dalton's chest sounded worse than he remembered from last week.

"You been takin' all the medicine I gave you?" Flaherty scribbled a few lines in the record, and leafed back to Dalton's previous visit note.

"Yeah. For all the good it's been doing me. I'm chilled all over, and my fever's worse than last week." He coughed and Flaherty heard the sound of loose phlegm. "And the damn cough won't go away."

"Okay. I don't think there's anything serious, Ricky. You've just got a bad chest cold."

"Don't feel like no chest cold I ever had before. I ain't gonna die am I, Doc?"

"Jesus Christ, Ricky. You're too stubborn to die. Here's a new prescription. It's stronger than the antibiotic I gave you last week. Have Stan fill it this afternoon." He handed Dalton the small sheet of paper. "Take it *instead* of the one I gave you. You got that?"

"I think so. I get the new pills from Stan. Take them instead of the others. What do I do with the old ones, Doc? Can I take 'em back? I already paid for them, you know."

"No, you can't take them back. Now get outta here before I charge you for another visit."

Dalton shuffled out of the room and Flaherty finished writing the visit note. He dropped the record in the completed pile and picked up the next file on his way to the other examining room. It was old Sarah Martinez. Her arthritis must be acting up again.

He stopped at the door to the room, then turned and walked back to his nurse's desk in the front of the office. He didn't think there was anything to get alarmed about, but Dalton wasn't reacting the way he expected.

"Ellen?"

"Yes, Patrick?" Ellen Synder, R.N., looked up from a stack of files.

"Give the CDC in Atlanta a call. See if they've heard anything about a resistant respiratory infection."

"Is there a problem with Mr. Dalton?"

"I'm not sure. Check it out for me. And make a note to follow up with him in a couple days. Just to be safe."

"Yes, sir."

Flaherty picked up the next record folder and headed back into the examining suites. Life was getting too complicated. He couldn't keep up with the latest medical discoveries any more than he could all the other changes in his profession. HMOs, PPOs, PSOs. Just a lot of alphabet soup. He had spent the last thirty-five years tending to the people of Tyler by himself and it looked like it was going to stay that way. Flaherty knew that there wasn't any bright, young doctor that was going to come and save his practice. When he dropped over, the good citizens of Tyler, however many were left, would have to find help up north in the medical factories. It was nothing he ever wanted to see.

He glanced at the cover of the record, then opened the door to the exam room.

"Sarah, how are we doing today?"

* * *

Braxton sat back in the painfully-uncomfortable plastic seat in the Dulles KLM gate area waiting for his flight to be called. With a CNN talking-head droning on in the background, he reflected on the morning's conversation with his CIA contact.

He had called "Mr. Smith" from SFO while he was waiting for the red-eye back to D.C., leaving a short message that he had decided to attend the conference. Slattery had returned the call in ten minutes and suggested they meet for breakfast the following morning in the Tysons Tower cafeteria.

Braxton wanted to get past the unpleasantness of seeing the agent again as quickly as possible so he had reluctantly agreed.

He had caught a few hours of sleep on the flight which had managed to arrive on time at 6:30 a.m. After a short cab ride to his apartment, quick shower and change of clothes, he had been ready for the encounter.

"What caused you to change your mind, Mr. Braxton?" Slattery had asked after laying down his breakfast burrito and coffee. He looked exactly the same as he had in Braxton's office: conservative business suit, thin leather brief case and expressionless countenance.

"Let's just call it civic duty. And it's Slattery, right?"

"Mr. Smith will be just fine for now, Mr. Braxton."

"Well Mr. Smith, you can just call me Adam. The formality seems a bit misplaced given what you probably know about me. So you want me to listen for news of Chinese encryption research?"

Slattery shifted uncomfortably in his chair. Looking back, Braxton should have realized this was not a positive sign.

"First of all, Adam, I do need to tell you that the information I'm going to give you is highly confidential. I would recommend that you not discuss this with anyone, including our mutual friend. It could be, well, dangerous."

If the spook's objective had been to get Braxton's attention, he had definitely succeeded.

"This doesn't sound like simply eavesdropping on cocktail party conversations."

"No. I'm afraid it's more complicated than that," Slattery continued. "We need you to contact someone for us. A Chinese attendee at the conference."

Braxton jerked straight up and leaned over the table putting his face directly opposite Slattery's. "Now wait a minute, Mr. Smith. If you think I'm going to run around like some TV superspy you're very wrong. We can stop this conversation right now."

"Please, Adam," Slattery raised his hands in defense. "Hear me out. We're not talking about a late night rendezvous or clandestine meeting. Just two scientists getting together to talk shop."

Braxton sat back and took a breath. He decided to hear the spook out. "What scientist?"

"I'll get to that. But first you need some background. Last week, one of our top cryptographic researchers, Kam Yang, was killed in a traffic accident. He had been working on advanced decryption algorithms."

"Why am I not surprised? Which encodings, Mr. Smith?"

"Let's say block ciphers."

"Okay. Let's say that. Like AES I presume. I'd be very surprised if he had made much progress."

"You might be surprised. No one thought it was possible to trisect a line until two high-school students did it a few years ago."

"Touché, Mr. Smith. You're up on your mathematics. But what does this Yang's death have to do with the meeting in Amsterdam?"

"Kam Yang's brother, Tak, will be attending the meeting. He's part of the Chinese delegation. We'd like you to speak with him."

"Right. What am I supposed to say? 'How'd you like to defect?'"

"Absolutely not!" Slattery nearly jumped across the table. He quickly regained his composure and continued. "Look, Mr. Braxton. Sorry. Adam. Kam Yang was doing very important work. Work he may have shared with his brother. We would simply like to get your opinion of whether Tak Yang is aware of what his brother was doing, and if that information is now in the hands of the Chinese."

"Why don't *you* ask him?"

"Surely you recognize the danger that would put Dr. Yang in. It is likely that he will be under surveillance by Chinese security. That's why we can't approach him directly. You, on the other hand, will be just another scientist at the conference. Use your judgment as to how best to start a conversation."

"So your concern is completely about Dr. Yang's safety?"

"Well, yes. I guess you could say that."

And very little about mine. "Why me?"

Slattery paused. "Your professional credentials are obvious, Adam. And we do have a . . . history of working together."

Braxton gasped. This guy was one piece of work. "Working together?" he shot back. "You refused to help us. We were nearly killed!"

"But look at you now," Slattery replied, his expression completely blank. "A successful businessman. Without any criminal record."

The last comment hit him like a slap in the face. He had been involved in three murders—one he had actually committed. Yet a shadowy Fed had offered him complete immunity. All in return for his signature on a confidentiality agreement. Everything about the Incident was now hidden behind a National Security Finding.

Could the CIA have been his rescuer? Maybe he did owe Slattery a debt after all.

Braxton held the silence until it had become too uncomfortable for either of them.

"So what do I do with this newfound information," he asked Slattery. "Assuming I get any?"

"Nothing suspicious. Just give me a call when you get back. We'll do lunch."

The agent's attempt at humor fell flat. *What the hell had he gotten into?*

Slattery returned to his burrito, giving a thankful break from the intensity of the conversation.

"Oh, there is one more thing, Mr. Smith," Braxton had said as he finished his taco.

"Yes, Adam?"

"I do intend to take you up on your offer of covering my travel expenses."

"Travel expenses? Oh, . . . yes. I see. We'll be glad to help. Within government per diems, of course."

So here he was, eight hours later, waiting—an *economy* ticket in his pocket—for his second all-night flight in a row. This time to a foreign country so he could spy for the CIA and investigate his ex-wife's murder.

What the hell am I doing?

PART TWO

The Consultant

Chapter 28

Krasnapolsky Hotel, Amsterdam, The Netherlands
Tuesday, 2:30 p.m.

BRAXTON LEANED BACK in his chair and fought off a yawn. Shuffling through the conference schedule he found the abstract of the talk: "Stochastic Anomolies of the Richards-Haberhoff Algorithm in Intra-Organization Communications - Dr. Henri Fabret, INRIA." INRIA was the French National Institute for Research in Computer Science and Automation. A name much too long for anyone—even French scientists—to remember so it was known in the community as simply INRIA.

Fabret was a young pony-tailed, wild-eyed researcher who was fervently explaining the mathematical details of an obscure encryption technique. Every time he wanted to emphasize a point—which was all too often—Fabret would pause, look to the side, and shake his head until his pony-tail would fall across his shoulder. Only then would he continue. The amazing aspect of the whole performance was that there were a number of attendees in the ornate Dutch ballroom who were actually paying attention.

Braxton was definitely getting too old for this conference stuff. The hours of sitting in hard folding chairs, the endless presentations by aging academic experts who had made their discoveries far too many years before, or aggressive young turks whose own discoveries were still too far in the future, the inedible chicken cordon-bleu and stale wine. He did enjoy renewing acquaintances with a few colleagues but they were the minority. Most were just anonymous, lonely faces searching for someone that might be interested in their work. As for Braxton, his back ached, his head hurt, and his eyes burned.

Fabret finished his talk with a characteristic flourish of gestures and the ballroom lights came up. He struggled through a few questions before the moderator thankfully called the session to a halt. Braxton used the interruption to excuse himself past four of his rowmates and escape.

He walked into the vaulted hotel atrium and took a seat beside an overgrown Areca palm. At least the plant wasn't likely to bother him.

The Grand Hotel Krasnapolsky was a beautiful structure, visually stunning with polished woods and painted frescos contrasting with soaring steel and sunlit glass. Directly opposite the Royal Palace, he was sure the hotel had seen the march of the aristocracy of the Continent. Now it was host to a coterie of international techno-nerds.

The plush, red brocade sedan in the lobby was well-worn but comfortable. His attention hadn't lasted very long; it was only the mid-afternoon break on the first day of the conference. And as far as drumming up business was concerned, he wouldn't get much out of this academic crowd. There was the meeting with Yang to attend to, but that would come later. What he needed to do was get started on why he really came to Amsterdam.

"Mr. Braxton! Hello!"

The loud, shrill voice shattered his concentration. He looked up to see a tall, well-dressed woman striding toward him. Her face was vaguely familiar but he couldn't associate it with a name. The outburst had centered the lobby's attention in their direction.

"Oh. Hello," he sputtered as he stood up.

"Sydney Marino," she said with a disarming smile, obviously sensing his confusion. "We met at Megan's apartment."

Damn! How could he have forgotten? He took her outstretched hand. "Miss Marino. Of course. I'm sorry. I guess I haven't gotten over the jet lag yet."

"That's okay. It happens to everyone. Although it does crush a fragile ego." She suddenly seemed to notice the attention she caused and lowered her voice a decibel or two. "I guess I shouldn't have yelled. But I certainly didn't expect to see you in Amsterdam. What are you doing here?"

"I'm attending a conference in the hotel. Weren't you here last week?"

"Yes, but something came up and I had to return. Everything is always urgent."

Braxton looked around and saw that they were still a focus for those in the lobby. Marino's animated style was hard to miss. "Would you like to sit down?" he asked.

"Oh, that would be nice, but I can't. I have to get down to Utrecht."

"I understand. It was good to see you again."

Marino paused, then flipped the smile into a wide grin. "What about later, though? A drink?"

"Ah, sure. Fine."

"Great! Here in the bar about 7:00?"

"Okay." Caught up in her enthusiasm Braxton didn't know what else to say.

"Super. See you." She spun on a toe and rushed off toward the entrance.

He watched as she handed something to an attendant. A few minutes later a car arrived and she disappeared into the afternoon sun.

What do you know? I just got picked up.

* * *

Tak Yang was a member of a panel discussion on governmental control of cryptographic technology. It was one of the few sessions Braxton had been able to endure. Actually, the topic was of considerable professional interest; he had been asked by many of his current clients to give them briefings on cryptographic export controls. While the panel session had disclosed little new information, the discussions had given him some ideas on a better presentation approach. He could always use a new "spin" to his proposals.

Yang had been the most insightful member of the panel. He spoke in polished King's English and seemed to even understand the less articulate questions of his colleagues. His descriptions of China's activities had been appropriately circumspect, but he had offered competent analyses of global political trends and positions.

The session had just completed and most of the attendees had rushed to dinner engagements and other appointments. A small group of questioners were still gathered around the panel participants at the front table. Braxton rose from his chair and headed to a corner by the rear door. He wanted to try to catch Yang as he left the hall.

Braxton's thoughts had slipped back to his conversation with Slattery when he suddenly saw a short black-haired man break from the group and walk toward the far door.

Damn! It was Yang. Should he try to catch the scientist now or wait for another opportunity? He couldn't take a chance on missing him altogether. What if he was leaving right after his presentation?

Braxton rushed across the room, knocking over a chair left haphazardly in the middle aisle. Yang stopped and turned at the unexpected noise.

"Dr. Yang!" Braxton called, and waved his hand.

Yang reached in his shirt pocket for a pair of gold-rimmed glasses, wrapped them around his ears, and squinted through the thick lenses at the tall American running toward him.

"Yes?"

Braxton took a breath after he had caught up to the scientist and tried to appear relaxed. "Dr. Yang. My name is Adam Braxton. I was very interested in your analysis of the business impact of controls. I was wondering if we could get together to discuss it further."

Yang glanced to each side, as if to see if anyone was watching. Then he peered back at the westerner.

"Mr. Bratton? What do you do?"

"It's *Braxton*, sir. Adam Braxton. I'm a security consultant in the United States. I was hoping we might be able to share some experiences."

"I see. Braxton. Yes, we could do that. Perhaps tomorrow at lunch? I understand the food is much better outside the hotel."

Braxton smiled. Even a Chinese scientist could smell a free meal. "I believe it is, sir. I'll meet you after the morning session. By the registration area. And I'll find an appropriate restaurant."

"That would be fine. Until tomorrow, Mr. Braxton."

Yang bowed slightly, then they shook hands and parted company in the crowded hallway.

Well, he had done it. At least set up a meeting. Now, how would he get the scientist to talk about his brother?

*   *   *

Braxton sat in the Krasnapolsky bar, twisting impatiently on a gold-plated bar stool and nursing an amber Talisker on the rocks. The bar was definitely old-world: rich in walnut paneling and soft leather chairs, smelling of tanned leather and expensive cigars. Oils of hunting scenes and windmill landscapes adorned the walls. Most of those sitting around the tables were in groups, paired by business interests or loneliness, so he had selected a stool along the brass-rimmed bartop. It was a great place to watch the other negotiations.

He glanced at his watch. 7:25. He would give her another five minutes then he was gone.

"Adam!"

The voice soared above the refined murmurs of the room's other occupants. He didn't need to identify the caller, but turned anyway and watched Marino stride through the entrance. Many quickly ignored the rude American, but a few, all of them men, took their time returning to their previous conversations.

"So sorry, Adam. I got hung up in traffic. Do you still have time?" She slid onto the stool next to him and placed her hand on his.

"Uh, sure. What would you like?"

"The usual, Karl," she called to the bartender.

"Yes, Miss Marino," the man replied.

"He seems to know you pretty well," Braxton said, hoping he didn't sound *too* jealous.

"Karl's a great guy," Marino replied innocently. "He's listened to a lot of my complaints over the past few months. How was your day? Is the conference interesting?"

"It's okay. There were a few good talks. Most of it was pretty stale though."

Karl returned and placed a tall, clear drink in front of Marino. She took a long swallow and seemed to relax.

"That tastes good. I'm sorry about your meetings. You really should get outside these stuffy walls. Amsterdam is a really cool city. And the countryside is beautiful."

"That could be tough. I didn't get a car."

"Oh? Then how about a little tour? Tomorrow's kinda light. I've got a meeting in the city in the afternoon, but I could free up the morning."

"I couldn't ask you to . . ."

She smiled and it lit up her whole face. "Not at all. And I really need to get away from work. It would be nice to do it with a friend. Where would you like to go?"

Braxton realized this was his chance to work on his *real* reason for coming to Amsterdam. He hated to take advantage of Marino, but he had to find out more about Vision One.

"I don't know. I've never been here before. Where's your office? Utrecht?"

"Yes."

"What's it like?"

"It's gotten pretty industrial lately but parts are still really quaint. And it is a beautiful ride."

"Then let's do that. Unless you think it's too much like work?"

"Not at all. How about 7:30?"

"That would be fine. I do need to be back here for a luncheon appointment. That okay?"

"No problem. Speaking of an appointment, I've got one tonight. Sorry I cut things so close. I don't budget my time very well I'm afraid."

Somehow that didn't surprise Braxton. The woman was completely out of control. In a cute sort of way.

"I'm glad you could come," he said. "I'll see you tomorrow, then."

"Great. I'll stop in front of the lobby and pick you up. 'Til tomorrow." Marino downed the remainder of her drink and hopped off the stool.

"Bye," he replied.

She turned to leave, then unexpectedly leaned over and kissed him on the cheek. "Ciao!"

He could feel the warm flush in his face as he watched her leave. A wave of turned heads followed her passage like a wake behind a speedboat. She was definitely a very attractive woman. He almost felt bad about using her this way. Then again, what did he really know about her?

"Karl?" he called to the bartender.

"Yes sir. Another drink?"

"No. Not yet. But tell me, what does Miss Marino drink?"

"The lady is very particular, sir. It is always the same. Avion. Mit gaz. And a slice of lemon."

Maybe not so out of control after all.

"Thank you, Karl. Maybe I will have another."

Chapter 29

"HE'S AS READY as he'll ever be." Slattery said. He was again sitting in Robinson's non-descript office at the NSA ostensibly to discuss their strategy after Braxton contacted Yang. Slattery didn't have a lot of confidence in Braxton's ability to pull off the meeting, but he had done all he could do. He just wished that Robinson had done the same. "Have you gotten anything new on Yang?"

"No. How do you think I would have? You did check out the Agency's files didn't you?"

Slattery took a deep breath. "Yes, Garrett. There wasn't anything."

Robinson shook his head in agreement. "Then I guess this consultant just has to go with what we gave him."

Which was precious little.

Robinson was being outwardly attentive but Slattery had been a field agent too long not to notice the slight pauses and drifting gaze. The analyst's mind was definitely on something else. What could be eating at him? Maybe Stroller was really on his back.

"We have to have the algorithm for the decryption, Roger. These militia attacks aren't going to stop with just two disruptions. This is just the start."

"You're right. They aren't random events. But something doesn't fit."

Robinson bowed his head and pressed his fingers into his temples until his forehead turned white. It hurt Slattery just to look. "You alright, Garrett?"

The analyst pulled his hands back to his lap. "Yeah, fine. Just a little headache. Are we covered in case the consultant gets in trouble?"

"I called our station chief in Amsterdam. He's keeping his assets on alert. But we can't put a tail on him at the conference. The place is already crawling with Chinese agents. If they get spooked they'll pull Yang back to Beijing."

"Why all the attention? Do they expect trouble?"

"Not from us, but there's already been some anti-China demonstrations. Human rights groups still get upset about China's behavior. Yang's on a very short leash. I don't know how close Braxton can even get."

"He'd better get damned close!" Robinson suddenly yelled across the desk. "This goddamn civilian was your idea, Slattery."

It took all of Slattery's training not to reach across the space and drive his hand into the wunderkind analyst's throat. But the conversation *was* taking an interesting turn. What had set Robinson off?

"I don't remember you having anything better, Garrett," Slattery replied in an infuriatingly calm tone. "You did ask for our help as I remember."

"Yes, of course, Roger. I'm sorry. I'm just so anxious about this militia threat."

Slattery searched Robinson's face for the truth, but the analyst had regained his composure. The professional's mask snapped back in place and Slattery had seen all he was to see for today.

* * *

Robinson spun out of the bed, grabbed his pants and went to look for a clean shirt. The Special Assistant had a penchant for ripping buttons and pockets in moments of passion, so he had started to stockpile laundered oxfords in her closet. Pushing innumerable blouses and suits aside—his area always migrated to the end of the pole—he found a respectable blue pinstripe.

"Garrett?" Flynn called from the bathroom.

"Yes?"

"You remember I asked you about Roger Slattery?"

Shit! Why did she have to bring up Slattery again? As if the conversation with him earlier this afternoon wasn't bad enough. "What about him?"

"Oh, nothing in particular. He's come over a few times to talk about the militia thing. Doesn't seem like a bad guy. Are you involved in any of that?"

"The militia? No. Claude's trying to stay out of it. We'll leave that battle between you and the CIA. We're the guys in the background, remember?"

"Some of my friends would say the shadows, Garrett. Like an illusion. By the way, put on the pink shirt, it makes you look really sexy."

He heard the rush of the shower and the rest of her comments were buried under the noise of streaming water.

Robinson spread the apparel back along the rod, and noticed the suit Flynn had worn at yesterday's meeting. Could she have left anything interesting? He turned back to the bathroom and, satisfied she was still occupied, stuck his hand in the jacket pocket. Empty. He reached farther into the closet and checked the breast pocket. Nothing. Reaching over to the other outside pocket, he felt an unusual stiffness. He pulled out a folded piece of notebook paper. One more look to the shower, and he opened the sheet.

Not a neat FBI memo, the sheet was a collage of handwritten letters. He remembered her doodling at the meeting, a decidedly unusual behavior for the intense agent. Across the top in bold capitals was IMAGER. The rest of the paper was filled with permutations of the six letters. Having seen enough, Robinson carefully refolded the paper and replaced it in the coat pocket.

He grabbed a tie and finished dressing. When she emerged from the bathroom, he gave her a quick peck on the cheek and headed out the door.

Waiting in the hallway for the elevator, the paper burned in his mind.

Damn Markovsky. He always has to be so clever.

Circled in the middle of the sheet had been the word "MIRAGE."

* * *

"Mr. Luckett, I believe?" Slattery stepped out from behind a row of cars and confronted the reporter. He had spent the last hour wandering the stores of the Falls Church strip mall, staking out the area for his meeting. He had felt stupid staring into the windows of beef cuts and designer clothes, walking among the housewives and whining children, but good tradecraft required the surveillance. It was unlikely Luckett was anything but what he seemed, but Slattery had learned long ago that first impressions could never be trusted. Not even his own.

"Well, Mr. Brown. Good to see you again."

"I'd like to keep this very short," Slattery replied. "What is it you'd like to tell me?"

"All business, huh? Okay. The arson, and *murder*, in Tyler was performed by Macon Holly's cell, but it was planned and staged by someone else. The same person who bought that old farm, buys the materiel, and directs the militia exercises. And the one who is coordinating all the militia operations. These are dangerous people, Slattery. And things are going to get a lot worse."

"That's quite a story, Mr. Luckett. Why don't you print it? I'm sure the *Post* would sell a lot of copies."

"If I had real evidence, I sure as hell would. But you know I don't. I'm just a poor hack reporter, Slattery. I don't have the resources to uncover dummy corporations, expose money transfers, and track clandestine communications. This is a very well-funded organization. They operate across the country and have all the participating cells under their control. I've done all I can, and lost a very good friend along the way. I do promise you though, if you don't do something I'll find a way to make all your lives miserable."

Slattery stared down at the smaller man and took a step forward. When he spoke, his voice was almost a whisper. "I'll forget that threat and chalk it up to frustration and remorse, Mr. Luckett. But don't *ever* do it again. I believe we all want the same thing: to see that those responsible for these acts of terrorism are punished. I have complete confidence that the proper authorities will see to that."

"So that's it? The 'proper authorities' will handle it? Jesus, Slattery, I thought you would be different. But you're the same as the rest. Nobody wants to buck the political line. You and Killer Carlson. Well, I'll find some way to write this story, with or without you."

"More threats, Mr. Luckett? Gil Converse, he's your editor right? I hear he's pretty much had it with your conspiracy theories. I don't imagine he's going to print anything new until you get your facts straight. And pissing me off isn't going to get you anywhere. Have a good day, Mr. Luckett."

"I hope you all rot in hell." Luckett spun on his heels and headed back to his car.

Slattery watched as the reporter got into a battered Escort and drove off. Luckett was undoubtedly the FBI's source. Of all the informants in the world, reporters were the worst. You never knew what was going to pop up on the next morning's front page.

Luckett would come back if he heard anything more. And God knows, they needed all the help they could get.

As he walked back to his car, Slattery thought about Amsterdam. He hoped to hell that Braxton could get something out of Yang. And manage not to get himself killed in the process.

Chapter 30

BRAXTON APPEARED AT the Krasnapolsky's entryway and searched for Marino. It was a crisp clear morning, the street still damp from an overnight rain. He watched as pedestrians made their way along the sidewalks, glancing down the canal and greeting the street vendors just opening their carts. It was so friendly, so casual. So unlike the hurried gruffness in …

"*Beep!*"

He jumped at the sound and finally noticed a bright red BMW 520i stopped along the street.

"Adam!" Marino called through an open window. "I didn't mean to startle you. I thought you saw me."

"My fault," he replied, climbing in. "I was daydreaming. This is a rental?"

"Yep. Vision One always goes first class." Marino jumped the car onto the Dam with a screech of tires.

"Must be nice. I usually get Corollas."

Marino maneuvered through the Amsterdam city streets, then onto the A2. As they neared Utrecht, she exited the motorway. They spent the next half-hour speeding past geometrically-furrowed fields dotted with quaint Dutch windmills accompanied by a running commentary on the history of the Netherlands by Marino. The carefree conversation almost made Braxton forget about why he was really in Holland.

He wasn't sure what he expected to find at Vision One. It had seemed so easy in D.C., just wrangle a trip to the facility and discover the secret he was looking for. But what was the secret? He didn't have any proof of Vision One's complicity in Megan's death, much less Lawson's. But he knew they were connected. He just had to figure out how.

"This is so idyllic," he finally said. "I never would have gotten out of that stuffy conference without you. It's hard to imagine you really get to work here."

"It is awfully nice," Marino replied as she down-shifted into a curve. "Quite a change from the sprawl of the Bay Area."

Braxton sensed this was his opportunity. "Is your office around here?"

"Actually, it's just ahead. Would you like to take a look?"

"That would be great," he replied as calmly as he could. His heart was racing almost as fast as the BMW. "But this was supposed to be a break from work."

Marino grinned. "No worries. I'm usually in and out in a flash. It will be nice to just tour around. With all the growth, keeping up with the people in the center is a constant struggle."

"There's a lot of comings and goings?"

"Oh, yes. Starting up any new facility is enough of a hassle, but with the IPO and European expansion the managers are really stretched. They're constantly bringing in someone new to solve the next problem that surfaces. And I'm supposed to keep up with it."

"I don't mean to be dense, Sydney, but what is it you actually *do*?"

She laughed. It was a relaxed, carefree gesture. Not unlike Megan's.

"You really are a technologist, Adam. I get asked that all the time by the researchers. They can't seem to figure why I get paid for just talking to people. When Vision One decided to come to Europe, they had a lot of concerns about the public's impression of the company. They didn't want to be just another US company looking to expand. They wanted the subsidiary to take on a real European flavor, but still maintain the technical excellence of the parent. As much as possible, the subsidiary is run by Europeans. It's important to get the right perception of the company in the customer's minds. Some of those customers are very large and very influential."

The speed of the BMW increased in tandem with Marino's speech. Her right hand had left the steering wheel and was waving across the windshield. Braxton glanced at the speedometer. It read 150 KPH.

"My job is to help manage the perception of all the stakeholders: customers, employees, and stockholders. I arrange interviews between the press and Vision One executives; place articles on the company in journals and magazines. I talk to industry consultants who are influential in setting people's perceptions. And I work with local governments to help them understand how Vision One can help their economies and create jobs."

She took a deep breath. Both hands returned to the wheel and the car slowed to a slightly less frantic speed. Braxton peeled his hand from the armrest and breathed his own sigh of relief.

"Sorry. Sometimes I get carried away. It really is exciting, though."

"I'm sure it is, Sydney. And somehow I feel you're very good at it."

She looked over at him and smiled again. "I try."

"Who exactly do you work for?"

"I was originally contacted by one of Vision One's board members, but I guess I mostly work for Paul Venton. He's one of the founders of Vision One."

"I remember Megan mentioning him. You 'guess' you work for him?"

"Well, the reality is I rarely ever see him. He lets me run things pretty independently. We exchange a lot of email, but I've only seen him twice in the last month. Mostly when I've arranged some kind of interview."

"What's he like?"

"Really intense. He's a super guy, but the company is his life. Most of the employees say Vee One stands for 'Venton is number one.' "

"That's not so odd for an entrepreneur."

"No. I've met lots, but Paul really is unique. He was a soldier once. Then he went back to school. After he graduated he stayed on as a professor. Became a real hot-shot researcher from the looks of his CV."

"How'd he get into business?"

"Got tired of seeing all his students and colleagues get rich in high-tech I imagine. He was doing breakthrough work in graphics and visualization and started doing a little consulting on the side. His work with both the government and private industry gave him the contacts he needed to set out on his own with Vision One."

"Is he married?"

"Only to Vision One."

Braxton noticed a road sign with the Vision One logo and barely had time to grab for the passenger safety handle before Marino yanked the wheel to the right.

Marino turned off the main road and into a parking lot in front of what could only be described as a huge glass cube. Braxton could just barely see the shadows of floors and windows behind the glistening facade. It had to be at least ten stories tall. A construction crew was hanging over the front face placing a small "Vision One" sign along the top edge. The building was devoid of any other adornments, save for spotlights on the corners. When he looked closer, he saw the lights were augmented by security cameras that swung slowly back and forth across each face.

Marino pulled into a space directly in front of the main entrance. The area was marked "Visitors Only."

She looked over at him sheepishly. "I usually have to park way in the back. But you're a visitor, right?"

Braxton nodded.

"Now before we go in, how would you like me to introduce you? I don't want you to be uncomfortable."

"How about as a researcher friend of yours? I don't want to bring up a lot of memories about Megan."

"Sure. I understand. A friend it is."

They walked through a huge set of plate glass doors and into a soaring teak and chrome lobby. The ceiling must have been four stories above their heads.

"*Guten* morgan, Margret," Marino said to an attractive blonde security guard at the reception desk.

"Good morning, Miss Marino," the woman replied in perfect English.

"How's Alex?"

"Oh, just fine, Miss Marino. He's starting nursery school this week."

"Super. You should be a very proud mother."

"Thank you. I am."

Marino signed them both in and took a plastic Vision One Visitor badge from the guard. "Mr. Braxton is with me. We'll be upstairs for a few hours."

"Yes, ma'am. Good to see you again."

They walked past the guard, deeper into the building until they came to an elevator lobby. Braxton saw the button plate and reached toward it but all he found was an unmarked slot.

"Not that one, Adam," Marino said. She took a few steps farther into the hallway and pressed another button. "That's the service elevator. It only goes downstairs."

"Interesting building," Braxton commented as they entered an elevator cab.

"Yes. It's built as a cube for heating and cooling efficiency. Of course the parallel with the HoloCube is a bonus. All the staff have offices on the outside walls. The interior is the labs, research libraries and computing centers. It seems to work out pretty well.

"Each floor focuses on one of Vision One's target markets. When a particular customer comes in, it looks like the whole building is focused for him. We're going to start at aerodynamics."

The elevator stopped at the fourth floor. When the doors opened, Braxton gasped. It was as if he had been transported back to the Smithsonian Air and Space Museum. Model airplanes hung from the ceiling and the walls were adorned with glossy photos of the best in aircraft technology. He spotted the new Airbus widebody, a Space Shuttle-like craft with European Space Agency markings and what looked like the SpaceX re-entry vehicle.

"Quite a gallery," Braxton commented.

"Yes. A&A has done a great job."

"A and A?"

"Aeronautics and Astronautics. That's what they call their division. These are all pictures of projects Vision One has worked on. Unfortunately, we can't show some of our best work. It's still classified."

They walked over to another reception desk and Marino signed the guest log.

"Morning, Greta," Marino said to the receptionist.

"Good morning, Miss Marino."

"Is Rolf around?"

"I believe he's in the lab." She reached for her phone. "I'll check for you."

"No. That's okay. We'll surprise him."

"Yes, ma'am."

"You really seem to know your way around here," Braxton said as they walked down a long hallway. "I haven't always had the same positive reception."

"The Vision One folks have really been great. 'Course it doesn't hurt that I work for the head man. But they've all been very supportive. I've pretty much got the run of the place. And I'm not here to take any of their jobs, so that makes it easier."

The hallway ran in a square around the inside of the building. On the "outside" of the corridor were the offices Marino had described. Most of the doors were open, although Braxton saw few inhabitants. The rooms at least looked familiar: stacks of files and journals covered every available surface. Vision One must employ a lot of scientists.

On the other side of the hall the doors were much less frequent and heavily secured. Most only had numbers, no descriptive name. The pair turned a corner and the inside wall changed to glass. Peering through, Braxton looked into a large room with over-sized flat-panel monitors hanging on the walls. Much too neat for a development laboratory, it was probably a customer demonstration room. A lone figure was sitting in a corner staring into a smaller monitor.

Marino swept her ID card through the access block and the door clicked open.

"Good morning, Rolf," she called out. "Got a minute?"

The man turned in his chair and watched as the visitors approached.

"Sydney, what are you doing here? I thought you had gone back to the States."

"Had some more work to do. I'd like to introduce you to a friend of mine, Adam Braxton. He's in Amsterdam for a conference and I wanted to show him around. Adam, this is Rolf Koenig, head of our A&A division in Europe."

Koenig rose from his chair and extended his hand. He looked about forty, tall and broad-shouldered, with short blonde hair and a deep tan. He had probably been an athlete in his younger days, but deep lines around his eyes suggested his priorities were now elsewhere.

"Mr. Braxton," he said. "Very good to meet you."

"Dr. Koenig," Braxton replied, taking his hand.

"Rolf, please. My days as an engineer are long past. I have been trying all morning to run our latest demo. It is all I can do to keep up with the young turks. I trust you are enjoying your visit to our country?"

"Yes. Very much. Sydney kindly offered to show me around Vision One."

"What is your specialty, Mr. Braxton?"

"I'm a consultant in computer security. I'm here for the cryptography conference."

"Excellent. Someone who can help us keep our secrets. Unfortunately it's become an increasing concern for us. With technology moving so rapidly, and product cycles shortening, we must be constantly aware of such threats. Competition has become quite fierce."

"I imagine many of your customers have the same concerns," Braxton added.

"Oh, yes!" Koenig laughed deeply. "This is a very serious thing for them as well."

"Rolf!" Marino interjected. "I didn't come here to have you two talk about business. Show Adam some of the work you're doing."

"Ah. Of course, Sydney." He turned to Braxton and lowered his voice only a bit. "She is a very focused individual, Mr. Braxton. In case you hadn't noticed."

"I *have* experienced a bit of that, Rolf," Braxton replied with a smile.

"Well, I will let you two be my first, what is the term, guinea pigs?" Koenig sat down in front of the monitor and began typing on a small keyboard.

"I will refrain from forcing you to sit through our marketing material, Mr. Braxton," he commented without looking up. "But I can assure you that it is spell-binding."

A few more taps at the keyboard, then Koenig pointed over the top of the monitor to the front of the room. "Have you ever seen our technological marvel in person?"

When Braxton followed the gesture, he saw two large shiny metallic cubes, one sitting on the floor and one hanging from the ceiling. They looked so benign he hadn't noticed them when he entered the room, but now he realized they were the HoloCube. They looked just like the pictures he had seen in magazine articles.

"No, I haven't," he replied. "Could I get a demonstration?"

"Of course," Koenig replied. "I believe your lovely escort would flail me if I didn't."

He pressed a single key.

Chapter 31

BRAXTON TURNED BACK to the device and saw that the space between the two metal cubes was now filled with a translucent image of a metal plate. Above and below the plate were layer upon layer of multi-colored lines.

"This is a recent simulation of airflow over a reusable entry vehicle. I'm afraid I can't mention the client. Re-entry into the atmosphere is a very complicated and dangerous proposition. Here you see the Mach flow patterns over the wings. If we introduce a small atmospheric perturbation," he clicked over an area of the wing, "you can see the result is quite disastrous." The colors changed suddenly, wildly varying between bright red and black. The structure began to vibrate then disappeared from the screen.

"Our simulation combines complex fluid dynamic flows with structural mechanics. Testing like this is simply too inaccurate to perform on physical models and too expensive, not to mention dangerous, to perform in real life. We are able to show the aeronautics designer the specific performance of his design over a wide range of conditions. And we do it safely, before the prototypes need to be built. Hundreds of configurations can be tested before committing to prototype production."

"I see. But how does the designer correct for that behavior?"

"An excellent question." Koenig restarted the simulation. "I will now add a certain pattern of small deflectors on the wings of the vehicle. You may have seen something similar on commercial aircraft." He typed a few commands and small nubs appeared on the wing surfaces. "This type of deflector has been used to modify the basic laminar airflow for many years. We have been able to add to its versatility by studying the precise placement patterns and even making the deflectors adaptive to different flow conditions. Let's see what happens now."

The turbulence was reintroduced, and a different pattern of flow appeared. At first the model was stable, but the end result was the same.

"Can the instability be completely corrected?" Braxton asked.

Koenig again smiled broadly. "Mr. Braxton. Would you have us give away our client's secrets?"

"Okay, okay," Marino interrupted. "I think Adam has seen enough of airplanes for one day. Thanks again, Rolf." She grabbed Braxton by the sleeve and pulled him toward the door.

"Very nice meeting you, Mr. Braxton," Koenig called as they walked away. "I hope you appreciate that you have both a very knowledgeable and attractive guide." Koenig turned and passed a private look to Marino. "I hope you enjoy your stay."

"Thank you," Braxton replied. "I'm sure I will."

"Koenig certainly understands the technology," Braxton said as he and Marino walked back to the elevators.

"Rolf's incredibly knowledgeable," she replied. "He's gotten us front page stories in *Aviation Week & Space Technology* with a single telephone call. And he's a joy to work with. Not at all like some of the other prima-donnas around here."

"He certainly seems to like you."

A flush came to Marino's cheeks. "Okay, so he is a bit of a flirt. Nothing I can't handle. Let me assure you, this job is a dream compared to some I've had. Being an independent consultant isn't all it's cut up to be."

Braxton couldn't help but smile as he thought back to some of his recent assignments. "You'll get no argument from me on that."

They passed through the reception area and Marino gave a quick wave to Greta.

A chime marked the arrival of the elevator. They stepped in and Marino pressed the button for the second floor.

"Where to now?" he asked.

"The only other major sector that's up and running is pharmaceuticals and biologics."

"P&B, right?"

"That's it! P&B's a big opportunity in Europe. Nearly all of the major pharma companies are headquartered over here. P&B isn't as advanced as A&A but some of the work they're doing is really interesting."

The doors opened and they stepped out into another reception area. This one, however, looked like a children's playroom. The walls were covered with huge pictures of multi-colored balls and rainbow-streaked landscapes. It was breathtaking, but completely other-worldly.

"Wow. I feel like I'm in some kind of abstract art school."

"I knew you'd agree with me. It is rather disorienting at first. The colors are just too garish. I've been trying to convince Hellie of that. Now I have a second opinion."

"Hellie?"

"Oh, I'm sorry. Helmut Plaeger is the Sector Director. Everyone calls him Hellie. This entry is his brainchild."

"Good morning, Miss Marino." The voice came from an attractive black woman behind the reception desk.

"Good morning, Naomi," Marino replied. She completed the requisite introductions, and signed them both in. "I'm going down to check out the lab. We won't be long."

This floor was similar to the one above, offices on the periphery and closed laboratories on the inside. As they walked down the hall, Braxton noticed one name plate in particular.

"Ben Lawson," he said. "Wasn't he Megan's friend?"

Marino stopped. When she turned back, her face had lost all its color. "Oh, yes. It was awful. I wonder why that plate is still there."

"Did you know him?"

"Not very well. He was on a special project for Paul. Not even Hellie knew what he was doing."

"Isn't that kind of strange?"

"Not necessarily. It could have been some classified work that Paul was managing. I don't get involved in those projects."

"Who took over after Lawson died?"

Marino paused and a wrinkle came to her normally smooth forehead. "That's interesting. I don't know. I thought I knew what everyone was doing in the sector. And I haven't seen any new faces. Maybe they had to drop the project."

"Probably."

"Enough of all that." She feigned a shiver. "Let's go find Hellie. He'll show you some really cool stuff."

What he really *wanted* to see was the inside of Lawson's office. What had the scientist been working on? And what had made him so afraid?

*　*　*

The blue mass slowly approached the barrier, preparing for its attack. It quivered as it progressed, constantly changing shape in response to the unseen protective forces. As it approached, the barrier became more defined. Rather than a solid wall, it was a lattice—regularly-spaced dense pillars creating an uncompromising obstacle. The intruder faced the ends of the pillars, their latticework extending indefinitely in every direction. Between the pillars were voids, seemingly open hallways to the rich interior, but the spaces were much too narrow for the bulbous craft to pass. It could never breach the barrier directly.

The object continued on, suddenly opening, exposing new colors of red, green, and white. A probe, a brilliant green ball, shot from the mass and hovered over the surface of the barrier. Then it dove into an open channel, dragging a multicolored thread behind. The thread twisted to the right, then the left, avoiding dangerous outcroppings that appeared from the surfaces of the pillars. Ever so slowly the thread made its way down the long channel.

Then it broke free! It had navigated the gauntlet and lived. Much of the object's mass was still on the outside, however, and it took several minutes more for the rest of the object to unravel and thread its way to the interior. Safely inside, the green ball curled its tail—or was the tail curling the ball—and recreated the compact, original mass.

"And that Mr. Braxton," Plaeger said proudly, "is how the Carleton-Rastov virus breaches a cell wall. What you have just seen was unimaginable a few years ago. No other system can show this result. It is truly amazing, is it not?"

"Breathtaking, Dr. Plaeger," replied Braxton, his eyes still transfixed on the HoloCube. "I've never seen a simulation like it."

"Our researchers are the world's finest. At first no one believed the virus could penetrate a cell wall without destroying it. It was simply too big. The secret was to understand the dynamics. In biotechnology, structure is everything."

"I do remember that the shape of a molecule is just as important as its chemical formula."

"Ah. Perhaps even more so. Molecules are not the one-dimensional structures their formula would suggest. In the real world, chains of atoms twist and turn into complex three-dimensional shapes. Why doesn't levo-glucose provide nourishment like its more common dextro-glucose sibling? Because it is twisted the wrong way and thus cannot be acted on by the enzymes in the stomach. The fit isn't right.

"Structure is critical everywhere in nature. The first level, primary structure, is just the chemical formula. The secondary structure is the next level of complexity. Think of the classic double helix of DNA. But few complex molecules stop here. If a cell's DNA only had a secondary structure it would be over ten meters long. The higher-order structures are what allows the incredibly dense packing of molecules. DNA's tertiary structure is another helix, its quaternary even more complex. The result is a mass of chromatin less than five nanometers in size."

"As I remember," Braxton replied, "these structures are driven by the electrical forces between the atoms. The resting structure of a molecule is that shape that minimizes the sum of all these forces. And that is what your program is displaying?"

"Exactly, Mr. Braxton! Just as it takes force to compress a car spring or to extend it, it takes energy to change the shape of a molecule from its resting structure. But when two molecules interact, their structures change. It is impossible to compare two resting structures and determine whether they fit. The analysis must consider the interactions between *all* the pieces of *both* molecules. It is only when we consider the interaction of the virus with that of the molecules in the cell wall that we see the result. Ah. But I see I lecture too much. Your friend is tapping her foot at me."

"I'm sorry, Hellie," Marino said impatiently. "But we do have to go. Mr. Braxton has another appointment." She started toward the door.

"Of course. Excuse me, Mr. Braxton. I am still too much of an academic. But you must come back so we can continue. I have to tell you how certain benign viruses could be used as cipher keys in molecular-coded encryption systems. It would be a breakthrough!"

"A very interesting proposition, Dr. Plaeger. I will make sure that we talk again."

"Adam!" Marino called from the hallway.

"Yes, Sydney. I'm coming." Braxton turned back to the scientist. "Thank you, Dr. Plaeger."

Marino waved her way past the reception desk and out to the elevators.

"I'm sorry, Adam. I thought Hellie would never stop talking. He can be pretty eccentric sometimes."

"No. I really enjoyed it. You were right. This *is* an amazing place."

"I had hoped you'd think so. I'm not a scientist, but I think it's pretty exciting just working around here. Everyone is so passionate about what they do. Thanks for letting me show you around."

She gave him a hug and kissed him lightly on the cheek. Braxton tried to take it in stride, but the lady was definitely having an effect on him.

As they arrived at the ground floor, Braxton noticed a man waiting in front of the service elevator that Marino had pointed out earlier. Far from looking like maintenance staff, he wore a long white lab coat over a starched shirt and tie. He slipped a card into the slot, the door opened, and he disappeared.

"Adam! What are you doing?"

He turned back and saw Marino standing at the guard's desk.

"Sorry, I got turned around."

Braxton waited until they had left the building before he posed the question.

"Did you see that man at the elevator?" he finally asked.

"What man?"

"He looked like a researcher. He went into the service elevator."

"Why would he do that?"

"I don't know. That's the point. Have you ever seen anybody go into that elevator?"

"Well, now that you mention it, no. When I came, someone just told me it was for the cleaning crews. Maybe it's for our classified work. We must need to have secure locations."

Braxton considered her response. They would need *somewhere* to conduct classified research. Could that be where Lawson had done his work?

"That's possible," he replied. "It sure would be interesting to find out where he went."

She turned and those huge eyes glared at him. "You must be joking! If you want to go snooping around there, you're going to have to do it yourself."

If that's what it takes, then that's exactly what I'll do.

Chapter 32

WISPY CLOUDS FILLED the Amsterdam sky and Braxton shivered against the damp salty breeze. After another white-knuckled ride back to Amsterdam, Marino had dropped him off at the hotel entrance just in time for his luncheon appointment. He had met Yang at the reception area and the scientist had insisted in sitting outside at a café along the Oudezijds Voorburgwal where he could watch the traffic on the canal. The luncheon crowds had returned to their offices, leaving the pair to complete their conversation in relative privacy. Only an occasional noisy tourist canal boat broke the quiet.

"Then you agree that international control of the technology is unlikely?" Braxton asked.

"Of course," Yang replied. "No sovereign state is going to relinquish what little power it already has over cryptography to an international body. We cannot agree on basic trade and tariff issues. Your own GATT is a farce."

"It is not *our* GATT, Dr. Yang."

"Of course. But to your original question, no. I see the future to continue to be driven by political and nationalistic forces."

"Surely the availability of cryptographic technology on the Internet will have the effect of leveling the playing field? Even without true controls."

"Perhaps in some locations. But not all countries subscribe to the unruly openness of your Internet. Some of us believe there are valid reasons for state supervision of certain types of information. Society needs rules, a certain structure. For the betterment of our citizens."

Braxton tried to read the Chinese scientist. His jet-black hair was carefully slicked back over his head, and the thick lenses of his glasses magnified his eyes until they overwhelmed his face. Was he the controlled bureaucrat-scientist he appeared to be, or was he simply being cautious with a stranger?

Could Yang believe Braxton had been sent there to check on him? In fact, hadn't he been?

"But enough of this. I must thank you for an excellent lunch, Mr. Braxton. It does wonders for an old man to get out in the fresh air."

"It was my pleasure, Dr. Yang. As I said, many of my clients do business around the world. I have a lot to learn about international issues."

"You underestimate yourself. Did you think I would not eventually recognize your name? The consultant who uncovered the Century Mole is known throughout the world. Even in my humble country."

Braxton blinked at the reference to his prior escapade. He still was amazed by the reaction to his brief moment of celebrity.

"The story is much grander than the facts, Dr. Yang. I assure you. I stumbled on something quite by accident and was lucky enough to see it through. That's all."

"I believe you call that fate? We actually have very little control over our lives, Mr. Braxton. Some, however, try to change their destiny. They meet with disaster." His eyes drifted to the canal, then out toward the dikes, the massive earth-works that protect this small country from the eternal sea. Was this what Yang had meant?

The mood of the conversation had suddenly changed. Braxton decided it was time.

"I must admit I am envious of your mastery of English, Dr. Yang. I can barely say hello in another language."

The scientist seemed to ignore the comment for a minute, preferring to stay within himself, but then slowly turned back to his companion.

"Thank you. I was raised in Hong Kong. English was as much a part of our lives then as Chinese. But lately it has been a struggle to maintain some fluency."

"You have been quite successful. Is the rest of your family in China?"

"Unfortunately not. No. My parents were diplomats of the past regime. They are no longer with us. My younger brother and I were separated after they died."

"Oh. I'm sorry. I have a brother also. Have you been able to locate yours?"

"He escaped to your country. He is a scientist also."

"You must miss him a great deal now that he is gone."

Damn! It was a stupid slip. He had tried to be so careful.

Yang's eyes opened round and clear. Braxton couldn't tell if the emotion was fear or only surprise. Then, just as quickly, his face returned to its previous opacity. He again looked out over the canal, but his eyes were different. They were now focused and alert. His head turned back, quickly scanning the surrounding tables and their occupants.

"You are indeed a surprising man, Mr. Braxton. This is not the place to discuss such things. If you know of my brother, we must talk. Tonight, at eight o'clock. *La Cochina* on the edge of the district."

"The red light district?"

"Yes. Is that not what you call it?"

"Uh, of course."

"Until tonight then. I must now return to the conference."

* * *

"Where's the crusade, Roger? The rhetoric? There's something missing here."

Slattery was updating Ikedo on the latest information from the advisory group meeting and his discussions with Flynn and Luckett. It was a "working lunch" in Slattery's office.

"If this was a political play there would be lots of PR," Ikedo continued between bites of his cheeseburger. "Letters to editors. Proclamations of independence. Have we received anything?"

"Nothing that I know of. But we do have these. Rachael just sent them over."

Slattery threw a stack of printouts on Ikedo's lap. They were copies of local newspaper articles on the recent attacks. One had a particularly ominous headline: "Revolution for Liberty Begins."

The junior agent scanned the sheets. "Looks like overzealous reporting to me. Anything more behind the stories than the standard newswire reports?"

"Nope."

"Then we ought to consider the alternative."

"Which is?"

"That this is all a ruse."

"A ruse? You think someone is organizing militia groups, plotting and executing military-style attacks just for fun?"

"I didn't say for *fun*, Roger," Ikedo said, correcting his colleague. "I said as a ruse. Everybody's behaving as if this is some kind of militia conspiracy. But the militia movement is all about fighting federalism. It's politics. It thrives on propaganda."

"If these attacks aren't politics, what are they?"

"They could be anything. Hate. Revenge. Or someone killing ten random people to hide the one real target. We don't have a clue. And what scares me is that whoever is behind all this isn't saying anything."

Slattery set down his burrito. He had been right bringing Ikedo in on this assignment. The analyst was looking at the situation from an entirely different viewpoint. It was similar to what Carlson had been saying at the meeting. "You could be right. Why should we all be off chasing militia groups when in reality we don't understand the motive? So what *do* we know?"

Ikedo ran through the points on his fingers. "Someone is organizing militia groups. These groups are executing small strikes against governmental targets. Large enough to require investigation but not serious enough to build significant public outcry. The intent seems to be an escalation of terror but there are no demands, no statements of responsibility. The objective seems to be confusion."

"Confusion or focus," Slattery replied.

"Focus?"

"Focusing our attention on the obvious. Like the magician who waves his right hand for us to follow while his left hand pulls the missing card."

Slattery's phone rang. He nodded to Ikedo then reached for the handset.

"Slattery," he answered.

"Afternoon, Roger. How's the spook business?"

"Jesus. Sam Fowler. What happened? Run out of fish in that lake of yours?"

Ikedo got up to leave but Slattery waved to him to stay.

"No way. Still loaded with bass, Roger. And still trying to get you to come out and visit."

"Absolutely. As soon as things slow down a bit around here."

"Been hearing that for years. You know, you really need to take a break every once in a while. While Beth still recognizes you."

The barb hit too close to home. Slattery had been a stranger again ever since Markovsky's first call. He didn't need this grief from the retired cop. "Okay, Sam. Enough of the prelims. What's up?"

"I need a favor. A background check on someone."

"Christ, Sam. You know I can't do that. Call one of your friends in the department."

"Bullshit, Roger. You owe me. And you know it. You never would have found the Cache without us."

"Yeah, and you all almost got killed doing it. Why don't you just stay retired?"

"Sydney Marino. With a wye. Works for a company called Vision One out in California."

Slattery scrawled the name on a pad. "Braxton involved in this one too?"

"It's personal, Roger. Isn't that enough? Just a quick check, then I'm back to the dock."

"I'll see what I can do. No promises. Call me in a couple days."

"Thanks. I'll be in touch."

Slattery put down the phone and leaned back in his chair. Odd time for his old friend to call.

"Anything important?" Ikedo asked.

"Not really. Just somebody trying to get me to take a vacation."

"Sounds like good advice."

"Yeah, well none of us get a vacation while this militia crap is still going on. Where were we?"

"You were talking about magic."

"Oh yeah. We need to figure out the trick. What is this all leading to? That's the only way we'll ever identify our magician."

After Ikedo left, Slattery stared down at the name on his pad. It would be easy to do a quick check on the name. It was the least he could do for the old cop.

For the rest of the day though, he couldn't get the image of that damn fishing camp out of his mind.

Chapter 33

I<small>T</small> <small>WAS ONE</small> helluva strange place for a meeting. Braxton had ignored the odd look he had gotten from the concierge when he asked for directions, but he never would have expected the reality of the restaurant. A thin building packed into a block of row houses, *La Cochina* was a Tex-Mex oasis on the edge of Amsterdam's red-light district. To say it was incongruous would be an understatement. A short flight of steps rose to an open door, from which a deafening blast of twangy country music was exploding. Hanging in windows on either side of the door were garish red-neon cacti, hiding who-knows-what activities inside.

He had approached the location with no small amount of anxiety. What if Yang told his countrymen of their meeting? Would they think Braxton was a spy?

Damn Slattery for getting me into this.

Braxton's heart pounded as he walked up the stairs. He took a deep breath.

Stop it! This wasn't some adolescent James Bond story. It was just a meeting between two scientists. That's all.

He stepped across the threshold.

He wouldn't have believed it, but the inside of *La Cochina* was even tackier than the outside. The walls were decorated with uncountable pieces of western junk—wagon wheels, cowboy boots, ropes, pieces of fence. They seemed to have been tossed randomly at the surfaces and then stuck there by some invisible force. The floor was covered in sawdust, with just enough beer and sweat added to make the concoction the consistency of molasses.

His ears must have accommodated to the music—they didn't hurt as much—but he still had trouble seeing through the dense tobacco smoke. No one seemed particularly interested in his entrance, so he probed deeper into the haze to look for his appointment. He thought he saw a bar to the left, then decided that Yang would prefer a booth and headed to the right. Halfway down the wall he found him.

"Dr. Yang. You picked a very interesting location." Yang stood up to greet his guest and Braxton saw that the scientist had "dressed-down" for the occasion. Instead of the strict black suit, Yang wore a pair of tailored gray slacks, blue pinpoint oxford, and dark blazer. He could have passed for a busy academic on any college campus. But where would he ever wear the outfit in China?

"It seemed appropriate to be less formal," the scientist replied seriously as they both sat down.

A Eurasian waitress in a red calico blouse and short denim skirt slithered through the crowd, took their order for two Grolsch beers, and disappeared back into the smoky haze.

Yang appeared in no hurry to start any conversation, so Braxton waited nervously until their beers arrived.

"Okay, Dr. Yang," he said finally. "What shall we talk about?"

"Well, first of all I would like to hear more about that adventure of yours. Especially how you were able to break the RSA trapdoor function. It must have been quite exciting."

Braxton didn't believe what he was hearing. He wants to hear about the Internet mole? He had been prepared for almost anything, but this?

"Look, Dr. Yang, I thought we were here to . . ."

"Please. I am very interested in how you cracked the algorithm. As one cryptoanalyst to another."

Yang's face appeared deadly serious. Okay, he could play along.

"I wish I could say I cracked anything, but the reality was that I was given the keyphrase. The journal's author gave me the hint just before he died. It took a few days to put it all together, but it was more blind luck than cryptanalysis. Oh, and to be specific the encoding was early PGP, not RSA."

Yang's stern look softened to what he probably considered a smile. "Excellent. Yes, that was exactly what I had heard."

"You had heard? What is this all about, doctor?"

"Please excuse my little ploy, but I had to know if you really were the famous Adam Braxton. These are sensitive times, and I must protect myself."

Yang had been giving him a test! He really was worried about security.

"I don't understand, Dr. Yang. Why is it so hard to talk about your brother?"

"Come now, Mr. Braxton. How would your government feel if your brother worked for the KGB? I have been under constant surveillance for decades. It is only due to his death that I was allowed to participate in this conference."

"You're right. I'm sorry. Did you hear from him often?"

"We communicated occasionally. A few times a year. With access to the Internet, we could exchange messages more frequently, but it still had to be hidden from the authorities."

"How could you be sure they weren't monitoring what you were sending?"

Yang paused as if he wasn't sure whether to answer. How was he going to get anything out of this man?

"Before I tell you anything more, Mr. Braxton, there is something I must know. You are not a member of your intelligence services, although I am sure they have sent you. As one scientist to another, was my brother's death really an accident?"

The question hung in the air like a Damocles sword. How could he answer it? Was it another test? What did Yang really know?

"Of course. I think, . . . Actually, Dr. Yang, I don't know. I read the newspaper reports. They all said it was an accident. What are you suggesting?"

"Thank you for your honesty. If I tell you what you want to know, you must promise me something. You must promise to find out what really happened. You are the only one I can trust. Do we have, as you say, a deal?"

What *could* he say? If he had any sense he would walk out right now and forget about this man, forget about Slattery. But there was something that kept nagging at him. Something that told him he needed to hear what Yang had to say. Before he could debate any longer, he said "Deal."

"Thank you. But I must warn you, there may be those who would choose to keep the truth hidden."

"Why, Dr. Yang? My understanding is that your brother was an exceptional cryptologist. Who would want to see him dead?"

"I am not sure myself, Mr. Braxton. But for some weeks before his death, my brother was concerned about something at his agency. What do you know of his work, specifically?"

"Actually, not very much. I understand he was an expert on mathematical cryptography. And that he was working on a specific class of algorithms."

"You are correct. My brother had found a technique to rapidly reverse the operations used in certain block ciphers. You are aware of the impact of this discovery?"

"Of course. It would open many different encryption schemes to discovery. Was AES one of the ciphers he worked on? Could he decrypt any of those messages?"

"It was not quite that easy. The process was still very time consuming, but given a particular cyphertext, he could usually break it in a few days."

The security of encryption schemes are evaluated by how long it would take a sophisticated eavesdropper, say the NSA, to decode the messages. Standard belief was that AES was secure for up to centuries of computer attack. Yang had brought it down to days! No wonder the CIA was so interested.

"Do you know the algorithm?"

"No, he would not share it. But he did send me a version of the decryption program."

"That is how you communicated."

"Yes," Yang said with a slight smile. "You must understand, Mr. Braxton, my brother was a very private man. And very patriotic. That is what I find so confusing. Why would he be afraid of those he worked with?"

"He was afraid? Afraid of who?"

"Excuse me. Your language is so difficult. Afraid is not correct. Confused is more accurate. You see, he had been monitoring a particular set of transactions. Something about military activity. He had discovered that they were working together. This surprised him. Do the branches of your military not work together?"

"I thought they did," Braxton replied. "Of course I'm sure they keep some secrets to themselves."

"He was very concerned. He had shared this with his group leader, but felt the information was not being acted upon. He feared some persons were keeping it to themselves."

"Why was it of such a concern? What was the activity?"

"I could not follow all he wrote. His last message contained something new. I believe the term was 'one half time'."

"Halftime? This had something to do with the messages?"

"Yes. That is what I assumed. Does this mean anything to you?"

"Nothing special. Halftime is just the break in the middle of American sporting events like football or basketball. I can't imagine what it could mean."

"That is unfortunate. I was hoping this would be meaningful to you."

"Dr. Yang. There is something I must ask you."

"Yes?"

"You said your brother was very private. Would he keep the algorithm to himself? Not share it with his colleagues?"

"You mean those with whom he worked?"

"Yes."

"Oh, no. What an odd question. Kam was very patriotic. He saw his discovery as a contribution to his adopted society. He would never have kept it from them. Why do you ask?"

"Oh, nothing of importance. Just a confusion I had. You have really helped me, Dr. Yang. I do appreciate it."

"Of course, Mr. Braxton, of course. I hope I have been of assistance to you. And your associates."

His associates? Oh. Slattery and his friends.

"Will you be having dinner?"

"I'm afraid not. While this milieu was quite appropriate for our discussion, the selection of food will not accommodate my digestion. If you will excuse me now, I will be on my way. Please do not attempt to follow me out. But you will remember our arrangement?"

"Yes, Dr. Yang. But how will I get in touch with you?"

"I'm sure we will meet again another time, Mr. Braxton. You are quite a popular celebrity you know."

Yang rose from the table, bowed slightly, and disappeared into the crowd.

Their waitress suddenly appeared, undoubtedly worried about her tip, and Braxton ordered another beer. He reviewed the menu, then decided that Yang may have been right. Since the conference began he had already eaten twice as much as he did normally, and Dutch-Tex-Mex probably wasn't what he needed.

Fifteen minutes later he paid his bill and got up to leave. He looked toward the door and noticed a couple moving through the milling crowd. The man suddenly turned and looked back in his direction. The smoke obscured his view but he was sure it was Roger Slattery!

Had the agent followed him to Amsterdam? Was he going to follow Yang?

Braxton pushed forward to try to get a better look but the crowd collapsed around him, making movement impossible. Damn! When he finally broke free they were gone.

Could it have been Slattery? What was he doing here? And who was the woman?

Chapter 34

WHY WAS THIS damn restaurant so busy? Braxton felt like a steer in a cattle drive. After jostling, shoving, and generally manhandling the unruly crowd, for which he received any number of unfriendly looks, Braxton finally discovered the reason they were all inside. The skies had opened and were releasing a torrent of water onto Amsterdam. He yanked the collar of his jacket over his head and ran down the stairs to the street, praying that there might be one empty taxi left in the city. He started in the direction of the hotel, walking backwards to watch for a possible ride.

Two blocks later, cold and thoroughly drenched, he saw a man leaving his cab and jumped in from the street side, giving neither the previous fare nor the driver any opportunity to refuse him. He barked his destination, then began a slow wringing of his clothes to try to remove some of the sopping moisture.

The vision from the restaurant pounded in his head. Was it really Slattery? Had he been watching the restaurant? Or was he there for another reason? It was paranoid to believe the agent would follow him to Amsterdam, but there was nothing wrong with a little caution.

He had just started on his left sleeve when the cab lurched to a stop in front of the Krasnapolsky. Braxton paid the driver and slid out, leaving a wet, dirty streak on the seat and a half-inch of standing water on the floor. The hotel concierge looked disdainfully as the ill-kempt American squeaked across the polished marble floor and into the elevator. The doors had nearly closed when he heard a shout from the lobby.

"Hold the elevator!"

He swiped his hand in the shrinking space between the doors, they reversed, and another dripping guest stepped in. She, there was no mistaking the voice, had been somewhat better prepared. A light nylon raincoat had kept most of her dry, although her carefully styled blonde hair hung limply around her head.

He knew there was no escape, it was only a matter of time.

"Adam!" Marino said when she finally lifted her head. "You look awful."

"Thanks. I could say the same about you."

"No, I mean you look so . . . wet."

"Yes, I think you're right. Pretty awful night isn't it?"

"Terrible. We went out after the meeting and all they wanted to do was drink and talk. I never got a thing to eat. And no one said anything about the start of the deluge."

The visit to Vision One still bothered him. Maybe he could pry some answers out of Marino in a more social setting. "I didn't get anything either. You want to grab a bite?"

"Okay. It'll probably do us both good. Give me fifteen minutes to clean up."

"Great. Meet you downstairs in the bar."

"No, let's do my room. Then I won't have to get dressed up. We can order something from room service."

The elevator stopped at the sixth floor and Marino stepped out.

"Sure, where are you?" he asked.

"603," she called back. "See 'ya."

* * *

Braxton took a quick shower, threw on a clean shirt and pair of slacks, and headed back down to the sixth floor. He didn't look great, but at least he was dry.

In the shower, he had tried to make sense out of the meeting with Yang. He couldn't really blame the scientist for being careful. It must have been nearly impossible for him with his brother working for the NSA. But could he really believe anything the man had said?

He stopped at room 603 and knocked on the door. It would be nice to spend more time with Marino. She was a bright, intelligent woman, a little hyper at times, but fun to be with. He could understand how she and Megan had become friends. They were a lot alike. Maybe tonight he would forget about Vision One and just enjoy himself.

No! This isn't about me.

This was about Megan. He was here to find out who killed her, and why. Nothing else mattered. If Marino couldn't help, then he'd do it himself.

The door opened, but all he saw was the inside of the room.

"Come on in, Adam," came a voice from behind the door.

He walked through the doorway and heard the door close behind him. When he turned around, Marino was standing wrapped in a long, white terrycloth robe, wet hair framing her face.

"Oh, I'm sorry," he said. "I'll wait downstairs."

"No, no. It's my fault. I'm running late. Why don't you order something from room service? I'll be done in a flash." She waved a hand in the direction of a sofa and disappeared into an adjoining room.

"What would you like?" he called.

"Some kind of salad. Some fruit. And an Irish coffee. I'm famished."

He grabbed the phone and placed the order, doubling it for himself.

Looking around, he saw another example of Vision One's obliging style. Marino's *suite* was a different world from his room upstairs. The sitting room held a sofa and two arm chairs, coffee table, and writing desk. Her purse sat on the desk's top and a briefcase stood alongside. A small corner bookcase held a variety of leather bound classics and a few well-worn paperbacks in French, English and German. The window looked out upon the Dam Square.

Feeling a bit self-conscious in an unfamiliar woman's hotel room, Braxton sat down on the sofa and tried to look relaxed. There wasn't any reason to be nervous, but he still felt like he was doing something wrong.

He jumped at a sound and looked up to see Marino still in her robe. She walked over to one of the arm chairs and sat down, pulling her legs around her like a contented cat.

"I just couldn't bear to get all dressed again," she said. "You don't mind do you?"

"Ah, no. That's fine."

"Great. Did you order?"

"Yes. They said it would be up in a few minutes."

"Super. It's a really great hotel, don't you think?"

"It seems to be. Although I must say your room's a lot nicer than mine."

She laughed and tossed her hair loose. It fell lightly around her face. She seemed completely at ease. "Don't I wish? It's really Vision One's suite. They let me use it when there's not someone important in from out of town."

"That sounds like a pretty good deal. Do you get it often?"

"Most of the time lately. I've been running back and forth between here and California nearly every week since I started. This way at least I have a familiar place to stay."

There was a knock on the door and Marino jumped up to get it.

"Hi, Willem," she said as a distinguished-looking middle-aged waiter entered with a tray.

"Good evening, Miss Marino. On the coffee table?"

"Yes, that'll be fine."

The waiter placed a silver tray with two steaming cups of coffee, two elegant salads, and a plate of assorted fruits on the small table.

"Here, I'll get it," Braxton said reaching for his wallet.

"Oh, no, Adam. It's all business. This one goes to Vision One. Just put it on my bill, Willem."

"Of course, ma'am. Thank you. Good night."

She showed the waiter to the door then sat down at the opposite end of the sofa from Braxton. Taking a coffee cup in both hands she brought the hot liquid to her lips.

"Umm. Just the thing for a night like this. Thanks for joining me."

"My pleasure," Braxton replied as he reached for a plate. "Do you know everyone in Amsterdam?"

She laughed. "You mean Willem? He's on the evening shift most all the time. I'm embarrassed to say, but I end up having quite a few dinners alone in my room these days. There's not much time for a social life."

"There must be lots of eligible men at Vision One."

"Oh, I guess. But they're all working so hard they don't even notice me."

Somehow Braxton found *that* hard to believe. Marino was a woman who looked attractive no matter what she wore. As she reached over for an apple, the front of her robe separated, revealing the sharp lines of delicate collarbones on smooth pink skin, and just a hint of a shadow beyond the vee of the opening. She seemed completely unaware of his observation.

Braxton started on his salad. It was definitely more appealing than the fare at *La Cochina*.

"How was your meeting today?" he said between bites.

"Not bad. It was with some local magazine editors. I'm trying to get some pieces placed. Then they took me to a perfectly awful Mexican restaurant, of all places. We could hardly hear each other, and I just couldn't eat anything. Where did you go?"

Mexican restaurant? Could she have been at *La Cochina*? Was she just covering for a meeting with Slattery? "Ah, we went to an Indian place. Had some ristaffel. It was very good."

"They have great Indian food here. We should go together sometime."

He had to find out where she had gone for dinner. But how?

"I hate to bother you, Sydney, but have you got any aspirin? I think today is finally taking its toll."

"Sure. I think. Let me check my bag." She bounded up and went back into the bedroom.

Braxton immediately headed for her purse. There had to be a receipt, a card, something. He opened the clasp and clawed through the contents: checkbook, compact, lipstick, credit cards.

God, why do women cram so much in a purse?

He gave up on the inside and checked the outer pockets.

Here he found something. A matchbook. He picked it up and read the cover:

Casa de Margarita

Mexican Cuisine in the Heart of Amsterdam

Not *La Cochina. It wasn't Marino. It probably wasn't Slattery either. What's happening to me?*

He unconsciously turned his head only to see Marino standing in the doorway, arms crossed defiantly over her chest. There was no question she had been there for some time.

"What the hell are you doing?" she demanded. Her normally creamy cheeks glowed crimson with fury.

"Sydney. I . . . I'm sorry. I thought . . ." His voice trailed off to a whisper.

"You thought what? You could steal something from me?"

"No! I wouldn't do that. It's Megan. I have to find out . . ."

"Find out what? What did you expect to find in my purse?"

The anger in her face frightened him. He had to calm her down. "I have to find out what happened."

"You know what happened," she countered. "She was killed in San Francisco. It was a terrible accident. What does that have to do with my purse?"

"Please. Come and sit down. I need to talk to you." He motioned toward the sofa.

Marino hesitated, threw the pills on the floor, and then slowly walked toward one of the arm chairs. Pulling the robe tight around her, she slipped down into the seat. Braxton returned to his spot on the sofa.

"I'm listening," she said flatly.

"The real reason I came to Amsterdam was to find out about Vision One. I don't believe Megan was killed by a thief. I think someone wanted her dead."

The grimace on Marino's face softened. "Adam, it's normal to deny something like this. But why blame it on Vision One? Why would they want to hurt Megan? She was one of their rising stars."

"I don't know why. That's why I'm here. But it has something to do with Ben Lawson's death as well."

For the next five minutes, Braxton recited his story. Like a lawyer summarizing his case, he explained each of the points: his dinner with Megan, her questions about Lawson, and then the call from Lieutenant Cassidy. He described his trip to San Francisco, the missing answering machine messages, the search of Megan's apartment, and finding Lawson's letter. Finally he explained Megan's hatred of violence and the incongruous defensive wounds.

His only conclusion: that someone, someone at Vision One, killed Benjamin Lawson and Megan Connelly to keep a secret safe.

"Alright," Marino replied when he had finished, "I'm still not completely convinced, but let's say I accept your argument. Why *were* you going through my purse?"

What could he say? That he thought she was a spying on him? With a CIA agent? God, what a fool he was. He had to come up with a story.

"I was looking for your ID." It was as plausible as anything.

"My ID? And what were you going to do with it? Dress up to look like me?"

"I don't know what I was going to do. I just have to get back into Vision One. To get into Lawson's office. I thought maybe I could just flash your badge."

"Adam, you saw the way they run security. You'd never get past the front desk."

Was this the end? How would he ever find Megan's killer now? Her stare burned through him. He dropped his head unable to meet her eyes.

"Why didn't you just ask me?"

He slowly raised his head. Had she really said that? "You'd go with me? You'd do that?"

She pointed a perfectly-manicured finger at him. "Don't get me wrong. I think you're *way* off base. But I also know, or think I know, how much you loved Megan. If this will help you put her death to rest, I'm willing to help. She was a friend of mine, too."

"Then let's go!" He jumped up from the sofa and headed for the door.

"Now? It's . . ." she looked down at a bare wrist.

"It's 8:30," Braxton answered. "There shouldn't be anybody else around by the time we get there."

"I suppose not. But can I get dressed first?"

Chapter 35

HOLLY LEANED OVER the map spread across the old trestle table. He had gathered what was left of his staff at the farmhouse to explain the logistics for the next exercise this coming weekend. Two cells from up north were coming down to the farm for a series of mock attacks. Not as big as the Gathering, but it would still take them the rest of the week to prepare the sites and arrange for places for everyone to stay. With Dalton out sick, they could barely finish the preparations.

And Holly knew he needed everything to go smoothly. There had been too many screw-ups already.

"Are the trucks ready to go, Tommy?" he asked.

"Yep, all set. I had the boys tighten the springs and rig the cargo covers."

"They don't know what they're for do they?"

"Hell no, Macon. Those good ole boys'll do whatever I ask 'em. Hey, I'm your Security Officer too, right? Ain't nobody gonna mess us up while I'm on watch."

"Right, Tommy." Wicks had become even more of a pain in the ass since his "promotion." Holly worried that maybe he had made a mistake in letting him deeper into their plans. "How about you Sean? Any problems getting enough ammo?"

"A couple of the new boys are bringing their stashes. We'll be fine on the rifles and sidearms. We're a little short on light mortar rounds but we'll get by. Can't be tearing up that much of the countryside anyway."

"Okay, but keep track of what gets used. And make sure those shotgun conversions are ready."

As Holly rolled up the map he caught movement out of the corner of his eye. Looking up, he saw Gary standing in the doorway. He had not even heard him come in. What was he doing here?

"Tommy, you've got to tighten up on security. The Feds are bound to be sneaking around now."

"I've got it covered, Macon. Ain't nobody getting in that don't belong."

It'll be your ass if they do, you bastard.

"Didn't see much in the paper, Macon," O'Grady said as they packed up. "Just that a fire burned down the courthouse. The others go okay?"

"Went great," Holly replied a little too loudly. "They'll try to keep all the rest out of the newspaper for as long as they can, but we know better. Six attacks all at the same time. No, they can't ignore us now."

"When do we go next?" Wicks asked.

Holly glanced over to their visitor. "Don't know. But after the last one, we'd better be ready anytime. Now y'all get back to town. We've still got a lot of work to do."

He waved the group away, nervous about the appearance of his benefactor. O'Grady left quickly, but Wicks lingered at the table. Holly figured he was going to try to cozy up to Gary. He had seen the two together, whispering in the shadows. Wicks thought Holly didn't know the kid was bucking for a better job with the Commander. It would serve him right to get one.

Gary finally gave up waiting and walked slowly over to the pair.

"Macon, we need to talk," he began.

"Should I go?" Wicks asked, more to Gary than to Holly.

"No, you can stay," Gary replied. "Actually it affects you, too. You're in charge of security now, right?"

"Yep."

"What's this about, Gary?" Macon didn't like the man's tone. And he really didn't like Wicks hanging around. If there was trouble, he didn't want it spread all over the cell.

"Where's Ricky, Macon?" Gary asked.

Shit. It was about Dalton. "Couldn't make it. Somethin' came up at the bar."

"Funny. I heard he'd been sick."

"Just a little cough. Ain't nothin' important."

"I didn't know Ricky was sick," Wicks interjected. "How come you didn't tell me, Macon?"

Holly glared at Wicks and saw a veiled smirk on his lips. The little bastard.

Don't think I don't know you were the one who told Gary. You'll get yours yet.

"So Ricky caught a bug," Holly explained. "He went to the doc. It ain't no big deal."

"The hell it isn't," Gary yelled slamming his hand on the table. "I told you to call me if anyone came down with anything. You know what we're doing here on the farm."

Beads of sweat ran down Holly's cheeks. He had heard Gary raise his voice before. It wasn't an experience he wanted to repeat. "Hey, take it easy. I said I'd tell you if anything funny happened. Ricky just caught a cold, that's all."

"No, Macon. That's not all." This time both of Gary's fists hit the table. The massive oak piece shook under the force. "You were given an order. I didn't say 'if you think it's important.' I said call me. And you didn't. Do you have any idea what you've done?"

"I didn't want nothing to happen to Ricky."

"That's not your responsibility! And don't you think it's a little late to be getting morality? It didn't bother you to kill Napes."

Why did he have to say that! Holly glanced over to Wicks and saw the shock on his face. How would he ever get out of this?

"You're incompetent, Holly," Gary yelled. "You're no good to the Covenant and you're no good to us."

Gary's voice was getting louder and louder. His head started to shake from side to side.

"I . . . I'm sorry, Gary. I shoulda called. It won't happen again." Holly was scared. It was like the man was having some kind of fit. Even Wicks had shrunk back from the table, trying to distance himself from the exchange.

"You're goddamn right it won't happen again, you stupid asshole. Why did I ever think you'd be able to pull this off?"

"You can't talk to me like that," Holly exclaimed.

"I can do anything I want, old man. And there's not a damn thing you can do about it." Gary's right hand flashed across his body and struck Holly square on his cheekbone. The older man spun back and had to grab the edge of the table for support.

"Nobody does that to me!" Holly yelled. He licked his lips and tasted the salty sting of blood.

"Well I do!" Gary replied. "I do anything I damn well want. You have a problem with that?"

Holly didn't know what to say. Gary had gone over the line. He was insane! Commander or no Commander this had to stop.

"Nothing to say, you weak old homo?" Gary continued. "Well I've got lots more to say. Sure glad you got rid of Napes for me. Made it a lot easier."

Made what easier? He couldn't mean . . .

"What?" Holly cried.

"That cute little Annie of yours. Now I can have her any time I want. She really likes the kinky stuff. Did you know that?"

"Shut up you bastard!" Without thinking, Holly's hand reached for his Colt.

"Bad move, old man," Gary whispered.

* * *

Wicks had never seen anyone move so fast. Before Holly could raise the weapon, Gary stepped into the militiaman, grabbed his arm, and spun, twisting the arm over his head. Then he yanked it down, levering it on his shoulder. Wicks heard a loud crack, and an ear-splitting scream as Holly's elbow snapped, tearing the collateral ligaments and severing the ulnar nerve.

Gary was still in motion, spinning back to face Holly, then burying the heel of his right hand in the man's solar plexus. Holly was thrown into the stone wall of the fireplace. He hit with a crack and slid slowly down to the floor.

When the whirlwind had finally stopped, Wicks looked up from his friend and saw Holly's Colt in Gary's hand. He had never even seen the exchange.

Holly sat writhing on the pine floor, his right forearm dangling pathetically from a bloody elbow.

"My god," Holly groaned. "My arm, I can't move it!"

Gary kicked Holly in the stomach and turned toward Wicks.

"No, Gary. No. I didn't do nothing. I won't tell anybody!"

"What's the matter, Tommy? I thought you were the tough guy." Gary's voice had returned to its ice-cold monotone. "It looks like your boss won't be able to run the cell anymore. You interested?"

"Sure, Gary. Sure. Whatever you want." Wicks was barely able to control the tremor in his voice.

"Good. I knew we could count on you. Now for your first assignment." He tossed Wicks the Colt.

"What do you want me to do?"

"Finish the job, Tommy."

"Kill Macon? He's my friend!"

"He's an impediment to the Covenant, Tommy. Do it." Gary slowly turned back to face the quivering Holly. "I won't tell you again."

Wicks looked at the gun, then down to Holly. He had known Macon Holly all his life. He was an old fool, sure, but Wicks didn't hate him. The man would be a cripple the rest of his life. Why did he have to kill him?

"Tommy, you can't," Holly pleaded.

Wicks glanced back to Gary. He had the gun. The mercenary was six feet away, just looking down at Holly. It would be so easy. And then the nightmare would be over.

As Wicks pointed the revolver, Gary turned his head and his hollow eyes took control of Wick's thoughts.

Holly *was* a fool. He hadn't recognized the power that Gary had offered. Power to take charge, to make people do whatever he wanted. To get back at all those that had taunted him in the past. Wicks knew what he wanted. Now he would have it.

The shot erupted into an avalanche of sound in the small room. He pulled it again. And again. Until the only sound was the click of the pin against an empty chamber.

Holly's body lay frozen on the floor in an expanding pool of dark liquid.

The silence of the aftermath was as frightening as Gary's outburst. Wicks felt like he had been turned to granite. What had he done? What was he getting into?

"Good job, son," Gary said softly. "I knew you were the leader we needed. First, get this cleaned up. No use in upsetting his family. Make it seem like an accident."

Wicks managed to get his mouth to move. "Yes. Sir." He slid one foot along the floor.

"It's Gary, son," he said with a frightening smile. "You're part of the family now."

"Yes sir, uh, Gary." Wicks actually took a step.

"Now about this Dalton. Where is he?"

"I don't know." Gary's smile disappeared. "But I can find out. He's probably at home."

"Good. He needs to be isolated, Tommy. Forever. We can't let him contact anyone else."

Jesus. He had gone to high school with Ricky. They had been on the football team together. But if he really was sick. "Okay."

"The doctor. You know who he is?"

"Doc Flaherty. He's got a clinic over in Cypress."

"Find out if he talked to anyone. Then take care of him. And his records."

"How am I gonna do that?"

Gary took a single step toward Wicks. "You've been telling me you're such a clever fellow, Tommy. You figure it out. You *can* do it, can't you?"

Wicks knew there was only one answer possible. "Yes. Absolutely."

"Very good, son." Gary moved the rest of the way to Wicks and rested his arm on the younger man's shoulder. It felt like an iron millstone.

"You're a very important part of the Covenant now, Tommy. Don't ever forget that."

"No, sir. Gary. I sure won't."

Gary motioned to the table. "Good. Now let's talk about this weekend's exercises."

* * *

Gary set the copy of Miyamoto Musashi's *Book of Five Rings* on the small table and stretched back on his bed. The passage from The Ground Book was especially prophetic:

> The Way of strategy is the Way of nature. When you appreciate the power of nature, knowing the rhythm of any situation, you will be able to hit the enemy naturally and strike naturally. . . . There is Timing in everything. . . . All things entail rising and falling timing.

The last few days had been telling. Holly had been trouble since the day they started: a little too thoughtful, a little too conservative.

Not the mindless, radical zealot Gary had desired. Well, now he was a little too dead.

Wicks would be able to carry out the last few steps. He was a spoiled, arrogant fool, but Gary had had no choice. The farm would still need to be taken care of. Perhaps he could fit Wicks into an appropriate part of that scenario.

Gary had packed and swept the motel room again. With each mission, his visibility increased. It was only a matter of time before someone broke. The end-game was near and he didn't want any loose ends left around for spying eyes.

The pills had finally taken effect and he would try to rest. As sleep overcame him, his message was already on the way to its destination.

Tyler sanction required. Situation stable.

Operation CHARLIE on schedule.

Tennessee component completed. HALFTIME proceeding smoothly.

Chapter 36

AﬀTER YET ANOTHER harrowing drive through the Dutch countryside, they arrived at Vision One and Megan signed them in, explaining to the security guard that she had left her briefcase upstairs. Braxton was introduced as her date for the evening. The guard listened impatiently, nodded his acceptance, and went back to his television. The Dutch national soccer team was playing France.

They took the elevator to P&B.

Marino nervously glanced up and down the hallway while Braxton pushed on the handle to Lawson's door. It clicked and the door swung open.

"Come on," he said, and pulled her into the office, closing the door behind them. Moonlight filtered through the smoked glass outside wall, providing just enough light to keep them from running into the furniture.

"Adam, this isn't a good idea. I don't know why I let you convince me to come. I could lose my job!"

"Dammit, Sydney, then leave!" he barked. "But I'm going to find out what happened to Megan and Ben Lawson. Something's wrong here. Are you going to help me or not?"

Marino shook her head but didn't move. "Help you do what, Adam? Hellie had the office cleaned out after Ben died. It's empty."

Braxton clicked on a small flashlight and panned it around the room.

"Where'd you get that? You have one handy every time you want to go breaking into people's offices?"

"I bought it today. Thought it might come in handy."

She was right. There was nothing but a desk, credenza, and file cabinet in the office, all modern, Scandinavian style in a deep-burgundy wood. The surfaces were clean and polished, the owners not allowing even a layer of dust to accumulate. Damn! What had he been thinking? They wouldn't have left anything behind.

"There's something here! I know it. Look in the drawers. Inside the cabinets. Lawson could have hidden something."

They spent the next ten minutes examining, scraping, and rubbing every hidden surface in the office. All they achieved were multiple cuts on the ends of every finger. Marino slammed the last drawer back into the file cabinet and turned to her partner-in-crime.

"That's it! I quit. There's nothing here, Adam. Let's get out before we get caught."

Braxton was leaned over the massive desk with his arms stuck deep into the middle drawer. He responded without looking up.

"Okay. I guess you're right." His voice reflected the tired frustration he felt. "It was a dumb idea anyway."

"No. It was not a dumb idea. You want there to be a logical explanation for Megan's death. It's just that sometimes life isn't logical. You know—shit happens."

"Yeah. Maybe I was looking for . . ."

"Looking for what, Adam?"

"Sydney! Have you got a compact?"

"Huh?"

"A compact. A makeup case. One of those round things with a mirror?"

"Sure. It's in my purse."

"Well can I have it?" His voice had gone from morose to manic.

Marino fumbled in the bag and finally pulled out a small round plastic case. "Here. What do you want it for?"

He grabbed the case, opened it, and dropped it into the drawer. He had almost missed it. It was just a rough spot on the underside of the top. But the rest had been so smooth. And there was something very regular about the scratches.

"Here! Look."

She came behind the desk and looked down as Braxton shown the light onto the mirror. Cut into the wood, backwards, so it could only be read with a mirror, were the numbers "7319879."

"What is it?" Marino asked.

"I don't know. It could be an account number, a computer password, a telephone number."

"Couldn't it be something from the manufacturer? A model number or something?"

"Not likely. That would be stamped or burned. This was obviously cut by hand. It had some important meaning for Lawson. We just have to figure out what. Have you got a pen?"

"Forgot that in your snooper spy kit, huh?"

"Please, Sydney."

"Okay, okay." She fumbled in her purse, produced a pen and scrap of paper, and copied the number.

"Now what?" she asked.

"Let's make a quick round of the floor."

They left Lawson's office to check out the rest of the floor. All the other offices were locked or empty. Their last destination was the customer demonstration room.

"Your folks really know how to keep a place clean," Braxton commented as they completed their search of the area.

"Paul's a real stickler on corporate security," Marino replied from the other side of the room. "I saw him chew out a programmer for leaving some listings in the demo room. The poor guy was shaking. It wasn't pretty."

"Whatever he does, it sure works. I've seen secure military facilities less sterile than this."

Marino glanced at her watch. "My god, Adam. We've been here nearly a half an hour. It only takes so long to find a briefcase. Security will come looking for us if we don't get downstairs."

"Okay, we may as well go. I certainly haven't found anything else. Thanks for putting up with this little escapade." He reached over and kissed her on the cheek.

"Well you certainly are a strange date. All this drama and you were only looking for a place to make-out."

They walked back through the dark halls to the elevator stack.

"What now, mister consultant?" Marino asked as they entered the elevator. "Are we done?"

"I don't know. I really believe we must have missed something." He reached for the "G" button then changed his mind and pressed "-1."

"Where are we going?"

"Just playing a hunch."

The elevator passed through the ground floor and stopped. The doors opened and Braxton gingerly looked out. The basement was a giant room of machinery. The space appeared to span the whole cross section of the building, only occasional thick concrete pillars breaking the open expanse. The floor and walls were painted a drab battleship gray, but multicolored pipes covered the ceiling, snaking between boilers and pumps.

"I'm gonna take a look," he said and stepped out into the dimly lit maze.

"Look at what?" Marino cried.

Braxton scanned what he could see of the area, then looked up and picked a particularly obvious purple pipe snaking its way across the ceiling. He jogged down the aisles between the electrical and HVAC components trying to keep the pipe in view. Barely missing protruding valve wheels and low cross-pipes, he finally stopped and turned to wait for his accomplice to catch up.

"Where are you going?" she demanded.

"Just checking the layout," he replied.

"Well, see. It *is* just the maintenance floor," Marino proudly stated.

"Okay, but what's below here?"

"Below here? Nothing. There wasn't any other floor on the panel."

"Then where do those pipes go?" All the ducting and pipe seemed to converge in the center of the huge area, just ahead of where they were standing. Most disappeared upwards, into the heart of the building, but a few seemed to go down. He pointed into the abyss.

"I don't know. And frankly I don't care. Enough is enough, Adam. Let's get out of here!"

Braxton sensed Marino was in no mood for further discussion so he followed her silently back to the elevator. Once again in the main lobby, he stopped and stared back at the elevators.

"Adam, come on," Marino pleaded.

"Not yet. I know we're missing something." He glanced over to the security desk and saw the guard look up at them briefly then return to his soccer game.

"I don't know where else we can look."

"What about the computer rooms in the center of the building? Can we get in there?"

There was a soft buzz and Braxton noticed the light above the first elevator come on.

"I doubt it. I've never even seen them. I wouldn't know how to get in."

The doors to the elevator opened and two men in white lab coats stepped out. They pulled cigarette packs out of their pockets and headed for the front door.

Braxton grabbed for Marino just as the doors started to close.

"What . . ."

He pulled her into the cab just as the doors slammed shut. Marino stood frozen as Braxton looked around. The cab appeared to be the same as the other elevators, except there was only one unmarked button on the control panel.

"Adam! We shouldn't be in here."

"Why not? I thought you said it was just a service elevator."

"That's what they told me."

"Then why would two guys looking like lab technicians be coming out of here?"

"I don't know. Maybe they were fixing something."

"Or maybe there's a secret lab."

"If there is, we're not supposed to be there."

"Well, let's take a look anyway." He reached over and pressed the button.

Chapter 37

THE ELEVATOR LURCHED and they could feel it going down. They stood next to each other, silently staring at a dark indicator above the doors. After about ten seconds the cab slowed to a stop.

"Seemed like a long trip for one floor," Braxton commented.

Again the door opened, but this time onto a very different vista.

They stepped into a tiny room, about ten feet wide by six feet deep. There were no windows, the walls were painted concrete block. Opposite the elevator was a single door; next to it, a plain black box with electronic keypad hung on the wall.

"I don't like this, Adam. It doesn't look like any parking garage I've ever seen."

"Where's your sense of adventure, Sydney?" He felt his heart beat a little faster. Would this help him understand what happened to Megan?

He reached for the door and tried the knob. No alarms went off, but neither did the knob turn. "Should we try Lawson's code?"

"Will it make any difference what I say?"

"No."

Marino took the paper from her purse and read each number while Braxton entered them into the keypad. The door responded with a click.

"You don't have to come in with me," he said. "But I'm going to check it out." He reached for the knob.

"I think I'll stay here."

"Suit yourself."

The pounding in his chest was getting louder. He turned the knob, pulled open the door, and went through. Ahead was a long, empty hallway. Light shown through glass doors and observation windows along each side. Not seeing anyone, he cautiously headed down the hall.

"*Clack.*"

He jumped and spun around. Shit! It had just been the door latch.

The throbbing moved into his head. His ears were filled with the sound of rushing blood. He crept up to the first window on the left and peered in.

He hadn't been in a chemistry lab since high school, but there was no mistaking the scene. Lab benches, test tube racks, microscopes, and centrifuges filled the room. Along with some equipment he didn't recognize.

Proceeding slowly down the hall, he checked out each room. They were all the same, complete chemistry labs. It was quite a set up. What were they doing in the basement of a computer software company?

As he approached the end of the hall he found not a wall, but a heavy door. Through a small window he saw another door, sandwiching what he assumed was some kind of airlock. The corridor continued past the second door with even more facilities on the other side. Inside the airlock he saw two white plastic isolation suits, dangling from hooks on the wall like medieval prisoners.

He stepped back, wary of the discovery and then noticed something that made him even more frightened: the symbol stenciled on the door. It was the purple circles of the international biohazard symbol. This wasn't just a chemistry lab, it was a *bio*chemistry lab. And whoever ran it, was dealing with some pretty heady stuff.

All those pictures of molecules and viruses upstairs, could they be for work here? Why would it be so hidden?

A sound broke his concentration. A grating along the floor. Someone was coming! He froze as if this would hide his presence.

Suddenly something brushed his back.

Braxton jumped to the side and raised his hands in a mock fighter's pose. His martial skills were a little rusty, but he'd at least try to put up a fight.

"Eeek!" Marino screamed.

"What are you doing scaring me like that?" Braxton's muscles relaxed but his stomach was locked in a knot. He felt sweat running down the inside of his shirt.

"I'm sorry, but you were gone so long. I got worried. What is this place?"

"It looks like some kind of a biochemistry lab. Did you ever hear of anything like this down here?"

"Never. I thought it was just Vision One."

"It may be, but they're sure into something other than computer graphics."

"Are you going to go any further? In there?" She pointed through the airtight door.

"Not without knowing what's inside. I'm not a fan of invisible microbes. Let's see what we can find in the labs."

They turned into the first laboratory and started searching. Marino checked the shelves while Braxton looked into the storage areas under the benches. After a few minutes of shoving dusty bottles back and forth all he had managed to do was remember how awful chemicals smelled.

"Nothing here," he said. "It's as clean as the rooms upstairs. I'll try the next one."

"Not without me," Marino replied as she hurried to catch up with him.

"Here's something." Braxton had gone into the next lab and was leaning over one of the bench tops.

"What is it?" she asked.

"It's some kind of laboratory notebook. Those researchers must have been working here when they went for a break."

"Do you understand any of it?"

"Not a bit. But this looks familiar." He had turned a page and was staring at a wildly colored picture of sticks and spheres.

"It's a picture of a molecule," Marino said. "Or at least part of a molecule. It's like the ones upstairs in P&B. Do you think that's what they're trying to make?"

"That sounds like a pretty good guess. I wonder what it is."

"Usually there's a legend somewhere on the picture. There!" She pointed to a line of tiny text at the bottom of the print.

"Lawson 423V85," Braxton read.

"Is this what he was working on?" Marino whispered.

The reference to the dead scientist brought a chill to the room. It took a moment for Braxton to recover.

"Okay," he finally replied. "First we check the lab books for anything else to help us identify what's going on here. Then we leave. I doubt whoever runs this lab would like our snooping around."

They spent the next five minutes flipping through notebook pages and searching the lab cabinets. Marino heard a sound and looked up to see Braxton carefully tearing pages out of one of the books.

"What are you doing?" she whispered.

"I needed something to write on. And I found some other pictures of Lawson's molecule. But I think we'd better get out of here."

He folded the sheets of paper and slid them into his jacket pocket. Then he took Marino's hand and they ran back down the corridor. Once back inside the security foyer, Marino reached for the elevator button.

"No!" Braxton shouted as he grabbed her hand.

"What's the matter?"

"That!" He pointed up to the indicator light. "It just went out. The elevator's going up. The technicians must be coming back. We've got to find a place to hide."

He pulled her back to the access door. "What's the combination?"

"731 something. I don't remember!"

"Where is it? You opened the door last!" He looked up and saw the indicator panel stop at "G."

Marino shuffled through her purse looking for the paper with the access code. The "G" light went out.

"Here. 7 3 1 9 8 7 9."

Braxton punched in the code. The lock clicked and they rushed through. He shoved the door shut and pulled Marino into the first lab. He hoped it was as unused as it looked.

"Where do we hide? What if they come in?" she cried.

"Here, behind the cabinet." They huddled behind a low cabinet next to the corridor window. Braxton poked his head above the cabinet, looked around, then ducked back down.

"Nobody yet," he whispered into Marino's ear.

The pair remained crouched together, waiting for the inevitable appearance of the lab workers.

Suddenly Marino coughed, the sharp sound echoing through the lab.

"What's the matter?" Braxton barked hoarsely.

"The chemicals. They're making me sick. I think I'm going to throw up."

Her face had turned a chalky white. He had been able to ignore the smell of the reagents while they were walking around, but here, clinging tightly to a storage cabinet, the odor was unbearable. He could pick out the pungent smell of ether, and sickening rotten-eggs of sulfur dioxide. The combination was enough to make anyone ill. But if Marino lost it, there was no way they could avoid detection.

He grabbed her by the shoulders and shook her as hard as he could. "Fight it! You can do it. You have to!"

"Clack." The lock on the door.

He put his arm around Marino and pulled her tight as they pressed against the wall. Her shaking frightened him almost as much as the researchers. What if she fainted? How would he get her out?

He heard the door open and then two men talking. They were speaking in a guttural, foreign language. He didn't understand a word. The voices grew louder as they approached the lab door.

"What are they saying?" he whispered.

"Shush!" she replied, holding her finger to her lips.

The voices passed the door and continued down the corridor.

"What did they say?" Braxton repeated.

"Oh, nothing important." Marino managed a faint smile. Beads of sweat collected along her jawline. "Just something about his date last night. He had a *really* good time."

"Jesus Christ," Braxton muttered.

They heard muffled conversation for a few more minutes.

"What now?" he asked.

"They're talking about checking some cultures. I think they're going into the other part of the lab."

There was a hissing sound followed by silence. Braxton stuck his head up to see what was happening.

"Where are they?" Marino asked.

"They're gone. They must be in the isolation area."

"Then let's get out of here before they come back!"

He led her back to the doorway and peeked around the jamb. The hall was empty.

"Time to go," he said.

They opened the security door as silently as they could and escaped into the security foyer.

Two minutes later, the elevator door opened back at the lobby level. Braxton put a finger to his lips and peered around the door to check on the security guard. He was still watching the television, but it was directly in the line of sight of their elevator.

Braxton fished in his pocket, pulled out a *kwartje* coin, and tossed it past the guard's desk toward the door. When it struck the marble floor, the guard turned, and Braxton yanked Marino out of the elevator and pulled her to the bank of doors on the opposite side, safely hidden from the eyes of the security guard.

"Are you okay?" he finally asked as he pressed the elevator call button.

"I think so. Where are we going now?"

"Nowhere. We're going out. Very calm and very normal."

The elevator annunciator rang, Braxton counted to five, and the pair stepped out into the lobby.

"Miss Marino," the guard said seeing them approach. "Have trouble finding your briefcase?"

She looked in horror at Braxton, then turned back to the guard, her winning smile firmly in place.

"Sure did. I guess I must have left it somewhere else. But to tell you the truth, I stopped in the lab to show my friend some demos and we got caught up playing Renegade Raider. He wouldn't let me leave until he showed me how he could get to the third level. Isn't that just like a man? You won't tell anyone will you?"

The guard looked at her sternly then let a slight smirk appear. "Okay, we'll keep it just between us."

"Thanks," Marino replied. "You have a good night."

"I'll try, Miss Marino. You too."

She signed them out and they walked slowly back to the parking lot. Aside from a slight wobble in her normally athletic stride, it was impossible to tell anything was wrong.

Until she collapsed like a rag doll in his arms.

Chapter 38

Amsterdam, The Netherlands
Thursday, 11:30 a.m.

BRAXTON LEANED BACK in his chair, looked over the railing and watched as sunlight sparkled off the ripples in the canal. The warm and brilliant Amsterdam morning was just the therapy he needed after a disturbing, restless, and all too short night.

There was something terribly wrong at Vision One. He had spent the better part of the morning sitting at a table in the café trying to put all the discoveries into some kind of context. Why was there a hidden biologics laboratory under the Vision One facility? Lawson must have known it was there. Why else would he have kept the access code? But did it have anything to do with his death? And how did Sydney Marino fit into the puzzle?

Why did there always have to be so many more questions than answers? He glanced at his watch and decided it was time to get back to the conference. He had to keep up his cover. A wave brought the surly waiter to the table with his check. The man had been scowling for the past hour, undoubtedly offended that the American had spent over two hours at his table ordering only a black coffee and plain croissant.

Braxton shoved a few bills under his plate and headed back up Damstraat toward the hotel. He had nearly reached the courtyard when he heard a voice calling his name.

"Mr. Braxton!"

He turned and saw Tak Yang waving from beside one of the front columns. What was the Chinese scientist doing? He was the one that had all the concerns about propriety. Braxton hesitated, but couldn't very well ignore the greeting in the midst of the other conference attendees, so he walked over to his colleague.

"Dr. Yang," he began, bowing slightly. "How good to see you again."

"Mr. Braxton. Please excuse my rudeness, but I am returning to Beijing this afternoon and wanted to be sure to thank you for your review of my manuscript."

Manuscript? What manuscript? "Why, uh, yes, of course. It was my pleasure."

"There were a few questions I had on your comments, however." Yang extracted a sheaf of papers from his leather satchel and held them up. "Perhaps you could explain them to me? I'm sure it is my poor understanding of your language."

"My comments? Well, certainly." Braxton took the offered papers from the scientist's hands.

"Excellent. I would be most grateful. I promise not to take too much of your very valuable time. Perhaps we could walk while we chat? It is such a beautiful day and I have a very long flight ahead of me."

Yang led Braxton across the Dam. They turned left on Nieuwezijds and continued behind the Palace.

"Okay, doctor. What is this really about?" Braxton said once they were out of earshot of the crowd.

"Thank you for playing along, Mr. Braxton. I thought of something last night and have been looking for you at the conference all morning."

"Ah, I had a meeting," he replied quickly. "Is this something about your brother?"

"Yes. It was something he said in his last letter. I hadn't considered it carefully until after our conversation. He said he was angry with someone at work."

"Angry? Did he get into a fight with someone?"

A look of shock appeared on Yang's face. "No. Of course not. My brother would never get into a physical disagreement. He was angry about this person's behavior. He felt he was misrepresenting his work. This is something that would have troubled him very much."

"Well, that behavior is not particularly uncommon in the NSA, or anywhere in government for that matter. Who was it?"

"He didn't say. But it must have been someone he worked with closely. He said . . ."

An elderly couple approached them on the path and Braxton stepped to his left, away from Yang, to avoid hitting them. It saved his life.

Frighteningly familiar explosions erupted around him. Something hit him hard, spinning him around and dropping him onto the brick walkway. He vaguely heard the roar of a car's engine, and then the explosions stopped, replaced by a cacophony of screams. He managed to open his eyes and saw three bodies lying on the path next to him. Then he felt a burning stake in his shoulder and the world faded into darkness.

* * *

Braxton fidgeted on the examining table. Waiting. It was like every other encounter he had ever had with a health care organization. Instants of impersonal imposition sandwiched between eras of inattention. There had to be a consulting opportunity here.

His last moments with Yang were still a blur. There were shots, then screams; people falling all around him. Other people had picked him up and put him in some kind of vehicle, probably an ambulance, and brought him here. People in white ripping his clothes, strapping him to machines.

When his head had finally cleared, he had asked someone where he was.

"There was a shooting," the face had said with a thick Dutch accent. "You're at Central Hospital in Amsterdam."

"My friend, Dr. Yang?" he had asked.

"I'm sorry," was the only reply.

Apparently he had suffered no serious injuries. They had taken his clothes, attended to what he assumed was a superficial bullet wound in his right shoulder, and left him in the examining room to freeze to death. Outside the room he saw his physician, a Dr. Magdar, speaking with two other men in dark suits. Maybe one of them would get him some clothes.

He hopped off the table and walked toward the door. Immediately Magdar rushed into the room, followed by his visitors.

"Mr. Braxton, please, you must sit down and rest. You have been through a very traumatic situation," said the dark-skinned physician in more heavily accented English.

"I feel fine, Doctor. I would like to get my clothes and get out of here."

"Yes. I understand. But I'm afraid the clothes you were wearing are quite unusable at this point. I will try to get something for you. Until then, Mr. Klaber would like to speak with you."

Magdar turned and left the room. The taller of the two men took a step forward and bowed stiffly. He was slim, about five feet ten, and dressed in a stylish double-breasted pin-stripe suit. Braxton couldn't decide if he was a cop or a diplomat.

"Mr. Braxton. I am Detective Hans Klaber from the Amsterdam police. This is my colleague, Detective Geffen." The shorter, plumper man nodded. "I would like to ask you a few questions if you are able."

Braxton had no desire to speak with any cop at this point, but he was sure he would never get out of here if he didn't.

"Of course, Detective Klaber. I'll tell you whatever I know."

"You are aware that Dr. Yang was killed?"

"Yes."

"You must understand this is a very delicate situation, Mr. Braxton. An incident of this type is upsetting under any circumstances, but to have it involve foreign visitors . . . . We must do everything we can to identify the perpetrators."

Okay, Klaber, get on with it. And where are those clothes?

"You were friends with Dr. Yang?"

"Not really. I only met him this week. He was doing some interesting work in cryptography. We spoke a few times during the conference."

"You were not at the conference this morning." A statement. How would Klaber know that?

"I had some work to do," Braxton replied. "Why is that relevant?"

"When did you meet Dr. Yang?" Klaber continued.

"Today? We spoke outside the hotel. He was leaving this afternoon and wanted to talk with me about a paper he was writing. It was a nice day and we decided to go for a walk."

"Whose idea was the walk?"

"Dr. Yang's."

"I see. Did he talk about anything other than this paper?"

"No." What was Klaber getting at? "Why do you ask?"

"Did he speak anything about his country? Was he happy there?"

"Dr. Yang spoke only of our work. Nothing else."

"Do you have any idea who might want to harm him?"

"As I said, Mr. Klaber, the only thing I know about Dr. Yang is his work in cryptography. I have no idea who might want to hurt him."

"Do you have many friends in China, Mr. Braxton?"

"I don't have any, Detective Klaber. I told you, Dr. Yang was simply a colleague."

"Yes. Of course. Did you get a look at any of the assassins?"

"No. I'm sorry. All I remember is being hit and then screams. I must have blacked out."

"How unfortunate." Klaber's eyes scanned the examining room, then stopped at Braxton's left shoulder.

"That's quite a scar you have on your shoulder, Mr. Braxton. Some kind of accident?"

How much did Klaber know about his past? It wasn't exactly a secret. But it had nothing to do with Yang.

"Yes, a hunting accident. Nothing serious, thankfully."

"I see. Was this . . . " Braxton heard a beep. Geffen reached into his pocket and opened a cell phone. He spoke a few words into the device then handed it to Klaber.

"Yes. Yes, sir. Of course, sir." Klaber's face turned to stone and he handed the cell phone to Braxton. "Someone would like to speak with you."

Braxton frowned and took the phone from the policeman. Who could be calling him here?

"Yes?"

A familiar voice came through the speaker. "Braxton. This is Mr. Smith. Can you talk?"

Braxton looked at the policemen, then turned and walked to a far corner. "I guess so. But they're still in the room."

"Don't worry about that. We won't get into any details."

"How did you find me?"

"The assassination of a Chinese scientist doesn't exactly go unnoticed. I was concerned about you and did some checking."

Braxton was sure that his own well-being was fairly far from the agent's focus, but he was glad someone knew where he was.

"Well, I'm okay. Just a flesh wound and a few cuts."

"Great, Adam. We're very relieved. Did you get a chance to have that conversation?"

This is what he really wanted. "Yes. But I'm not sure it will be much help."

"That's for us to decide. When are you coming back?"

"I don't know. I hadn't thought about it." What time was it? He felt like he had been here for hours. It must be at least dinnertime, his stomach was starting to growl. No point in rushing now. "Probably tomorrow."

"That's fine. Let's meet at your office on Saturday. Say about noon?"

"Okay. Noon at my office. Oh, by the way, do you know our friend in Maryland's supervisor?"

"You mean Yang?"

"Yes."

"Yeah, I do. Why?"

"That will give us something to talk about. I won't have any more trouble here will I?"

"No. I'll take care of everything. Let me talk to Klaber."

Braxton walked back toward the cops and handed Klaber the phone. As the detective spoke, his face tightened and his tone again became deferential.

Dr. Madgar suddenly appeared at the door. He was carrying a stack of clothes. "Mr. Braxton, we have been able to find something for you to wear. I hope they will fit satisfactorily."

Geffen took the bundle from the doctor and handed it to Braxton. He set it down on the table and separated the contents. Flannel shirt, size medium. Jeans, waist 44. Penny loafers, size 43. He wasn't an expert on European sizes, but they seemed about right.

"This looks fine, doctor," he replied. "Thank you."

As Braxton started dressing, Klaber flipped the phone closed and handed it back to Geffen. He didn't look pleased.

"For a simple consultant you have very powerful friends, Mr. Braxton. The original call was from our Minister of Defense. I have been asked to provide you our full assistance. Is there anything else you would like to tell us?"

"No. I've told you everything I know. Do *you* have any idea who would want to kill Dr. Yang?"

"There are many possibilities: terrorists hoping to create an international situation, Chinese expatriates, common street criminals. You can be sure we will investigate all the possibilities."

"Thank you, Detective," Braxton said sincerely. "Dr. Yang was a brilliant scientist. I hope you find out who wanted him dead."

Braxton had nearly finished buttoning the shirt when he heard Klaber say, "If he was their target."

"What?"

"Well, *you* were walking with Dr. Yang."

Chapter 39

WICKS PACED THE porch of the farmhouse waiting for his friend to arrive. He felt like shit. It had taken most of the night to clean up the mess. Now he had to start damage control.

The familiar blue Dodge van pulled up to the house and the driver stepped out.

"What the hell are you doing calling me out here at ten in the morning?" O'Grady yelled, slamming the van's door.

"I told you. We've got to talk. Come on in." He led O'Grady into the kitchen and headed for the refrigerator. "What do ya want?"

O'Grady waved his hand away. "I want to know what's going on! Elizabeth's been callin' me all night. Asking about Macon. Where the hell is he?"

"He's gone," Wicks said flatly taking a swig of his beer.

"What do you mean he's *gone*? Where'd he go without telling his family?"

"Stop your goddamn whining, Sean. He's dead! Okay? We gotta figure out what to do to or we're gonna be next."

O'Grady grabbed for the table. "Dead! How? What happened?"

"It was Gary. He found out Macon was the one that let the Fed in." Wicks figured a lie was safer for everyone.

"And he just killed him? How do you know?"

"Gary called me early this morning. He said Macon had jeopardized the whole operation. He also thinks Macon killed Cal to cover his tracks."

"His own son-in-law? Jesus, I don't believe it."

"Oh, cut the bleeding heart shit, Sean. You hated Cal just like the rest of us. And you know Macon was getting soft. Lost his guts

I'd say." Wicks tossed his bottle in the sink and reached in the refrigerator for another.

"Why'd Gary call you?"

"He asked me to take over the cell."

Wicks could see the shock on the Irishman's face. He couldn't screw this up. Without O'Grady's support they'd all be buried with Macon in a week.

"I don't know why," Wicks continued. "And I damn well didn't ask him. All I know is that we're in this together now, Sean. You want to run the cell that's fine with me. But I sure as hell don't want Gary sending Alexander in here to clean us up."

O'Grady pulled up a chair and dropped down. Wicks waited him out.

"Okay, you want to play big shot with Gary that's fine with me. For now. What do we need to do?"

"I figure we just keep our mouths shut," Wicks said. He was still shaking but maybe they could get through this. "Nobody knows what happened to Macon. Maybe he just flipped out. But we've got to keep the exercises on schedule. That'll keep Gary off our backs until we can figure out a plan. You okay with that?"

"Yeah. I've got some more conversions to do but I'll get 'em done."

"Good. I'll go through Macon's papers and see what I can find. We play it according to the plan and get through this weekend."

"Whatever you say, *boss*. I'll get back to the store. Call me if you need anything."

"There is one other loose end I need some help with, Sean."

* * *

"This is bullshit, Tommy. I can't do this. Doc and Ricky ain't never done anything to nobody." They were sitting in O'Grady's van outside Doc Flaherty's office. It was a cool Georgia night; a sea of stars twinkled in the rural sky. In the office, a single light shone from a rear window.

"It's a little late for that don't you think?" Wicks replied with a sneer. "I was at the courthouse. Remember?"

O'Grady glared at his friend from the driver's seat. "That was different. Maybe Macon did go nuts. Who knew all this was gonna happen?"

"Get over it, Sean. We've got work to do. If either of these guys blows what we've been doin', the Feds'll have us in Jesup with old Charlie. And it won't be for just shootin' at a couple of Troopers." He paused before voicing the other option. "Or maybe you'd rather tell Gary to piss off."

O'Grady shuddered and shook his head.

"Then let's go," Wicks commanded.

They were dressed in fatigues, assault boots, and black knit hoods. Those and the other items in the back of the van had been scrounged at the farm. Gary had enough materiel stashed there for a dozen assault exercises.

Wicks jumped out of the van and headed for the front door.

He pulled off his hood and knocked. A light came on over the entrance.

"Tommy?" Flaherty said as he opened the door.

"Sorry to bother you, Doc. I just came from Ricky's house. He's doing real bad. I think you oughtta come take a look."

"Damn," Flaherty said. "I was hoping that last round of antibiotics would do the trick. Come on in while I get some things. You're lucky to catch me. I was about ready to head home."

Wicks nodded, but luck had nothing to do with it. He and O'Grady had been watching the office since mid-afternoon. They knew only Flaherty was inside.

He stepped across the threshold and closed the door. "Waiting for any patients, Doc?" he asked.

"Nope. Just finishin' up today's records. Let me file 'em away and we can go."

Flaherty walked down the hall and disappeared into one of the back rooms. When he reappeared, he had a stack of folders in his hand. Then he turned and went through a door behind the reception area. Wicks followed him.

They entered a room filled with tall metal book shelves, all overloaded with manila folders.

Flaherty dropped his files on a small table and turned to Wicks. "You shouldn't be in here, Tommy," he said. "It's our medical records room. I'll meet you in the lobby when I'm done."

Suddenly a bell sounded throughout the small house. Wicks spun around and tried to decide what to do. Was it an alarm?

"Sorry," Flaherty commented walking to the door. "That's my telephone. I set it on the bell when I'm alone in the office. It'll just take a second."

Wicks made a decision. "Sorry, Doc. I don't think so."

As Flaherty passed, Wicks pulled a Glock from his waistband and slammed the handle of the automatic into the side of the aging physician's head. The brittle bones splintered under the force and sliced into the side of his brain. He fell to the floor like a handful of pick-up sticks.

Wicks quickly scanned the shelves and found that the old country doctor had refused to bend to even the slightest hint of modern filing procedures. No fancy color codes on these files. They were all in alphabetical order.

He ran his finger across the labels, looking for his objective. Yanking out a file, he opened it and read the notation:

Ricky Dalton - bachelor, barkeeper, militia

Wicks folded the file and stuffed it in his jacket pocket. Then he grabbed Flaherty's hands and dragged him to the front door.

The bell was still ringing when he called to O'Grady.

* * *

They drove to Dalton's small farmhouse on the other side of town. The place was known to everyone in Tyler: the Dalton family had lived here for almost seventy years.

Wicks and O'Grady crawled into the rear of the van, collected their bags and hopped out the rear doors. O'Grady ran to place the packages while Wicks headed for the front door.

There was no way he wanted to even get near this disease-ridden piece of crap, but he had to be sure Dalton was there. There had been too many mistakes already.

He knocked, then, hearing no response, tried the doorknob. It turned and he went inside.

"Ricky?" he called from the front room.

Nothing.

"*Ricky!*"

"Who's that?" came a weak voice from upstairs.

Wicks galloped up the stairs and found Dalton in a large bedroom on the second floor. He was lying in bed covered in enough blankets to bury a horse. His face was ashen grey.

Dalton looked up when Wicks came to the door. "Tommy? Is that you?"

"Yeah, Ricky. It's me." Wicks stayed in the doorway, not wanting to get any closer than was necessary.

"I ain't doin' so good, Tommy. Really feel like shit." Dalton coughed and Wicks instinctively covered his mouth with his arm. He had to get out of this tomb.

"I know, Ricky. I brought the Doc for you. He'll be here soon."

"Thanks, Tommy." The words were slow and frail. "You're a good friend."

"Eh, yeah. You just stay put. Just a couple minutes."

Wicks took the stairs two at a time, then rushed out the door. Once he'd cleared the porch, he stopped and bent over to catch his breath. When he looked up, O'Grady was dragging Flaherty's body out of the van.

"You okay?" O'Grady called. "You look like shit. Ricky there?"

"I'm fine. Ricky's in bed upstairs. Everything set?"

"Yeah, but I could use a little goddamn help here."

They dragged Flaherty into the farmhouse. The Irishman went back to the van while Wicks pulled Dalton's medical record from his pocket and lit it with a small butane lighter. The file smoldered for a moment then burst into flames. Once he was sure the record had caught, he tossed the paper torch under a low-hanging curtain. The flames reached up for the cheap material, slid off, then grabbed firm. It would be enough.

O'Grady already had the van running when Wicks hopped in the passenger seat.

"How long?" Wicks asked.

"Two minutes," O'Grady replied. "I was gettin' worried."

"Let's get outta here. We're done."

The blue van drove quietly off into the night, only a faint flicker emanating from the farmhouse. Two minutes later the structure erupted into a volcano of flame.

Dalton had always said that as the last of his family, he wanted to die in his home.

Well, the old sot got his wish.

Days later, the unfortunate accident would be blamed on a gas leak and subsequent explosion.

*   *   *

Gary stepped from the woods and jogged back to his car. The flames from Dalton's home cast soft, dancing shadows as he traced back across the field.

So far Wicks had lived up to his bravado. The exercises this weekend shouldn't be a problem. Even *he* could keep the cell, or what was left of it, together for a few more days.

One more week and the watcher could leave Tyler, Georgia behind. Shepard had finished the molds. It would be a spectacular op—quite something to put on his resume.

Gary smiled. If only he could let anyone read it.

Chapter 40

Hotel Krasnapolsky, Amsterdam, The Netherlands
Friday, 8:00 a.m.

BRAXTON WOKE WITH his shoulder throbbing. He groped over the bedside table for the aspirin and codeine prescription Dr. Magdar had given him, swallowed two of the pills, and collapsed back into bed, knowing he was now far too awake to ever get back to sleep.

After Slattery's telephone call, Klaber had pressed for another hour to get Braxton to confess to something. The Inspector had eventually given up, and, with Braxton dressed in the clothes Magdar had provided, had driven him back to the Krasnapolsky. The consultant had then asked the concierge for two favors: first, to confirm his return to the States the next day, and second, to see that he was not disturbed until then.

That had been eighteen hours ago, and the second request had certainly been followed. He reached for the phone to check on the first.

"Good morning, Mr. Braxton," came the deep male voice from the front desk. "I hope you are feeling better today."

"Yes, thank you," Braxton replied, rotating his now less painful, but still quite stiff, shoulder. "Do I have any messages?"

"Yes, sir. Three. From last evening. The first is from Hendrick. He has confirmed your flight from Schiphol today. We will have a driver waiting for you at 10:30."

"Oh, that won't be necessary, I can catch a cab."

"Oh no. It would be our pleasure, Mr. Braxton. To make up for the unpleasantness of your stay. We have also taken the liberty to refuse certain, shall I say unseemly requests, from reporters. There have been a number of stories on the television and in the tabloids. The Krasnapolsky believed you would like to avoid these contacts."

"Why yes, thank you very much. It was very kind of you."

"Our pleasure, Mr. Braxton."

Now Braxton understood why Vision One had chosen the Grand Hotel Krasnapolsky. No hotel in the States would have avoided the opportunity for that publicity.

"The next message is from a Mr. Fowler, in the United States. He inquired as to your status. He was quite insistent in speaking with you."

"I can imagine. I pity whoever had to take the call."

"Yes, sir. There is a notation about that. He asked that you call him as soon as possible. The last call was from one of our guests. Miss Marino. She was very concerned about your health but understood our request to not bother you. She also asked that you call. Would you like me to put you through?"

Did he really want to talk to Marino now? She would likely want to help take care of him. And he didn't want to deal with that baggage now.

"No, thank you. Just leave a message for her. Thank her for her concern and tell her I'll get back to her after I return to Washington."

"Yes, sir. I will leave it in her mailbox. Is there anything else?"

"Could you call the number for Mr. Fowler?"

"Of course, sir."

There was a short pause, then Braxton heard a weak "Hello?"

"Morning, Sam. What's up?"

"Adam? It's goddamn . . . 2:00 a.m. What the hell are you doing calling me now?"

Shit. He had forgotten the time difference. "Sorry, Sam. I just woke up and got your message."

"Are you okay? We heard there was a shooting."

"Yeah. Just a scrape on my shoulder. I was lucky."

"You're damn right. Were you with the Chinese guy that got killed?"

Guess news does travel fast.

"We were walking together. The attack, I guess that's what it was, is still kind of a blur."

"This have anything to do with that Marino gal?"

Braxton considered the question. No, they couldn't be connected. "I don't think so, Sam. But did you get anything on her yet?"

"So far she looks clean, but I've still got a couple of feelers still out."

"Thanks. But I need you to do another check. Name is Kam Yang."

"Yang? Isn't that the name of the scientist that was killed over there?"

"That was Tak Yang. Kam was his brother. He was killed in a car accident a week or two ago."

"Helluva coincidence."

"That's what I'm worried about. The accident happened somewhere around D.C. See what you can find out."

"Will do. When are you coming back?"

"Today. It'll be good to get home." That was an understatement. "Oh, don't ask Slattery about Yang."

"Why not?"

"I think Yang was a spook. Probably NSA."

"Shit, Adam. I told you not to get messed up with those guys. Roger involved in all this?"

"Yeah. I'll explain when I get back. Give me a call tomorrow."

"For sure. You take care of yourself."

"Thanks. Now get your butt back to bed."

* * *

Gary drove the rental up the dirt road and stopped in front of the farmhouse. It was a warm Georgia morning and a light breeze carried the sweet smells of jasmine and magnolia through the car's open windows. This truly was a beautiful property. Rich Georgia clay, row after row of flowering shrubs, wide stands of pecan trees, and rolling verdant meadows. An ideal place to retire. Too bad he'd never have the chance.

Entering the house, he saw Wicks and O'Grady arguing across the trestle table.

"What's the talk in town?" Gary asked. "Any trouble?"

"Trouble? Shit, the whole town's in a panic!" O'Grady's thick Irish brogue rang through the meeting room. "How do you think they'd feel? First Brown gets killed, then Macon and Cal disappear, now Ricky and Doc Flaherty go under. Everybody's wonderin' who's next."

"Come on, Sean," Wicks responded, putting his hands on his

partner's shoulder. "It ain't that bad. Sure folks are upset. But they'll get over it."

"We gotta stop this, Tommy. Just for now. I know what we're doin' is important. But if we don't have the support of the town they'll turn us all in."

So. The old gunrunner did have some smarts. *Maybe I picked the wrong guy.*

"Shit," Wicks answered. "Nobody's gonna say anything, Sean. You just don't know these folks."

"Actually, I agree with Sean," Gary replied. "All the trouble has given us too much visibility. We need to quiet things down. Give folks a chance to get back to normal. After the exercise we'll shut down for a while. That okay with you, Tommy?"

"Sure, Gary," Wicks said. "Absolutely right. Get things back to normal."

"And you can sit out CHARLIE," Gary added. "We've got more than enough cells ready to make our point. You get the teams through the training this weekend and I'll take it from there. Oh, and we're just about done in the lab. When the boys are finished, you can go down and clear everything out. I'll give you a call."

"We'll take care of everything, Gary. There won't be any more screw ups."

"I know, Tommy. I know. We're all counting on you. And Sean."

He could almost see the gleam in Wick's eye. The little bastard couldn't wait to get downstairs. Well, it would be worth waiting for.

* * *

"Cindy! What are you doing here?" Tracomb said as he entered the closet. Cindy Falmouth was a Biochem that worked in another section of NCC. Tracomb had seen her a few times at company events.

"Gina asked me to swap times with her. She had a doctor's appointment."

"Well, welcome to Satisfaction Central. Make any customers happy today?"

"Come on, George," she replied as she straightened up the area around the telephone. "This isn't so bad. It's important we all understand what our customers want."

"What they want is for us to get their orders to them. Something I can't do sitting in front of this damn phone. You buy all that quality crap?"

"Yes, I do. Up to a point. Maybe Phillips does get carried away but he's trying to make a difference. You ought to give him a chance."

Tracomb furrowed his brow and crossed his arms in front of his chest. "Hey, I'm here aren't I? Woodruff straight out refused."

"I heard. I think he's wrong."

"We'll see. So far there haven't been any repercussions. But if I were him, I'd be updating my resume." Tracomb took his position in front of the phone and started down the customer list.

Falmouth started out the door, then turned. "Oh, I meant to ask you about one of your entries."

"Which one?"

She came back to the desk and leafed through a few pages in the customer listing. "This one. The CDC. What is this mark?" She pointed to a light pencil scrawl in the margin.

"It's a question mark. What does it look like?" Who made her the Quality Police all of a sudden?

"Okay, but what does it mean? Did you contact them?"

"Yeah. I called. The contact name's wrong." Falmouth gave him a sour look. "What's the big deal?"

"For starters we ought to know who's buying our cultures. But more important, the strain is 252M."

"So? It's still just *Chlamydia*."

"Not exactly. DZ252M is an abnormal variant of *Chlamydophila Pneumoniae*. Same family, different genus. It's Biosafety Level 4; same as Ebola and Hanta. It's resistant to all known antibiotics. If it got out . . ."

Tracomb's mouth fell open. "Shit. How the hell was I supposed to know that? I'm not in Bacteriology."

Bastards. Now some executive's gonna rake me over the coals.

"Take it easy, George. Let's just call the CDC back and see if we can figure out what happened to the shipment."

Maybe she was right. If he could trace the requester now, no one would need to know he screwed up the first time around. He reached for the phone, dialed the CDC, and heard the same polite southern voice.

"This is George Tracomb from NCC. I called last week. We're trying to trace an order to Dr. Weaver."

"Yes sir. I remember. But I'm sorry, there is no Dr. Weaver on staff."

"Is there anyone whose name is close? Maybe I'm pronouncing it wrong." He spelled the name for the receptionist.

"There's still no match on the clinical list, sir."

"You're telling me there's no one named Weaver at the CDC?" he yelled into the phone. What the hell could have happened?

"Well, no," the voice replied. "There was a Randy Weaver in the support group. I believe he worked in the mailroom. But he quit about four weeks ago."

Right after the shipment. Randy Weaver. Wasn't he the guy at . . . Ruby Ridge? Oh, shit. Tracomb swallowed and the bitter taste of bile filled in his throat.

"Uh, thanks. I guess we'll just have to double-check our records. So, thanks. Good-bye." He slammed down the phone.

"George, what's the matter? You're white as a sheet!"

"We screwed-up, Cindy. Bad. What's the extension for security?"

Chapter 41

FROM THE FRYING pan into the fire. Slattery had barely finished with the aftermath of yesterday's Amsterdam shooting when Flynn had called. She wanted him at the NCTC to review the militia strategy.

They'd better come up with some answers soon. Something was going on and the longer it stayed hidden the more worried he became.

He had invited Ikedo for company and was packing up his papers when the phone rang.

"Slattery."

"Afternoon, Roger. Did I catch you at a bad time?"

It was Fowler. How was he going to handle him this time?

"Hello, Sam. Actually I was on my way out."

"Well, this won't take but a minute. Any word on that Marino gal?"

Slattery took a deep breath. "Nothing significant, Sam. Just your average citizen."

"Oh, I see. I've had a little trouble getting back to her family. You have a hometown?"

"Hey, you expect me to do all your work for you?"

"Just looking for some help, Roger. No problem is there?"

"No. Of course not. She just came up clean. I really gotta go, Sam. Talk to you later."

"Sure, Roger. I hear you. Later."

He slammed down the phone. The noose around his neck just got a little tighter.

* * *

Slattery settled into his chair in one of the FBI conference rooms at the NCTC. The map on the far wall mimicked the one he had seen at the DNI's meeting. Red pins highlighted the latest militia attacks. Photos and reports papered most of the other walls. Peppered among the documents were far too many large hand-written question marks. The wastebaskets were filled with foam containers and empty pizza boxes.

They had already gone through the obligatory introductions: Manny Ikedo from the CIA, Carol Courington and Tony Lasalle from the Serial Crimes Unit. Slattery recognized the rumpled clothes and lethargic demeanors as signs of long hours in a confined space. The FBI pair had spent too many days in this room already. Even Flynn had lost some of her edge.

"Looks like your war room, Mary Ellen," he commented.

"The Serial Crimes Team had started it up after the first attacks," Flynn responded, "and we kinda took it over once everything escalated. We still run operations out of the SIOC downtown, but all the thinking gets done in here. You'll have to excuse the look of the place. A lot of the team have been living in here the past week."

The Strategic Information and Operations Center was the FBI's latest $20 million high-tech baby. Located at FBI Headquarters in D.C., it was designed to handle up to five major crises at once. All fiber optics, high-speed computers, and video walls. Unfortunately there had already been nine militia attacks. The hotshot designers must be having seizures.

"Well, Manny and I really appreciate your inviting us over. We've been trying to figure out what the motive for these attacks could be, and frankly, we don't buy the militia revolution angle."

"We would have expected to have received some demands, Director Flynn," Ikedo said, picking up on the thread. "Extortion or at least political rhetoric. Something like the Unibomber's manifesto. The lack of demands suggests there may be an alternate explanation."

Slattery watched as Flynn sized up his associate. Her response would determine how far this exchange was going to go.

"Mary Ellen, please," Flynn replied to Ikedo. "We have far much too much to do to get hung up on formalities. I have to agree with you, Roger. We have been thinking along similar lines."

"Have your teams uncovered anything new on the person behind all this?" Ikedo asked.

"Nothing directly. But we have traced the explosives that were used. Carol?"

The bleary-eyed female agent opened her folder. "The composition of the Semtex matched that of a shipment that was stolen from the Razorback Armory, outside of Little Rock, Arkansas. The theft was reported over a month ago."

"Anything else taken?" Ikedo asked.

"Yes. A case of ignitors, seven light mortar launchers, and ten crates of 9mm ammunition."

"Jesus," Slattery said. "How did they get all that out?"

"Just drove up and loaded it," Flynn replied. "They had all the right paperwork with all the right signatures. Nobody knew anything was wrong until we traced the Semtex composition from the manufacturer. A couple of Army captains in Arkansas are up shit creek about now."

"Everything points to a very sophisticated and knowledgeable coordination," Ikedo added. "How can we get any information on the leader?"

"A good question," Flynn responded. "Unless we have some new outside information," she turned her eyes back to Slattery, "the only way we know is to get it from inside the militia groups."

"None of your informants have heard anything?" Ikedo asked.

"No. No one we deal with has any idea who's pulling the strings. It's like he knows exactly where we are all the time."

"A leak?"

"Possibly, but not necessarily. As I said to the DNI, this has not been a major focus area for us. Sure, we have contacts in the big organizations, but the groups are so splintered, and there are so many of them, it wouldn't be hard for a terrorist to find the clean ones."

"It sounds like our only option is to break one of the involved cells," Slattery said. "Have we got any possibles?"

"Tony's run the latest correlations," Flynn replied turning to the young agent. "What have we got?"

Lasalle passed out a sheet of facts and statistics. "With only two sets of attacks we're going on a lot of guesswork, but the best bets are one cell in Tennessee and another in Georgia. Both are very close to two attack locations, and fit the psychological profile of vulnerable militia cells. The members are all local with no apparent connections to other groups other than local militia gatherings."

"The one in Georgia," Slattery asked. "Is this the same cell you were investigating previously?"

"Yes," Flynn replied. "And to answer your next question, we still have no idea what happened to Agent Thomas."

Everyone in the room fell momentarily silent, respecting the memory of a fallen comrade.

"Why not just go in and shake them up?" Slattery asked.

"You heard Carlson," Flynn replied. "If I go in on our analyses alone, without any corroboration, he'll have our heads. And it could jeopardize any evidence we do get."

"How about if you had an independent source?" Slattery asked.

Flynn's eyes bored into the agent. "Roger, you better not be holding anything back from me."

"Something new, Mary Ellen. Another source. Nothing I'd bet my career on by itself, but the source confirms outside involvement in the Georgia farm, and the cell's activities."

"Who is it, Roger?"

Slattery knew this was coming. He didn't want to divulge Luckett's identity just yet, but had to provide some verification.

"I think he's the source of your original tip on the Georgia farm."

Flynn looked over at Courington and Lasalle. They both nodded.

"Then let's go for it," she said.

"Can you get a warrant with just this?" Ikedo asked.

"Absolutely," Flynn responded with an uncharacteristic grin. "Judge Wilfred Campbell had an office in the Middleton Courthouse. Lost the autographed Georgia Tech football he had kept for forty years in that fire. He'll sign anything I give him if it'll help catch the arsonists."

"Okay, what about timing?" Slattery asked.

"We may have something there," Courington said. "As you know, we still have the Tyler farm under surveillance. They have a pretty set pattern when they're preparing for practice exercises. We saw the pattern before last weekend's activities and have observed that pattern again this week. I believe the farm will be crawling with militiamen this weekend."

"The more the merrier for interrogation," Ikedo commented. "But can you set something up that fast?"

"We'll get it set up," Flynn said without hesitation. "Don't worry about that."

Somehow Slattery had no doubt the Special Assistant could get it done.

"If there's anything we can do, Mary Ellen," Slattery added.

"Thank you, Roger. For now, just keep that source handy in case I get in any hot water."

"Will do. I guess we'll leave the rest to you."

Flynn nodded and Slattery gathered up his papers. The others followed his lead, packed up, and headed for the hall.

As they were filing out, Flynn touched Slattery's shoulder.

"Can I have a minute, Roger?"

"Sure."

They waited until the others had left the room.

"It's about IMAGER."

"Come on, Mary Ellen. I've told you all I know."

Flynn raised her hands in defense. "No. I understand that. Don't talk, just listen. I've been hearing things about IMAGER. That it may not be real. If this is something another intel agency cooked up, it will be big trouble for everybody involved. I just wanted to warn you. I hope you're out of the way if it ignites."

Slattery stood expressionless. He knew Flynn was fishing. She was looking for any twitch, any confirmation. But her instincts were right, however she got them. "Another intel agency." Who else was there except the NSA? When she gets her proof, Robinson will be history, clever or not.

"Thank you for coming, Roger," she finally said. "And for your help. By the way, I really like your colleague. Bring him along anytime."

"Thanks, Mary Ellen. I'll tell him."

Slattery turned and left the conference room to find Ikedo.

"So what do you think of our Special Assistant, Manny?" he asked when he had caught up to the agent. "All you expected?"

"Quite a lady, Roger. I'll bet she gets just about anything she sets her sights on."

Slattery thought back to Flynn's last comment. "Probably does, Manny. But I'd be careful if I were you. I think she may have you in those sights."

* * *

"What's happening?" Robinson cried into the burner cell phone. He was cowering inside his Lexus in a not very hospitable southwest D.C. neighborhood.

"Robinson? What the hell are you doing calling me here?"

"I want to know what happened in Amsterdam. Who killed Yang?" Robinson raised his head and scanned the neighborhood. But not out of fear of identification.

"How the hell am I supposed to know? He was a goddamn commie for Christ's sake. Who cares?"

"But he was with Slattery's consultant."

"Yeah. And he was your hotshot cryptologist's brother. So what? The damn consultant didn't find out anything did he?"

"How could he? There was nothing to find out. You didn't have anything to do with . . ."

"Jesus Christ, Garrett. I've got more important things to do than orchestrate a sanction on an unknown Chinese scientist in Amsterdam. What's the matter with you?"

A group of three teenagers gathered on the corner across from Robinson's parking place.

"I . . . I think we may have a problem."

"Problem?" The voice turned cold and deadly quiet. "What kind of a problem?"

"I think the FBI may know about IMAGER."

"The FBI? You mean Flynn, right? What does the bitch know? Tell me, Garrett."

The order came through loud and clear. "I'm not sure, sir. I just think we need to be careful. She's been acting strangely the last few days."

"Shit! I told you to be careful around her. She's a goddamn viper. But you had to keep up your damn tryst. How deep is the intrusion?"

"I think it's just the CIA cover."

"You'd better damn well find out if that's all! And come up with some kind of story if we need to go public."

"I'll find out."

"Good. Now about this consultant. He's not going to be a problem is he?"

"No. No way. Slattery will take care of him." At least Robinson hoped so.

"Make sure." There was a pause, then the voice returned in a lighter tone. "And loosen up, Garrett. Everything's going just fine."

"Going fine? We have no goddamn idea where anything is going. Seven people are already dead!" He stole a glance and the youths were now pointing in his direction. Shit!

"We know more than you think. There's nothing to worry about."

"Sure, sure. But what about the message? Shouldn't we tell someone?"

"Tell them what? We've got some screwy message about some fairy tale operation? Do you know what it means?"

"No, but we still . . ."

"Why?" the voice demanded. "To show our hand? Let our enemies run to ground? Then we'd never find out what they're up to. No. We tough it out until we know for sure."

"But it's all happened. It's the truth."

The line went silent. All Robinson could hear was the throbbing of his blood in the earpiece.

"Listen, Garrett," the voice began slowly. "There is no absolute truth. You know as well as I do that absolute truth requires absolute knowledge. And we're not quite that good yet. Until we know more we keep our mouths shut. I'm not going to have you jeopardize this breakthrough by telling everybody in Washington you can read their mail.

"You and your whole goddamn organization get paid to support the policies of this administration. Not to go off and get some bleeding heart conscience. Remember that and you'll live a long and happy life. Now get off this line. And keep your zipper shut for a while. I'll find a way to derail Flynn."

The line went dead and Robinson threw the phone on the passenger seat. Two seconds later the neighborhood and his young admirers disappeared in a storm of dirt and gravel.

Chapter 42

Cerberus Consulting, Tysons Corner, Virginia
Saturday, 7:30 a.m.

HIS BIOLOGICAL CLOCK completely broken, Braxton had awakened with a start at 5:30 a.m. He tossed and turned for another half hour, finally deciding there was no way he was getting back to sleep. He showered, dressed, and drove to his office. At least he'd be able to get an early start on the backlog of work from his trip.

The yellow Virginia sun hung low in a hazy blue sky. He felt physically relieved to be out from under the gray Amsterdam weather. It had been an ill-conceived journey that had answered none of his questions and left him even more confused about Megan than before he left. Did her death have anything to do with Lawson's? Was Lawson's death an accident? And what was the meaning of the laboratory under Vision One?

It would be over an hour before Karen arrived, so he picked up a cold Coke and a bag of bagels from the downstairs all-night deli. Carefully balancing his purchases and his briefcase, he waited patiently for the elevator in the lobby. When it arrived, an oriental man brushed past him hurrying to get in the empty cab. Braxton shuddered. The sight of the man brought back painful memories. He had tried to put the encounters with Yang out of his mind. They had yielded little information, and nearly gotten him killed.

No more cloak and dagger, he promised himself. Why the hell should he help the CIA with their problems? They had already caused him more trouble than they could ever repay.

Arriving at his desk, the workload was even worse than he had imagined. The stack of phone messages was an inch thick, his voice mailbox was filled, and his blinking email icon had become a dangerously red beacon. He was afraid to even check how many messages were waiting.

While he had been gone, he had tried to keep up with daily calls to Karen, but after the attack he had simply asked if she could come in on Saturday to help him with the backlog.

Procrastinating long enough, he decided to first check his voice mail. The most urgent messages would be there. He logged into VIRNA and settled in.

Most of his messages were from clients, wanting to know the status of some report or clarifications on some proposal, but the sixth one yanked a knot in his stomach.

"Adam. It's Susan. I heard about Amsterdam on the news. How awful! Are you okay? Please give me a call."

Her voice had the same soft sincerity he remembered so painfully. He had shared something unique with her once, and the transformation of that relationship still left a void. It was uncomfortable having her still care so much.

He punched out of VIRNA and dialed her number at the Senate Office Building. It rang three times.

"You have reached the office of Susan Goddard, Media Relations Director for Senator Wilson Lexington. I can't take your call right now. Please leave a message after the tone and I'll get right back to you."

Jesus! It was seven thirty on a Saturday. Of course she wasn't there. "It's Adam. Ah, Adam Braxton. I'm fine, thanks. Uh, good-bye."

He dropped the phone into its cradle and started breathing again. His hands were damp with sweat. Maybe he still cared more than he had thought.

* * *

Karen arrived a little after eight and knocked lightly on the wall. They exchanged greetings after which she softly pulled the door closed and left him to the daunting task of catching up.

It took him an hour and a half to finish with VIRNA and sort Karen's paper messages. Throughout the morning's effort, his eyes would occasionally stray to the briefcase lying in the chair next to his desk. Inside were the notebook pages he had taken from the Vision One laboratory. They were like magnets pulling at his mind through the scuffed leather case. Tiny irritants at first, beckoning benignly. Then, little by little, increasing their siren's song until he couldn't think of anything else.

Finally at 9:45, after stumbling through a particularly difficult response to a contentious client at Accenture, he couldn't stand it any longer. He grabbed the case, pulled out the papers and spread them over the top of the other work lying on his desk. There in front of him were the brightly colored pictures of some other-worldly object. The renderings of an infinitesimally small molecule that somehow linked Vision One with the death of Benjamin Lawson. And, he was sure, ended Megan's life as well.

He pulled a magnifying glass out of his desk drawer and scoured the pictures for any kind of identification. All he found was the code number Marino had already spotted. And there was no way they'd get what it meant from Vision One.

Frustrated he shoved the pictures aside. What was going on in that laboratory? Were the scientists in the basement at Vision One *making* the molecules that had been designed upstairs?

A buzz broke his concentration and he saw the intercom light blinking on his phone.

"Yes, Karen?"

"Sam Fowler's here, Adam. He wants to know if you have a few minutes."

"Absolutely! Send him in." The consultant needed the break and it might help to have a friend to talk to.

A huge black man entered the office and went straight for the refrigerator tucked in a corner behind the door. Six foot three and at least two hundred-thirty pounds, a faded green polo shirt rolled over the waistband of wrinkled khaki pants, the ex-D.C. cop certainly hadn't slimmed down since his retirement. Braxton noticed the slight limp that he still carried from their last adventure.

"Got anything good?" Fowler asked.

"Look for yourself, Sam. No beer if that's what you mean."

Fowler shook his head. "Not for me. Pat ordered me to lose weight. Something diet?"

"I think so."

Fowler pulled out a Diet Dr. Pepper and sat down in one of the chairs by the coffee table.

"I didn't expect to see you this early."

"Had an appointment with a client in McLean. Stopped on the way back."

"Another roving husband?"

"Actually this one's a roving wife. Hot shot lawyer. The husband thinks she's got too many out-of-town clients."

"I don't understand how you stand it."

Fowler flashed a wide grin. "Oh. It ain't so bad. And it gives me an excuse to get out of the house. You doin' okay?"

"Yeah. But I'd feel a lot better if I could ever get past all the crap that came in while I was gone." He waved his arms over the mess on his desk.

"The bane of the working class, Adam."

"Thanks for all the sympathy. Speaking of working, how about the stuff you were supposed to do for me? Find out anything?"

"Not as much I would have liked. I talked with Trooper Alesi, the cop that covered the Yang accident. The guy was definitely NSA. Alesi got the investigation yanked out from under him, but he checked the records for me anyway. Ruled an accident, no evidence otherwise. Yang was broadsided by a stolen two-ton pickup, no identifiable prints, no suspects."

"Well, that doesn't help much. How about Marino?"

"That's a little different. A cursory check looked fine. I called a buddy on the San Francisco force, he checked her out back there. Everything was okay, at least from the time she arrived a little over two months ago."

"What about before then?" Braxton curled his eyebrows at his friend.

"That's the problem. There is no before then. Her references look okay on the surface but they don't pan out if you dig. It's like she just appeared out of thin air."

"How did she ever get a job at a company like Vision One with a record like that?"

"Good question. Did you ask her?"

Braxton thought back to their conversation on the way to Utrecht. "Come to think of it, yes. She said something about a recommendation from someone on their Board of Directors."

"Well, that would explain it. No one's gonna question a Director's recommendation."

"But who *is* she?"

"I didn't know what else to do, so I took a chance and called Slattery." Braxton's mouth dropped open. "Take it easy. I didn't use your name and I didn't know you were running an op with him."

Braxton scowled at his friend. "I was not running an op, Sam."

"Okay, whatever. Anyway, he's a friend and he owed me a favor."

"So what did he say?" *Dammit, Sam. Get to the point!*

"Stonewalled me completely. No information." He took a swig of the soda. "My bet is he ran across a red flag."

"Red flag?"

"An alert on a dossier or background check. Usually means the target's undercover."

"Undercover? Marino is a cop?"

"A cop or a spook. Could be in a protection program but from what I've heard, it didn't sound like this was anybody trying to hide out."

Marino is a spy? Maybe it *was* her with Slattery! What were they doing in Amsterdam? Checking on him?

"Adam?"

"Oh, I'm sorry, Sam. I don't believe it. What the hell is going on?"

"I think that's my question, buddy. How about you start at the top for me?"

Braxton related his first meeting with Marino, and his suspicions around his ex-wife's death. Then the request from Slattery to contact Yang's brother. And finally the meetings in Amsterdam and the discovery of the laboratory at Vision One.

"You have been a busy boy," Fowler commented when his friend had completed the story. "You're damn lucky you weren't hurt worse. Made any sense of it yet?"

"Not a bit, Sam. I know Megan's death is tied to that lab, but I don't know how. I was trying to work something out when you came in. You're a hotshot detective. Maybe you can find something I couldn't."

Braxton motioned his friend over to the desk and showed him the papers.

"Jesus, Adam. What is all this?"

"Pages I took from a lab notebook at Vision One. They're pictures of some kind of molecule."

"Looks more like some kind of Walt Disney Rorschach Test."

"That's just the false-coloring of the modeling program. Each colored sphere represents a different type of atom: black for carbon, white for hydrogen, and blue for oxygen."

"I didn't think atoms were just simple balls."

"They're not. This is just an easy way to represent the way they link together. The size of each sphere has something to do with the density function of the outer electron shell. It approximates the average bonding length so you can tell how far apart the individual atoms are."

Fowler's eyes glazed over. "Right. If you say so. Chemistry was a lot easier when I was in school: a molecule was just a floppy handful of balls connected by springs."

"Yeah, I know. I'm not so up to date myself. That's part of my problem."

"So you don't know what this thing is?"

"Nope. All we have is the ID number. This 'Lawson 423V85'." He pointed to the marking in the corner of the page.

"Okay if I take a look?"

"Sure." Braxton stepped back and let Fowler examine the pages. He picked up each one, turning it over in his huge hands, holding it up to the morning light coming through Braxton's windows.

"Have you looked on the back of the pictures?"

"The back? Yeah. I've gone over every inch of those pages."

"Jesus, Adam. I hope you're a helluva lot better consultant than you are a detective. You're too used to your damn computers. These pictures are pasted on the pages. Just like the good old days. We need to look on the *back* of the pictures, and under them. Someone could have written something there."

"You mean like 'put picture of molecule so-and-so here'?"

"That's what we need to find out."

Chapter 43

BRAXTON GRABBED ONE of the notebook pages from Fowler and held it up. The color printouts *had* been pasted onto the notebook pages. Why hadn't he seen that?

"Have you got something sharp?" Fowler asked. "A knife?"

"Yes! In my desk."

Braxton pulled open his desk drawer, reached in and handed Fowler a red Swiss Army knife that had to be at least an inch thick.

"Normal consultant fare?" Fowler asked, turning the instrument over in his hand.

"Well, you never know when you might need to break open a computer."

Fowler completed his visual analysis, then deftly pulled out a thin blade. Carefully working from one corner of the torn page, he began to peel back the picture.

"Anybody gonna miss these?" Fowler asked as he slowly cut through the adhesive.

Braxton hesitated. He hadn't really thought about his break-in as having any ramifications. They seemed to get away fine. But what if there were surveillance cameras inside? Did Vision One know he was there? Could that have been what happened in Amsterdam?

"I . . . I don't know."

"Well, too late to worry about that now."

A minute later Fowler had extracted the picture. He turned it over.

"Damn," Braxton said. There was nothing on the back of the drawing nor on the facing page.

Fowler took the next page and performed the same operation. Still nothing. One page left.

When the last picture had been freed, they slowly turned it over. There on the back, in neat hand printing was: *"Chlamydophila Pneumoniae."*

"What the hell is that?"

"I don't know, but I'm going to find out. Now it's my turn to do some detective work."

Braxton sat back down at his desk and began typing.

"Let's try PubMed first. It's the web interface to the National Library of Medicine. They index every major medical journal article and monograph."

The search produced a list of eleven citations. Braxton clicked on the first, a year-old New England Journal of Medicine article.

As he waded through the medical-ese of the article, the buzz of his intercom again interrupted his plans.

"Yes, Karen?"

"There is a Mr. Smith here, Adam. He says he has an appointment with you."

Smith? Shit. Braxton had forgotten all about the appointment he had made in Amsterdam. It seemed like a century ago.

He turned to Fowler and whispered "It's Slattery."

"Roger's here?" Fowler asked.

"Sorry, Karen," he said into the intercom. "I forgot to mention it. Give me a minute and then send him in."

Braxton gathered up the Vision One papers and stuffed them in his top drawer.

"You want me to go?" Fowler asked.

"How'd you like to be a little bird on the wall?" Braxton replied. "I could use the backup."

Two minutes later, Braxton was sitting calmly at his desk as the CIA agent came through the door. Slattery walked toward him and Braxton could see his eyes scanning the room. The door to the adjoining conference room was uncharacteristically ajar.

"Agent Slattery," Braxton said as he came around the desk.

"Mr. Braxton," the agent stiffly replied as they shook hands. His eyes shifted from the consultant and began roaming over the top of the desk. "How are you feeling after the trip back?"

Braxton suddenly thought of his computer screen. The NEJM article was still there! Stealing a look, he saw the streaming star field of his security wallpaper.

"Fine," he replied with a sigh. "Just fine." He motioned for the agent to take a seat on the couch. "Actually, I have a ton of work to get caught up on. I'd like to get this over with as soon as possible."

"Of course. You seem to have recovered from the, ah, accident quite well."

Jesus. He didn't have time for the spook to start playing mind games with him. "Look Agent Slattery, we both know my history and we both know Dr. Yang's death wasn't an accident. I'm not about to dwell on what happened. I happened to be in the wrong place at the wrong time. What I'd like to know, however, is if my actions had anything to do with his murder."

"I really don't know, Adam. Did you do anything that might have caused anyone to worry?"

"How am I supposed to know? Isn't that more in your field of expertise? I had a couple of conversations with one of my peers at a scientific convention. That's what it was supposed to look like, right?" He realized he had leaned forward in his chair and begun to shout at the agent. His heart was pounding in his chest. Calm down. It won't do any good to yell. He took a deep breath and sat back.

"Your emotion is certainly understandable," Slattery replied. "I hope you realize we had no idea there would be violence involved."

I'm sure you didn't. You might not get the information you want.

"Of course, Mr. Slattery. Has Klaber found out anything about the murder?"

For the first time, Slattery hesitated, holding Braxton's attention. "Nothing yet. But it's still very early for any breakthroughs. I'm sure they'll locate the guilty parties."

"I'm sure."

"Well, what did Mr. Yang have to say, Adam? I can call you Adam?"

"No. You cannot. Unfortunately, I don't think I was able to find out very much about Dr. Yang's work."

"Had he been in contact with his brother recently?"

"He said they had exchanged some electronic mail over the past few weeks."

"And these were about?"

"Family conversations mostly, according to Tak. Catching up on news, that kind of stuff. They did encode their messages with Kam Yang's programs, but Tak assured me he did not have knowledge of the algorithm itself."

Slattery took no notes. He just sat, seemingly relaxed, watching his informant. Braxton wondered how many others the agent had approached in this way. Were any of his friends spying on *him* in the name of national security?

"I see. And this was the extent of their communications?"

"Tak did say that his brother would occasionally mention something about work. Recently, he said that his brother was concerned that his information was not being handled properly. He was afraid his boss was withholding things from the higher-ups. Is that possible?"

"I can't imagine that would happen. And we certainly did get the information from his decodings."

"All of it?"

"Yes, Mr. Braxton. That's why you asked me about Yang's supervisor?"

"That and one more thing."

Slattery cocked his head. "Yes?"

"Yang was sure his brother would never hold anything back from the NSA. Patriotic was the word he used. Who told you Kam Yang withheld the decryption algorithm?"

"I don't think that is relevant, Mr. Braxton."

"Of course, just asking." Braxton wished Fowler could be watching the agent's face. He didn't see a slip. But the old detective might have been able to pick up something he had missed.

"Is this the kind of information you wanted, Mr. Slattery?" Braxton continued.

"We had obviously hoped for a more positive result, but intelligence is hardly ever that straightforward. We will certainly take Dr. Yang's comments on his brother into our analyses. You are aware, Mr. Braxton, that everything he told you might not be true. He could have had any number of reasons for coloring the truth: jealousy for his brother's life in the United States, revenge for his untimely death, or even protection of his position if he thought you could be an agent for the Chinese government. I wouldn't dwell too much on trying to figure this all out. We'll take it from here."

"That's fine with me."

"I hope the remainder of your trip was less harrowing. Was the conference valuable?"

"As a matter of fact, yes. I learned a lot of very interesting things. But if that's all, Agent Slattery," Braxton rose to emphasize the point, "I really must get back to work."

Slattery stood to face the consultant. "Certainly, Mr. Braxton. Again, on behalf of the government of the United States, let me express our thanks for your help. I'm sorry your trip had such a traumatic end."

"I suppose you're welcome, Agent Slattery. But I must tell you I am not interested in any more cooperation with your employer. This has not been a pleasant experience."

"Of course. I understand. I don't believe there will be any further need for us to contact you."

Braxton escorted the agent to the door, but stopped before pulling it open.

"Agent Slattery?"

"Yes?"

"You are sure Dr. Yang was the target of the attack?"

Slattery again paused before responding. Did the spook know more about the murder than he had explained?

"Of course," he finally responded. "Who else could it have been?"

"I don't know. It was just something that Klaber said before I left."

Slattery smiled. It only made Braxton feel sicker.

"Is there some reason you think he was not the target?"

"No. Not really." Braxton prayed Slattery couldn't see into his thoughts.

"Then it had to be Dr. Yang, didn't it? Good afternoon, Mr. Braxton."

Braxton escorted the agent to the outer door, and watched him walk down the hall toward the elevators. By the time he returned to his office, Fowler was already on the sofa with a new Dr. Pepper.

"A real warm-hearted guy isn't he, Adam?"

"Oh yeah. A real charmer. What do you think?" He pulled a Coke from the refrigerator and joined his friend on the sofa.

"I believe he was straight with you. From what I heard he tried to play it as a routine debrief. But a couple times he was too anxious. Pushed a little too hard for what you had. I'd guess the comments about this Yang's bosses were news to him. Roger's not one that likes getting lied to. I'd say he's on a slow burn right now trying to figure out how to verify what you told him."

"Well I hope it fries him. I want nothing more to do with him. What I do want is more information on this *Chlamydia* thing."

Chapter 44

ROGER SLATTERY HATED housework. Yet here he was, wasting a beautiful afternoon washing dishes and picking up all over his Fairfax townhouse. Why couldn't he be sitting in front of the TV watching CNN and sipping a cold beer? It wasn't his fault that he hadn't lifted a solitary finger since his wife Beth had left on Monday to visit their daughter in Roanoke. Or that she had called while he was on the way to his meeting with Braxton saying she would be coming home a day early.

Yeah, life's a real bitch.

He straightened a picture on the mantle and took a moment to reflect on the image. It was a shot from a family picnic in Great Falls Park. Taken when? Must have been ten years ago. John was wearing his favorite high school sweatshirt and Katy still had her hair in braids. Now there're both off on their own and he was about to be a grandfather. All in all they turned out pretty well.

That was mostly due to Beth, he had to admit. He hadn't been around nearly as much as he should have. There was Katy's senior play—he had been in Egypt—and John's championship basketball game—there had been an important debriefing at the Farm. And numerous other events where fathers were supposed to appear. Beth and the kids said they understood, but he wondered if they really did. If they really knew how important his work was. If only he could tell them everything – the lives saved, the catastrophes averted. But his trainers had been right. This was the price of living in the shadows.

He was home more now, of course. Getting a little long-in-the-tooth to go hustling all over the globe. But he still had a role to play. And he still loved every minute of it. Or almost every minute.

He was scraping a smear of pizza off the glass-top coffee table when the phone rang.

"Slattery."

"Roger. It's Peter. Sorry to bother you on a Saturday."

The hairs raised on the back of Slattery's neck. In all the years he had worked for him, Markovsky had only called him at home five times. And each one brought back painful memories.

"Right. What's up?"

"Something's come up. Are you busy?"

"Yeah. You want me to come in anyway?" Markovsky had been dodging Slattery's calls ever since the last meeting at the NCTC. Now he wanted to get together. He deserved to get his chain yanked.

"No. We don't have time. I'll have a car pick you up in a half-hour. We're going to a meeting."

Shit. It was sounding worse and worse. He'd probably be gone when Beth returned. Again.

"Okay. I'll get cleaned up. May I ask where we're going?"

"1600 Pennsylvania Avenue."

*   *   *

After entering the White House through the West Wing entrance, Markovsky led Slattery past an array of stone-faced Marines, through the labyrinthine hallways, and to a stairway that took them down to the first security level. His boss had described the meeting as a simple briefing, but from the number of Secret Service guards wallpapering the passages, he feared something more. This dread wasn't lessened by the presence of the colleague walking beside him.

It had been years since Slattery had been in one of the secure situation rooms. The walls had been given a fresh coat of paint, and new faces stared out from within the picture frames, but other than those minor differences, the area felt the same as it had during Desert Storm. The same cheap deodorant smells, the same shadow-less indirect lighting. A synthetic, antiseptic land where time stood still. There was never any day or night; no morning or evening. Just the unrelenting, oppressive tension of crisis. A place where a man could age years in just a few days. This was not a location to which he had had any desire to return.

They entered the room and Slattery knew his instincts were still intact. Sitting at the table were President Matthews, and DNI Carlson. The only question was whether this was an update or an inquisition.

"Mr. President," Carlson began, "I believe you know Peter Markovsky?"

Matthews nodded as the Deputy Director came forward.

"Mr. President," Markovsky replied. "I have brought two of my colleagues for background, Mr. Roger Slattery and Dr. Harriet Hawthorne."

The trio took seats at the end of the table.

"Slattery, Hawthorne," Matthews repeated. "What's this about Steven?"

"I needed to brief you on new developments in the militia situation," Carlson explained. "We continue to believe that these activities are being coordinated by external forces. And the FBI has recently uncovered some rather disturbing news."

"By external do you mean foreign?" Matthews asked.

"I believe Peter can best answer that," Carlson replied, looking over to the Deputy Director. Markovsky hesitated, then responded.

"Mr. President. We really don't have that level of information yet."

"But your informant is foreign, is he not?"

"Yes, sir. But his information came from domestic sources. We should be careful before drawing any conclusions."

"Okay. So we still don't know *who*. You have something on *what*?"

"We believe so, sir," Markovsky replied. "As the General said, the FBI has uncovered some new information: the hijacking of an active biological agent going from National Culture Collection to the CDC."

"Hijacking?" Matthews asked.

"Actually, sir," Carlson added dryly, "a package was stolen from the CDC's mailroom."

"Their *mailroom*?" The President showed an uncommon look of surprise.

"Yes, sir," Markovsky responded.

Carlson turned toward Matthews and added quietly, "We will need to speak with Secretary Tomlinson about this later, Mr. President."

Fascinated, Slattery watched the DNI work the discussion. Tomlinson was the Secretary of HHS. Carlson didn't miss a chance to take a swipe at his moderate colleagues, even if they were of his own party.

"What is this thing anyway?" Matthews asked, concern obvious on his face. "Anthrax? Ebola?"

"It's called *Chlamydophila Pneumoniae*, Mr. President," Markovsky answered.

"*Chlamydia*? Isn't that some kind of venereal disease?"

"Ah, no, sir. That's *Chlamydia Trachomatis. C. Pneumoniae* is genetically related, but with very different biological activity."

"Then I've never heard of it."

"Neither had the rest of us, sir," Markovsky replied. "That's why I brought Dr. Hawthorne. She is our Section Chief for Chemical and Biological Warfare." He turned to the woman sitting next to Slattery. "Dr. Hawthorne?"

"Mr. President," Hawthorne began slowly. "Most forms of *C. Pneumoniae* are relatively benign. It is a gram-negative *coccobacillus* bacteria whose infections are easily cured by any number of common antibiotics. Unfortunately, the stolen strain is unique. It is quite virulent and antibiotic resistant."

"Okay," Matthews said. "But at least we're not dealing with something really serious. Ebola or something like that."

"I'm sorry, sir," Hawthorne replied, "but this *is* worse. In CBW terms, Ebola is not that interesting. It is much *too* virulent. Perhaps satisfactory for tactical uses, but certainly not strategic. A really effective agent is slow acting and hidden, like HIV. This gives the biological agent an opportunity for maximal exposure before it is identified. And by then it is too late."

Slattery couldn't help but notice the gleam in the scientist's eye as she described the gruesome process. Hawthorne was a thin, intense researcher who had headed the CBW section for as long as Slattery could remember. She was another CIA "lifer" who would rather die at her desk than retire. There was no question of her loyalty, or her dedication; you could hear the intensity in her voice.

Her hair was pulled back tight, the streaks of gray her chevrons of authority. Cool hazel eyes stared out from dark hollow sockets. Few people really scared Slattery, but he had never felt comfortable around Hawthorne. Seeing her reminded him of pictures of the Holocaust.

"You're suggesting HIV could be a weapon?" Carlson asked.

"Oh, not really. It *would* be fairly effective except for two factors. First, its method of infection, intimate sexual contact, is too limited for most uses. It could be used against a highly inbred faction, perhaps an Arab ruling family, but then its second factor applies. The course of the disease is *too* long acting. Targets can remain functional for decades. This significantly limits its practical military or political use.

"So you see, the perfect CBW weapon must have a critical balance of toxicity, contagion, specificity, psychological effect, and ease of distribution. Anthrax, for example, is highly toxic, contagious, has excellent terror factors, but the vector is easily recognized and quite indiscriminant. Not ideal characteristics. Thus it has tactical value, but cannot be considered strategic."

"So what the hell does all this have to do with this *Chlamydia*?" Matthews asked.

"A not unreasonable microbe, Mr. President," Hawthorne replied. "*C. Pneumoniae* has been studied for a number of years as a possible contributing factor to heart disease. It appears to infect the arterial wall and cause lesions which in turn lead to atherosclerosis. If this continues over long periods it can lead to heart attacks or strokes."

"You mean we could cure heart disease with antibiotics?" the President asked.

"An insightful leap, Mr. President. But a little overstated, unfortunately. There are too many additional factors."

"Then this doesn't sound like a very good weapon." Carlson added.

"Not in its common form," Hawthorne continued. "But we identified a mutation. It is highly virulent. Very rapid acting with a substantial predisposition for the coronary arteries. Two weeks after infection, a thirty-year-old has the cardiovascular system of an octogenarian. As an additional benefit, without specialized testing death appears natural. Quite effective as a strategic weapon."

"You knew about this bug?" Matthews looked incredulous.

"Well, ah, yes, Mr. President. It was isolated in the early nineties. But since we didn't have an effective counter-agent we have kept it in storage."

"You're telling me we don't have a vaccine."

"That is correct, Mr. President."

Matthews paused and sat back in his chair. The rest of the room sat quietly waiting for his inevitable analysis. "So what we've got is a killer bacteria in the hands of a bunch of para-military fanatics. How much trouble are we in, Dr. Hawthorne?"

"The specific prognosis is dependent on many factors, of course. Including how much of the bacteria has been duplicated from the original culture. An outbreak would not be completely devastating, but it could infect up to 20% of our population if effectively dispersed. At a conservative 50% mortality that could cause a Class B."

Matthews' forehead wrinkled. "What the hell is a 'Class B'?"

"I'm sorry, sir. I meant a Class B catastrophe. Back in the eighties, Rand was working on ways to classify disasters, both natural and man-made. The old 'so many millions of lives lost' just wasn't relevant in today's complex world. The true impact of a disaster has a lot more to do with the damage to a society's capacity to function than simply the number of people killed. Twenty million people killed in an earthquake in rural China has significantly lesser impact than two million on Wall Street or Pennsylvania Avenue."

"Unless you're Chinese," whispered Carlson.

Hawthorne scowled at the DNI and continued. "It has to do with the impact on the culture. Rand identified three levels of catastrophe, A, B, and C. The event, or more correctly the damage caused by the event, is classified by the time needed to return the societal function to its previous state. A level C disaster is relatively minor. The infrastructure can be rebuilt in five to ten years. Something like the San Francisco earthquake of '89. A Class B event takes longer to recover, approximately a generation. The damage from World War II was a Class B. It took us over twenty-five years to bring the world, mostly Europe and Japan, back to a stable, functional capability. Class A catastrophes take significantly greater than a generation. In fact, they could have incalculable ramifications."

The scientist's explanation brought a somber stillness to the room. Slattery had dealt with more than his share of psychotic terrorists, but Hawthorne's off-hand analysis of the end of the world was enough to scare even this hardened agent.

"What *would* be a Class A event, Dr. Hawthorne?" Carlson asked.

"Let's see. A population explosion in the Far East could be Class A. That could destroy a major culture like China or India. Or an environmental accident. Global warming causing a melting of the polar icecaps. You realize, of course that 50% of our population lies within 50 miles of a coastline. Major population centers would be underwater. This could be an 'A'. Then of course, there was the meteor that hit the Yucatan. This was the ultimate Class A. We don't have a lot of experience here, Mr. President, but the simulations have been rather illuminating."

"Yes, thank you, Dr. Hawthorne," Markovsky said with a shiver in his voice. "We appreciate that background."

"So the good news, Mr. President," Carlson interjected, "is that we're only looking at a *possible* Class B. And there would be no physical infrastructure damage."

"You see that as 'good news,' Steven? We could only lose ten percent of our population? Five of our states eradicated? Only take a generation to recover?" Matthews stood up, towering over the other participants, and turned a frigid gaze on the figures around the table.

"Let me make this very clear. This kind of disaster is *not* going to occur on my shift. This is not the legacy I want left in the history books. You figure out who the hell has this damn bug and you stomp them out."

The President's eyes stopped at Carlson. "I want this problem eliminated, Steven. Is that clear?"

"Yes, Mr. President," Carlson responded. "Perfectly clear."

"And, Peter. You *will* resolve this IMAGER situation. I won't have infighting among my teams."

"Absolutely, Mr. President," Markovsky answered.

Matthews headed to the door. "One more thing," he added, "I don't want to see one word of *any* of this on the evening news."

Chapter 45

"GODDAMN ASSHOLE," WICKS yelled out his window as he swerved onto the shoulder and blew past the right side of a shiny red Toyota with Michigan plates. The car had been crawling along Georgia 480 at 45 miles an hour. *Friggin' Yankee!*

Wick's truck showered the Toyota with gravel as he cut back into the lane. He had spent all day down in Columbus at his John Deere distributor asking for a thirty-day extension on his account. The man had acted like a goddamn banker. It wasn't anything the distributor hadn't given to his buddies over in Phenix City. Maybe their next exercise should be at *his* house.

All Wicks wanted to do now was get home and change. The other cells would have already started arriving at the farm. There'd be hell to pay if he wasn't there. He had wanted to check with O'Grady about the arrangements, but the trip to Columbus had taken all day. He'd call when he got home.

The ring of his cell phone broke his temporary calm. He prayed it was O'Grady.

"Tommy Wicks," he said into the phone.

"I need you to go down to the farm, Tommy."

Shit. It was Gary.

"Now?"

"Yes! I've been trying to get you all day. Why aren't you there now?"

"Uh, I had to get some supplies. Down in Columbus. Took me all day."

"Well get up there now. We've cleaned out the lab. I want you to close it up before the exercises start. Can't have anybody sneaking around down there."

"Okay, I'll be there." At least now he'd get to see what's in that damn secret lab.

"Good. Talk to you later, Tommy."

Shit. He'd already passed the turnoff for the farm. He spun the truck into a one-eighty and headed back down GA 480.

*   *   *

They were gathered fifty yards down from the main entrance to the Citizens for Liberty farm. The assault teams had been waiting since daybreak for clearance to enter, and the sweltering heat was beginning to take its toll.

Special Agent Randolph Washington ducked into the converted Airstream RV that served as the team's command and control center. The interior was packed with radio scanners, video monitors, and satellite communications equipment. Two FBI communications specialists sat squeezed in the narrow space between the walls of dials and blinking lights. Washington's boss, Agent-in-Charge Warren Wesley Bradley sat at a small table in the far end.

"How's it goin' Randy?" Bradley asked.

"It's hot, goddamn it! When you gonna let us loose, Wes? My guys are gonna mutiny if we don't get started."

"Just tell 'em one of those stories of yours. That'll put 'em to sleep."

Bradley turned to one of the techs. "What's the word from AirRover, Chris?" AirRover was the FBI's newest RRV, Remote Reconnaissance Vehicle. The drone was a three-foot wingspan airplane, equipped with radio remote control and real-time video. For safe, clandestine aerial surveillance it was the best in the world.

"Everything looks quiet," replied the younger specialist. "Two cells arrived about an hour ago. They're setting up in the west clearing. Ringo and Santee took teams to cover them."

"What about the farmhouse?" Washington asked.

"Nothing new. Three men went inside a couple hours ago. Probably getting ready for dinner by now."

"It's time to go, Wes," Washington said to his boss. "We can't wait any longer."

"Okay. Pass the word, Chris. We go in fifteen minutes. Give me a yell if you see anything new."

"Yes sir, will do."

"Take care, Randy," Bradley called as Washington left the trailer.

"You got it," Washington replied, stepping back into the sticky Georgia afternoon. The break inside the air-conditioned Airstream had only made his return more uncomfortable. He was already soaked to the skin with sweat. Between his fatigues, camouflage paint, Class 3 body armor, and ten pounds of electronics there wasn't any way to stay comfortable. He had to get his team into the field before all their energy was drained.

He walked over to a group of five agents kneeling under an ancient pecan tree. From their bobbing and shifting he could tell they were as uncomfortable as he was. They would be the primary assault team, hitting the farmhouse, backed up by other FBI and ATF teams now deployed throughout the surrounding farmland.

"Shit, Randy. It's hotter than a barbeque pit out here. When do we go?" It was Greg Franklin, Washington's partner. They had worked together for five years now, ever since Franklin had graduated from Quantico. Washington thought of the reckless recruit as his protégé and was always on guard for his safety.

"Just wanted to make sure you were warmed up. Let's do it."

Washington pulled out his field map and laid it out on the grass in front of them.

"Our target is the farmhouse. Chris says there's only three of the militiamen inside. Greg, you take Paul and Ted to the rear. Dave, Alex, and I will hit the front. After the house is clear, we'll check the out buildings. I don't expect problems but watch yourselves anyway."

"No sweat, Randy. We can take care of these local yahoos." Nods around the circle echoed Franklin's assessment.

"Just remember, these guys don't seem to care what happens to them." Washington adjusted his radio headset. "Everybody on-line?"

One by one, his team members reported in. Equipment checked, they half-timed through the woods and down to the access road.

* * *

If he hadn't been coming from an unfamiliar direction, Wicks probably wouldn't have noticed. He had been looking for the dirt access way leading to the farm when he noticed an out-of-place Airstream trailer parked by the side of the road. At first glance it looked like any other RV, well-worn and covered with decals proclaiming the glories of Luray Caverns and Iron Mountain, but what was it doing parked on the side of this lonesome stretch of highway?

Wicks slowed down to get a better look and noticed the multiple radio antennas sticking out from every possible surface. Danger signals flashed in his head. As he drove past, he noticed a group of men running through the dense forest. They were dressed in black like commandos, not the normal camouflaging of his militia colleagues.

It could only be one thing. Feds.

Shit! Gary had said they were safe. No one would catch on until it was too late.

Sean was undoubtedly already there. Should he try to warn him?

He reached down for his phone. But what could he do? They were already there!

Wicks saw the access road coming up on his right. Everything looked normal. Maybe it was just his imagination.

He punched his foot on the accelerator and sped toward Tyler.

* * *

"Still clear, Chris?"

Washington and his team were huddled behind a derelict Ford tractor, one hundred yards from the front of the militia farmhouse.

"No change, Randy," came the electronic response. "Still quiet."

"Okay. Greg, you in place?"

"Sittin' pretty, Randy. Behind the old shed out back."

"See any movement?"

"Caught a couple of heads in the back window. Probably the kitchen."

"Sounds good. Stay put and we'll move to the front. When we break through close the door on 'em."

"Roger that. We'll be waiting."

Washington motioned to his team and they ran to the front of the farmhouse, spreading out along the rotting wood porch. Washington slid along the clapboard, ducking under the occasional window. He was just about ready to go.

CRACK!

Washington whipped his head around and saw Alex Carpentier frozen, his boot sticking through a splintered floorboard. Shit! He heard movement inside the house.

"Now, now!" he screamed into the headset.

He dashed for the front door, threw his not insignificant weight against the barrier, and rolled through the opening as the door gave way. Popping up in a shooter's stance he scanned the area.

"FBI!" Washington yelled.

Dave Gorpa flew through the doorway and raced into the room to the left. Carpentier came next, running down the hall after a shadow that disappeared around a far corner.

Washington followed his squad and saw Gorpa cuffing a man in his room. Moving down the hall, he spotted Carpentier pinning another on the floor of the kitchen.

Two down. Where the hell was the third?

* * *

Franklin heard the order and dashed with his team to the door at the rear of the farmhouse. As he hopped up on the back porch, the door in front of him flew open and a huge man dressed in fatigues ran through, knocking the agent to the floorboards. Convinced of his ability to avoid capture, the terrorist ignored the FBI agent rushing toward him from the storage shed. Ted Asahi was a second generation Nippon-American, with little sympathy for the self-styled revolutionaries out to "save" his native country. He was also a black belt in both aikido and Isshin-ryu karate, which boded poorly for the success of the escape.

Franklin watched the encounter with a grin as Asahi met the man's momentum with a precisely executed *kote gaeshi*, directing the militiaman's forward motion into a deep spiral, driving him to the ground and converting his kinetic energy into heat and pressure. Concentrating the pressure to a leverage point at the man's shoulder, the terrorist hit the ground with a resounding crack. Franklin had never been able to understand how Asahi made it look so effortless.

The comm crackled. "Greg. Two down inside. You get number three?"

"Three secured. Ted took him down clean."

"Good work, Ted."

"Thanks, boss," Asahi replied, finally breaking his radio silence.

"We're clear here. Backup's coming in for the pick-up. We're gonna take a look around."

"Roger that," Franklin replied. "See you inside."

He was headed up to the house when he remembered the small shed.

"Randy, I'm going to check out the back shed. May find something interesting."

"Okay, but take Ted and check-in if you find anything."

Franklin saw that Asahi had already started toward him so he moved on ahead to the shed. It was a small structure, little more than an over-sized out-house, weathered clapboard siding with an asphalt tarpaper roof. There was a small lean-to attached to the back, next to a poorly kept vegetable garden. Franklin pulled on the plank door and it gave easily and smoothly.

Looking inside, the shed seemed to be a storeroom: sacks of seed and fertilizer, rakes, shovels and other tools leaning along the walls. A well-worn path had been beaten in the dirt floor from the door to the far wall. He walked over and knocked on the wall with the butt of his M16. One section seemed to vibrate more than the others. He grabbed a slat and yanked. The wall suddenly came loose and swung back toward him.

Behind the wall, a concrete staircase led down into darkness. It was clearly a recent addition, in stark contrast to the rest of the farm's structures. The camouflage of the passage had been well-conceived. This was obviously a very professional operation. But what kind of operation?

Franklin pulled out a flashlight and shone it down the steps. All he could see was a landing in the darkness.

He turned hearing a sound and saw Asahi enter. "Ted, I found something."

"What is it?"

"Some kind of underground passage. I'm going down to check it out."

"Greg!" The call came from his headset. "It's Randy. Wait for the rest of the team. You don't know where it goes. We'll be done here soon enough."

Franklin was tired of waiting for everyone else. He had discovered the passage, and he was going to find out where it went.

"Sorry, Randy. I missed that. I'll report back as soon as I find something."

Waving off Asahi's grimace, he held the flashlight high in his left hand, got a firm grip on the assault rifle with his right, and started down the stairs.

When he reached the landing he discovered a heavy sealed door. Shining his light through a thick glass porthole in the door, he saw an apparently empty room filled with desks of some type. He tried the door latch and it unlocked easily. Standing to the side, he took a deep breathe, swung back the door, and spun into the room.

His flashlight scanned across the space. A laboratory! The desks were lab tables, covered with beakers, bottles and test tubes. Around the room were additional pieces of technical equipment. And the place smelled like his college chemistry lab.

"Randy, it's Greg. Found something real interesting."

Washington's reply came a second later. "It's about time. What have you got?"

"Some kind of underground laboratory." As he replied, he made a tour of the room's perimeter, looking for anything that would help him identify the militia's goals. "Looks like a chemical operation. First class setup."

"Explosives?"

"Probably not. Too extensive. If I had to guess, it'd be drugs."

"Well, that's one way to fund a revolution. Don't touch anything, the lab boys will figure it out."

"No problem. I've got no interest in messing with . . ."

He had made a complete circle of the room and was back to the door. The dust he had kicked up disclosed an odd red shimmer in the space across the opening. He knelt down and saw that the beam was coming from a small box on one side of the doorframe. A red light on the box was flashing rapidly.

"Oh, shit."

*　*　*

Washington was searching the cabinets in the kitchen when he heard Franklin's expletive.

"Greg? What was that? Repeat!"

He turned to look out the kitchen's rear window toward the shed. At first it was just a muffled rumble. Then a spear of flame burst from the shed and the ground around the structure jumped. Next came a deafening roar as sod, trees, and dirt flew into the air, followed by a cloud of dark smoke and more flames.

The explosion shattered the window Washington was facing, spewing shards of glass everywhere, but the agent stood transfixed, unable to take his eyes off the devastation that moments before had been a bucolic garden.

"Greg!" he yelled into his microphone. "Greg!"

Chapter 46

Tyler, Georgia
Sunday, 12:15 a.m.

THE APPEARANCE OF the FBI at the farm had driven Wicks into a panic. With Holly gone, they would blame *him* for all the trouble! And what had he done? Just what Gary had told him to. It wasn't his fault. He was just playing along.

Shit, Gary was crazy. The mercenary might have killed him!

He had to get away and think. O'Grady and the others would give up his name as soon as they had a chance. They would be pointing the finger at him! He knew he didn't have much time before the Feds would be on his tail.

He had rushed home, thrown some clothes in a duffel bag, and taken off in his wife's Chevy Malibu. Lou Ann had been screaming questions at him—she could be such a bitch—but he had just ignored her. What the hell did she have to worry about? The Feds weren't after her. Anyway, the less she knew the better.

There was this motel down toward Columbus that he and Donna, his secretary at the dealership, used when they needed to get away. Wicks knew the owner; he could keep his mouth shut for a fifty. A few days to think and then he'd resurface. That'd do it. He'd have everything worked out by then.

On the way south, Wicks pulled off at a Speedway Liquor. He needed something to calm his nerves.

* * *

27 . . . 28 . . . 29. Times four is one hundred sixteen. Damn! Still not high enough.

Flynn was marking time at the corner of M and 31st Streets, hoping she had gotten her pulse rate up enough to call it a morning. Frustrated, she turned down 31st toward the jogging path along the B&O Canal.

She could have gone into work and used the training room at headquarters, but it was a beautiful, sunny morning and she needed the fresh air. They had tracked the progress in Georgia all evening the night before. She hadn't gotten home until midnight. Now after seven hours of solid sleep, she almost felt normal. No point in ruining that by going back to the office just yet.

The booby-trapped lab had been a frightening development. Besides another agent's death, two more had been injured in the blast. What the hell were these bastards doing?

The rest of the raid had gone smoothly. One of the cell's leaders was still missing, but Flynn was sure he'd be captured by the end of the day. Someone had better break. She needed to show some progress to Carlson and the advisory group. Her job depended on it.

She turned left at the foot of the hill and headed east. The path ahead was clear. With few other runners out this early on a Sunday, she shouldn't have any trouble getting her pulse rate up.

Damn she hated running! What a useless form of exercise. It was a helluva time for Robinson to take a vow of chastity. Working out with him was a lot more fun than this. He'd lived this long without any morals. Why the hell did he . . .

Ouch!

Her right foot slipped on a loose rock in the pathway and she fell hard to the dirt.

Dammit! That'll teach me to not watch where I'm going.

"Can I help?"

Flynn looked up and saw another jogger framed in the bright sun. Where had he come from? An arm reached out in her direction.

"Looks like you took quite a tumble," the shadow said.

She reached up and grabbed the outstretched hand. "Thanks."

Pulling herself off the ground, she leaned back against the metal railing that separated the path from a ten-foot drop to the canal bed.

"You, okay?" the man asked.

"I think so. Wasn't paying enough attention."

"I bet you were thinking about work. Jogging is supposed to be a way to get away from your job, not be an extension of it."

He was slim and tall, over six feet, with slicked-back black hair and wearing a light blue jogging suit, unadorned except for a prominent Nike swish. His voice was deep and resonant, with a playful lilt that was missing from those she normally dealt with. Maybe this run hadn't been such a bad idea after all.

"How's your leg?" he asked.

Flynn took a tentative step, then shifted her weight onto the foot. A little sore but nothing major.

"It feels fine," she said. "Just a stupid mistake. Thanks for stopping."

"No problem," he said with a smile. "Y'all be careful now." Before she could reply, he gave her a quick nod and sprinted away down the path.

Damn. Another opportunity down the drain.

* * *

Wicks sat quietly in the chair trying to make sense out of the last eight hours. It was hard to do anything else, handcuffed to the immobile table.

After finishing the bottle of Jack Daniel's he had finally passed out. Then he had been rolling in white Gulf Shore sand with Donna, when a loud crash broke him out of the surreal splendor. Five men, dressed all in black, had stormed into the motel room and thrown him on the floor. Everyone was yelling. He couldn't understand anything. It sounded like the building was being torn apart.

One of the men said something to him, he couldn't tell what, and he shook his head. This seemed to anger the man and Wicks felt a heavy boot crush his side. Then something hit his head and things went fuzzy.

He vaguely remembered getting dressed, being handcuffed, and thrown into the back seat of a car. He had no idea how long he had traveled; he must have passed out somewhere along the way. He awoke when another set of men, this time in street clothes, dragged him out of the car and through the back door of an old building. His watch said it was 8:30, he assumed it was the morning. Now he sat here, chained to the desk like a goddamn criminal, wondering what was going to happen next.

They would certainly interrogate him. The room was tiny and filled with the smell of sweaty exertion. Or was it the smell of fear? The walls and floor were tile—to make them easier to clean—and the light above his head was covered with wire mesh. Across from him, the wall was covered with a huge mirror. He tried to look into it but it only reflected the visage of an ugly, disheveled man, so he turned away. But he knew what was behind it. He had seen the TV shows. It was his interrogators, waiting for the right moment to make their entrance.

What would they do to him? He hadn't ever believed all that stuff about the cops beating people to death. They didn't do that now, did they? Anyway, what had he done? Burned an old building? Collected some guns? Shit, he'd tell 'em to go to hell. Gary had told him if there was ever any trouble to just call his lawyer. The shyster could take care of anything. He'd show them. Yeah, that's what he'd do.

He felt better now. He was ready.

The door creaked open and two men in dark blue suits entered. One was white, with a short blonde crew-cut and rough, poxy complexion. He stared at Wicks for a moment, then slowly took off his coat and hung it over the back of a chair. The other man was the biggest black Wicks had ever seen. He must have been a football lineman. His head sat flat on his shoulders as if his neck had been stuffed down into his body. When he took off his coat, the sleeves of his shirt strained against the mass of his biceps.

He didn't feel so confident anymore.

"Thomas Wicks?" the white man said.

"I want to see my lawyer," Wicks responded with as much bravado as he could. He kept his eyes on the white man.

"He asked if you were Thomas Wicks," the black man said. "Answer the man, boy."

Wicks jerked toward the black man. "Boy! Who you calling a boy, monkey?"

"I don't know, *boy*. Who are you?" The black stared down at Wicks from over the table.

Wicks started to jump up but the handcuffs held him back. Damn. Don't let them get to you. It's all a game. He settled back in the chair.

"Yeah, I'm Tommy Wicks. Who the hell are you? And where am I?"

"I'm Agent-in-Charge Bradley and this is Special Agent Washington," the white agent responded. "We're with the FBI. You are in FBI headquarters in Atlanta."

Shit, Atlanta. They are serious. Okay here goes. Act indignant.

"What am I doing here? Where's my family? Are they okay?"

"Your family's just fine," Bradley said. "They're back in Tyler. You're the one we want, not them."

Okay. That's all they're going to get. "I said I want a lawyer. I ain't sayin' nothing else."

Washington leaned so close over the table that Wicks could smell stale coffee on his breath. "I guess that's your choice, boy. But if I were you I'd consider doin' a little talkin' first. You're in for a mighty rough ride otherwise."

"Whadda you mean? My lawyer'll have me outta here before dinner. You can't keep me locked up for breakin' some gun laws."

"Gun laws?" Washington replied smiling. "Is that what you think this is about? Read him the charges again, Wes. Maybe he didn't hear them the first time."

Bradley reached into his pocket and pulled out a small notebook.

"Mr. Thomas Wicks. You are charged with thirty counts of possession of illegal firearms, thirty counts of concealing dangerous weapons, two counts of arson, six counts of attempted murder, and four counts of first degree murder."

"Two of 'em Federal agents," Washington added. "You're in a pile of shit, *boy*."

Murder! There was no way they could know about Holly.

"I didn't murder anybody! What're you talkin' about?"

"We're talking about *murder*, you damn redneck bastard." The words spit from Washington's mouth. "We know it was your cell that torched the newspaper office and the courthouse."

"I didn't kill nobody!"

"And we know it was your cell that set the booby trap on the farm. That was my team trapped in your goddamn laboratory. My partner that died. If I had my way, I'd start breakin' you apart, one bone at a time."

"Hey, wait a minute! I didn't know about any booby trap. I never went near that lab. He wouldn't let me!"

"Who wouldn't let you?" Bradley calmly asked.

"I said I want to talk to my lawyer." They knew too much. He was scared and wasn't gonna say another thing. Gary's lawyer would get him out of this.

"Where'd a small-time punk like you get a lawyer, Tommy? Where's he from?"

"Uh, none of your damn business. Just give me a phone. I get a call right?"

"Sure, Tommy, Sure. Here. Use my phone." Washington reached into his pocket and handed Wicks a cell phone.

"Randy," Bradley interrupted. "I don't think this is a good . . ."

Washington shook his head firmly. "Hey, don't worry, Wes. I got a real strong feeling Tommy here is doing the right thing. He wants to call his lawyer, and we need to let him."

Wicks looked suspiciously at the phone. Why was the chimp being so helpful? Shit, probably just doesn't know any better. He flipped open the mouthpiece.

"I need my wallet," Wicks said.

"Don't know the number, huh?" Washington said with a smile. The cop disappeared and returned a minute later with the wallet in his hand. He tossed it on the table. "Here you go, Tommy."

Wicks picked up the wallet with his free hand and extracted the small piece of paper he had hidden in a torn corner of the billfold. He carefully typed in the numbers and hit send. As he looked up, the huge black still had the sickening grin on his face.

The call connected and began ringing. Wicks felt his heart pounding like a machine gun.

"We're sorry. The number you have dialed is not in service. Please check the number and dial again."

The message repeated twice before disconnecting. Wicks slowly set the phone back on the table. Gary had set him up. What could he do?

"What's the matter, Tommy?" Washington asked. "Your lawyer too busy to talk to you?"

"I want a deal. I want immunity . . ."

Washington slammed his fist on the table. Wicks felt the wood shudder under the force. "The only deal you're going to get is the chance to be alive a year from now. That's a better deal than you gave my partner. This is it, Tommy boy. Your last chance."

"Where did you get the number?" Bradley asked softly. "If there's somebody else involved, you really should tell us. We'll do what we can to help you."

What could he do? He was just a pawn. The mercenary was the bad guy.

Wicks turned to Bradley. "Gary. It was all Gary. He gave the orders. Got the guns and planned the attacks. Told us what to do. *He* killed all those folks! We were too scared to do anything."

Bradley and Washington looked back at one another. What were they thinking? Did they believe him?

"An imaginary friend Gary, huh?" Washington finally replied. "Gee, Tommy, that's not the way we heard it. Your friend Sean O'Grady says you gave all the orders. And it was you that killed the publisher and the janitor at the courthouse."

That goddamn Irish sot. Why the hell couldn't he keep his mouth shut? Goddamn it! He wasn't going to take the fall for this alone.

"I'll tell you what *really* happened," Wicks began. "It wasn't me. It was Sean! The guy called him a drunk and Sean went crazy. 'String the monkey up' he said. *That's* the truth."

Chapter 47

FLYNN'S STRIDE HAD taken on a slight lopsidedness, but she seemed to have avoided any serious damage. And she was now paying a lot more attention to where she was going. Ahead, another runner turned onto the path and jogged toward her. He was shorter than her earlier good Samaritan, and stocky, with a blonde crew cut. Probably military, unfortunately. They were *always* married.

Her thoughts drifted back to Robinson. He *had* been acting strangely lately, ever since this militia thing broke. Maybe she should talk to Carlson about him. It wouldn't be that surprising if Markovsky and Stroller had cooked up something. And then there was the IMAGER anagram. That was pure Robinson. What if . . .

Jesus! Why won't this guy get over? He was only about ten yards away now, but running directly at her, leaving her little room between him and the railing. She wasn't going to take the time to go around him on the other side. She'd just force her way past the thoughtless creep.

A flash of light caught the corner of her eye; a glint of sunlight off polished metal that was moving straight toward her! She reacted instinctively, flattening herself against the railing in avoidance, swinging up her left arm in a parry, and driving her right fist at her attacker's solar plexus.

A searing pain ripped her left arm, and she let out a scream, more from surprise than pain. Her attacker stumbled back and looked quickly around. Other joggers had reacted to the yell and were heading in their direction. The man looked back at Flynn briefly, then ran up the slope and disappeared into an alley between the M Street buildings.

The adrenaline rush faded and Flynn began to feel shaky. She was completely astonished by the attack. Looking down, she saw that the arm of her sweatshirt was soaked with blood. What the hell had just happened?

*   *   *

Things had gotten a little easier. The agents had let him take a piss and given him a cold drink. Washington had disappeared for the moment—which made Wicks a lot more comfortable—and Bradley had brought a stenographer in to take his statement. He was surprised how easily the words came out.

"Tell us more about this friend of yours, Tommy. What's his last name?"

"I don't know. He never said. It was always Gary. We all just did what he said."

"Why, Tommy?" Bradley asked. "Why would you do what some stranger wanted?"

"We were all suspicious at first. But he knew everyone: Casey, up north; Shepard in Tennessee. And he could get anything. Automatics, explosives, anything. He said he just wanted to help us."

"When did you first meet him?"

"About a year ago. Macon, Macon Holly, he was in charge then."

"Where is this Holly now?"

"He . . . he had an accident," Wicks stuttered. They didn't need to know everything, did they? "Shot himself."

"Are you sure Holly's death was an accident?" Bradley pushed. "Could this Gary have had anything to do with it?"

"I don't know. Maybe. He said it was an accident."

"Okay. What did Gary do after this Holly died?"

"It seemed like he kinda took over. Everybody listened to him. He was talkin' about the Covenant and how we all need to work together."

"What's the Covenant, Tommy?" Bradley asked.

"You know, the Covenant. Gary made us all sign it when he first came. It was all about liberty, getting our rights back. Stopping the Feds, ah, stopping the government from taking our rights away. The Jews controlling our money. The blacks takin' our jobs. Getting out of our private lives, out of our business. That's what we talked about."

"Is that what you believe, Tommy?"

"Well, yeah. Where's my rights? I work hard. But I gotta hire who they say. Treat 'em better than I treat my family. And if I fire anybody, I get sued. Ain't nobody carin' about *my* rights. Just everybody else's. That ain't fair."

"And destroying the county records. That was about protecting your rights?"

"We had to show 'em. That they just couldn't push us around anymore. Gary said there were lots of us that felt the same way. We were all going to get together and take the government back. Get rid of all the bleeding-heart liberals and fag-lovers."

"That's what Gary said, 'take the government back'?"

"Yeah. It was all part of the Covenant. The Commander was going to put things right."

"Who's the Commander, Tommy?"

"Gary's boss. Gary said he was a soldier. The Commander was in charge. The Commander was organizing the groups all over the country. We were gonna work together."

"This Commander have a name? What does he look like?"

Wicks screwed his face. He really *didn't* know anything about the Commander. "Ain't nobody ever seen him. Gary just talked about him all the time. Never said what his name was though."

"Didn't you ever ask about him? Didn't anybody ever question Gary?"

What was wrong with these guys? Why don't they understand?

"You didn't question Gary. Ever. He was crazy, I tell you. I saw him break a guy's arm for just messin' around at an exercise. Reached out and snapped it like that." Wicks waved his arms to demonstrate.

"Okay, Tommy. Let's take a break. I want you to work with one of our artists. Let's find out what this Gary looks like."

* * *

"What do you think, Randy? You believe all this Covenant shit?"

Bradley had stepped out of the room and joined his agent at the viewing mirror.

"I don't know," Washington replied. "This asshole seems too scared to make up a story like this but who could tell? It does jibe with the stuff we've been hearing about somebody coordinating these groups. I'll check with D.C. to see what they've got."

"Thanks. As soon as I've got a sketch I'll fax it to Quantico. Maybe we'll get lucky."

"I hope so."

"And nice call on the lawyer. I didn't know what you were up to."

Washington tossed back his head and smiled. "Thanks for not pulling the plug. No way this asshole had a lawyer ready. I figured he'd been set up. But you better keep me away from him. It was all I could do to keep from wringing the bastard's neck."

* * *

Wicks spent the next hour describing Gary to the FBI artist. Instead of a pencil and pad, however, this "artist" used a computer to compose the face. Wicks was pleased with the result, it was a pretty good likeness. That would count for something, wouldn't it? Not that he expected anyone would ever catch the slippery mercenary.

When they had finished, one of Bradley's flunkeys took him down to a cell block in the basement of the building. Jesus, it was cold and dank. How was he going to get any sleep here?

As they walked down the corridor between the cells he saw O'Grady sitting on a bunk on his left. He prayed they wouldn't put him in the same cell as his squealer *ex*-friend. The guard passed O'Grady's cell and the gate on the next cell slid open.

"Hey, Tommy!" O'Grady whispered once the guard had disappeared. "This shit's a piece of cake. Just got knocked around a little. You okay?"

Wicks walked up to the front corner of the cell. "Okay? You goddamn bastard. What were you thinkin'? Telling 'em I did all that shit? If I ever get my hands on you . . ."

"Jesus, Tommy. Tell me you didn't fall for that crap. That's standard cop procedure. Tellin' you the other guy squealed. You didn't tell 'em anything, did you?"

"Uh. Well. I thought you were tryin' to set me up for the fall. How was I supposed to know?"

O'Grady dropped his head into his hands. "Shit, Tommy. You stupid asshole. You just killed both of us."

Chapter 48

THE SUN WAS just rising over the horizon when Agent in Charge Bradley turned into the gravel parking lot. He drove past the flickering "Providence View Motel" sign and searched for the unit number Washington had given in his message.

A sign in the office window proclaimed "Georgia's Finest Lodging," but all Bradley saw was a run-down fifties road stop whose time had passed with the coming of the Interstates. An all-too-familiar ending for much of this part of Bradley's home state.

He shouldn't have worried about spotting the unit. It was framed with two unmistakable Government Issue vehicles and a flashing Georgia Patrol car.

"What have we got Randy?" Bradley called as he walked up to the door marked "113."

"The desk clerk called us at six this morning," Washington replied, leading his boss past the patrolman and into the unit. Four other FBI agents were carefully but thoroughly disassembling the contents of the room. "He recognized the face on the flyer we left. Gary rented this room from him three months ago. Plunked down cash for six months."

"Didn't this guy think that was a little strange?"

"Gary said he was a salesman. Wanted to have a place to call home when he was in the area. The owner grabbed the money and forgot about it."

"Get the M.O. out to the other teams," Bradley replied. "Found anything here yet?"

"Not very much." Washington pointed over to a plywood desk in the corner of the room. "Looks like he cleaned the place pretty well."

"Makes sense. He's a pro. Motel have WiFi?"

"Nope," Washington answered. His smile suggested that was way above the amenities offered by the motel's management.

"Check the cell towers anyway. Maybe we'll get lucky. What about prints?"

"We lifted some partials earlier. Sent them in, but I doubt they're good enough for a match."

"You never know. The boys in Quantico can do some pretty fancy magic."

"Thump."

The pair turned to see two of the agents flipping a flowered double mattress. They were giving the room a very thorough check.

"When was Gary here last?" Bradley asked.

"He left Saturday. 'In a hurry' according to the clerk. Probably right after the raid."

Washington shuffled absentmindedly from one foot to another. Bradley felt sorry for his agent. This time there was nothing the ex-athlete's physical prowess could do to help them. It was tearing him up inside.

"Sorry to call you out on this, Wes," Washington finally said. "Not the big break we wanted. Hear anything from the other teams?"

"The Tennessee lead came through. The head of the local cell coughed up his contact right away. Called himself Terry. They had a possible informer and this Terry told them to make a lesson out of it. Burned his house down and killed his whole family. These assholes are nuts, Randy."

"Did they find any of the goddamn bacteria?"

"No. No labs, no bugs. But Terry did have a plastic molding made."

"Some kind of weapon?"

"I don't know. Quantico's got it too."

"Damn. Doesn't sound like anything that's gonna get us very far. I was hoping we'd have an ID by now."

"Well, we'd better find something soon," Bradley said shaking his head. "From what I hear, all the rest of the teams are coming up empty too. And D.C.'s flipping out. Somebody's head must be in a vice."

"Hey, Randy," called a female agent sticking her head out from under the desk. "What do you make of this?"

* * *

"Tell me again why I'm sitting in this car with you," Braxton asked. Of all the places he could be on a gorgeous Monday morning, sitting in the back of a stretch limousine with Roger Slattery was pretty low on his list.

"I told you everything I know, Adam," the agent responded. "I got a call from my boss, Deputy Director Markovsky, saying he wanted me to bring you to the White House."

Braxton let the use of his first name slide by. No point in making an awkward situation worse. "Why does he want to talk to me? And at the White House?"

"Don't know why. As to the where, if he has to be in the White House, he'll sometimes just squeeze short appointments between other meetings. Sit back and enjoy yourself. Have you been to the White House before?"

"Not by invitation. How about you?"

"A few times. Most of them not ones I like to remember. Nothing like this."

Braxton hoped the agent was right. He had actually been taking the day off, finally getting a chance to finish reading the Sunday Post in his Falls Church apartment. Slattery's call had been quite a shock. At first he had been skeptical, concerned about some CIA plot against him, but the agent's near pleading tone had finally convinced him. He had cleaned up—it *was* the White House—and waited for the limo.

They rolled through the Southwest Gate and pulled to a stop. As they got out, Braxton noticed three commercial vehicles along the driveway, their sides proclaiming North Capital Landscaping, Central Irrigation, and Washington Audio Systems.

"What's going on?" Braxton asked his host as they passed into the West Wing Entrance.

"Oh, probably just sprucing up for the ceremony on Wednesday."

"The signing of the intelligence exchange agreement?"

"Yeah, another big photo op for the administration. Gotta have everything look good."

"You're not happy with the agreement? I would have thought this would be a big help to you."

"It's nothing but a chance for the big chiefs to ruffle their feathers for the voters. Everybody agrees to play nice and share their intel, unless of course it involves information collected on their partners. There's still too much parochial thinking in the world. It's just another 'feel-good' announcement that makes the good guys look better, but won't stop the bad guys."

"Why Agent Slattery, you're not the federal lackey I thought you were."

Slattery glared back at Braxton who only returned a toothy smile. It was the least he could do in return for the agent's ruining of his day.

They passed easily through the Secret Service check-in and down a long hall. Braxton looked into one large room and saw a crowd milling around. A few looked up as they passed.

"The Press Briefing Room," Slattery commented.

As they walked farther down the hallway, Braxton was struck with the quiet of the residence. He felt that he should talk in whispers, as a small statement of respect. The most powerful man in the world lived and worked here. It wouldn't do to disturb his concentration.

A short elegantly-dressed man met them around one corner.

"You must be Mr. Braxton," he said extending his hand. "I'm Peter Markovsky, Deputy Director of the CIA. Thank you for coming in on such short notice."

Braxton returned the firm handshake. "Mr. Slattery was very insistent, Mr. Markovsky. But I would like to know why I'm here."

"Of course. A few of us had some additional questions for you. This seemed to be the most convenient place to get together."

"Convenient?" Braxton asked.

"Yes. One of those interested is the Director of National Intelligence."

Braxton looked over to Slattery and saw that the agent was as surprised as he was.

"Please, follow me," Markovsky said.

The trio had started down the hall when the Deputy Director turned to his agent.

"I can take Mr. Braxton from here, Roger. We'll be out in a few minutes."

Braxton saw Slattery fall behind, another surprised look on his face, as he and Markovsky continued down the hall. If he hadn't been in the White House, he would have felt like a death row convict being escorted for a last, long walk.

They stopped, and Markovsky opened a door. "This is the Roosevelt Room," he said.

It was a relatively plain room, furnished with comfortable chairs and Early American reproductions. Two features stood out. The first was a rousing equestrian portrait of Teddy Roosevelt hanging above a fireplace mantel. The second was a grim man sitting at one side of a long conference table. Braxton recognized him as General Steven Carlson, the Director of National Intelligence. There was no one else in the room.

Markovsky paused for a moment, perhaps waiting for Carlson to stand, but the DNI stayed put. Finally, Markovsky concluded the introduction. "Ah, General Carlson, this is Mr. Adam Braxton. Mr. Braxton, I'm sure you recognize DNI Carlson."

"General Carlson," Braxton said. "Pleased to meet you."

"Sit down, please." It was an order. Markovsky and Braxton took seats opposite the DNI.

"First of all, Mr. Braxton," Carlson began, "I am aware of your relationship with Agent Slattery and the CIA. While I do not agree with the Agency's, or their friends', handling of this Yang affair, I do sympathize with their desire to keep secret the loss of a critical intelligence capability. As a civilian, I will also ignore your clumsy efforts at making contact with the Chinese scientist which undoubtedly cost him his life. I place this blame on Mr. Markovsky."

"General," Braxton responded, "I really don't think . . ."

"Braxton, I don't give a rat's ass what you think. You're here to listen, not to talk. The obviously ill-conceived request by the CIA," Carlson glared at Markovsky, "did not give you the authority to go breaking into commercial buildings and destroying invaluable private property. They should know better than to send a wit-less scientist on an intelligence mission."

"Wit-less scientist?" What was he talking about? Did he know about Vision One? But we didn't destroy anything!

"I don't know what you thought you were doing sneaking around the Vision One facility, and I really don't care. I just want to make it perfectly clear that you are *never* to discuss your little escapade with anyone, and should you attempt to do so, you will find yourself in a federal prison for the rest of your life. I believe you are familiar with these confidentiality requirements."

What was Carlson doing? Braxton had never been spoken to like this in his life. And Markovsky seemed as shocked as he did. The Deputy Director's face was scarlet. Had the DNI lost his mind?

"General. I don't understand. We didn't destroy anything! Sydney Marino and I found . . ."

"Damn it, Braxton, shut the hell up!" Carlson's voice echoed through the room. "The ephemeral Miss Marino, eh? Well, perhaps she'll verify your story. If we ever find her. She seems to have disappeared. And I suppose it would come as a surprise to you that the underground security vault at Vision One in Utrecht was destroyed last night? Luckily they had another backup of all their documents off premises. We don't have any *proof* of your involvement in that fire, but it is quite a coincidence don't you think?"

"Vault?" Braxton exclaimed. "It wasn't a vault it was . . ."

"What now, Mr. Braxton? You're going to tell us it was some nefarious secret laboratory?" Carlson shook his head. "We are all aware of the unfortunate death of your ex-wife. I suppose I can understand your need to blame someone. But this doesn't allow you to go off and create shadow conspiracies. I suggest you go back to your cubicle and keep a very low profile. Now get out of here before I change my mind about being so lenient."

Markovsky looked around as if he didn't know what to do, then stood up and pulled Braxton off his chair.

"Thank you, General," the Deputy Director said demurely.

"Thank you for what?" Braxton whispered to Markovsky when they were out of the hall. Getting no response, Braxton simply fumed to himself. As he passed the Secret Service guards he saw a look of disdain in their eyes. He had no doubt that Carlson's outbursts had made it outside the small room.

"See that Mr. Braxton gets home safely, Roger," Markovsky finally said when they met Slattery in the entryway. "And give me a call when you get back." The Deputy Director immediately turned away and disappeared into another hallway.

"Ready to go back, Adam?" Slattery said cheerfully.

"You can go to hell, Slattery," Braxton whispered. "All of you!"

He walked up to the nearest Marine guard. "I presume I can get a taxi around here?"

Chapter 49

"THAT'S THE STATUS of the investigation, General. It's clear Vision One has been withholding critical information on their progress. How would you like us to proceed?" Captain Edward Fraser closed the folder in front of him and looked over to the imposing figure at the end of the table.

Army General William Robert Yancey, head of the Defense Intelligence Agency, tapped his fingers on the long conference table. The sound echoed like a war drum through the small room. Splayed on the walls of the sanctum were the photographs of distinguished officers and commemorative plaques recognizing heroic deeds performed by their agency. Unfortunately, most were unknown except by the few who frequented these halls. Even their sister agency, the CIA, was at least glamorized by the public. The DIA acted in the background, their work unappreciated, and usually demeaned, by the rest of the intelligence community. This was a perception not lost on the attendees of the meeting.

"That's an issue we'll have to take up later, Ed. Right now, the most important thing is to make sure our tracks are covered. We have to find some way to recover from *your* screw-up, wouldn't you say Lieutenant?"

Yancey turned to the only other figure in the room. Army Lieutenant Sydney Walker, Intelligence Analyst II, looked up from her notes and returned her General's penetrating stare. She had known the briefing would come down to this confrontation. Walker took a deep breath and began her defense.

"I don't see how I could have reacted any differently, sir. The civilian had an agenda that was in direct convergence with ours. I felt it was critical that we intersect Mr. Braxton's initiative if only to mediate any adverse incidents. As a result we were able to develop new intelligence that supported our hypothesis."

"But in doing so, you blew your cover. Your behavior eliminated any opportunity to return you to Vision One. You screwed up, Lieutenant, and put the operation in jeopardy."

She glanced over to Fraser for support, but he refused to acknowledge her.

Not a big surprise. Her boss was an Academy lowest-quartile whose main goal was to avoid doing anything that would draw attention to his incompetence.

"Braxton would have been exposed in any case, and perhaps captured," she replied. "My identification was unfortunate, but there is still no evidence that Vision One suspects my real mission. We can just confront them with the evidence."

"I hardly think your word would stand up in an inquiry, Lieutenant. The courts don't look kindly to breaking and entering."

"We didn't . . ."

"That's quite enough, Lieutenant," Yancey barked. "We obviously should have sent a more experienced man to do this job. Your little midnight affair with the civilian may have blown our only chance to find out what is really going on at Vision One."

"There must be something . . ." Walker pleaded.

"There's an inspection team on the way now, Lieutenant," Fraser finally replied. "They'll be at Vision One tomorrow."

"And you better hope they find something to support your story, little lady," Yancey concluded. "Or I'll have your ass in Alaska inspecting igloos for security violations."

* * *

"What the hell happened in there?" Slattery screamed into the telephone.

"Roger," Markovsky calmly replied. "I thought you'd be calling. What did our Mr. Braxton have to say after the meeting?"

"He told me to go to hell and took a taxi home. I've been trying to get you for hours!"

"I just got back to the office. It's been quite a day."

"Okay, so *what happened?*"

"You'd never believe it. Carlson reamed your friend's ass. He implied he knew all about our game with Claude. I gathered he didn't think much of our strategy, but it was Braxton's extracurricular activities that really pissed him off."

"What activities?"

"You remember his ex-wife got killed a few weeks ago?"

"Yeah, but what does that have to do with us?"

"Apparently he thinks her employer, some company called Vision One, had something to do with her death. So when he was in Amsterdam, he and a lady friend go and sneak around the place. They broke into some secure area. God knows what else they did. Carlson was purple with rage. I thought he was going to put the guy under house arrest. He said if he ever heard of him again he'd throw him in Leavenworth."

Shit! That was why Braxton agreed to go to Amsterdam. So we could pay for his goddamn B&E.

"Who was this friend of his?"

"Some woman named Marino. Carlson didn't seem too worried about her though. Mostly just chewed out Braxton."

Marino? So that was Fowler's game. He and Braxton *are* still working together.

"So what do we do now?" Slattery asked.

"With Braxton, not a goddamn thing. Don't talk to him. Don't go near him. I don't believe you knew what this asshole was going to do, but we can't give Carlson any more ammunition. Just keep working with Flynn and the rest of the advisory group. We do have a real problem to solve."

Slattery hated to bring it up, but he hadn't had a chance to talk to his boss in days. And the story had smelled funny from the beginning. "Have you read my report on Braxton?"

"Yes." The response was cold and flat.

"What do you think about what Yang said about Robinson? Any chance he's lying to us about the algorithm?"

"Why? What would it gain him?"

"I don't know, but it's put us in one helluva position."

"I can't believe it. Robinson's ass is in a vise for not getting the algorithm out of Yang. Claude would never put up with it."

"If he knew. Did you say Carlson knew about IMAGER?"

"It seemed like it."

"Who told him? And why?"

There was a pause on the phone. "Good question, Roger. I suppose Claude could have felt there would be too much pressure. But he should have told me first. I'll find out."

"Anything *else*, Peter?" Slattery replied in the most sarcastic tone he could manage.

"No. Bad luck getting caught in this, Roger. Just keep your head down for a while. If I find out what really set Carlson off, I'll get back to you. Oh, and don't forget about the advisory group meeting this afternoon."

"Thanks. Just what I need is more face time with Carlson. I'll bring my body armor.

"You know somebody's stonewalling us, right? It could be Stroller, Robinson, or even Carlson. But we'd better figure out who it is. And fast."

* * *

Everything had been put in place, everything was ready. Gary hit the "Send" key and relaxed for the first time in months.

```
CHARLIE on schedule.

HALFTIME preparations complete. Ready to execute.

Tyler camp compromised. All connections destroyed.
```

He swallowed the handful of pills and closed his eyes. How much time did he have left? Enough to spend the bounty he had collected?

It really didn't matter. The money was simply a way to keep score. What did those religious fanatics know about real terrorism? Indiscriminate bombs. Suicide squads. They were nothing. He was the best. He had told his bosses and they had laughed at him. Well, they weren't laughing now.

The move on Tyler had been faster than he had expected. He doubted the FBI could have done it by themselves, the Agency was undoubtedly involved. Even the gut-less bureaucrats would have recognized the threat by now.

Wicks was a particularly unfortunate loose end. The spine-less sycophant would spill his guts if the FBI pinched him. There wasn't much he could tell, and the booby trap had done its work, but the error bothered the mercenary's sense of closure. Under other circumstances he would have sanctioned the informant on principle, but the damage was done and he had another assignment to complete.

He had had to leave Tyler quickly but had found a motel in Phenix City where he could go to ground. He was about to leave this latest home when his cell phone chimed a new message. He clicked it open and read the text.

`Consultant becoming dangerous.`

`Sanction approved.`

Mail from the Commander was very unusual. They had decided direct field communication should be minimized. The plans had been finalized months ago; every step worked out in excruciating detail, every option listed and prioritized. There was no need for polite thank-you's. Just concise status updates.

Gary shook his head. The request was ill-timed. He still had a few last-minute duties left, but it wouldn't do to cross his paymaster. He would take care of the primary mission then handle this new one. It shouldn't take too long.

Chapter 50

"Do you bring me to these meetings as a form of medieval punishment, Peter?" Slattery asked as they settled into the chairs in another SCIF in the NCTC. "What will it be today? A group inquisition?"

The CIA agent had fumed all morning over Carlson's attack on Braxton. It wasn't that he liked the consultant all that much—he could be an arrogant sonuvabitch—but he couldn't put up with bureaucrats taking their frustration out on civilians. He was sure Carlson was pissed at the CIA for getting Braxton involved, pissed at NSA for lying about their screw-up, and pissed at Braxton for violating Vision One, one of the country's high-tech hotshots. Unfortunately for the consultant, he was the only one over whom the DNI had any real clout.

Slattery had paced back and forth in his office all morning, ranting at the stupidity of the "system." He hadn't been talking *to* anyone; he simply needed to vent the anger inside.

And just when he was beginning to calm down, it was time for the meeting at the NCTC. What could be next?

"Our friends were busy this weekend, Roger," Markovsky said, ignoring his subordinate's previous question. "Carlson has an update for the group."

"Did we learn anything from the Georgia raid?"

"You know about that?"

"Yeah. I talked with Flynn on Friday."

"I don't know any details. I'm sure Mary Ellen will tell us if she found out anything."

The rest of the advisory group members filed in, Stroller and

Robinson trailing, looking like a pair of beaten puppies. Carlson must have finally gotten around to them.

The activity in the room froze when Flynn entered. Slattery feared something unexpected had happened. The FBI Special Assistant looked especially dour. Which might be explained by the white cloth sling supporting her left arm.

Slattery tapped Markovsky on the shoulder.

"What happened to Mary Ellen?"

"She had a run-in with a mugger yesterday," he replied. "He cut her forearm pretty badly, but she seems okay."

Jesus. This town was getting dangerous. *I wonder how the mugger made out?*

"Everyone seems to be here so let's get started," Carlson finally announced. "There have been a number of militia developments over the weekend. The situation is becoming increasingly serious. Mary Ellen, would you please give us a summary of these events?"

Flynn rose and walked to the front of the room. Her movements were slow and deliberate. The injury was definitely having some effect. The now-familiar annotated map of the United States appeared behind her, dots of blue and green pinpointing the previous militia activity.

"Late last week," the Special Assistant began, "we received corroboration from an informant that the activities of the Citizens for Liberty militia organization in Georgia were being directed by an external group. And that this cell had been involved in the Tyler and Middleton arsons. As a result we obtained a search warrant for the cell's center of operations, a local farm. This warrant was executed late Saturday afternoon by a combined team from the FBI, ATF, and Georgia Patrol." The country-wide map dissolved into a close-up of the Tyler farm. "We arrested thirty-seven militia members on a variety of state and federal weapons charges."

"Were there any casualties, Mary Ellen?" Delacroix asked.

"Unfortunately yes, Admiral. We had no problem making the arrests, but one of our agents discovered a laboratory buried in a hidden bunker. The bunker was booby trapped. The laboratory was completely destroyed and Agent Gregory Franklin was killed."

The room went silent. This was the second agent Flynn had lost. Slattery knew what she was going though. He had lost a few of his own on even successful operations.

"What kind of a laboratory was it, Mary Ellen?" Delacroix continued. His voice had lost its usual hard edge.

"Quantico has only started the analysis," Flynn replied. "But from what we can tell it was a very sophisticated biochemical facility. Far beyond anything required for simple explosives. We believe it may have been used to culture the *Chlamydophila Pneumoniae* stolen from the CDC. Atlanta is performing similar analyses."

Slattery watched the faces react when Flynn named the microbe. It appeared everyone had heard the news despite their efforts to keep it under wraps.

"Excuse me, Mary Ellen," Stroller interrupted, "but is there any chance the bacteria was destroyed in the explosion?"

"The resulting fire would certainly have neutralized any active material in the lab. But we have no proof that cultures weren't taken away earlier. It has been a month since the theft."

"Have you gotten anything out of the goddamn terrorists?" Delacroix demanded.

"Very little from most," Flynn responded. "They seem to have just been happy to just play soldier every few weeks at training exercises. The leader of the Tyler cell was more cooperative, however. He confirmed that the cells were being coordinated by someone called the Commander. No one has ever seen him, *if* he even exists. All their contact was with a man called Gary. This Gary bought all the weapons, directed all the operations. Including the Tyler and Middleton attacks. We've developed this sketch of the man."

A drawing of a face appeared on the screen. There was nothing remarkable about the features, yet Slattery felt a chill cut through him. Something about the face was familiar.

"So who is this man?" Markovsky asked.

"We do not have any identification at this time. We're checking all the local motels, bars, and gas stations. We'll find him."

"Do you think this one man is responsible for all the attacks?" Garcia asked.

"I really don't know, Jerry," Flynn replied. "It seems unlikely that one person could coordinate all these groups. I expect there is a small team involved, reporting to this Commander. Once we have this Gary, we'll track down the rest."

"Is this all your arrests came up with?" added Delacroix.

"They also pointed us to additional cells in Tennessee and South Carolina, Admiral" Flynn added. "We're checking them out now. We'll have more information in the next twenty-four hours."

"If this is all we have, General," Stroller said to Carlson, "I would rather Mary Ellen was out trying to find whoever is behind all this rather than sitting in this meeting."

"That might be easier to do if we had any consistent background intelligence," Flynn countered.

The Special Assistant's words hung in the air like a thundercloud. Carlson glared at Flynn, then back at Stroller. Stroller sat deathly still, his mouth agape. Slattery just held his breath.

"Unfortunately, there *is* more," Flynn finally continued. "There has been another round of attacks. This time on state office buildings." The US map reappeared, but now blotched with points of red overpowering those in blue and green. "Twelve attacks on offices all over the country. Another doubling of activity."

"Any evidence of biological warfare?" Garcia asked.

"No. Only arson. Apparently designed to destroy records. And induce fear."

"Any loss of life?" It was Admiral Delacroix.

"Three deaths, seven other injuries. All civilians, all fire related. Any occupants were cleared under gunpoint. We still don't believe that any of the deaths were planned. They appear to be due to the poor training of the militia terrorists. This Commander is continuing to play on the sympathy of the conservatives. As long as there are no mass killings, it's still a 'bloodless revolution.' "

"Same M.O. as the other attacks?" Markovsky asked.

"Yes, Peter. Again, they were very well planned. The terrorists used automatic weapons and high tech explosives. There was one deviation from the previous attacks, however. They all occurred at midnight *local* time. Unfortunately, we didn't make the time connection until it was too late. We could have warned the West Coast offices."

"Why didn't your prisoners tell you about this attack?" Delacroix asked.

"They only knew that a third attack was being planned. The Tyler militia was not going to take part in Operation CHARLIE, as they called it. They were never told about the schedule or the targets until the last minute."

"ALPHA, BRAVO, CHARLIE," recited Delacroix. "I wonder how far it goes?"

"It's not going any farther," Carlson announced, rising from his chair. "Your job is to stop this *now*, Mary Ellen. What is your plan?"

"Our forensic investigative teams are already exhausted from the previous nine attacks. We don't have the resources to cover over twice as many more. We'll do what we can at the sites, but I don't expect a lot of additional evidence. Our focus is now on this Gary and his associates. With the Tyler cell broken we can work back through the other cells and identify their contacts. Once we crack one, he'll lead us to the Commander."

"And how long will this take, Mary Ellen?" Carlson pressed.

Slattery was again reminded why he hated bureaucrats. There was no way any law enforcement officer could put a deadline on an investigation. There were too many unknowns. But Carlson wasn't going to be satisfied until Flynn was all the way out on that wobbly plank. All he cared about was having a scapegoat. And leaving the dirty work to the foot soldiers.

Flynn stood her ground and returned Carlson's stare. "Seventy-two hours, General."

Shit. She's dead.

"We'll hold you to that," the DNI replied.

"Yes sir. I know you will."

Flynn walked back to her seat as Carlson turned to face the others. "I agree with Claude that we should now cut this meeting short and let you get back to managing your teams. I did think, however, that giving everyone a consistent overview of the situation was important. We cannot afford any miscommunication. I know you all will do everything possible to resolve this crisis." He focused his gaze on Stroller. "We have, unfortunately, lost our earlier intel on these groups. I expect you all to give Mary Ellen and Jerry your full support."

"General Carlson?" The query came from David Scott, the normally reticent State Department representative.

"Yes, David?" Carlson answered.

"I think we need to consider another aspect of the attacks. Besides the obvious escalation in numbers, there is also an escalation in targets. From local, to county, to state institutions. The next step is clear. We should alert all the Federal Office Buildings. We can't afford another Oklahoma City."

"Excellent point, David. Please coordinate a response with Mary Ellen.

"One final item. There is no way we can now keep this quiet. And David's analysis will not be lost on the media. By tomorrow I expect to see reports of these attacks in every paper in the nation. We *must* find out who is behind this. If this government cannot protect its citizens and its institutions, we will surely descend into anarchy."

Chapter 51

"YOU WANTED TO see me, sir?" Walker marched up to Yancey's desk and gave her best salute. Out of the corner of her eye, she saw Fraser cowering behind a report on the side of the room.

The General had paged her just to be sure everyone else in the complex knew she was being called on the carpet. She had been an intrusion on the DIA's old boy network ever since she had signed on, and they never missed a chance to run her through the office gauntlet.

"At ease, Lieutenant," Yancey mumbled without looking up from his desk.

Walker stepped to parade rest and waited for the inevitable barrage. To her side, Fraser set the report in his lap and waited like an obedient servant.

After about two minutes, Yancey's head slowly raised. The General's eyes were bloodshot and even more hollow than usual. It must have been a bad night.

"I've been reading the results of the inspection, Lieutenant," he began. "I'm afraid it's not quite what we had hoped."

"They found the security level didn't they, sir?" she asked. "And the laboratory?"

"Oh, yes," Yancey replied softly. "They found the security level."

Well, so far so good. Now they can't deny what we found.

"But there wasn't any goddamn laboratory!" He jumped from his chair and slammed his fist on the desktop. "The whole area is nothing but charred rubble. Whatever *was* in there was destroyed by a fire over the weekend. And by the way, Vision One says it was a document vault."

"A document vault?" Walker cried. "The lab was there. A full Level 4."

"So *you* say!" Yancey yelled back. "Here, you read the goddamn report." He threw the file at her. She held her ground as it struck her chest and fell to the floor.

"You screwed up big time, Lieutenant," Yancey continued. "You and your goddamn boyfriend."

"He was not my boyfriend, *sir.*"

"I really don't give a rat's ass if he was your long-lost father, Lieutenant. He's in as much trouble as you over this."

"Braxton? What trouble?"

"I'm sure it comes as a surprise to you, Lieutenant, but the DoD doesn't look kindly to people breaking into their contractor's sites."

"But there was no damage. We didn't touch anything. What are they going to do?"

"He's just a civilian," Fraser interrupted. "Why would we care about him, Lieutenant?"

"Because he does have a connection to us, sir." Walker directed the reply to her boss. "He was a witness. We should find out what he knows about Vision One."

"He doesn't know jack shit, little lady," Yancey said. "And I can assure you he will have nothing more to do with this operation. As of yesterday, like you, Mr. Braxton is out of the game."

* * *

God, what a day!

Braxton had tried to finish up two new proposals but he had still been so upset from his meeting at the White House he could barely concentrate. He had tried to call Fowler, hoping to have someone to complain to, but the detective had been out of town on another assignment. He had finally given up, and wasted the rest of the afternoon in mindless bliss playing FreeCell on his PC.

At 6:30 he threw the incomplete documents into his briefcase and dragged out of his office. Maybe a quick meal would get him going. *Will it be leftover pizza or leftover Chinese?*

On the way to his car, he passed the newspaper stands at the entrance to the parking garage. A headline on the afternoon *Post* caught his attention.

Militia Attacks Escalate - FBI Denies Conspiracy

He dropped four quarters into the slot, pulled out the paper, and scanned the article.

```
Militia groups all over the nation last night
escalated their fight against the government by
attacking twelve state office buildings. These
attacks follow earlier engagements at . . .
```

"Nice story don't you think?"

Braxton jumped at the unexpected voice. He turned and saw a smallish, disheveled man looking over his shoulder.

"I hope I didn't startle you, Mr. Braxton," the man said. "My name is Taylor Luckett. I'm a reporter for the *Post*. That's my story. I'd like to talk to you for a moment if I may."

A reporter? Why would a reporter want to talk to me? Oh, of course. Yang's murder.

"I'm sorry mister, Luckett was it? I have a meeting to get to. And I really don't have anything to say about the events in Amsterdam." He turned back toward the garage.

"At 6:30? That wouldn't be a meeting with Mr. Slattery would it?"

The agent's name stopped Braxton cold. He spun around to face the reporter.

"I see you're familiar with his real name," Luckett said. "I wasn't sure."

"I don't know who you're talking about. I suggest you leave me alone, Mr. Luckett."

"Come on, Braxton. Let's cut the shit. I saw you in the White House with Slattery. You obviously know him. And you do seem to have a penchant for getting yourself into high-profile trouble."

Braxton tried to look offended but doubted the reporter was fooled. What could he do?

"I still have nothing to say to you, *Mister* Luckett."

"That's fine. Just listen for one minute. Then decide what side I'm on. It might be worth your while."

Luckett paused and Braxton considered what to say. He didn't like standing around in a parking garage with this Woodward and Bernstein wannabe, but if there was a chance he could explain what happened at the White House . . . .

"One minute, Mr. Luckett."

"For the past two months I've been researching a story on the militia movement. A few weeks ago, a friend gave me information on something much bigger. Have you read anything on recent militia attacks?"

"I don't know. Maybe. Weren't there a couple of fires set?"

"Yes. About two weeks ago three small town newspaper offices were burned down. All were anti-militia. Three different parts of the country, all at the same time. Then last week, while you were in Amsterdam, there were six more fires at county courthouses. All over the country, all at the same time."

Nine cases of arson? He hadn't heard of all those.

"And now last night, there were twelve more attacks on state offices."

"What are you suggesting, Mr. Luckett?"

"I'm not *suggesting* anything, Braxton. I'm telling you that someone is organizing militia groups. He's coordinating terrorist attacks. And he's not going to stop."

"What does this have to do with me? I don't know anything about any conspiracy."

"Roger Slattery is the CIA's top counterterrorism agent. He's now sitting on the Director of National Intelligence's personal advisory group. The agencies are keeping the truth about the attacks buried while they try to figure out what's going on. But they're getting nowhere. No one has ever coordinated these groups before. They hardly even talked to each other. But someone is changing all that."

That's the connection! Coordinated militia attacks. That's what Yang meant when he said our military groups were working together. It was 'militia' not 'military'! And that's why Slattery needed the decryption algorithm.

"What do you want from me, Mr. Luckett?"

"I want to share information. I don't trust Slattery, the CIA, the FBI, or the goddamn administration to get this right. That friend of mine I mentioned? The militia killed him because he wrote the truth. I don't know how you're connected, but I think you're an honest guy. I took this chance because I need your help. Tell me what you know. Maybe we can stop this before it gets any worse." Luckett glanced down at his watch. "Well, my minute's up. What do you say?"

This was all coming too fast. He needed time to think. And to find out more about this reporter.

"You tell an interesting story, Mr. Luckett. Let me sleep on it. I'll give you a call if I think of anything that might help."

Braxton turned his back on Luckett and walked slowly toward his car. His heart was pounding like a jackhammer. Could there be a connection between the militia and Amsterdam? Could that be why Carlson came down on him so hard? Or did this Luckett have some other motive?

"Oh, Braxton," Luckett called. "Don't wait too long. Folks close to this problem have a nasty habit of getting hurt. But I guess you already know that."

Chapter 52

Braxton leaned back in the overly-soft Scandinavian sofa and whistled a sigh of fatigue. There was something very wrong with the events around him but he was unable to put them into any kind of pattern. Megan's death, Vision One, a militia conspiracy; seemingly unrelated events but with a mind of their own. As if some master puppeteer was pulling the strings of a troupe of marionettes. Daring the audience to piece together the story line. Unfortunately, he at least, was missing the point.

After the encounter with Luckett, Braxton had passed on dinner and poured a strong tumbler of Talisker scotch instead. He had planned to put all the questions out of his head and spend the rest of the evening falling into a calming stupor. That, among all of his other worries was why he answered the knock on his door with such enmity.

"Who is it?" he growled from across the room at the intrusion.

Nothing.

Shit! He pulled himself up and trudged over to the door. The dark, smoky liquid had begun its magic and he felt a slight wobble to his step.

"What!"

A quiet voice drifted through the door. "Adam. It's Sydney. I need to talk to you."

Sydney? Sidney who? Oh, Jesus. Sydney! He twisted the deadbolt and pulled the door back against the security chain. Peering through the crack, he spied his previous partner-in-crime. She was as attractive as ever, but her face had an unease he had never before seen. Damn, what more can she do to me now?

"Well, the disappearing Miss Marino. How good to see you. What do you want?"

"We need to talk. Please let me in." Her voice was almost pleading. She checked the hallway behind her as if expecting someone to come through the shadows. She was not at all acting like the self-possessed PR expert.

"I think I'd rather not, Miss Marino, or whoever you are." The words stumbled awkwardly out of his mouth. He shook his head to clear his thoughts. "I've been called a liar, my reputation is shot to hell, and I feel like shit. When I needed your help, you were nowhere to be found. No thanks, I think I'll pass on anything you have to tell me. Have a good life."

He wanted to simply slam the door in her face and get on with his life, but something stopped him. Before he could gather the strength to pull away, her voice reached through the opening and held him fast.

"I'm sorry, Adam. You're right. I lied to you. But we have to talk. It's about the *Chlamydia*."

So she does know about that! Goddamit, it was time *somebody* told him what was going on. It may as well be her. He unhooked the chain and pulled open the door.

"Alright, get in here and sit down. You've got a lot of explaining to do. But first I'm getting something to sober me up."

He made her sit quietly while he brewed a double-strength pot of green tea and took two aspirins. While he waited for the caffeine to kick in, he peered around the corner of the kitchen at his guest. She was dressed conservatively for the sophisticated, outgoing woman he remembered. Dark blue suit, raincoat.

Was it raining outside? He didn't even know.

Her blonde hair was pulled back tightly, revealing a child-like innocence in her face. It had been like that in Amsterdam. Which woman was she?

"Where should we start?" He chose one of the easy chairs and set the cup down on the end table. It was the last he would see it that evening.

She slowly raised her head and stared straight at him. He didn't know whether to be relieved or scared.

"My name really is Sydney. Sydney Walker. I'm a Lieutenant in the US Army, assigned to Pentagon Intelligence, the Defense

Intelligence Agency. My job was to infiltrate and gather intelligence on Vision One. But something went terribly wrong."

Braxton felt all the air leave the room. He could barely breathe. "So you *are* a spook," he finally exclaimed. "But why investigate Vision One?"

"Vision One gets a lot of government contracts. Some are public, and some, well, not so public. *C. Pneumoniae* was used in Desert Storm as a biological agent."

"Wait a minute," he interrupted. "I found that name, too. From the pages in the lab notebooks. I looked it up. It's not all that dangerous. And easily cured by antibiotics. It isn't any secret weapon."

"I know the background. But there are special strains that are very virulent. They've been developed over the years as part of the CBW program at Fort Detrick. We had a vaccine, but the bacteria mutated again. I don't understand the details, but Vision One was supposed to be designing a new antibiotic. It was taking much too long. We thought they might be hiding something from us so I was sent in."

"How did you get in?"

"Oh, it wasn't that hard. General Hastings is on their Board. It only took a call."

That's what Sam had said. Must be nice to have powerful friends. All his seem to want to do is screw him.

"So how did I fit into your neat little plan?"

"You didn't. Not at first. I really did know Megan. She was a great lady. It was a terrible accident, Adam. You've got to believe that."

"I don't know what to believe any more, Sydney. People seem to have this habit of lying to me."

"I know. I'm sorry. It *was* wonderful to see you in Amsterdam. And when you said you were going back out to Vision One I had to go with you. If you were caught it could have brought too much attention."

"Apparently we were caught. Do you know how?"

"Vision One security checked the access logs and then the video surveillance tapes. After my superiors found out, they were adamant that I couldn't surface. 'Sydney Marino had to disappear', they said. It was too dangerous and Venton would undoubtedly suspect we had had something to do with the break-in. They wouldn't let me corroborate your story. As long as it was just you, they had deniability."

"*Deniability?*" Braxton yelled across the table. "They crucified me. My reputation could be shot. Just so you could have 'deniability'? Bull shit!"

He knew he was attacking the messenger but he couldn't help it. And anyway, she *was* one of "them."

"I know, Adam. I know it's late, but maybe I can help. That's why I came."

"Help? How?"

"I heard something when we were in the laboratory. I didn't tell you."

"You mean when the lab techs came through? I thought you said they were discussing their sex lives."

"They were. But they also said they were duplicating the antibiotic. Vision One has the cure, Adam. It exists."

"So they did what you wanted. Why would they hide it from you?"

"Why do you think? Money. A new antibiotic could be worth billions of dollars. They wanted to get it to market first."

"I thought we had all the antibiotics we needed?"

"That's what everybody thought in the eighties. So the mainstream drug companies quit doing antibiotic research. They went on to other projects: Alzheimer's drugs, TPA, Viagra. Unfortunately a lot of bacteria developed mutations, resistant strains. Like what happened with *C. Pneumoniae*. This made it a great biological warfare agent. But we needed a way to control it. Once we had the antibiotic we would have time to develop a vaccine."

"And now Vision One made you one. So why don't you and your SEALs just go get it?"

"That's the Navy, Adam. We have the Rangers. Anyway, Venton denies it. I assume you know the lab is gone. Without that, there's nothing to find. It's my word against Venton's. And I'm not all that credible right now, either."

Braxton shrugged his shoulders. "So? What does this have to do with me?"

"Dammit, Adam. I could get court-marshaled for telling you this! I'm trying to help you."

"Yeah, thanks. Next time just keep your help to yourself. I'd rather have my life back."

"I've read your file. You have friends in the community. Contact them. You can make them understand."

"And save your ass at the same time I suppose."

Walker's face dropped. He had gone too far.

"Sydney. I'm sorry. I didn't mean it that way. I'm strung out too. I don't have any more credibility with my contacts than you have with yours. The Director of National Intelligence threatened to throw me in jail! You get paid to save the world. I don't. There's nothing I can do."

"Apparently not. Whatever you say."

Walker stood up and immediately headed for the door. Braxton didn't bother to move.

Before she disappeared into the hallway she turned back to him. "You can be a really great guy, Adam Braxton. But Megan was right. Sometimes you'd rather lock yourself in a little room and hide rather than take a chance on really making a difference."

The sound of the slamming door echoed through his apartment. What was he supposed to do? This wasn't his problem. He had other things to worry about.

* * *

Robinson rolled over and stared at the glowing face of his alarm clock. 1:50 a.m. Five minutes later than the last time he had looked.

He hadn't gotten a solid night's sleep since Kam Yang's death. And his cold-turkey avoidance of Flynn hadn't helped. Night after night he traced every crack in the ceiling, studied every pattern in the texture.

It had gotten too personal. He had always worked in the background. Setting things in motion and watching the reactions. Now he was part of the play and the ramifications were much too close. People he knew were being affected. Being killed.

He closed his eyes and tried to visualize his last vacation to St. John. When was it? Three years ago? He was climbing on the rocks, walking in the sand, . . .

The insistent buzz slowly pulled him back to his bedroom. Away from the sun, away from the surf. He reached over and grabbed the phone.

"Hello?" he said sleepily.

"What are you doing calling me again?" said the angry voice.

What the hell? Oh, it's him. "You're getting back to me now? It's 2:00 a.m.!"

"Keeping the country safe is not a nine-to-five job, Garrett. Now why did you call?"

"Did you see the latest decryption?"

"Yes." The response was flat. Without emotion. What was wrong with him?

"So what should we do?" Robinson asked. He pulled himself up against the headboard.

"Didn't we already have this discussion? We don't do a goddamn thing."

"But it's that consultant. Braxton. They're after him. We should warn him."

"Warn him! Hasn't he done enough damage already? Look, Garrett." The voice dropped to nearly a whisper. "If this information helped us with the attacks, of course we'd release it. But it doesn't. And the cost would be too high. We must keep the algorithm secret a little longer."

"I'm tired, sir. Very tired."

"I know, Garrett. We both know what a burden knowledge can be. But your country is counting on you. Let's see what happens. We'll talk later this week."

"Yes, sir." He was too tired to argue.

"Now get back to sleep, son."

Robinson collapsed back onto the bed. Nothing was clear any more. What should he do now?

Chapter 53

"BRAXTON! CAN WE talk?"

The muffled voice came out of the darkness in a corner of the Tysons Tower parking garage. Braxton had just parked his car and started toward the elevator. He recognized the voice and just kept walking.

"Adam. Please."

Jesus. Why does everyone want to talk in the goddamn garage? He turned to face the voice.

"Look, Mr. Smith. Mr. Slattery. Whatever your name is. I don't have time for any more of this. I tried to get the information you asked for. I nearly got killed doing it. And as a reward I get threatened again. Only this time by my own government. No, I don't think we have anything to talk about. I should have listened to Sam and told you to go to hell."

Braxton's voice had grown louder and angrier with every sentence. He took a deep breath and let his pulse return to normal. What the hell did Slattery want now?

"I understand you're angry. I didn't have any idea Carlson was going to set you up like that. We, *I*, appreciate the information you gave us. I can promise you that it will be used. I just can't give you any more details."

Still playing the cool spook, eh, Slattery? Well, maybe I'll try a little fishing and see what I catch.

"I hope so, Slattery. For Tak Yang's sake. Oh, by the way, you wouldn't be interested in any information on *Chlamydophila Pneumoniae* would you?"

The reaction was instantaneous. Nothing major, just a twitch above the eyes, a tightening of the neck. But for a professional agent it was a scream. Braxton had caught a big one.

"Well, did I get your attention, Mr. Slattery?"

"What do you know about that, Braxton?" Slattery's tone had a razor-sharp edge.

"I know of someone who has a very strong interest in that particular microbe. Maybe we can share some information. You tell me how Yang figures into the recent militia activity and I'll tell you about *C. Pneumoniae*."

"Militia? I don't know what you mean."

"Okay. Have it your way. There's no militia conspiracy. No coordination. And nobody cares about *Chlamydia*. See you around Slattery."

Braxton turned, walked toward the elevator, and started counting. He got to four.

"Stop. Okay, we'll talk." Slattery walked up to face the consultant. Braxton felt the power of the man as he stood just inches away. "Look, Braxton. If any of what I'm about to tell you gets public, I will personally break every bone in your body—very slowly. This is a national security issue. I don't imagine I need to explain the potential penalties for both of us."

"Okay, Slattery, I'm duly impressed. Let's get on with it."

The agent took a step backward and Braxton's heart slowed a bit. "About two weeks ago, Kam Yang decoded an Internet message that suggested an external group was organizing the activities of a number of militia groups. Since then, these groups have executed a series of coordinated attacks on local and state institutions. Eleven people have already been killed, including two FBI Agents."

Braxton just stood and listened. This was old news, except for the FBI murders.

"We don't know what further attacks may be planned," Slattery continued, "because Kam Yang was killed in the traffic accident. And with him the ability to decode the messages. We have to find out who's behind this and what is their objective."

"So you sent me to get the algorithm from his brother?"

"Yes."

"But he didn't have it and said his brother wouldn't have kept it a secret. Why would the NSA tell you different?"

"I still don't know."

"Shit, Slattery. You're the one from the world of secrets and lies. If you don't know, who does?"

"Good question, Adam."

"Okay, so these militia groups are working together. You want to know who is behind it. What does this have to do with *C. Pneumoniae*?"

"Not yet. Your turn. What do *you* know about it?"

Slattery's cold stare cut into the consultant. He had to find the connection that would explain Megan's death. Unfortunately the CIA agent was his only shot.

"You know I went snooping around the Vision One facility in Utrecht last week?"

"And caused quite a stir among some of their friends in the Pentagon it seems."

The Pentagon. DoD. So that *was* where the pressure began.

"Apparently. When I was there with Marino, we discovered a hidden biological laboratory. Heavy-duty biohazard stuff. As best as I can figure, the scientists upstairs were designing molecules and the ones downstairs were cooking them up."

"How do you know this has anything to do with *Chlamydia*?"

"I lifted some pages out of their lab notebooks." Slattery's eyes popped. "When I got back here, Sam and I discovered they were descriptions of *Chlamydophila Pneumoniae*."

"Sam knows about this too?"

Braxton would have enjoyed shocking the spook, if the subject wasn't so frightening.

"Yes. I hope that's not a problem." Braxton enjoyed watching Slattery shake his head in frustration. It was time to poke the spook again.

"Oh, Marino's a DIA agent, in case you didn't know."

"Your friend Marino is DoD? Jesus Christ."

Braxton let the surprises sink in, then got back on track. "Your turn again, Slattery. What's the connection?"

The agent again paused. "We raided one of the militia cells last week."

"The one in Georgia?"

"Yeah."

"I read about it."

"Not all about it. One of the FBI agents found a bio lab buried in their farm. It was booby trapped. The agent was blown to bits along with the lab."

"I'm sorry. Did you find any *C. Pneumoniae* there?"

"No, all the material was destroyed in the explosion. But about a month ago, the CDC discovered that a *C. Pneumoniae* sample was stolen from their mailroom. An hour from the Georgia farm."

That was it! From the labs of the CDC to a backyard kitchen of death run by a bunch of political extremists. And Vision One was stonewalling on the cure.

"What are they going to do with it?" Braxton asked.

"That's what we're trying to find out. You knew about the militia connection didn't you?"

"Not all of it. I got some ideas from a friend."

"That friend wouldn't possibly be a reporter?"

Braxton tried to stay cool, but the probe came too quickly. He needed to get back on the offensive.

"Speaking of friends, did you know who Marino was?"

"No," Slattery responded. "There was a flag on her file. I couldn't check any further without raising alarms. And that was not something I was too anxious to do. What was she doing at Vision One?"

"Look, that's it, Slattery. All I know. Now get out of here. And out of my life."

"Nothing I would like better, Adam. One last piece of advice, though. I'm sorry about your ex-wife, but leave Vision One alone. You got your hand slapped the other day. Don't give anyone an excuse to do anything more. These are bad folks. And I can't help you if you get in their sights."

"Thanks for the advice. But I never wanted your help, and I'll not be asking." Braxton spun on his heel and walked to the stairway. He wasn't going to stand around there any longer.

When he reached the first step he turned and called back to the agent.

"Oh, Slattery. You do have an antidote for this bug don't you?"

"I don't think that's relevant, Mr. Braxton."

"Oh, yeah. Right. It's a secret. If I were you, Slattery, I'd talk to some of your friends about their secrets."

* * *

"Everything is ready, Mr. President," Dawson announced. They were gathered in the Oval Office for a final review of the next day's events. "The State Dinner will begin at 7:00 this evening; the signing ceremony will be in the Rose Garden at noon tomorrow. It looks like the weather will be ideal."

"Have the press details been worked out?" Matthews asked his Press Secretary.

"Yes, sir," Newington replied. "Invitations to the dinner went out to the lead anchors of NBC, CBS, ABC, Fox and CNN. They will all be attending. There will be limited taping permitted at the reception tonight. We'll get spots on the 11:00 news programs. The real attention will be tomorrow. We will have live coverage beginning at 11:30 a.m. on all the networks. After the signing ceremony, you'll hold a short press conference. It will be a real showcase, sir."

"Thank you, Warren," the President replied. "It sounds like you've got quite a party set up."

"This will be a significant event for your presidency," Secretary of State Donovan Fletcher added. "It will guarantee your place in history."

"I'd rather it guaranteed my re-election in November, Donovan. In case you hadn't noticed, the approval ratings have begun to slide."

"I'm sure it's just the post-convention doldrums, Mr. President," Fletcher replied. "The signing of the intelligence exchange agreement will make every American sleep more soundly at night."

"I wish I had your confidence. I'm especially concerned about the domestic policy numbers. Are we likely to get any questions on this militia problem, Steven?"

"I don't think so, Mr. President," Carlson said. "We'll be sure to keep Luckett out of the corps. My team has been meeting . . ."

"Yes, Steven," Matthews interrupted. "I know what you've been doing. But we don't seem to be making any progress. *Get me some answers.*"

"Yes, sir," Carlson replied quietly.

"Warren." Matthews started down his action list. "Work with Steven to put together Q&A's for the militia events. I don't want any surprises. Get me a draft this afternoon."

"Yes, Mr. President."

"Donovan. The electorate will identify most closely with the Brits. Keep PM MacAlister close to me. Who else is up front Chad?"

"Besides yourself, the V.P., Speaker Andersen, DNI Carlson and SecState Fletcher will be on the podium. The rest of the Cabinet, Joint Chiefs, House and Senate leaders, and the Supreme Court will be in the first rows. We'll fill the spare seats with some Congressional staffers."

"Good way to hand out some favors, Chad. Just make sure they're photogenic. One more thing. Put LaRoche at the end of the table. I don't know why the French keep electing the ugliest men as their Presidents."

* * *

The Lincoln Memorial cast long shadows from the late afternoon sun as Braxton walked up the Colorado marble steps to the sculpture. He saw his appointment sitting on the top step writing in a small notebook. Luckett looked up in time to see the consultant approach.

"I was wondering when I'd get your call, Braxton," he said.

"Just had some checking to do, Mr. Luckett. Believe it or not, lately I've run into a few people who don't always tell the truth." Braxton swiped his hand across the marble step and squatted down.

"Can't imagine who that might be. Nice place for a rendezvous, by the way."

"Thanks. I'm sorry about your friend. George Brown, right?"

Luckett stared off across the reflecting pool toward the Washington Monument then returned his focus to Braxton. "Yeah. He was a good reporter. They're not going to get away with this." Luckett's easy going attitude transformed into a steely-cold hate. His story had turned very personal.

"Have you heard anything more about the militia attacks?" Luckett asked.

"I read the FBI raided the Georgia cell."

"Yeah. Interrogated everybody. The militia's contact was a mercenary named Gary. The FBI's got a nationwide manhunt out, but my guess is this guy'll just disappear back into the shadows. They'll never catch him. So what *is* your role in all this?"

Braxton had spent all morning on the story he would give to Luckett. He hoped it was enough to keep them both out of jail. "As far as I can tell, the CIA was monitoring electronic communications about the conspiracy between this Gary and his boss. A couple weeks ago, the encoding changed in the messages. They couldn't read it any more. Slattery asked me to try to try to see if there were any new encryption schemes being described at the conference in Amsterdam."

Luckett listened intently to the description, his eyes never leaving Braxton's.

"And I suppose the deaths of the Yang brothers were just a coincidence."

"You've done your homework, Luckett. Let's say there are a lot of loose ends."

"Okay, we'll leave that one for now. Did you find anything in Amsterdam that would help?"

"No. But there is another connection here. The FBI discovered a biological lab buried on the Georgia farm. The militia, or at least this Gary's friends, were replicating a microbe they stole from the CDC. Something called *Chlamydophila Pneumoniae*. And it's not the common venereal disease."

"Germ warfare!" Luckett exclaimed. "No militia group has ever done anything like that! How bad is this stuff?"

Every time Braxton told his story it made him even more depressed. How were they ever going to stop this madness?

"Normally pretty benign," he continued. "Common antibiotics can usually kill it. But if this Gary has found a strain that's resistant it could be disastrous."

"Jesus. They used it yet?"

"I don't think so. That's probably why the Feds want Gary so badly. But if he's good enough to put all this together, I doubt he'll leave anything behind."

Luckett paused, then said, "Well, he did make one slip."

"What!"

"The FBI tracked him to a motel outside of Atlanta. Raided it early this morning."

"You've got good contacts, Mr. Luckett."

"Taylor, please. I do have a few friends left."

"Did they find anything?"

"Gary was long gone and had emptied the place, but the cleaners found a scrap of paper under a table leg. And it had some writing on it."

"What did it say?"

"All it had was 'Yale 82.' "

"What does it mean?"

"Beats me. You're the Ivy Leaguer from Boston."

"Boston College is not Ivy League, Taylor," Braxton replied. He visualized the scrap of paper and possible connections flashed through his head. "Yale University? A class year. Or a basketball score."

"Or the start of a combination," Luckett added. "Yale makes locks, too."

Braxton shook his head. "I vote for the University. I think we need to do a little research."

"*We?* I appreciate all the information, Mr. Braxton, but I can take it from here."

"Sorry, Mr. Luckett. We're partners now. That's the way I work. Anyway, I've got just the resource we need for this investigation. Meet me at National tomorrow morning. We're taking a trip to New Haven."

Chapter 54

THE FLIGHT TO New Haven was thankfully short. Braxton hated flying twin turbo-props. It was like huddling in an over-sized beach ball in a hurricane. The reason they never served meals was because no passenger could ever keep one down.

Luckett disappeared behind the morning's *New York Times*, leaving Braxton by himself to work out a strategy for the day. What they had was a tiny clue to a huge puzzle. Hopefully the trip would let them connect a few more of the pieces.

"So who is this guy Cavendish?" Luckett asked in the taxi on the way to Yale.

"Professor Duncan Cavendish, Taylor."

"Great. Sounds like a snooty Brit to me."

Braxton nodded. "Close. A Brit who went to Yale on scholarship and adopted Yale, New Haven, Connecticut, and the United States the way a lonely child adopts a lost puppy. I always thought he was angry over missing out on the British Empire and was looking for the next best thing. He's a renowned expert on early American History. He could recite every battle of the American Revolutionary War, who won, who lost, and all the political ramifications."

"How did you run into this guy? I thought you were some kind of computer geek."

"I'm a computer *scientist*, Taylor. But I always had a love of history. Cavendish was a Visiting Professor at Boston College when I was a junior. I took a couple of courses from him and we became friends. I've tried to keep in touch over the years."

"Can he really be of any help? We're not looking for ancient history here."

"His avocation is keeping track of everything at Yale worth remembering. If something happened here thirty years ago, the Professor will know it."

The taxi dropped them off on College Street and Braxton led Luckett into a grassy valley enclosed by the ivied buildings of Yale's Cross Campus.

"Are you sure this is the right place, Adam?" Luckett asked as they approached an imposing Gothic building. "It looks like a church."

"It's Sterling Memorial Library, Taylor," Braxton replied with a smile. "And you haven't seen anything yet."

Braxton had already noticed a portly gentleman in a sport coat and tie standing like a Beefeater guard at the top of the entrance steps. He took the steps two at a time and stuck out his hand.

"Adam!" the man roared, ignoring the hand and wrapping Braxton in a bear hug. "How good to see you. I was so surprised when I received your phone call."

Braxton extracted himself from the embrace. "Professor Cavendish. Good to see you as well. This is Taylor Luckett, ah, a colleague of mine."

"Mr. Luckett. Very good to meet you." Cavendish downgraded to a hand shake for the reporter. "Now come along inside and tell me more about this important search."

They followed Cavendish through the massive arched wooden doors and into the interior of the library.

"Is this your first time at Yale, Mr. Luckett?" Cavendish asked as they walked down the main aisle.

"Taylor?" Braxton repeated, not hearing a response.

He turned and saw Luckett standing transfixed ten feet behind them just inside the doors.

"It *is* a church," Luckett finally whispered, staring up at the vaulted ceiling sixty feet above their heads.

"No, but it was designed for study and contemplation," Braxton explained after he retraced his steps. "Complete with stone arches, clerestory windows, stone and wood carvings and over three thousand stained-glass windows."

"Actually, there are thirty-three hundred," Cavendish corrected.

Braxton shook his head. "Of course, Professor. But we really should get going. Is there somewhere we can talk? It's quite important."

"Certainly," Cavendish said. "We're going to my favorite lair."

Braxton grabbed Luckett's coat sleeve and pulled him forward. Cavendish led them down the long main aisle, then took a right at the altar—which looked suspiciously like a circulation desk—through a breathtaking limestone cloister to the north wing—and finally into a room marked "Manuscripts and Archives."

It was a quiet, dim reading room where they took seats on opposite sides of a huge oak table. Braxton would have felt uncomfortable carrying on a discussion in the chamber, except for the dearth of students. Looking at his watch, he realized that 10:30 was a little early even for Ivy Leaguers.

"We're looking for someone, or something, having to do with Yale in '82," Braxton began. "Unfortunately that's about all we know. I believe whatever it is, however, was memorable. A famous person, a significant event. Taylor and I are very grateful for any help you can give us, Professor."

"Think nothing of it, Adam. I have missed our discussions over the past few years. I trust you have kept yourself busy?"

"Yes, Professor. A little too busy sometimes. But if we could get started."

"Oh, yes. Now the records are a bit sketchy before nineteen hundred, but I'm sure I can find . . ."

"Excuse me, Professor," Luckett interrupted. "But we're looking for *nineteen* eighty-two. Not eighteen eighty-two."

"Oh." The excitement drained from Cavendish's face. "Nineteen eighty-two?"

"Yes, Professor," Braxton replied. "I'm sorry I wasn't clearer."

"So recent," Cavendish said sadly. "Well, that *will* be significantly easier. We should start with the *Yale Banner*. That's our yearbook. We can branch out to specific clubs and organizations from there. The Class of 1982. Let's see what I can remember."

*　*　*

"Find anything, Taylor?" Braxton asked. In the past half-hour, he and Luckett had gone through a stack of eleven books Cavendish had deposited on their table. "I don't see anything that could connect to . . . our friends."

"Me either. All pretty standard stuff. No familiar faces, no special events."

"These are all the Yearbooks for 1982?" Braxton asked his host.

"Yes, all the Yearbooks and Activities Guides. But I can assure you that a number of very significant events occurred that year. Why there was the dedication of the new statue in the west courtyard, . . ."

"Yes, Professor," Braxton interjected. "I'm sorry. We didn't mean that nothing important happened. Just nothing that fits our parameters."

"I see. Well, are you looking for anyone in particular?"

"I'm afraid I really don't know. It might not even be a *someone*. But something about 1982 was significant."

"Oh," Cavendish replied wrinkling his forehead. "Then you didn't mean the *class* of 1982. You meant the year."

"Well, yes," Luckett replied. "I guess we did."

"Then you shouldn't just look at these. You need to look into the next year too." Cavendish got up and again disappeared into the stacks. When he returned, he dropped another pile of books onto the table.

"Perhaps, these will help," he said.

Luckett shook his head and rubbed his eyes. "Now I remember why I wanted to get out of college so badly," he whispered to Braxton.

"Look at the silver lining, Taylor," Braxton replied. "At least he gets the books for us."

"Professor, Cavendish," Luckett asked as they began their new search. "Do you remember whether there were any significant events in the first semester that year? A violent demonstration? Sit-in?"

"Oh, heavens no. Nothing like that. We had our small demonstrations but nothing untoward. Certainly nothing like those barbarians up north."

"Barbarians?" Braxton asked.

"Yes. In Cambridge."

"Oh, you mean Harvard," Luckett said.

"Sometimes they are so very, well, uncivilized. I have never been able to understand why they are held in such high esteem."

"Yeah, I always wonder about that too," Luckett added.

"It's like The Game," Cavendish said.

"The game?" Braxton asked. "What game?"

"*The* Game." Cavendish looked at the pair as if they were idiots. "The Harvard-Yale game."

"Oh, the football game," Braxton said. God, why can't Cavendish just let us do our work? After two hours of historical ramblings, even he had run out of patience with the academic.

"Of course. We always have a remarkable team. But Harvard has much, well, beefier players, you know." Cavendish's eyebrows crowned in a knowing look. "It's their more liberal admission policy, you know."

"Yes, I see, Professor. But, if you don't mind I think we'd better get back to these yearbooks." Braxton turned back to his book in hopes of shutting the old academic off.

"If you would like I can go back through the archives and see if we have any other details on the teams." Cavendish rose, but continued his discourse on the way to the stacks. "Let's see. I think the newspaper reports would be in section B73 . . ."

"No thank you, Professor. I'm sorry, but I really don't think you need to do that. You have been very helpful, however. Thank you." Braxton buried his head into the doings of the Yale Glee Club.

"Oh. Well, yes. I see." The professor shuffled back to his desk at the front of the room. "It was quite a good game, Adam. Despite the result, of course."

Cavendish was almost past. They were nearly free.

"And that horrid prank. It got most of the publicity."

Braxton's head popped up. "Prank? What prank?"

"Some unruly MIT students tried to disrupt the game. Jealousy, I imagine. It was disgusting."

"What did they do?"

"A big balloon appeared in the middle of the field around halftime and . . ."

"*Halftime?*" Braxton exclaimed.

"It got bigger and bigger then just burst. The foolish affair was over in a few seconds but it was in all the headlines the next day. Can you imagine? It made a mockery of the day."

The consultant got up and put his arm around Cavendish. "Yes. I'm sure it was awful. But perhaps we should have a look at those archives after all."

* * *

Braxton and Luckett spent the next forty five minutes in the microfilm room, searching the newspaper archives for any articles on the ill-fated football game. The professor had been right on one account: while the game itself had received brief coverage in the sports pages—Yale had lost 45 to 7—the MIT prank had made the front page. From the *New Haven Register*, to associated articles in the *Boston Globe* and *Herald American*, the technology students' escapade caught the attention of both communities.

Desiring to take some of the polish off their snobbish neighbors in Cambridge, four fraternity brothers from the Massachusetts Institute of Technology planned a surprise during the Harvard-Yale football game. At a break in play during the second quarter, the stadium attendees observed a black balloon appearing out of the turf near the middle of the field. As it grew bigger, the letters "MIT" painted on the sides became clearly visible. Eventually, after growing to over six feet in diameter, the balloon finally burst, leaving nothing behind but torn shreds of rubber and white talc.

Beyond the sensational headlines, the newspapers continued the story, giving a surprising amount of detail. From what Braxton was able to piece together, the escapade was called a "hack," which was then defined as an elaborate, often technological, prank. Hacks were executed according to a strict code of ethics requiring them to be good-natured, non-destructive, and safe, yet often needing significant planning and engineering finesse.

Could this "hack" be the reference on Gary's note? What could a college student prank have to do with a militia rebellion?

Braxton had asked Cavendish if he knew of any other descriptions of the event and the professor had gone back upstairs. He reappeared ten minutes later holding a worn, oversized paperback book. The title was *The Journal of the Institute for Hacks, Tom Foolery and Pranks at MIT* by the MIT Press. As Braxton thumbed through the pages, he saw that the volume was a testament to the ingenuity of youthful engineering students. It actually brought back memories of his own student days at B.C., although his efforts seemed amateurish compared to changing a hotel marquee to your fraternity's name, reconstructing a campus patrol car on the top of a huge domed building, and creating a stained-glass cathedral in the university's main lobby.

The book had a whole chapter devoted to the Harvard-Yale '82 hack, including additional articles reprinted from the *Globe* that showed the actual construction drawings of the inflation device. It was a six-inch by three-foot cylinder into which was packed the balloon, a Freon canister driving a hydraulic ram, an electric inflation pump, and necessary control valves. Electric power was supplied by one hundred feet of cable that the students had buried under the sod of the field during multiple midnight "raids." The cable had finally been brought to an unused electric circuit in a stadium tool shed. At the chosen moment, it was plugged in by one of the students and the hack initiated.

Braxton couldn't help but think how today students could miniaturize the plan. Tiny pumps run on batteries. Wireless activation. It would still be a fantastic feat.

He stared at the drawing again and realized why it seemed familiar. It looked almost like a sprinkler head. Something that would be used in an irrigation system.

An irrigation system! The signing at the White House. My God!

He grabbed for his cell. There was no signal.

"Where are you going, Adam?" Luckett asked as the consultant raced for the stairway. "I have some other references here."

"I've got to get outside," Braxton yelled back. "I know what's going to happen!"

Chapter 55

"WE'RE TEN MINUTES late already Chad. Were the hell is the DNI?"

The President paced back and forth in front of his desk like a mechanical toy as his Chief of Staff rushed into the Oval Office from the reception area. Matthews hated being late for anything. The only thing he hated more was incompetence on the part of his staff.

"Millie just got a call from him, sir," Dawson began. "He's stuck on I-395. Some kind of accident. He said to go ahead without them."

"Well, wasn't that thoughtful of him. Damn right we'll go ahead without him. Is the Speaker here?"

"Yes, sir. He, the V.P. and SecState are in the hall. Everyone else is outside already."

"Then let's do it, Mr. Dawson. It's time to put another glow on the campaign."

*   *   *

"Slattery."

Slattery had answered his private line with his usual warm greeting. Braxton knew he had to stay calm. He had to make the spook understand.

"It's Adam. Adam Braxton. It's *happening*. Now!" He caught his breath. Calm down. Speak slowly. Blood pounded in his ears.

"Adam? What are you talking about? *What's* happening?"

"The militia. The *Chlamydia*." He couldn't make sentences. Words just popped from his mouth. "Sprinklers in the White House irrigation system. Today. At the signing."

"What are you saying? Are you *sure?*"

"Yes, goddamn it." He was screaming into the phone. "It happened at the Harvard-Yale game in '82. You've got to stop them!"

The line went dead.

* * *

President Matthews stood regally behind his podium as the Prime Minister of Great Britain warbled on about the historic value of the agreement. He would probably invoke the names of Chamberlain and Churchill. It would make for great sound bites.

The Washington weather had cooperated fully: bright yellow sun, clear blue sky, hardly any breeze. A bit humid for some of the other heads of state—Chancellor Kellogg from Germany was constantly squirming in his seat—but Matthews loved it. One of his greatest gifts was the ability to look comfortable under any circumstances, from the frozen steppes of China to the sweltering heat of the Brazilian rain forest. He had conquered them all, including the blistering intensity of the White House Press Briefing Room.

He looked out across the Rose Garden, now filled with the elite of world leaders. It was such an idyllic location. The garden had been trimmed and pruned, washed and watered. Every leaf and bud in its place. He did miss the sweet smell of the lilacs, they wouldn't bloom again until May, but there was a new scent in the air. He couldn't quite place it.

I'll have to check with Millie later. She would surely know.

This would be a landmark day. He could feel it. The agreement would be another ribbon on his chest. Another point the opposition could not refute come November. Yes, they would all remember this day.

Why are all those beepers going off?

* * *

The Commander sat on the edge of the hotel room couch, his eyes fixed on the flat panel TV. Since early that morning he had watched the mind-numbing news reports, the endless procession of dignitaries and the banal speeches leading to the signing.

At each phase his pulse had ratcheted higher. When all the murdering lackeys had been present, he had sent the signal. His heart pounded until he had felt it would surely explode.

Everything had been so perfect: the stolen culture, the militia diversion, the custom atomizer, and the preparation for the event.

What had happened?

Suddenly the participants had jumped up and run from the Rose Garden. They ran like the cowards they were. Away from their destiny.

He threw the half-empty coffee pot by his side at the television screen.

How could his plan have been discovered? It had to be that damn consultant. Well, soon he would be history along with the rest of them.

PART THREE

The Commander

Chapter 56

BRAXTON STEPPED OUT of the elevator at Tysons Tower, his travel bag slung over his shoulder, and trudged down the hall toward his office. It was much too late to be trying to get any work done, but he did have another meeting with Takagawa in the morning. He'd never get up in time to prepare *before* it, so it was now or never. Maybe he could grab a few minutes of sleep on the office sofa.

After the call to Slattery, he and Luckett had gathered all the information on the Harvard-Yale hack, said their thank-you's to Cavendish, and took a cab back to Tweed New Haven Airport. They discovered the next available flight wasn't until 7:30 that evening, so they spent the remaining hours in the Runway Bar nursing a few beers and watching for any news on the signing. At 6:00 Airport CNN had finally announced that the event had been marred by a bomb scare. Everyone had been evacuated, the talking head had reported, but there had been no bomb and no one had been injured. Undeterred by this good news, the anchor had gone back to descriptions of the latest Midwest flooding.

"Well, I guess someone got the message," Braxton had commented. But was their discovery in time?

The flight to National had been another vertigo-inducing turbo prop and neither Braxton nor Luckett had the stomach to carry on a conversation. They spent the flight in silence, each pondering how he would find out what had really happened at the White House. A curt goodbye was all they could muster at National. It was then that he had decided he needed to return to his office.

Braxton fumbled with his ring of keys and finally found the one to his outer office door. Turning the tumbler, he thought he heard a noise. He looked up and down the hall, but saw nothing.

Why did he ever let himself get involved in all this? What he needed most right now was some rest.

He opened the door and groped for the light switch. Chu had left her space as neat as ever. He had to give her a raise this year. She had been doing twice the work of any other assistant he had ever had, and still managed to keep the office presentable.

As he opened the door to his inner office, he saw a flash of light to his right. What was going on?

Braxton pushed back his door and the light from the reception area flooded into his office.

"Jesus Christ!" he exclaimed upon seeing the chaos. Drawers were pulled open and papers thrown all over his desk and the floor. Someone had been ransacking his files!

He jumped at another sound. Someone was *still* here! The noise came from the direction of the connecting conference room. The door was ajar; this was the source of the flash of light. He ran into the room in time to see a form rush out the now open door to the hallway. Without thinking, he took off after the shape.

The flapping of soft-soled shoes echoed through the empty hallway. Braxton's office was at one corner of the huge rectangular building. The elevator and stairway complex sat in the center. The intruder had turned right, probably the way he had initially approached the office; but it was the long way back to his exit. Braxton turned left, then made a quick right down the longer hallway toward the stairs. He would now be nearly even with the trespasser.

Braxton pushed his exhausted body as far as it would go. Faster! He had to find out who this was!

His brain commanded his legs to turn the corner into the elevator cross-aisle, but, in what he would later recognize as a life-saving twist of fate, they wouldn't respond. They were out of control, pumping up and down like the pistons of a runaway steam engine. He overran the near corner, but did manage to lean his body enough to direct his substantial momentum into the wall at the opposite side.

He struck the surface at full speed: first his legs, then his chest, then his head smashed into the unforgiving cold tile. Braxton slid to the floor, unable to move. When he looked up, he was staring up at a slim, black-clad figure holding the biggest silver automatic pistol he had ever seen. The man's face was covered with a ski mask, but his eyes! They were black holes in circles of pure white. His mind screamed for escape but he couldn't draw away from those eyes.

The man slowly raised the automatic and Braxton knew his end had come. All he could think of was Megan. Soon he would be with her again.

In the distance Braxton heard a bell ring. The man with the hollow eyes paused, lowered his gun and walked toward the consultant. Never releasing Braxton from the hold of his hollow eyes, he leaned over and put something in the consultant's shirt pocket.

"Tell your friend I'm back," he whispered through the mask.

He gave Braxton a final wink, and disappeared through the stairway door.

Freed of the mysterious force, Braxton slipped into unconsciousness.

* * *

Slattery squinted through bleary eyes at the flashing red and blue lights ringing the entrance to the Tysons office building. He shook off the hypnotizing effect of the blinkers and searched for his FBI colleague.

As if the excitement at the White House hadn't been enough, Flynn had woken him out of a very sound sleep, barked out a confusing sequence of events, and asked—or was it told—him to meet her. He had apologized to Beth, thrown on what clothes he could find in the dark, and drove off into the night.

Slattery turned onto Tysons One Place and saw a familiar dark Ford sedan. He pulled up behind. Flynn, dressed in a dark-green workout suit and matching FBI cap, met him on the curb.

"Looks like you've got quite a party going, Mary Ellen. What happened?"

"Somebody broke into Adam Braxton's office," Flynn replied. "They were rifling the place when he came back tonight."

"Braxton?" Slattery asked. "I don't know . . ."

"Oh, cut the shit, Roger. I've been talking to Peter. I know all about IMAGER, the Yangs, Braxton, and the *Chlamydia* attack on the White House. You guys are all nuts, you do know that don't you? I told you to be careful. Did you realize IMAGER is an anagram of MIRAGE?"

He shook his head hopelessly. Shit. Robinson's set us all up.

"I called because I wasn't sure what happened to Braxton," she continued.

"Is he okay?"

"As it turns out, yeah. Knocked himself out chasing the intruder. Lucky thing too, he just missed a bullet."

"A bullet? Doesn't sound like your typical break-in. Anything missing?"

"Nothing obvious. From what I heard of the scene, it'll be tomorrow before anybody can make any sense out of the mess."

"Any ID on the shooter?"

"Not yet. The Fairfax County detectives are still trying to get a coherent statement out of Braxton."

Slattery looked across the street to the tower. The three Fairfax County police cars were still standing guard around the entrance. He spotted at least two other FBI cars lurking in the shadows. What wasn't Flynn telling him?

"What brings the FBI out on a simple B&E?"

"Just lucky," Flynn replied. "One of my boys caught it on the radio. I recognized Braxton's name. I didn't know whether it was serious or not, so I called. Sorry to drag you out for nothing."

"Not a problem. I haven't had a good midnight op for years. Oh, how's the injury?"

She flexed her left arm. "Much better, thanks."

"Glad to hear it. You gonna hang around?"

"Maybe for a while. See if we can help out the locals."

"I'll leave it to you then. Goodnight." He turned, headed back to his car, then stopped. "One thing more, Mary Ellen."

"Yes, Roger?"

"Let's keep this little meeting just between us. Braxton's still on the Agency's shit list and I don't need the grief."

Flynn nodded. "Understood," she replied with a smile.

"But I would like to get a look at the police report when you get done."

* * *

"Ouch!" Braxton yelled as a strange man dabbed an alcohol swab on a cut above his right eye. He was lying on the couch in his office watching some kind of paramedic tend to his wounds. Around him, a crowd of men was studying the results of the intruder's search. Two were dressed in Fairfax County Police uniforms and two more wore plainclothes. One was wearing a dark jacket with "FBI" printed on the back.

Holding him forward was Karen Chu.

"Oh just lie still," Chu ordered. "You're acting like a baby. They're trying to help you." She eased his head back down as the EMT took away the painful swab and searched in a briefcase for a bandage.

"Thanks for all the compassion." He pushed his head up from the sofa only to have Chu press him back down, none too softly.

"You are *not* getting up, Adam Braxton," she ordered. "Just lie back and rest."

"You're sure you don't want us to take you to the hospital, sir?" the EMT asked as he taped a bandage across Braxton's forehead. "You really should get that bruise looked at."

"I'm just fine, and I'm not going to any hospital. Thanks for your help though. I do appreciate it."

"Yes, sir. If you have any dizziness, . . ."

"Yes, I know. I'll get it checked out right away."

The paramedic shook his head and packed up his things. Braxton didn't have time to deal with hospitals or doctors. He had to figure out what had happened tonight. And why.

"What time is it anyway?" he asked Chu.

"It's 3:00 a.m."

"3:00 a.m.! What are you doing here?"

"Besides you, my name's the only one on the building's emergency list. The police called me. And *someone* needs to look after you."

"I'm fine. Really."

"You're lucky you're still alive, according to what I heard. Did that thief really try to shoot you?"

"Ah, I don't know. No. I don't remember. The thief. Did he take anything?"

"Not that I can tell so far. But he seemed mostly interested in your desk. You'll have to check that when you're feeling better."

"I can do that . . ." He started to sit up again, but his head began to spin and he collapsed back down even before Chu could get to him.

"Adam Braxton, you stay put. You need to rest. I'll be back in a minute." Chu gathered the discards of the first aid kit and disappeared from his view.

The next hour was spent with the Fairfax Police, specifically a young detective named Wilson. Courteous and thorough, he had taken the consultant's statement, asked a few questions, then returned to the team who were searching the office for any evidence the intruder might have left.

"Mr. Braxton?" Detective Wilson reappeared at Braxton's couch.

"Yes, Detective?"

"We're about ready to go, sir. You going to be alright?"

"Yes, thank you. I'll be fine. Karen will take good care of me. Did you find anything?"

"Well, we took a number of prints but I imagine they will all be yours and Mrs. Chu's. We won't know much more until you have a chance to see if anything is missing. I'll leave my card. Give us a call when you've done an inventory."

"I'll try to get to that later today, Detective. Thank you."

Wilson stepped away then stopped and turned back. "You know, Mr. Braxton, I wish I could be more positive, but it is unlikely that we will be able to find the guy that did this. I'm not aware of any similar B&E's in the area. Security is too tight in these buildings. I also checked the security tapes. There's no record of an intruder. Whoever this guy was, he looks like a pro. You're sure there's nothing valuable here? Something someone would want very badly?"

"Nothing that I know of, Detective. All I have here are work records: Contracts, reports - that kind of thing."

"You're in security, right?"

"I do consulting in information security, yes."

"What about the records of some of your clients? Something that would help someone break into their systems?"

"I suppose someone might think that, but all I have here are summary reports. No secret codes or incriminating files. When I have found security holes, my clients fill them immediately. I can't imagine what anyone would want."

"Well, someone wanted something, Mr. Braxton. Do check your records. And if I were you, I'd be a little more careful for a while."

"Thank you, Detective. I'll certainly try. But I do have one question."

"Yes, sir?"

"Why is the FBI here? They don't usually accompany you on a break-in do they?"

Wilson smiled. "Not hardly. Just professional interest. They were in the building on another case and heard the intruder's shot. They called us after they found you. Lucky coincidence, don't you think? They could have saved your life."

"Oh, yes, Detective. Quite a lucky coincidence."

After Wilson left with the investigation team, Braxton was finally alone with his thoughts. He knew this was not a random break-in. Someone *did* want something from his office and he was afraid he knew what it was. His discovery of the Vision One lab seemed to be public knowledge.

He reached into his pocket and pulled out the card the intruder had put there. It was John Smith's business card; the one from his desk on which he had written Slattery's name. Braxton had decided not to mention the man's message to the police. But what did it mean?

And what was the FBI doing in his building?

Chapter 57

The White House, Washington, D.C.
Thursday, 9:00 a.m.

THE PRESIDENT LOOKED up from the militia intelligence estimate his DNI had just delivered when his Chief of Staff entered. Dawson stopped in the middle of the Seal, waiting like the apocryphal messenger for his punishment. Carlson stood quietly by the side of the Resolute desk.

"Yes, Chad?" Matthews asked.

"The Emergency Response Team from AMRIID has completed their analysis, Mr. President."

AMRIID, the Army Medical Research Institute of Infectious Disease. Better known as the Doctors of Death from Fort Detrick. Matthews knew he wasn't going to like this message.

"And?" the President barked.

"I'm afraid there's no doubt, sir. The *C. Pneumoniae* was released. We found the fake sprinklers. Custom molded. Radio controlled release. Quite sophisticated devices, sir."

"Shit. Everyone was exposed?"

"We have to assume so. The winds were appropriate to carry the microbe over the dignitaries and across the VIP seats."

Jesus. What have those fools done now? Why did we ever start playing with this stuff?

"I have a full list of the attendees, Mr. President," Dawson added. "We'll alert each of them, confidentially of course, as to the possible danger."

Matthews turned his head away from his visitors. He had thought about what he would do all night. God help us all.

"No we will not," the President finally replied.

"What?" Dawson exclaimed.

"I said we are not contacting *anyone*, Chad," Matthews continued. "There's no way to know you've been exposed. Right, Steven?"

"Yes, that's what Dr. Hawthorne believes," Carlson replied. "The only symptoms look like the flu."

"Then we're not notifying anyone. What are we going to say? 'Hello, Prime Minister MacAlister. You were just exposed to an incurable disease. You've probably got two weeks to live. Hope you had a nice visit.' How will it look if seven of the world's leaders are assassinated in Washington? We would lose all credibility in our foreign policy. We'd be a pariah." Matthews hung his head and drove his fingertips into his temples. How could this have happened?

"Has everyone bought into the bomb threat?"

"It would appear so," Dawson said. "That was enough of a shock."

"Good. Let everybody be shocked. It will keep them occupied. Who discovered the plot?"

"Slattery from the CIA," Carlson responded. "You met him at the briefing. He called the Secret Service crisis line."

"Well I'm glad someone is doing their job. Make sure he gets a citation or something." Matthews stood and looked down on his visitors. "The reality of this attack does not leave this room. Chad, you keep the White House secure. Work the Service through Bigelow. Make up some interesting story for the press. Steven, you make sure the Response Team keeps their mouths shut. And the CIA. Confiscate the reports."

Matthews turned and stared out the windowed wall of the Oval Office, across the lawn where his home, the country's home, had been defiled. What more could any of them have done?

"I only have one more question," he said without moving. "Do we have an antidote for this thing?"

"Mr. President," Carlson replied. "Dr. Hawthorne said that . . ."

"I remember what she said. I also know that more crap goes on at Fort Detrick than even SecDef Sorenson knows. Find the answer, Steven. If you don't, forget what's going to happen to the rest of the world. Think of what's going to happen to this country."

* * *

Braxton shook his head and forced his eyes open. Jesus, he hadn't even realized he was dreaming. Hadn't he just been talking to

Karen? Then he had been running through a dark tunnel. Flashes of light were all around him. Why had he been running? Was he running after someone? Or away from someone? He couldn't remember.

He glanced down at his watch: 1:00 p.m. Damn, the day was half gone.

He pulled himself up and spun on his butt, carefully setting his feet on the carpet. Jesus his head hurt! He looked around at the disaster that had struck his office. The intruder had been bad enough, but the Fairfax cops had made it worse. Now there was dust everywhere and a horrible chemical smell. He had better start cleaning up.

His legs weren't nearly as sore as his head and they successfully raised his body to vertical. After a brief moment of vertigo, his head cleared and he began a slow survey of his office. He had apparently interrupted the intruder as he was going through the desk: the drawers were still open and papers had been tossed across the floor. It would take him the rest of the day to clean up this mess.

"Adam! What are you doing?"

Braxton jumped at the voice and spun around, grabbing for his desk to keep from falling over. Chu stood in the doorway.

"My God, Karen, what are you trying to do, frighten me to death?"

"I heard a noise," she answered sheepishly.

"I didn't think you were here. You haven't been here all night have you?"

"Well, yes. I couldn't just leave you alone."

Braxton shook his head at her dedication. He really didn't deserve her. "I'm fine now. So you can go home. Russell must want to kill me."

"Russell's not getting home until five. I'll finish up a couple reports and then go. But you should go home yourself."

"I managed to get some sleep, actually. I'll just check my mail and straighten up the office. Tell anybody that calls I'm out."

"Okay." She smiled a "that's what mothers are for" smile and turned to go back to her desk.

"Karen?" Braxton called.

"Yes?"

"I'm really sorry you had to come in. But . . . thanks for last night."

She nodded. "I'm glad I could be here, Adam. Are you really okay? Is there anything else going on?"

Damn. She could sense his problems better than he did. He couldn't get her caught up in this mess.

"Not now, Karen," he replied softly. "Give me a chance to get settled. We'll talk later."

Chu disappeared into the front office, and Braxton returned to the disaster that was his desk. He carefully knelt down, picked up a handful of papers, and piled them on an empty spot on his desk. Then he took a few more steps and picked up more sheets, returning them to the same pile.

Fifteen minutes later he sat exhausted in his chair, looking at two feet of paper wondering how he could have ever squirreled away that much in three rather small desk drawers. He was tempted to simply throw the whole pile in the wastebasket—how valuable could they be? —but thought better of it, and began to scan each page for its relevancy.

He had barely started when Chu's voice came over the intercom.

"Adam, Mr. Smith is on the phone. He says he needs to talk with you."

Smith? Oh, Slattery. Wonder what took him so long?

"Sure, Karen. I'll take it."

He punched a glowing button. "Braxton."

"Adam. I just heard about the break-in. Are you alright?"

"Just a little bruised. I'm fine."

"What did they want?"

"No idea. There doesn't seem to be anything missing."

"Well, I'm really glad you're okay. You take care of yourself now."

That's all? Nothing about the White House? Where's my "thank you for saving the country, Adam"?

"Uh, Mr. Smith! Wait."

"Yes, Adam?"

"About the bomb scare. Was the alert in time?"

"Bomb? Oh, at the White House. Yes, everything is fine. Lucky it was only a false alarm."

"Yeah. Lucky. Well, I'm pretty tired right now. But there is one other thing. Do you know anyone with albino eyes?"

"Albino eyes?"

"Yeah. Eyes with no color."

"Not that I can think of. Why?"

"Oh, just someone I met. Thanks for the call."

"Uh, sure. Hope you're feeling better."

Braxton slammed down the phone in disgust. No thanks. No congratulations. No nothing. *He* knew the attack was real. But they weren't going to admit it. The bastards.

Why did I ever expect anything else from them?

As he tried to calm down, his eyes wandered to the small refrigerator sitting in the corner. He had avoided checking for the file, preferring to believe the intruder was a common burglar. But there was no hiding the reality of the break-in. The detective had said he was a pro. And Braxton had seen the cold dedication in the hollow eyes.

He limped over to the appliance, reached under it, and pulled out the small drainage tray. Taped to the bottom in a plastic freezer bag was the Vision One file. With the *C. Pneumoniae* diagrams and Braxton's notes from his Internet search. This was what the intruder was after. He was sure. This was what may have already taken countless lives.

Braxton opened the file. What had he missed? What should he do with it now?

*   *   *

Slattery sat at his desk rubbing a tired set of eyes. He hadn't gotten back to sleep until 2:00 a.m. and had been back in Langley at 8:00.

The latest intelligence findings on militia activity lay strewn over his desk. Things had been frighteningly quiet since the Tyler raid. The FBI had a few more leads now, but how many other groups were still hidden? Waiting for their moment to rise up and strike.

He felt so helpless. They had to find this Gary.

The call to Braxton had been a horrible mistake. He was sure the consultant hadn't believed either his concern, which was real, or his White House explanation, which, of course, wasn't. And what did his question about the strange eyes mean? It couldn't be . . .

His private phone rang. "Slattery," he grunted.

"Roger, Steven Carlson."

Jesus! The DNI.

What have I done now?

"General. Good afternoon."

"Steven, please. It's only appropriate after all we've been through. I just came from a meeting with the President. He wanted me to express our thanks for your alert yesterday. Someday you'll have to tell me how you figured it out."

"Uh, yes sir. Certainly. Thank you." Too bad it was a black-listed civilian who discovered it. "I just wish we could have uncovered the plan sooner."

"So do we all, Roger. Has anyone taken any responsibility for the . . . bomb scare?"

"No sir. I was just going over the FBI militia reports. There doesn't seem to be any response. We need to keep working to tie the White House attack to these extremists."

"Well, that's another reason for my call, Roger. Both the President and I feel that it's very important that we keep this whole affair under wraps for now. There are global security issues we must evaluate. I'd like to ask you not to repeat anything of this activity."

"I certainly agree with your assessment, sir, but I have to report . . ."

"Nothing, Roger. No reports. No findings. We can't afford to have any record. And don't worry about Peter. I'm meeting with him later this afternoon. Does that cover it?"

"Yes, sir. That about covers it," Slattery said with a bit of an edge.

The phone went silent. All he heard was calm regular breathing. Shit! What did he think he was doing playing smart-ass with the DNI?

"I appreciate your trepidation, Roger," Carlson finally said. "But this is an extraordinary situation which requires extraordinary measures. I expect you will discuss this with Peter. He's a good man."

What could he say? Carlson *had* covered all the bases.

"Yes, General. I understand. Thank you for your call."

"And thank you, Roger," Carlson concluded. "Be assured that we will remember your contribution."

Slattery stared into the phone. Was that a promise or a threat?

* * *

Braxton was halfway through the last pile of paper on his desk when he heard a knock and looked up to see Chu in the doorway.

"I'm sorry to bother you, Adam. But I think you need to see this. She had a FedEx package in her hand.

"I'm kinda tired, Karen. Maybe later."

"You need to look at this, Adam. It's *very* important."

Her voice had an urgency that scared him. "Sure," he replied. "Of course."

When she brought the package to his desk, he saw that she had already opened it. It was a single sheet of paper: a business letter on Lockheed-Martin letterhead. Scanning the content, his eyes locked on one particular paragraph:

```
... Due to unforeseen business changes, we regret
that we must terminate our consulting contract with
you effective today. Please return all confidential
materials in your possession as soon as possible.
Our contracts administrator will contact you
regarding outstanding invoices. We are sorry . . .
```

"What the hell are they doing!" he yelled. "This is a hundred thousand dollar contract! We just started it."

"That's why I thought you'd want to see it," she replied firmly.

He had to calm down. This was *his* problem, not hers. The meetings in Pentagon City had gone perfectly. He had done all the right things: clarified the problem, identified the influencers, met with the decision makers, and answered the objections. They had been anxious to get started on the security review. What had gone wrong?

"Of course, Karen. I'm sorry I snapped at you."

"Should I call Kevin?"

Kevin O'Malley was Braxton's corporate attorney. "Yes. And fax him the letter."

"But it won't help, will it?"

"Probably not. The contract says thirty days' notice, but it would cost more to fight Lockheed than we'd ever get. It's just gone. What the hell happened?"

Chu stood uncomfortably, shifting her weight from one foot to the other. "I think I know," she said quietly.

"You know? How?"

"I have a neighbor, Trudy. She's a contracts manager at Lockheed Federal now. I called her when I saw the letter."

"What did she say?"

"She didn't want to get involved, Adam. I had to pull in some very old IOUs. You have to promise not to use her name, *ever.*"

"I promise, Karen; I promise. What did she say?"

"It came from their funding agency. The Pentagon. They dropped some hints that they didn't like your name on the consultants list. It doesn't take long for something like that to have an effect."

The Pentagon. DoD. Carlson. Vision One. It was a chain that was trying to drag him into an abyss. His head dropped into his hands.

Chu stepped back into her office and silently closed the door behind her.

God, why does everything happen at once?

Chapter 58

Cerberus Consulting, Tysons Corner, Virginia
Thursday, 5:15 p.m.

BRAXTON HAD HAD enough. There was no way he was going to get anything more accomplished today. He picked up his briefcase and began collecting some papers, more out of habit than a belief he'd get any work done at home.

Finished stuffing the files inside, he closed the top of the case and saw a man standing in his office doorway.

"Jesus, Slattery! Can't you just knock?"

"Sorry, Adam. But we have to talk. I saw your secretary leave, and came up. This *is* better than the parking garage isn't it?"

Braxton latched his case and set it on the floor. "I guess you recognized my message after all. That is what this is about isn't it?"

"The man with the albino eyes is the one that attacked you?"

"All business now, huh? Okay, we'll make this short. I'm very tired, and I'm very angry. Yes, he had albino eyes. And he pointed a very big gun at me. Then he said, 'tell your friend I'm back' and stuck your card in my pocket."

"My card? How did he . . ."

"He found it on my desk. Bad luck, I guess. That's it. I presume you won't tell me who he was, so I won't ask. I've given you the message. Now I'm going home."

He picked up his briefcase and walked indignantly past the agent.

"Lock up when you're through." On the way out the door he turned. "You know, Slattery, you're no better than he is."

* * *

"Braxton," he groaned into the telephone. Looking over to his alarm clock he saw it was only 8:45 p.m. It felt like the middle of the night.

After the confrontation with Slattery, he had taken a taxi home. There was no way he could have faced Northern Virginia traffic in the state he had been in. He had taken a shower and collapsed into bed. All he had wanted was a good night's sleep.

"Adam! Are you alright?"

The soft female voice was all too familiar. It was Susan Goddard. His stomach started to twist which only made his head hurt more.

"Oh. Hello, Susan."

"I heard about the break-in on the TV. Is everything okay?" Her voice sounded dry and raspy.

"Yes. I'm fine. Just bruised up a bit. It was stupid trying to chase him."

"Do you know who it was? What he wanted?"

"Ah, no. No idea at all. Probably just someone looking for some office equipment to steal."

"Adam, I hate to ask, but you're not mixed up in anything are you? I mean the incident in Amsterdam and now this."

Leave it to Susan to cut to the bone. He had to change the subject.

"Nothing but a string of bad luck, Susan. How about you? You sound a little hoarse."

"Just a touch of the flu. Probably working too hard."

"You running everything on the Hill yet?"

"Not hardly. I can barely keep up with the Senator."

"Tell him to take it easy on you," Braxton said. "You deserve a break."

"Senator Lexington's really great, actually. He even invited me to the White House yesterday."

Yesterday? No. It couldn't be. "The White House? When, Susan?"

"For the intelligence agreement signing. I'm sure you heard about the bomb scare. Wasn't it awful? Who would do something like that?"

"I . . . I really don't know. I'm pretty tired, Susan. I think I better call it a night."

"Oh. Of course. I'm sorry, Adam. I just wanted to make sure you were okay."

"I'm glad you called. But please take care of yourself. I hear there's some really bad bugs out there."

"Don't worry. I'm sure it's just one of those three-day things. Call me when you get feeling better, Adam. It would be nice to see you again."

"Yeah. Me too, Susan. Good night."

Braxton set the receiver back in the cradle. Why did she have to be there? He knew his discovery had been too late. He had heard it in Slattery's voice.

Goddamit! He couldn't let this happen to her. She had saved his life once. He had to try to save hers.

He reached for the phone.

* * *

He had started with D.C. Capitol Hill, Georgetown. They would be ideal for the gregarious Miss Walker. Lots of Sam's. Lots of Steve's. Even a Sarah or two. But no Sydney and no S. Walker.

Perhaps only Sydney Marino was outgoing. Not Sydney Walker. She *had* seemed much more subdued in his apartment. He picked up the phone and began relentless badgering of the Northern Virginia 411 operator.

There had been five S. Walkers in Fairfax County, and all had been misses. Two more in Arlington County and three in Alexandria County. Also misses. Frustrated, he moved on to the Maryland operator.

Listing number four in Bethesda was ringing.

"Hello."

Pay dirt.

"Good evening, Sydney," he said in his most upbeat tone. "It's Adam."

"Adam? . . . Oh! Adam. The newscast. I heard . . ."

"Yes, yes. I'm fine. They missed again. We need to talk. Now."

"Now?"

"Yes. *Now.*"

* * *

The Legal Sea Foods in Tyson's Galleria was busy but sedate at 9:30 p.m. The twenty-somethings had departed to more social surroundings leaving the restaurant to the serious diners. The couple had started with a round of drinks: Walker opted for a glass of Chardonnay while Braxton ordered a double Talisker.

"It's good to see you again, Adam. I hated the way we left it."

He still couldn't decide whether he could believe anything the woman said. But he was running out of options. He had to take the chance.

"I need to know something," he asked abruptly.

"Okay, what?"

"Do you know what happened at the White House?"

"The White House? What do you mean? When?"

"At the signing."

"Oh. You mean the bomb scare. Who could have done such an awful thing? Thank God it was only a hoax."

He watched her face. The huge dark eyes, the gentle curve of her nose, the smooth, sensuous lines of her lips. God, she was good. Would he even know if she *was* lying?

"It wasn't a hoax, Sydney. It was real. Someone released the *Chlamydia* during the ceremony."

"What!" Her voice leapt above the casual dinner conversation. She glanced quickly around, then lowered her tone to a whisper. "Who . . . who would do such a thing?"

"Are you ready to order?"

Their heads snapped up to see a young, well-scrubbed waiter standing alongside the table.

"Ah, yes," Braxton replied. "Sydney?"

Walker ordered a Seafood Caesar Salad and Braxton seconded the choice. He wasn't up to making any more decisions tonight.

"No one knows who's responsible," the consultant continued after their waiter was safely out of earshot. "The FBI and CIA are trying to make a connection to those militia attacks. They think the bacteria was cultured on a farm in Georgia."

"But Amsterdam, we saw . . ."

"Yes. That's what keeps bothering me."

"It could just be a coincidence," she said. Her voice had changed. It was calm, analytical. "It might have nothing to do with Vision One."

"Maybe. But I'm not convinced. Do your bosses know about the exposure?"

"I don't know. I told you, I'm not on anybody's most-likely-to-succeed list right now. But I haven't heard any rumors either."

"Then nobody is talking to anyone else." His voice was getting louder, but he couldn't stop himself. "DoD is so spooked over our little escapade that they're stone-walling everybody else. And the CIA and FBI are so obsessed with the militia threat they're blind to Vision One."

Walker slowly set her knife and fork on the side of her plate. When she looked up, Braxton knew he was about to be interrogated.

"Why the concern now, Adam? You knew about all this last week and you didn't give a damn. Or so you said. I doubt this is some abiding concern over the people in the current administration."

"Actually you're wrong. This *is* about people." Or at least one person. "I don't care if nobody else wants to do anything. I'm not going to just sit around when I *can* do something."

"But what, Adam? What can you do?"

"I don't know yet. But I'm sick of all this political bullshit, Sydney. I'm sick of nobody caring why Megan was murdered, I'm sick of being chewed out by Carlson, and I'm *really* sick of your bosses trying to ruin my business."

"What!"

"DoD is telling all their contractors to quit doing business with me. This is now *very* personal. I'm going to find out who killed Megan, and I'm going to find out what happened to that *Chlamydia* antibiotic."

He could feel the blood rushing to his face. Attacking Walker wouldn't get him anywhere. He paused and took a deep breath.

"But I need your help."

His companion considered the request with a calculating calm. It seemed like an eternity.

"Well, it's not like I've got a lot of other things I'm working on," Walker replied with a smile. "What do you want me to do?"

* * *

"Would you like anything else, sir?"

The young waitress stood before him, impatiently tapping her pencil on the order pad. His hazel eyes looked up at her, noticing her attention dart across the aisle. She had already written off the tip from this overworked businessman and was sizing up the opportunities elsewhere. His was not a face she would remember.

"No, thank you," Gary replied. "Just leave the check please."

She dropped the slip on the table and moved promptly to a well-dressed quartet on his right. As always, contact lenses made him invisible.

The consultant certainly did get around. Gary had followed him over the past twenty-four hours: the chaos at his office, his trip home, and now a late night rendezvous with this woman. A friend, but not a close one. There was caution in both their demeanors. It could have been a first date, but they were much too serious. The conversation was subdued, accusatory, not meant to impress or console.

A business colleague perhaps? Or something more ominous? Someone with whom to share information?

He had only been asked to search for information. Somehow the consultant may have gotten access to background on *C. Pneumoniae*. There had been nothing in his apartment or office, although he had to admit Braxton's arrival was ill-timed. He had not had time to cover his presence. The shot had been simply a warning, something to distance him from the nosy consultant.

But where had the cavalry come from? He had had barely enough time to exit through the service entrance before the cops and FBI arrived. Who could have called them? And what was the FBI doing at a simple breaking-and-entering? You'd think he had broken into the White House.

Then there was the card. How could *he* be connected to this consultant? But then he had been there. Gary had seen his face.

He shook his head to knock the image out of his mind. He had waited so long. Maybe it was time to repay the old debts.

Braxton and his companion rose to leave. Gary folded a small stack of bills, placed them over the check, and picked up his coat. He doubted there would be any late-night liaison between this pair. It was time to drop the consultant and investigate more interesting possibilities.

Chapter 59

"THANK YOU ALL for coming," Carlson began, standing at the front of the conference table. "I apologize for the hastily called meeting, but events have out-stepped our ability to adequately communicate plans and strategies. It is critically important that we continue to coordinate our activities and not duplicate efforts. Mary Ellen, would you please begin with a summary of the FBI's investigation?"

Slattery watched Flynn confidently stride to the front of the room. Amid the escalating crises, Carlson seemed to have forgotten about the punitive deadline he had forced on the Special Assistant.

"In the week since the raid on the Tyler farm," Flynn began, "we have traced connections to twenty-five other militia cells in ten states." The map behind the Special Assistant revealed the locations in glowing red circles. "In fifteen cases we discovered evidence that linked the cell to one of the militia attacks. We are continuing to investigate additional cells, but personally, I believe we have identified all of the cells that participated in the assaults."

"Was there any commonality in the cells, Mary Ellen?" asked Garcia.

"Some, Jerry. All the cells were small, and relatively isolated in the overall militia movement. Their views were extreme and had a history of violence against authority, principally the Federal Government. It was clear they were selected only after a very thorough analysis."

"What about this Gary?" Carlson asked. "Was he involved with all the cells?"

"At first we didn't think so. Their contacts all had different names. Terry, Mike, Oren. And never a last name. But then we started building a profile. It was always the same man. He used different names, but it was always the same man. The coordinator is our Gary."

Something finally clicked in Slattery's head. He looked over to the map then down to his notes. Could he have missed the connection?

"Is there any progress on identifying him?" Stroller asked.

"Nothing yet. We're still cross checking fingerprints from his various motels, but all we have are undifferentiated partials at best. The profile has been sent to every law enforcement agency in the country, as well as Interpol. He won't escape, and we've completely disconnected him from his cells."

"The cells you know about," Stroller added.

"*All* of his cells, Claude," Flynn responded firmly. "He's impotent. It's only a matter of time until we locate him." She reached into the folder in front of her and pulled out a sheet of paper. "We just completed a new sketch of Gary. Tony will pass copies around. It's already on the wire to every field office in the country."

"What about the bomb threat at the White House, Mary Ellen?" Delacroix asked. "Is there any connection?"

Slattery glanced over at Carlson. He was stone-faced. Maybe he *had* been able to put a lid on the *C. Pneumoniae* attack.

"Not that we can determine at this time, Admiral. The evidence on the source of the scare is so sketchy we have no reason to believe the events are connected. If there are no further questions," Flynn said picking up her papers, "that's all I have at the moment. I will be sure to update all of you with any breaking news."

"Thank you very much, Mary Ellen," Carlson said. His demeanor was uncharacteristically cordial. "Unfortunately, until we catch this Gary, I'm afraid that many of our questions will remain unanswered. Jerry, could you update us on Homeland activity?"

"Of course, General," Garcia responded.

Slattery only half-listened to the succeeding updates from Garcia and Delacroix, instead staring intensely at the artist's sketch of their nemesis. He felt sick to his stomach. It wasn't the taut, young face he remembered but it had been seven years. He dropped his head to his hands and rubbed his eyes until they screamed for relief.

Flynn had provided two tantalizing clues. But it was only circumstantial. He'd have to address the one discrepancy personally.

"If there are no other updates," Carlson's voice broke through Slattery's concentration. "Despite Mary Ellen's reservations, I'd like to stress the importance of determining the linkage, if there is any, between the militia attacks and the White House bomb threat. I expect all of you to report any progress to my office and the other group members. We will be on emergency schedule until you are notified otherwise. Thank you."

There were a few glances around the table, but Carlson made a prompt exit, and the other members slowly filed out. Slattery held back, waiting until Flynn had sent her entourage on their way. It seemed she wanted to talk as well.

"What's up, Roger?" Flynn asked. "You've been watching me all morning. I will assume it's not my new outfit."

Slattery quickly checked out the Special Assistant's dark blue pinstripe suit. Trim, and packed in all the right places. His reaction, or lack of one, was simply another sign of his impending senility.

"Sorry, Mary Ellen," the agent replied, "It's a lovely suit. But a couple of things you said hit a nerve. Where did Gary use those aliases?"

"Let's see, Terry in Chattanooga, Oren in Eugene, Mike in Grand Rapids, . . ."

"So it was Gary in Georgia, Terry in Tennessee, Oren in Oregon, and Mike in Michigan?"

"Well, yes. That is rather interesting isn't it? I thought he was just using Senator's first names."

A shiver went up Slattery's spine. He had to find out.

"I noticed you didn't give Gary's eye color. No one remembered?"

"Certainly they did. There were a few discrepancies, but we're sure his eyes were colorless. Some kind of crazy albino mutation."

Albino eyes! God, it *was* him. Slattery looked back down at the facsimile. It had always been the eyes.

He was shaking with anger. How much time had they lost already?

"You never said anything about his eyes," Slattery accused.

"Of course we did," Flynn replied. "It's in the bulletins."

"I've *read* the bulletins, Mary Ellen. Eye color was 'NA', not available. Here, I pulled this off Intelink this morning."

He held out a sheet of paper and she grabbed it away from him.

"Shit! Somebody didn't understand 'None' so they put in 'NA.' I'll send the damn clerk to Frozen Toe, Alaska. We'll get it fixed." She looked up and gasped. "You okay, Roger? You look like you've seen a ghost."

"Singer," Slattery whispered.

"What did you say?"

"Gary. His name is Singer, Alfred Whitehead Singer. I worked with him at the Farm. And he was the one that attacked Braxton."

Flynn's perfectly-shaped mouth fell wide open.

*   *   *

Vision One was the key. Braxton knew it. Somehow Megan's death was tied into that laboratory and *C. Pneumoniae*. But who could have had her killed? And why?

Yesterday he had meticulously gone through the Vision One web site, but it was nothing but marketing fluff and self-congratulatory rhetoric. He needed to know about what made the company tick.

One of his friends had once said, "When all else fails, follow the money." So that was what he did.

He had logged onto the SEC site and pulled down everything they had on the company. The filings for Vision One's Initial Public Offering had been a treasure chest of goodies. Between the corporate hype and the legal disclaimers he found details on the Founders, Board of Directors, facilities, and consultants. No wonder DoD was after him, they practically ran Vision One. The lists of Army, Navy, and Air Force brass read like a Joint Chiefs' Christmas party guest list.

Venton still controlled 30% of the company himself, however. There was no way anything went on without his knowledge, especially that laboratory. Who else would have that information? And whose side was he really on?

It had been time to dig a little deeper on Paul Venton.

So he had spent most of last night filling out a dossier on the Chairman and President of Vision One. He had extracted information from the web sites of the Library of Congress, DoD,

DoE, and NSF. There were five private sites in the US and Europe devoted to customers of Vision One, and even one site that purported to know all the "secrets" of Vision One's clandestine support of FEMA's shadow government.

Once he moved away from the corporate information, however, he was stymied. He knew there were people that claimed they could get anything on an individual electronically, but unfortunately he wasn't one of them.

This morning, he had finally stacked up the sheets of printouts and slid them into a manila folder. This was not an area where he had the requisite expertise.

Fortunately, he knew someone who did.

* * *

"How are you feeling, Mr. President?" Dawson asked as he walked into the Lincoln Bedroom.

"Like shit, Chad," replied Matthews. "How do I look?"

"Ah, a little brighter than yesterday, sir."

"You'll never make a politician, Chad. You're a terrible liar."

Matthews lay quietly but uncomfortably in the huge four poster bed, staring out at his Chief of Staff through a tent of hazy plastic. The team from Walter Reed had transformed the famous bedroom into a makeshift isolation ward. He had learned that even as President, he was ruled by the laws of modern medicine. The bedsheets were harsh and scratchy. The air under the tent was stale and smelled of balms and antiseptics. Even his voice, which had grown steadily weaker, was now metallic and flat, picked up by a miniature CIA microphone and amplified by a modified Secret Service receiver.

The distortions of his world through this protective curtain had increased over the past few days, and he didn't know whether they were due to the aging of the material or his own deteriorating mental state.

Dawson's eyes wandered over the bedside table and its pyramid of medicine bottles.

"They've got me on another cocktail of antibiotics," Matthews explained. "A mouthful of horse pills six times a day. They even wake me up in the middle of the night. I'm beginning to think they're all quacks."

"Your physicians are the best in the country, Mr. President. In the world. They're doing everything they can."

"I know, I know. It's just so damn frustrating." He coughed and felt the painful contractions pulse across his chest. A wad of phlegm pushed through his bronchi and lodged in his throat. He fought the urge to spit it out and swallowed hard.

His head dropped back onto the pillow. He was so tired. "Our own bug, Chad. *Our bug*! What the hell were they thinking?"

Dawson stood quietly, leaving the question to dissipate in the air.

"Any news from Fort Detrick?" the President asked, sitting back up to face his Chief of Staff.

"They're working on the new antibiotic. There's some real progress. We just have to give them a bit more time."

"I have always valued your frank opinions, Chad. Don't start with D.C. double-speak now. Translation: they don't have a goddamn clue. We're on our own. What's happening with the other members of the signing party?"

"We're trying to keep the investigation as low key as possible, of course. Of the sixty-five US government officials we have determined that fifty-two have demonstrated symptoms. Thirty-one are sufficiently incapacitated to be unable to go to their workplace. This includes five members of the Supreme Court, ten members of the House, and seven Senators. All of the signators except LaRoche have significantly reduced their public appearances. There does seem to be some correlation with age. I'm sorry, sir."

Matthews waved off the apology. "At least you seem to have come through okay."

"So it appears, Mr. President. There are times when I do feel, well, a little guilty about that."

Matthews considered the confession. He could not let his disability destroy his team. They were all that now stood against the forces of anarchy.

"You must never let that affect you, Chad. None of us is prescient. We must accept God's will and move ahead." He felt another wave of fatigue and fell back into the soft pillow. "How could we have let this happen?"

"There was nothing we could have done, Mr. President. Short of locking you up in a bombproof room for your term. That's the horror of terrorism. It strikes at our greatest weakness: our openness."

"Which is also our greatest strength, Chad. Never forget that. What has happened here may result in personal tragedies, but it must never be allowed to weaken our resolve to lead the world into freedom."

Enough flowery eulogies, dammit. You're still President, act like it.

"Call Steven. I'd like to go over the intelligence daily with him."

Chapter 60

"GARY'S REAL NAME is Singer, Alfred Whitehead Singer." Slattery was addressing a team of twenty agents in the FBI conference room. He recognized Carol Courington and Tony Lasalle from their previous meeting. Flynn sat calmly in the back of the room. "Manny, please give everyone a copy of the file. This is Singer's personnel file. Some confidential agency data has been purged, but otherwise you've got everything we do.

"Singer's father was a Yale philosophy professor. Alfred North Whitehead, the famous English philosopher, was his idol. Gave the name to his son the way you'd name a prize. Unfortunately, the father died when Singer was three. He was then raised by his mother, an elementary school teacher. She smothered him, and he never developed what we could call normal social skills. His shyness, coupled with an apparent ease at achieving scholastic success, was seen by his peers as an aloof superiority that even more alienated him. He always saw himself as an outsider.

"Singer was a trouble-maker at school but bright, and won a scholarship to Princeton. His profile was perfect and we recruited him when he was twenty-one. Selected for special ops duty at twenty-five. Clandestine operations, overseas duty in the Middle East, Southeast Asia, South America. Did his job very well. Retired seven years ago. That's what's in the file.

"Now what's *not* in the file. Singer liked his job too much. Got a thrill out of the op, turned paranoid whenever we brought him out. The albino eyes were a detriment, too easy to remember, but he was damn good. He proposed some rather unorthodox missions and was retired. We had heard rumors he was free-lancing but ignored them. Our mistake. He's smart, tough, and utterly amoral. You can't trust anything he says. He had a pretentious affectation to pick his cover name based on his location. It was his signature. I always felt it would get him killed someday."

"Any ideas how to catch him, Roger?" Flynn asked.

"We can't be sure that the op is over. If you *have* shut down his militia cells, it will cut off his ability to execute. That will leave Singer and his Commander. It's an opportunity to catch his boss. But he's on the run. He'll try to disappear. We need to get him before that happens."

"Can't be that hard to find a psychopath with albino eyes," commented a young female agent.

"Do not underestimate this man," Slattery ordered. His eyes drilled into the agent. "He can act as normal as anyone. And your different informants were correct; he changes his eye color at will with colored contact lenses. He only leaves them out when he *wants* to be remembered."

The agent shrunk back in her chair from the reprimand. Another lesson learned, Slattery hoped.

"Agent Slattery," asked Tony Lasalle. "You seem to know a lot about Singer. Did you work with him?"

Slattery paused. How honest did he really need to be? "Yes. He was in my class at the Farm. He scared me even then. I was also his last case officer." *And I was the one that forced his retirement.*

After a few moments of silence, Flynn rose to take back control of the briefing. "That's all for now. Roger, thank you very much for taking the time to brief us. Now it's our turn. Carol, I want copies of Singer's file to all the field teams in an hour. We don't have long to catch this bastard. Now move!"

"One last thing," Slattery added. "Singer is extremely dangerous. He will not be taken alive."

Slattery let the implication hang in the air as the agents slowly filed out. He motioned to Ikedo and the junior agent followed.

"Okay, Roger," Flynn said after everyone had left. "How do you know it was Gary at Braxton's?"

"Braxton told me. Gary found my card on his desk. Told the consultant to tell me he was back."

"Shit. There wasn't anything in the report!"

"Yeah. He didn't tell the cops. Didn't mention the eyes either. Braxton can be a real pain in the ass sometimes."

"I oughta throw his ass in jail."

"Maybe later, Mary Ellen. For now, tell me why you *really* were at his apartment."

She wrinkled her forehead, then cracked a half-hearted smile. "I'm sorry, Roger. But what I have to tell you can't leave this room. We were at Braxton's because we knew someone was going after him."

"You knew? How?"

"We picked it up from Garrett Robinson's phone."

The realization took only a second. "You tapped the phone of an NSA employee?"

"Damn right we did." The smile disappeared. "Every goddamn phone we could find. The bastard's been stonewalling everybody about IMAGER."

"Wait a minute. I know Carlson found out about the IMAGER ploy. So Garrett was playing games, covering his ass. That doesn't give you the right to tap his phone."

"He didn't *lose* the decryption capability, Roger. He's had it all along. He just buried the intel after Yang died. I got the tap because we knew he'd been lying to everyone."

Slattery remembered what Tak Yang had said: his brother's supervisor was keeping information to himself.

"But why? Why would he keep the messages secret?"

"Isn't he mister schemes within schemes? I can't imagine why. But that's what I'm going to find out."

The edge on Flynn's voice would have cut through steel. What else was going on here?

Flynn looked up as a man walked by the door to the conference room. He gave a thumbs-up sign.

"What's that about?" Slattery asked.

"We're going to check out Robinson's apartment. Want to come?"

"His apartment! You got a search warrant?" She grinned and nodded. The pleasure on her face was absolutely frightening. "Sure. Can I bring Manny?"

"Love to have him along," Flynn replied.

* * *

"Don't you *ever* eat anything healthy?" Braxton asked, putting down his tray of Chicken Caesar Salad. Across the table in the Tysons Tower cafeteria, Luckett was devouring two of the greasiest pieces of pepperoni pizza the consultant had ever seen.

"Hi, Adam. I'm really glad you called. It's good to get out and have a real meal for a change. You know pizza has all three of the most important food groups: bread, cheese and meat. It's the perfect meal. *That*," he pointed to Braxton's tray, "on the other hand, is nothing but rabbit food."

"Let's debate nutrition another time, Taylor. It's been a long week. How are things at the *Post*?"

"With no more militia attacks, I'm back to working on the latest corruption charges from the Mayor's office. Lots to do but nothing very exciting."

"What's the take on the White House bomb scare?"

"Everybody's accepting the party line. We've done a couple of background stories on Iraq and the IRA, but nobody's taking it very seriously. And no one has connected Matthews' mysterious flu. They figure he's just over-tired."

"I guess that's good. You think DoD is working on a vaccine?"

"I bet they've got Fort Detrick and Walter Reed going full bore. But nothing's coming out on it. My contacts are afraid to talk to me."

"That's too bad. I need some help."

Luckett looked at the consultant warily. "What kind, Adam? No more trips in little airplanes I hope."

"Nope. It's Vision One. I think Venton is behind all this but I can't find the connection. I pulled some corporate information, but I couldn't find anything on the man." He handed a folder to Luckett. "Here's what I got off the Web. I was hoping you could get some more details."

Luckett took the file and skipped through the pages. "Pretty dull stuff. What are you looking for?"

"I'm not sure, unfortunately. There has to be something in Venton's background that would explain destroying the lab. I was hoping you could check him out."

"Sure, why not? It's more interesting than tracking down feather-bedding meter maids." He folded the file and stuffed it into a pocket of his raincoat. "You look pretty ragged, Adam. You okay?"

Braxton hesitated. Did he really want to pull Luckett into his problems? But hadn't he already?

"I've been better," he finally replied. "DoD is on my back. Getting my clients to cancel contracts. If I don't find a way out of this mess, I'll be out of business in a couple of months. I *really* want to find the bastard that's doing this to me."

"Funny how things change when they get personal, isn't it? I'll get what I can, and give you a call later today." Luckett wiped his lips with a paper napkin and gathered up his trash. "You know," he said, as he walked toward the trash bin, "this is going to make one helluva story. If anyone will ever let me print it."

* * *

Flynn's driver took the Special Assistant, Slattery, and Ikedo to Robinson's apartment on Connecticut Avenue. Another car with four additional FBI agents followed. They presented the search warrant to the building attendant, and the man led them to Apartment 301, a comfortable two bedroom suite that overlooked Rock Creek Park.

Slattery still couldn't believe that Robinson had lied to them all. Why did he need to concoct such a strange story? And why involve Yang's brother? But how else would he have known about Braxton?

The apartment was sparsely but elegantly decorated in wood and leather. A few MOMA prints hung on the walls. Simple, tasteful, and professional. Slattery never would have picked the spook for Scandinavian modern.

"Kevin, you and Aaron take the bedroom. It's across there." Flynn pointed to a doorway off to the left. "Tony and Carol, you check the living room. Roger and I will go through the study."

"You seem pretty familiar with the place, Mary Ellen," Slattery commented as she led them into a converted bedroom. "Been here before?"

"Yes. Some kind of party I think."

Slattery didn't think he was getting the whole truth. Maybe there *was* a reason Flynn was taking the developments so personally.

The study echoed the style of the rest of the apartment. A plain cherry desk sat against one wall, topped by a large monitor and keyboard. The system unit sat alongside. The desk's surface was completely clear of clutter; a stack of magazines sat on the only other piece of furniture, a double drawer credenza.

Normally, Slattery would have expected piles of work-related papers, but this was no ordinary man. An NSA employee couldn't exactly bring his work home, any more than Slattery could.

Of course there were those special times. And they deserved a special place.

Flynn started on the credenza. Soon she had piles of folders strewn all over the floor.

"How about I take a look at the PC?" Ikedo asked.

Slattery looked over and saw Flynn was still engrossed in her search. "Sure," he replied. "Give it a try."

Feeling useless with both his colleagues busy, Slattery went for his own tour of the apartment.

The other agents were busy with their assignments and paid no attention to their CIA guest. He was looking for something a little out of place, a little different. Nothing as obvious as a safe. A real spy would have his stash off-site, but Robinson was arrogant enough to believe he could keep it in a more accessible location.

He started in the kitchen, checking the drawers and cabinets. Inside the nooks, behind the canned vegetables and cereal boxes. After rifling the frozen food in the refrigerator, Slattery decided it was time to move on.

Next came the two bathrooms. The medicine chests, often a prime source of insight, were unremarkable. It seemed Robinson kept himself going on aspirin and a full regimen of multivitamins. Even the toilet tanks came up empty.

He wandered out into the hall to select his next target. Courington and Lasalle were still busy in the bedroom, and Ikedo and Flynn were keeping each other company in the study.

As he stood there he heard a sound, like a motor, and was hit in the face with a blast of cool air. Looking over he saw the air vent. The edges of the metal cover were painted to the wall. Whoever last decorated the apartment hadn't felt the need to remove the plates and covers and paint behind them. Pretty sloppy work for such an up-scale building.

He now knew his next target.

"What are you doing?" Lasalle asked when he noticed Slattery crawling along the floor.

"Looking for cracks," the CIA agent replied. "Well, well. You have a pocket knife, Tony?"

Chapter 61

Braxton HAD DONE all he could until Luckett got back to him. He had shuffled papers ever since the meeting, biding time until it was late enough to go home and fix some dinner. One concern kept gnawing at him, however. It had only been a day since they talked, but he had to know for sure.

"Hello?" The voice on the other end of the line was weak and raspy. It was what he had feared.

"Susan?"

"Oh. Adam. It's so good to hear from you. Are you alright?" Her voice picked up a bit.

"I'm fine. But how are you? Your office said you were out."

"More like down and out since Wednesday night. This damn flu just keeps getting worse. I've spent the last two days in bed with aspirin and chicken soup. Now I can barely keep anything down." She coughed and it echoed down the phone line. "I'm sorry, Adam. I didn't mean to complain. What did you want?"

"Ah, nothing really. I just wanted to check on you."

"Well you must be psychic. Is this a new skill you've picked up?"

He laughed. It felt good.

"Just bad timing probably. Can I do anything for you?"

"No. Thank you. But how about you take me out to a big fancy dinner when I get better? Anything but chicken."

"It's a deal. Have you seen a doctor?"

"I dragged into my HMO yesterday. They said it was a virus and there was nothing they could do."

Unfortunately that was closer to the truth than they knew.

"Okay, but if you get worse or need anything give me a call."

"Yes, *doctor*. I'll take my medicine and call you in the morning." She was trying, but her voice was strained. The initial burst of energy had drained away.

"Take care of yourself, Susan," he said softly.

"You too, Adam. Bye."

It was fifteen minutes before he had gathered the strength to go home.

* * *

Slattery spread the sheets of paper across the glass top of Robinson's coffee table as Flynn and Ikedo joined him on the plush leather sofa. Behind the vent cover he had found a piece of string tied to a protruding nail. When he'd pulled up on the string, a large envelope had been dangling invisibly in the airshaft. And inside the envelope had been these very illuminating documents.

"It's every goddamn communication between Gary and the Commander," Flynn exclaimed.

"Here's the last one I saw," Slattery pointed to a sheet about a third of the way across the table.

"There's nothing all that specific," Ikedo said. "Everything's in code words and innuendo."

"But there's enough to draw some pretty reasonable conclusions," Flynn replied harshly. "We could have known CHARLIE was about to happen. We could have guessed about HALFTIME!" She slapped her hands on the table. "What the hell did Garrett think he was doing?"

"What did you hear on that phone call, Mary Ellen?" Slattery asked.

"What phone call?" Flynn snapped.

"The one you *tapped*."

"Oh. That one. We heard Gary was after Braxton. That's why we were tailing him. We knew he was out of town and had agents waiting for him at Reagan National. They followed him to his office. When they went upstairs they found him unconscious. I called you as soon as I heard."

"You probably saved his life. Who else was on the phone?"

"We don't know. The call came from a burner cell in Alexandria. Garrett wanted to warn Braxton, but the other guy talked him out of it. He's a real smooth operator."

"Can we hear the tape?" Ikedo asked.

"Sure."

"Maybe we can recognize the voice," Slattery added.

"Worth a try I guess. The lab boys are doing a voiceprint, but without any suspects we don't have anyone to match it to. We'll have to get it out of Garrett."

"Director Flynn?" The voice came from the hallway.

"Yes?"

One of the FBI agents appeared in the entryway. "We've got Garrett Robinson downstairs. He's pretty pissed. Screaming about NSA privilege. National security."

"Tell him he can stuff his privilege up his ass. Arrest him and take him to headquarters. Full handcuffs. Let him stew for a while. If I see him now I'll strangle him myself."

* * *

Luckett had spent the afternoon calling in favors and collecting a substantial dossier on Paul Venton and Vision One. Now, stretched out on the sofa in his Arlington condo, he could take a new look at the target of Braxton's investigation. It was very enlightening.

In the middle of reviewing some recent loan applications, he heard a knock on his door.

Who could that be?

He stuffed the file under a sofa cushion and went to check out the interruption.

"Yes?" he called.

"Excuse me, Mr. Luckett," said a deep voice with a slight southern twang. "I'm Special Agent Davis from the FBI. I'd like to speak with you a minute."

The FBI? What could they want? "What's this about, Agent Davis?"

"Ah, I'd rather not discuss it through the door, sir. I'm following up on some of your recent stories. About Georgia."

Well, they finally decided they'd talk to someone with some real information. It was about time.

Luckett released two deadbolts and pulled the door back against the security chain.

"Could I see some ID, please?"

"Certainly, Mr. Luckett."

Davis held up an FBI identification card and Luckett unhooked the chain.

"Come on in, Agent."

"Thank you, sir."

The Agent walked into the entranceway and stood at a casual attention. He was medium height, probably mid-thirties, with soft, unremarkable features. His attire included gray slacks, blue sport coat, and a pair of gold-rim dark glasses. Missing was the haughty arrogance Luckett had experienced all too often with Fibbies.

"Would you like to sit down?" the reporter asked.

"No, thank you. I don't want to take up too much of your time."

"So, how can I help you?"

"First of all, Mr. Luckett, let me say how impressed the Bureau has been with your articles on the militia. You can appreciate that we can't publicly comment on the material, but it is required reading for the team."

"What team is that?"

"The Militia Crisis Team, sir. We're in charge of the investigation of the militia attacks."

"I thought those were all over."

"We certainly hope the attacks are over. But not our investigation. Right now we're looking into some inconsistencies from certain sources. Have you ever spoken with Mr. Adam Braxton?"

Braxton? Why would they be asking him about the consultant? How much did they know about the trip to Yale?

"I believe I have met him, why?"

"Off the record, Mr. Luckett? This is sensitive information."

"Okay, Agent Davis. Off the record." For now.

"We have reason to believe that Mr. Braxton may be withholding information on the militia attacks."

"Withholding information! I find that *very* hard to believe. He has always been, well, quite helpful."

"Yes, sir." Davis nodded as if he had heard all this before. "But we believe he is now under a lot of pressure from some of his clients, the Department of Defense in particular, to hide certain information which could assist us."

"Why are you asking me?"

"Honestly, sir, we know you have met with Mr. Braxton a

number of times recently. Most recently lunchtime today. We also know you were a close friend of George Brown, and assume you want to see his killers brought to justice. If Mr. Braxton has said anything to you about the attacks, it could very well be the clue we need."

"No. I can't believe Adam would hide anything from the FBI."

"You are aware of his precarious financial condition? If he should lose a few clients, he could be bankrupt. This is a powerful motivator, Mr. Luckett."

Braxton had said they were pressuring him, but bankrupt? Luckett never knew it was this bad. Still, would he have hidden anything? After what happened at the White House?

"I'm sorry, Agent Davis. But I still don't believe Adam could withhold information. He told you about Vision One didn't he?"

"Vision One?"

"Yes. The company his ex-wife worked for." Don't these incompetents know anything?

"Oh, Vision One. Yes, I'm sorry. He did mention them, but he never gave us any details. Does he have any evidence of their involvement?"

"You know he does! He was in their laboratory in Amsterdam. We know about the *Chlamydia* bacteria What more do you need?" Why was Davis playing him along like this?

"What exactly has Braxton told you about *C. Pneumoniae*, Mr. Luckett?"

Davis was making him very uncomfortable. Why was he asking things he should know?

"Excuse me, Agent Davis. I've told you all I know about Adam Braxton. If I were you, I'd quit persecuting the victims and start trying to find these murderers. A lot of us would like to see some justice coming out of the FBI for a change. So if you don't mind . . ." Luckett turned and went to the door.

"But I do mind, Luckett," the man snarled, taking off his glasses. "Sun Tzu said 'Humanity and justice are the principles on which to govern a state, but not an army; opportunism and flexibility, on the other hand, are military rather than civic virtues.' And right now, I'm about to take advantage of an opportunity."

* * *

Slattery stood in front of the one-way mirror as Flynn walked slowly into the interrogation room. Since they had returned from Robinson's she had cleaned up in the ladies' room, read Robinson's file—faxed from the NSA—twice, yelled at two of her assistants, and returned to the ladies' room. Now every hair was in place and every seam in line. She had made herself as ready as she could.

He had sent Ikedo back to Langley to pull some files. This was going to get rough. If what Slattery thought was true, she should never be in that room with him. It was like a surgeon operating on her lover. Emotions had a funny way of affecting a professional's skills. He hoped she was up to it.

Robinson sat motionless behind the metal table. He stared straight ahead, into the mirror, ignoring the entrance of his inquisitor.

Flynn sat down facing Robinson. "We found the file, Garrett."

He looked through her.

"It's just us. You and me. Why, Garrett? Why?"

Still no response.

"People were killed!" She stood and her voice raised with her stature. "What were you doing, goddamn it?"

Shit! She was losing it. He grabbed onto the frame of the window. But he couldn't go in. It was her case.

"Two agents died from your actions. Or your inactions. Why?"

Silence.

"They had wives and children. What did they ever do to you?"

Silence.

"How many other people have you screwed on this one?" She was screaming now. "Talk to me, you goddamn bastard."

He turned to return her gaze. "It was necessary," he said calmly. "For the greater good."

She sat back down. "Who was on the phone, Garrett?" Now softly. Like one lover to another.

"Sorry, Mary Ellen. I can't. It's complicated."

"It's your only chance, Garrett. This is treason." She was pleading with him. For the FBI, or for herself?

Slattery choked the window frame as he waited for the answer.

Finally, Robinson stared back into the mirror. "I'd like to call my lawyer, please," he said.

*   *   *

Gary rolled off the edge of the queen-sized bed and shuffled into the study. Tonight he would treat himself to a real home, with a real bed. Hopefully for a real night's rest. Too bad he couldn't say the same for the condo's owner.

He pecked out the message, and hit "Send."

```
Consultant narrowing focus to your location.

Will expedite sanction.
```

The pain had been gnawing inside him all day. Eating away. The attacks were more frequent now; three or four times a week. But there was still work to do. Loose ends to be removed and cauterized, unfinished business to be tended to. His revenge would be satisfying, and absolute.

Gary staggered back to the bed, glancing only briefly into the blood-soaked living room, and collapsed into a drug-assisted coma.

Chapter 62

SLATTERY HAD AWAKENED at 6:00, replaying the interrogation in his head, hoping for some new realization of the identity of the Commander. Beth had finally given him a gentle nudge; their private code that said it was okay for him to get up and go to work. She could read the news reports as well as anyone and, being married to a spy for too many years to count, could tell what wasn't being said. She had squeezed his hand, turned over and gone back to sleep.

He had arrived at 7:00 and begun reviewing the overnight updates.

"Roger?"

Slattery looked up from the latest FBI incident report and saw Ikedo standing in the doorway. "What's up, Manny?" he asked.

"Mary Ellen sent the Robinson wiretap recording over last night. I just sent it to you. Thought you might want to check it out."

"Mary Ellen, huh? And she sent it to you. I told you to look out for that lady."

A flush appeared on Ikedo's cheeks. "Come on, Roger. Give me a break."

No snappy retort from his usually razor-sharp colleague? He might have hit a raw nerve. Unfortunately.

"Come on in," Slattery replied. "Call it up. We'll listen together."

Ikedo moved behind Slattery's desk and opened the Intelink file.

"Hello?" It was a vague, sleepy voice.

"What are you doing calling me again?" A deeper voice. Strong and accusatory.

"You're getting back to me now? It's 1:00 a.m.!" The first voice again. Now recognizable as Robinson.

"Keeping the country safe is not a nine to five job, Garrett. Now why did you call?"

"Did you see the latest decryption?"

"Yes."

"So what should we do?" Robinson.

"Didn't we already have this discussion? We don't do a goddamn thing."

"But it's that consultant. Braxton. They're after him. We should warn him."

"Warn him! Hasn't he done enough damage already? Look, Garrett, if this information helped us with the attacks, of course we'd release it. But it doesn't. And the cost would be so high. We must keep the algorithm a secret a little longer." The other voice softened. Became manipulative.

"I'm tired, sir. Very tired."

"I know, Garrett. We both know what a burden this knowledge can be. But your country is counting on you. Let's see what happens. We'll talk later this week."

"Yes, sir."

"Now get back to sleep, son."

They both stared at the monitor in silence. Slattery grabbed the mouse, clicked on the rewind icon, then hit "Play" again.

They listened to the conversation twice more. Slattery wrinkled his forehead until his eyes hurt. There was something familiar about the words and the phrasing.

"What's the matter, Roger?"

"Oh, nothing. Thought I recognized something. What do you think?"

"Interesting conversation," Ikedo began in his best analyst voice. "From what I've heard about Robinson, he's a real hot shot. And an arrogant bastard. But here he was . . . well, deferential. All the 'sir' stuff."

"Yeah. It sure didn't sound like the Robinson I talked to. And the other guy really knew how to play him."

"What do we know about Robinson's background?" Ikedo asked.

"Background? Not much. Well-educated obviously. Been in the NSA about . . ."

Ikedo waved his hand at his boss. "No. Before that. It sounded like Robinson was talking to a superior. Was he in the military?"

Slattery cocked his head. "I don't know. But we're damn well going to find out. What's Mary Ellen's number?"

"555-1703," came the rapid reply.

Her private line. Slattery's smile belied the concerns his ploy raised.

He reached for the phone and punched a number. "Mary Ellen? Roger Slattery. I want the full jacket on Robinson, especially any military background. We may have a lead on your accomplice."

* * *

Braxton had decided he would get some well-needed rest by taking Saturday off. He *was* stretched out on the sofa in his apartment and re-runs of NCIS *were* on the TV. He tried to convince himself the open laptop sitting on the coffee table didn't really count as work.

The phone rang and he leapt for the handset.

"Adam Braxton."

"Adam, it's Taylor Luckett."

"Hi, Taylor. I was hoping you'd call. Did you find anything?"

"Adam. I need to see you." The reporter's voice was weak and strained.

"What's the matter? Are you okay?"

"Yes. I . . . I found something. Meet me tonight. At the memorial. Ten o'clock. Like before."

"Taylor? Why? What have you found?"

He hung up.

Maybe Luckett had found something! They *would* get to the bottom of this nightmare.

But it was a very odd call.

* * *

"Here's the file, Roger. I pulled it off Intelink and made a couple printouts." Ikedo dropped a folder on the senior agent's desk. "Robinson enlisted in the Marines after he graduated from Penn State. Went to intel training after Parris Island. Initially assigned to DIA by the Pentagon, then to NSA. Stayed on after his tour."

Slattery thumbed through the sheets in the file. "We need the names, Manny. Who did he serve under?"

"Thought you might want that. Mary Ellen has a few friends at the Pentagon." Ikedo pulled another sheet from the folder he was holding and slid it over to his boss. "I ran it against DoD's active file. Nothing clicked."

Slattery ran his finger down the list. Two-thirds of the way down it skidded to a stop.

"Shit!" he exclaimed.

"You found something?"

"Sometimes computers just can't do the work for you, Manny."

Slattery reached for the phone. "What was Mary Ellen's number again?"

* * *

After calling Flynn, Slattery had known the next steps were up to others far above his pay grade. He had left Ikedo to continue researching Robinson, and had returned home, attempting to make up to Beth for his absence by rushing around the house doing menial chores like mowing the grass.

As expected, Markovsky had called at 4:15 and told him to get ready for another meeting at the White House. A CIA staff car had arrived ten minutes later and driven him into the city.

He dreaded these visits. All they had ever brought was trouble. Interacting with the politicians was one reason he had never sought management positions at the Agency. That and his penchant for blunt truth-saying.

Unlike his usual brusque military reception, however, he was met by a friendly female Secret Service agent who escorted Slattery up the stairs to the second floor of the White House. This was the First Family's private residence. Only close friends and the ever-present Secret Service frequented these halls. What had he done now?

The agent opened a door. Slattery walked through and immediately stopped short, shocked by the bizarre scene before him. It was the Lincoln Bedroom, but decorated as he never could have imagined. The President lay motionless in a huge bed, clear plastic drapes separating him from the two individuals standing alongside. Mary Ellen Flynn stood silently to Slattery's left, looking ashen in shock, while Peter Markovsky was positioned on his right, near the President's plastic tomb. To Slattery it looked like nothing short of a wake.

He was shaken out of his introspection by a metallic electronic voice. It took a few seconds before he realized it was the voice of the man behind the curtain.

"Mr. Slattery," said the voice. "Thank you very much for coming. My apologies for the rather depressing atmosphere."

"Roger, Mary Ellen," said Markovsky, "the President wanted to meet with you in person. As I was saying, Mr. President, it was Agents Flynn and Slattery who discovered the connection."

"I wish I could say congratulations," Matthews added, "but somehow I just don't feel that is appropriate. We do all appreciate your work, and the difficulties under which it was performed."

Slattery looked at Flynn and realized that for the first time since he had known her she was speechless.

"I'm sure I speak for Mary Ellen, Mr. President," Slattery responded, "when I say we would much prefer that the outcome had been quite different."

"Thank you, Mr. Slattery," replied Matthews. "So do we all."

There was a knock on the door and all eyes turned to see the identity of the next visitor.

"Peter?" said a surprised DNI as he walked into the room. Carlson quickly scanned the others in the room, then walked abruptly past them to the President's bed.

"You wanted to see me, sir?" he asked.

"Yes, Steven." Matthews replied. He pushed a plain manila folder through an overlap in the drapes. "I was wondering what you thought of this?"

Carlson took the packet and glanced through the contents.

"My God!" he exclaimed. "Are these really other messages on the militia conspiracy? Where did you get them?"

"We have discovered that Garrett Robinson had the deciphering capability all along," Matthews explained. "He's under arrest at FBI headquarters."

"Robinson? From the NSA? Why would he do such a thing?"

"We're not sure, but we think under some misguided sense of loyalty to another conspirator. Someone who wanted this information kept secret. Someone *I* would call a traitor. You've never seen any of these before, Steven?"

"Certainly not, Mr. President." Carlson stretched himself to full military attention.

"Perhaps you'd better look at the last message."

Carlson's countenance cracked slightly. He reopened the folder and pulled out the bottom sheet of paper.

Slattery watched with a mixture of hatred and satisfaction as the color slowly drained from the DNI's face.

"This seems to be a conversation, Mr. President. Where did you get it?"

"It's a transcription of a *telephone* conversation, Steven. The FBI tapped Robinson's phone when we discovered he was withholding IMAGER intelligence. Don't you want to know where we found the other documents?"

"I assumed you had gotten them from him."

"Not quite. We got them from his co-conspirator."

"Oh. So you know who he is?"

"Yes." The pain was obvious in Matthews' face, but Slattery understood his need to confront Carlson his own way. "We searched your home this morning, Steven. We found them there."

"My house! You can't . . ." He looked to Markovsky, then over to Slattery and Flynn. "Mr. President. No. There must be some mistake." Carlson stepped closer to the tent enclosing the President.

"There is no mistake. We did a voiceprint on the tap. The search of your home simply confirmed it." Matthews paused. Slattery wondered if the President had the strength to continue "Why, Steven? How could you do this to us? To me?"

The ex-Marine reached out with shaking hands. "I . . . I didn't do this. I couldn't, sir. Joseph, you've got to believe me."

Carlson nudged even closer to the bed, leaning as if to better convince his Commander in Chief.

A hand suddenly shot through the plastic curtain, grabbed Carlson's coat collar, and yanked him into the tent. Slattery jumped forward in defense, but Flynn pulled him back. She gave him a quick look of assurance.

"You missed the earlier party," Matthews hissed, "so I want to introduce you to our little visitor, *C. Pneumoniae.*"

Carlson struggled to pull back from the sickly man, but Mathews' grip held him firmly in place. The President's voice was hoarse, but Slattery felt the same strength that had taken the man to the most powerful post in the world.

"What I believe Steven, is that your actions disgraced this administration and our country. I will never allow you to again represent a single American citizen, much less be a part of this administration. Whether or not this damn bug has its way.

"If I could, I'd hang you from this bedpost right now. But others are more temperate. You are going to resign from government service tonight, *forever*. If you do not, I will have you brought up for treason. You'll never see another day of freedom."

Matthews released his grip and Carlson recoiled back into the room. As he neared them, Slattery and Flynn unconsciously leaned back, distancing themselves from the invisible curse hanging over the soldier.

"I did it for you, sir," Carlson suddenly pleaded. His voice was halting and weak. He was no longer "Killer" Carlson. "The polls. I had to protect you. To ensure your re-election. I . . . I didn't know about the virus."

Matthews stared blankly at the man who used to be his closest friend. "And I no longer know about you, Steven. Get out of my sight."

Carlson managed to pull himself erect. "I'll prepare the document, now, Mr. President," Carlson said. Eyes straight ahead, he marched slowly past Markovsky, Flynn, and Slattery, then through the door into the hall, closely followed by two Secret Service agents. An eerie silence hung heavy in the room.

"These events are not to leave this room," Matthews finally stated. "I will not put the country through it. You will see that the conditions are carried out, Mary Ellen."

"Yes, Mr. President."

"What about Kam Yang and the attack on Mary Ellen?" Slattery asked. "Do we just forget about them?"

"There's no evidence the General had any part in either incident, Roger," Markovsky replied calmly. "Unless Robinson opens up, which I doubt he will even if he knows anything, these are questions we'll never have answered."

Slattery wiped a bead of sweat from his forehead. It was a stupid question. He should have known better than to stick his nose into politics. It always came out bloody.

He looked over to the bed and saw a frightening weariness wash over Matthews' face. The strength he had brought against his adversary withered away.

"If there's nothing else, Peter," Matthews said weakly, "I'd like to take a short nap."

Chapter 63

Lincoln Memorial, Washington, D.C.
Saturday, 10:00 p.m.

I HATE THESE stupid meetings!

Braxton once again trudged up the steps of the Lincoln Memorial, looking for some sign of Luckett. At this time of the night, the memorial's floodlights provided the only protection from the hidden demons of the Washington night. He had noticed a shadow at the top of the steps; a shape barely visible behind one of the massive Tennessee Marble columns.

Luckett must really enjoy playing these hide-and-seek games.

When he reached the top of the first level, the form became more distinct. It was clearly a man, sitting on the monument floor, hunched over. His chest lay against his raised thighs. The rumpled coat confirmed this was his favorite reporter.

"Taylor!" the consultant called. "It's Adam. Quit loafing. Let's get on with this."

There was no recognition from the shape. It could be someone else, but who else would be here this time of the night? Why was he just sitting there?

"What was so important?"

Braxton jogged up the last few steps and walked over to his friend.

"Taylor?"

A chill cut through him despite the mild spring evening. No. It couldn't be happening again.

He reached over and touched Luckett's shoulder. The body shuddered, then slowly leaned away from him, falling onto its side against the cold floor.

"My God!" Braxton whispered.

The man's face was unrecognizable. It had been brutally beaten.

He leaned down to look closer, moving his eyes down the body. Dark red stains covered the wrinkled white dress shirt. Farther down, two bloody clumps lay against his abdomen. Only when Braxton looked closer did he realize they were Luckett's hands sticking out from the sleeves of his coat.

He reached down and lifted one of the clumps. Nimble fingers that once pecked out exposés and investigative reports were now nothing but fragments of skin and bone tied together by silken white threads. Braxton felt sick to his stomach. Who could have done this?

"Aaaaagh."

He almost missed the low animal-like groan.

"Taylor? Can you hear me?"

"Adam." The word came invisibly from the mass of red and black that had once been the reporter's face.

"Taylor. Who did this? Why?"

"Vision . . . not . . . who we expected." The voice was even weaker than before.

Braxton fought off his repulsion and drew closer to the source of the sound.

"Vision One? What about them? What isn't who we expected?"

"Not . . . in Amsterdam . . . not who . . ."

The voice dissolved into a meaningless rattle.

"Taylor! Please." Braxton shook the body trying to force some response. "What about Amsterdam?"

The rattle stopped. Then there was nothing but silence.

Memories. Another time. Another place. Running for his life.

No! This time he wasn't going to run away.

Emotionally drained, Braxton knelt to sit down next to his friend. As he did, a bullet passed over his head, its whine tearing through the fabric of the night. The projectile ricocheted off the column next to him, sending a rain of marble chips over Luckett's lifeless body.

Braxton spun onto the floor of the monument. Another bullet struck above him and he scrambled frantically past the second row of columns.

A third shot. This one lower, about a foot off the ground, only inches behind his feet. Braxton huddled behind the column, trying to hide himself from the deadly fire.

The wail of police sirens rose from the distance. More memories. They had thought of everything. It was a very efficient setup.

Where was the sniper? Braxton edged his head around the column and was blinded by the glare of the floodlights. They masked the whole area around the memorial.

The assassin couldn't be straight ahead, that was the reflecting pool. He had to be to one side or another.

He had been kneeling down toward Luckett. The shrapnel had scattered to his right. So the shooter had been on his left. Where? In the trees along the circle? He peeked out again and spotted the shadow of a Park Service Information Kiosk behind the lights. It was a perfect blind for the hunter. How could he use that to his advantage?

Braxton turned his head to look for another escape route and gasped at the sight of the overpowering statue behind him. Nineteen feet tall, cut from white Georgia Marble, President Abraham Lincoln stared down at him disapprovingly. "Why are you here?" he seemed to say. "Defacing my monument. Get out!"

Braxton gingerly crawled into the monument's interior. When he looked back through the columns, he could no longer see the kiosk. There was no line of sight for the assassin. He was safe, temporarily.

But how could he escape? There had to be stairs, something. Off to his right he saw a sign: "Elevator." He ran to the door and pulled. It was locked.

The only other door in the interior—which he discovered was also locked—led to the Gift Shop.

The sirens were growing louder. Would they be protection or a fatal invitation? Staying where he was sounded less and less like a promising strategy. Better to live to fight another day.

Bullshit! Better to live.

He had to go back out through the pillars. But he *didn't* have to go down the great stairway. The main portion of the monument, along with the grand colonnade, sat on a pedestal about ten feet high, which itself sat on a larger base. A gravel pathway ran along the top of the base. If he could get to that pathway, he could go around the monument, and climb—or jump—down the sheer fifteen foot drop to the ground. By keeping the memorial between himself and the assassin, he might be able to get away.

He started at the far right of the entryway. Gathering his

courage, he took a breath, then ran past the corner directly toward one of the front columns. A shot screamed past his head, burying itself in the marble exterior. He grabbed the flutes of the pillar for strength, and looked right to the five columns that marked the next steps in his escape.

Flashes of red appeared beyond the searing white lamps. If the assassin hadn't moved, Braxton could run to the end of the colonnade, down to the pathway, over the side of the base, and across the grassy lawn to safety. If he had . . .

He dashed across the open space to the next pillar.

Braxton moved in bursts—frantic dashes to a column, anxious waiting as he huddled behind it—fear and adrenaline always in command. His heart pounded, filling his ears with deafening rushes, blocking any other sounds. All he cared about was the pathway ten feet below.

Racing to the last column, he decided there was no point in stopping. He blew by the upright, bounded off the end of the pedestal, and strode down three meter-high blocks to the base plateau.

* * *

Braxton glanced over his shoulder and stared through the taxi's rear window, straining to identify the cars streaming behind them. Had he seen any of them before? The rain and fog, which had begun a few minutes before, was making it nearly impossible to decide.

No. There was no way anyone followed him. He was safe–for the moment.

After his run from the Monument, he had flagged a cab on Memorial Bridge and directed the driver to an apartment building in Bethesda. The taxi slid to a stop on the slick pavement, Braxton paid the fare, and dashed through the rain into the lobby of the high rise. Running his finger down the resident's list, he stopped at "S. Walker" and pressed the small black button beside the name.

"Hello?" came a soft tinny voice.

"It's Adam," he replied. "Adam Braxton. I've got to talk to you."

"Adam? What's wrong? Did you find out something?"

"Yes. We have to talk. Hurry."

"Eh, sure. Come on up. Ten oh-four."

He heard an electronic buzz and pushed open the door.

* * *

"He's dead?" Walker cried.

"Yes. It was awful. I'd never seen anything like it."

Sydney Walker had greeted the agitated consultant at her door and led him into a small, neat apartment. She had been dressed informally, Georgetown University sweatshirt, jeans, and sneakers. Braxton had been immediately stuck by the knick-knacks and curios spread everywhere, from colorful Japanese cloisonné trays to delicate Hummel figurines. Just what you'd expect from a well-traveled spook.

He had immediately requested a drink and she had disappeared, returning with a tumbler filled with Scotch, and a glass of white wine for herself. The story of his meeting with Luckett had filled the next half-hour.

"Who would have done this?" she asked.

Braxton shook his head. "Taylor didn't say. He just tried to talk about Vision One."

"Vision One? They did this to him? But why would they . . . torture him so?"

"I can only guess that whoever did this was trying to find out what Taylor knew. And apparently was after me as well. Taylor was the bait."

"That's awful. Do you think Taylor really discovered something?"

Braxton rubbed his forehead. What was it Luckett had said?

"He said something about it not being Amsterdam. Not what we thought."

"What not being Amsterdam?"

"I don't *know* Sydney. That's all he said." His hands were shaking. He had to calm down.

"I'm sorry, Adam." She reached over and placed her hand on his shoulder. It actually did make him feel better. "What do we do now?"

"I don't know." His head fell back into his hands. "I was afraid to go home. I'm sorry I bothered you."

"Oh, stop it, Adam Braxton. Don't start feeling sorry for yourself now. I've got something to show you." Walker stood up and went over to a small desk in the corner of the living room. When she returned she had a folder in her hand. "But first of all you need to contact the police. Someone was bound to see you at the Memorial."

"Okay. In a minute. But I've got to think this through. They'll want to talk to me. Drag me down to some goddamn interrogation room. I'd like to be able to live long enough to get there."

"I'm sure they'd protect you."

He curled his nose at her. "Sure. I'm everybody's favorite person right now. Guess what the DNI would say if he found out I was getting Luckett to investigate Vision One? How would the DIA feel about your involvement?"

Walker's silence was enough of an answer.

"So what have *you* found?" he asked.

"I've been trying to figure out what Paul would have done. We know he was soaking DoD for money to develop an antibiotic for *C. Pneumoniae*. According to the lab tech documents, he had found it, but needed more time to work out the manufacturing process."

"Then we came along."

"Right. He couldn't afford to have his project discovered so he buried it."

"You mean torched it. But why would he destroy his own lab?"

"I don't think he really did. I think he packed up the lab, moved it somewhere else, then set the underground facility on fire to cover its real use."

"And concoct that archive story to bury us."

"Paul is a very bright man. And very practical. The structural damage from the fire was minimal. I'll bet he didn't lose one full day of work in the rest of the Vision One building."

"That's still a helluva chance to take. What if the fire had gotten out of control? It could have destroyed his building."

"Not if he knew what he was doing. It's the only explanation that makes sense. Who else would have wanted to destroy the lab? Who else *could* have? You saw the security."

"Okay, say I buy this. Venton moved his lab and set a fire for a cover. But where did he take it?"

"That's what I've been working on. It has to be fairly big, he couldn't do it in a house. Probably a commercial property for the power and other utilities. I checked all the ownership records and . . ."

Braxton curled his brow at his companion.

"Okay, *I* didn't do it. I've got a friend in the Department of Justice. He pulled some strings. Anyway, no new property transfers in Venton's name or Vision One. Anywhere, including Amsterdam."

"What about property he already owned?"

"We checked that too. There's nothing in Amsterdam except the new Vision One building."

Suddenly something clicked.

"That's what Taylor said," Braxton cried. "'It's not in Amsterdam.' He meant the lab."

"Then where could it be?"

"What about California?"

Walker's mouth opened, but no words came out. Her eyes drifted up to the ceiling.

"Maybe, just maybe," she said.

"Maybe *what*, Sydney!"

"A lot of the old-timers at Vision One would reminisce about their first facility. It was a small warehouse on Alameda Island. They were only there a few years but everybody talked about it like it was their family home. They said Venton never sold it out of sentimentality."

"Maybe it was more like practicality," Braxton replied. "A place to hide a little biological moonlighting. Not like he hasn't done it before. I'm thinking we need to visit that island in the bay. You up for it?"

"Who's buying the ticket?"

"I'm losing my business, remember? Dutch treat."

Walker shook her head. "Why do I let you talk me into these midnight escapades?"

"It's only a plane ride."

"Okay, okay. But I've got to pack a few things first." She turned and walked toward the front hallway. "Don't you have a call to make?" she asked.

"Oh, right."

Braxton picked up the phone and punched a number. Seven rings later a sleepy voice answered.

"Hello?"

"Sam? It's Adam."

"Adam?" Fowler replied. "What are you doing calling me now? I'm in bed."

"Sorry, Sam, but it's been a busy night."

"I don't want to hear this, do I?"

Braxton hated it when the huge man whined. "Taylor Luckett was killed tonight. Tortured."

"What!"

"I was supposed to meet him at the Lincoln Memorial. Someone got to him first."

"Who would want to kill the reporter?"

"We were looking for something that connected the militia attacks to Vision One. Taylor must have found something."

"What do the D.C. cops say?"

"I didn't stay to find out. They started taking target practice at me, so I split."

"Jesus, Adam. Where are you? What are you going to do?"

Before Braxton could answer he heard a knock at the door. Walker appeared from a doorway in the hall and stared back at him, a look of fear on her face.

"Go see who it is," he whispered, waving his hand in the direction of the door.

"What?" came the voice from the phone.

"Sorry, Sam. That's why I called. We're going to San Francisco."

"Yes, who is it?" Walker called through the door.

"Why are you going to San Francisco?" Fowler pressed. "And who's we?"

"Venton has another building," Braxton replied. "We think he moved the lab there."

"Adam, who is *we?*" the ex-cop repeated.

"FBI, ma'am. Special Agent Davis." The deep, resonant voice echoed through the apartment like thunder. Braxton's head spun toward the door. "I'd like to talk to you about Adam Braxton."

"Shit!" Braxton whispered.

* * *

"Adam? Braxton!"

The line went dead. Fowler slammed down the phone and fell back onto the mattress.

"Braxton again?" his wife asked from the other side of the bed. "Please leave it alone, Sam. You know what happened last time." She rolled over and stretched her arm across his chest.

What the hell was the damn consultant doing now? Braxton was in over his head again, and this time Fowler was in no position to help. He had no authority. No cavalry to call. There was only one option. Braxton would be pissed as hell, if he lived long enough.

"I can't, honey. I just can't." He tenderly set her arm aside and reached back for the phone.

Chapter 64

"W̲HAT DO I do, Adam?" Walker whispered. Braxton had joined her at the apartment door.

"Stall," he replied quietly. "Ask to see his badge."

Walker turned back to the door. "Could I see your badge please? We've had some trouble in the building lately."

"Certainly, ma'am," the voice said.

"Now what?" she asked, turning back to the inside of the apartment.

Braxton pushed her aside and squinted through the security fisheye. He saw an average-sized man holding an FBI identification card in front of his face. As he watched, the card slid down, exposing the features behind. What he saw turned his body as cold as the black voids staring back at him.

"Adam? What's wrong? Is the badge real?"

He grabbed her arm and pulled her away from the door. "It's the man who attacked me at my office."

"My God!" Walker gasped. "How did he find you?"

"How did he find *you?*" Braxton's heart was racing. Seeing those eyes had revived the terror of that night. "And I bet this is the same man who killed Taylor. We've got to get out of here!"

They needed time. Braxton's eyes scanned the room for ideas. Nothing.

The pounding in his head was becoming unbearable. He could barely think. *What can we do?*

"Tell him you have to get dressed," he finally whispered. "It will give us a couple of minutes."

"But there's no . . ."

"Do it!"

She nodded and leaned back toward the door.

"I've got to get some clothes on. I'll be right back."

"Yes, ma'am. This won't take very long, by the way."

Braxton pulled her back into the living room.

"How can we get out?" he asked.

"That's what I was trying to tell you. There isn't any other way out. What are we going to do?"

"Well, staying here will not be very pleasant, I assure you." He scanned the room looking for something. Anything. His eyes stopped at the balcony sliding doors. "What's out there?"

"Just the balcony," she replied, as he ran for the doors. "Where are you going? We're ten stories up!"

Braxton slid open the door and stuck his head into the night. A cold, damp wind slapped him in the face. It was still raining, but the balcony of the apartment above acted as a canopy and shielded him from the brunt of the storm.

"Get a coat and some clothes. And hurry. He won't wait much longer. Go!"

Walker disappeared back into the room off the hallway, then returned a few seconds later in a light nylon jacket and carrying a small duffel bag. Braxton had had barely enough time to think through their next step.

"Don't look so surprised," Walker said to his obvious confusion. "I had a go-bag ready. Now what do we do?"

"We're going to pay an unexpected visit to your neighbors."

He pulled her out to the balcony, grabbed her bag, and nonchalantly tossed the duffel over her railing and onto the matching balcony of the adjoining apartment.

"Adam," Walker cried. "You can't be serious."

"It's our only chance, Sydney. Watch me. It's not that hard."

So much for the pep talk. It had been two years since he had done any serious rock-climbing; he hoped he still had a few of those skills left.

It wasn't all that much of a leap. Only a short four-foot space separated the two railings. All he had to do was ignore the hundred-foot drop to the concrete pavement below.

Braxton grabbed a plastic patio chair and pulled it next to the railing. He stepped onto the chair and climbed up to the side railing, trying to get a foothold on the slick metal bar while balancing against the damp brick of the building exterior. He took a deep breath and, never looking down, swung out his right leg until it touched the neighboring railing.

Another breath and he reached out with his right arm, digging his fingers around a protruding brick face. He flattened his body against the wall and finally exhaled. Turning his head, he saw the lights of the D.C. skyline through the rain.

"Adam? Are you alright?"

The voice seemed miles away. All of a sudden he felt very tired. Why was he having so much trouble concentrating?

"*Adam!*"

Another breath and he yanked his right arm with all the strength he had. His body pivoted over his lead foot and he fell awkwardly onto the far landing.

"Are you okay?" Walker called across the space.

"Yes," he yelled back, pulling himself up. "It's easy. Now it's your turn."

"Adam, I can't."

"You *have* to, Sydney. He won't wait much longer. Just crawl up and give me your hand. I'll pull you over."

She took one look back into the apartment and put her foot up on the chair. Her next step was to the railing. As she stood balanced at the brink, Braxton saw her eyes wander downward.

"No!" he yelled. "Don't look down. That's *not* where you're going. Look at me."

Her head came up. Tears welled in her eyes. He had to get her over.

"Reach over and give me your hand. You can do it."

Walker extended her arm. Her hand barely passed the railing.

"Come on, Sydney, I know you did far worse than this in boot camp. Reach over and grab my hand."

He thrust his hand out into the rain. Walker leaned forward and their fingers met. He stretched farther and grabbed her wrist. Her fingernails dug into the soft skin of his forearm.

"Okay. Good. Now I'm going to slowly pull you over. Shift your weight to your front leg then step over to my railing. We'll rest then. Keep looking at me. Okay?"

Walker hesitated then nodded. He pulled back carefully, watching her body rise up to the railing.

"That's great. Now just step over. I'll take your other hand. We're almost there."

Walker's back leg moved over the railing. Braxton felt the nails dig deeper into his skin. Her foot came across and she was there, straddling the chasm. He reached for her other hand.

The sound of the crash exploded through the still-open patio door. Walker snapped her head toward the sound, losing both concentration and footing. Braxton grabbed for her other hand as her sneaker slid off the wet railing.

She fell straight down into the darkness.

Braxton desperately grabbed for her wrists, praying he could stop the fatal descent. His grip held, but her momentum slammed him against the railing, shooting a crushing pain through his chest. His arms felt like they were being pulled out of their sockets.

Swinging like a trapeze artist, Walker's stomach struck the edge of the balcony, the impact knocking her breath away and muffling a scream of terror.

The man had given up waiting. They had only seconds before he would discover them. Braxton looked down and saw Sydney dangling lifeless at the ends of his arms. Her legs were too far below the balcony slab to help him raise her up.

"Sydney!" he called. "I'm going to pull you up. But you have to help. Can you hear me? Sydney!"

"Yes! Please hurry, Adam. Please." Her voice was weak and gasping.

"Okay. Here we go."

He willed the pain away, closed his eyes, and pulled.

What happened next, Braxton saw, or imagined, in slow motion. Walker's head appeared, slowly rising above the slab and up to the railing. Then her body materialized, jumping toward him like an attacking animal, leaping the railing, and knocking him over. When he opened his eyes, he was flat on his back with Walker lying over him. They shared one glance and time returned to normal.

"We've got to go," he whispered. "He's in your apartment."

Walker rolled over him and hopped to her feet. Apparently there was nothing seriously damaged. He followed, stepped to the door, and grabbed the handle. Saying a short prayer he yanked and felt it give.

"Guess they don't worry about burglars up here," he said, throwing it open wide. "Let's get out of here."

"My bag!" she yelled.

"Go on. I'll get it." He pushed her inside and reached down for the duffel.

"Braxton!"

The voice came from across the void. He turned toward the voice, saw a flash of light, and jumped back through the door. No time for the duffel now. They had to get out.

The apartment was a mirror of Walker's. He followed her in a dash for the door, knocking over an end table and lamp in the darkness. Another scream, this time a woman's, echoed through the apartment.

When Braxton reached the door, Walker was fumbling with three different locks.

"Hurry, Sydney," he begged. "Hurry."

The door finally flew open and they rushed into the hall.

"The stairs," she cried hoarsely.

"Okay," Braxton replied and they took off down the hallway. Turning a corner, Braxton saw a figure disappearing into one of the elevators. It was only ten yards away.

"The elevator. We can make it." His lungs burned with every step, but the attacker would only be seconds behind them.

He ran even harder, grabbed Walker's jacket, and pulled her through the closing doors.

The doors shut and he collapsed onto the back of the cab. They were safe.

Looking up, he saw an elderly woman pressing herself into a back corner. He couldn't blame her. Walker was bruised, bloody, soaking wet, and gasping for air. He probably looked worse. His chest and arms screamed with pain. If they could only get away from the building they might have a chance.

"Ahhhhhhhh!" the woman yelled.

The gun appeared like an arrow between the doors. It was the same huge, silver automatic he had seen in Tysons. Their companion shrieked again, and Braxton stood frozen, again staring into the bore of the weapon.

Walker suddenly jumped forward and reached for the weapon, grabbing the top of the slider and slipping her finger in front of the hammer. She jerked her hand down, savagely twisting the pistol. Braxton heard a loud snap, followed by an excruciating scream. The pistol dropped to the floor and the hand disappeared back behind the doors.

He felt a lurch and the floor fell beneath him.

*   *   *

"Are you okay?" he asked.

"I think so," Walker replied. She was shivering against the wall of the elevator cab. "I guess I should thank you for saving my life."

"I could say the same, but we'd better save that until we're sure we've gotten away. This guy can be pretty persistent." He reached down, picked up the pistol, and stuck it in his pocket. "That was a pretty neat move, Sydney."

"I don't even remember what happened. It was all automatic. I saw the gun and just reacted. I guess all that training wasn't wasted after all."

As the elevator chimed off the floors, Braxton watched the lights count down to one.

"It's usually pretty easy to catch a cab around the corner," Walker said.

"It'll be hell to get one tonight in the rain," he replied. "Where's the nearest Metro station?"

"Down a couple of blocks. It's not too far."

"Then let's go for it."

He pushed Walker against the sidewall and cocked the automatic.

"I'm sorry ma'am," he said quietly to the cowering woman, "but you might want to move up here, out of sight when the doors open." She stared at him blankly, then slid along the cab wall and pressed herself into the front corner.

Nothing surprised him anymore. If the attacker was waiting for them, Braxton was going to be ready.

The doors slowly pulled back. He counted to three, spun out of the cab into a shooter's crouch and scanned the gun across the lobby. It was empty.

"Sydney. Let's go!"

He took her hand and they ran through the outside door into the Bethesda night.

* * *

"What the hell are you doing calling me at midnight!" Slattery yelled into the phone.

"Why should you get to sleep if I can't, Roger?" Fowler screamed back. "Braxton's in trouble. Taylor Luckett was killed tonight. The cops might think he's involved."

"Jesus. Is he?"

"Sort of. But he didn't do it."

"Where is he?"

"I'm not sure. I think they're going to San Francisco. Something about Vision One."

"They?"

"I don't know who he's with. I thought I heard a woman's voice in the background."

"Shit. Walker."

"Who the hell is Walker?"

"It's Sydney Marino's real name. His conspirator from Amsterdam. She's with DIA. Or was. When are they going?"

"They may already be on their way."

Slattery went silent. Fowler held his breath. The spook had to make the next move.

"You know that man is trying to end my career don't you? Pack a bag. I'll meet you at Dulles at 6:00 a.m."

"In the morning?"

"Yes, the *morning*, godammit. Get us two tickets to SFO. In the meantime use some of your contacts and make sure he hasn't already been picked up by the locals."

Chapter 65

SLATTERY FLASHED HIS ID at the Dulles security guard and was escorted around the checkpoint scanners. Once he was clear, he saw Fowler pacing back and forth just outside the security area. Dark blue windbreaker, black rumpled pants, crepe sole broughams. The man would look like a cop until the day he died. A lone nylon athletic bag hung at the end of one arm.

"Hey, Sam. How are you doing?" he said slapping his friend hard on his back.

"Pretty lousy considering it's 6:30 a.m. and I haven't gotten any sleep. Where the hell have you been?"

"Got tied up. You get our tickets?"

"Yeah. You *are* going to pay for this aren't you?" Fowler handed over a ticket envelope.

"Absolutely. Uncle Sam never reneges on an obligation."

"Right. Just remember I only take cash these days. Anyway, thanks for helping out here. I think our friend is in way over his head."

"He's *your* friend, Sam. I've got a case to close and Braxton is just one of the players."

Fowler shook his head. "Whatever you say, Roger. By the way, what did you tell your bosses about this little trip?"

"Somewhere in the stack of leads was one from San Francisco," Slattery explained. "I told everybody I was going to follow it up."

"And they believed you?"

"It'll work for a while."

Fowler looked down at his watch. "Time to catch the train. We're on a 7:30 to SFO."

They walked to the AeroTrain hall for the C and D Gates and caught a car a few minutes later. Fowler dropped into the first seat he could find. Slattery stayed standing at his side.

"All the non-stops were filled," Fowler explained as the shuttle lurched forward. "So we've got to stop in Denver."

"Shit," Slattery murmured. "Did you find out anything about Luckett?"

"I called a couple of friends on the force. Worst goddamn murder they'd seen in years. Luckett's hands were crushed and his face bashed in. Somebody must have wanted that information real bad."

"What about Braxton?"

"They got an anonymous call about a shooting. When the black and whites got there they saw somebody running away. No ID, but they did find Braxton's prints on an envelope in Luckett's pocket. He's just wanted for questioning at the moment, but if he doesn't show they'll put out a warrant."

"Great. Any identity on the killer?"

"Nope. But he shot the hell out of the Memorial. Forensics was still gathering the slugs."

Slattery stood silently as the shuttle moved under the tarmac of the airport, adding pieces to his mosaic. Why did everything keep coming back to Braxton? And why did he keep coming up right?

"We found out who was coordinating the militia attacks," he said quietly.

"No shit!" Fowler exclaimed a little too loudly. "Who?"

The shuttle slowed into its berth, then jerked to a stop.

"It's a long story. Buy me a coffee and I'll tell you."

"Sounds good. I could use a breakfast taco."

Slattery punched the ex-cop in his stomach. "You know, Sam, you really have been putting on weight lately."

* * *

The Alameda Skillet was a 50's style greasy-spoon squatting along the channel between Alameda Island and the Oakland mainland. It had somehow survived the closing of the Naval Air Station in the eighties, and now prospered on the new wave of high tech companies expanding from the over-crowded—and over-priced—Peninsula to the west.

Braxton squirmed on the hard wooden bench at the diner's window, nursing his fourth can of Coke. If Walker didn't get back soon he was going to explode.

The past twelve hours had been an exercise in evasion. They had taken the Metro to Reagan National, then an airport shuttle bus up to BWI. In Baltimore, Walker rented a car and they drove up to Philadelphia International Airport, stopping along the way to raid ATMs, dump the assassin's gun in a roadside culvert and get a change of clothes at an all-night Wal-Mart. It had been all Braxton could do to get his companion to enter the store, much less buy anything off the rack.

They had spent a fitful, uncomfortable night in the United Red Carpet Club on Walker's frequent-flyer card. There had been little conversation; they were both too exhausted, and too frightened, to pass the time in idle chat. About 3:00 a.m. Walker had gone to the restroom. When she returned she had some positive news.

"I called a friend in Amsterdam," she had said. "Paul left for California last week. They don't know when he'll be back. Maybe our guess was right."

They had taken the first flight to San Francisco, arriving at SFO mid-morning California time. Walker had rented another car and driven up the peninsula and across the Bay Bridge to Alameda. She had dropped Braxton off to watch the old Vision One building, then driven back to Palo Alto to find out what she could at Vision One headquarters.

So he had sat here for the past three hours, staring out the window at the two story brick building across the street. A squarish, plain structure, only a faded shadow of "Vision One" etched into the brick above the entrance served to remind an observer of the structure's hallowed history. Since he had arrived, Braxton had only seen about fifteen people coming and going, all of them casually dressed youngsters. Pretty odd for an abandoned warehouse. None of the visitors matched the description Walker had given him for Paul Venton.

Walker reappeared in the diner at 2:30.

"Jesus, Sydney," Braxton complained. "Where have you *been*?"

"I went to Vision One remember?"

"No, Sydney. Where have you *really* been? That's hardly the outfit you had this morning." Walker was now dressed in a trim gray pants suit and white turtleneck sweater. Despite their sleepless night she glowed like an angel.

"There's this great Nordstrom in Palo Alto. I couldn't stand those other clothes. Do I look okay?"

"If you ask me, you always look good, Sydney."

"You're sweet. I got some things for you too," she said, sliding onto the bench across from him. "They're in a bag in the car."

"So much for keeping a low profile. Now what did you find out about Venton?"

"My friends in Palo Alto said they knew he was in the area, but he hasn't showed there at all. Did you seen him?

"Nope. There have been some people in and out but no one that looked like Venton. Maybe he's not around."

"Oh, no. He's there. If he's keeping his normal hours, he was across the street by 6:30 this morning."

"Even on Sunday?"

"Every day."

Braxton suddenly stood up and grabbed his jacket.

"Where are you going?" Walker asked.

"First I'm going to the john. I thought you'd never get back. Then I'm gonna check out this building while it's still light. You know, while you were gone I was thinking. What if . . ."

"Adam?" she interrupted.

"Yes?"

"Could you change your clothes? Please? You look like a refugee from the waterfront. I'd hate to get arrested *before* we get into any real trouble."

* * *

"Detective Fowler?" A short oriental man approached the pair as they walked out of the jetway.

"Inspector Huang?" Fowler replied.

"Welcome to San Francisco," Huang said with a bow.

"Roger, this is Inspector Anthony Huang, from the SFPD. He worked on Megan Braxton's case. Inspector Huang, this is Roger Slattery, he's a . . . government representative."

"Please, call me Tony. Mr. Slattery." Another bow.

Slattery returned the bow. "We really appreciate your help, Inspector. You understand, however, that this is an unofficial visit?"

"Yes. Sam briefed me on his call from the plane. I'll accept the explanation, for now." The cop's eye's twinkled and Slattery breathed a sigh of relief. He hadn't really wanted Fowler to involve any of the locals, but they would have wasted hours without some help. His friend's instincts were still intact.

"Come, let's get you started on your search." Huang led them down the concourse. "We have determined that a Miss S. Walker arrived with her brother this morning and subsequently rented a car."

"Her brother?" Fowler asked.

"Undoubtedly an alias for your Mr. Braxton. I've got a bulletin out on the car, but this is a very large metropolitan area. Do you have any idea of their destination?"

"It has something to do with Vision One," Fowler explained. "Their offices are in Palo Alto."

"Yes. I am familiar with the company. We use some of their products in forensic reconstruction. But the car rental agent remembers Miss Walker asking about a map of the East Bay. Alameda in particular."

"Alameda?" Fowler asked. Why would they want to go there?"

"Could there be another facility there?" Slattery responded. "Or the homes of some of the executives?"

"I can have someone check, Mr. Slattery."

"Thanks, Tony," said Fowler. "That'd be great. But for now Roger and I'll check out Palo Alto."

* * *

Braxton and Walker finished their fisherman's platter—which wasn't actually all that bad for the West Coast—paid the bill, and walked out into the mild California weather. The setting sun cast long shadows as they walked across the street to the channel. Water lapped up at the seawall giving a soft, melodic background to their stroll. If anyone had been watching, they would have seemed just another pair of lovers enjoying the romantic evening.

"I really like the new clothes," Braxton commented, modeling his khakis and sweater for her. "You can do my shopping anytime."

"You really do need to get out more. Your other clothes are kinda, well, out-of-date. And you can look quite dashing."

He wasn't sure he liked Walker's comment, but figured it was probably true. Ever since Megan had left, well . . .

"So where are we going?"

Her question knocked him out of his dream. "What's the rush? You're not enjoying the company?"

"I'm flattered but I thought you had other things on your mind."

Braxton stopped and took Walker's hand. "You know you don't have to do this. It's my fight."

She returned his solemn stare. "We've been through this before, Adam. Megan was my friend, too. And we both know neither of us is safe until we find who's behind all this."

He leaned over and kissed her on the cheek. "Then I guess we'd better get started."

He led her farther down the street. "Vision One is the next building ahead. There's a service entrance on the side. One of the people inside took a cigarette break this afternoon and I taped the door after he went back in."

"Not bad for an amateur. But what if someone noticed it?"

"Ah . . . we think of something else."

They continued toward the building and, after checking for prying eyes, turned into the alley. Braxton led her to the entrance and reached for the door. It squeaked open. The tape was still in place.

"Wait!" Walker cried as he was about to enter. She reached into her new duffel bag and pulled out two long magnesium flashlights. "I thought we might need these."

"Always prepared," he said smiling. He took a final look up and down the dark alley, and pulled her into the building.

*   *   *

"This was a helluva waste of an afternoon." Fowler tossed another cup of coffee out of the car window onto Calle Escondido in Palo Alto. Across the street stood a sprawling glass and concrete building with a stainless steel "Vision One" pushing through the top story.

"You've wasted a lot more time than one afternoon on a stakeout, Sam," Slattery replied from behind the wheel of their Taurus. He rubbed a stiff and sore neck.

"Yeah, but I didn't have a friend's life hanging on those."

"Look, Sam. We've done all we can. Nobody we've talked to has seen or heard from either Braxton or Walker."

"Or they have and aren't willing to tell us. Dammit, Roger. They're here somewhere. We both know it." He hit the dashboard with his huge fist.

"Jesus, Sam. Take it easy. We talked to the employees. We've driven around for hours searching for their car. What more can we do but wait? I'm open to any good ideas."

"Okay. What about this Alameda Island? We could go there."

"And do what? We don't even have a place to start."

Fowler leaned back in the seat and sulked. Slattery welcomed the silence.

"What's your angle on this, Roger?" Fowler finally asked. "You think the killer and Vision One are connected?"

Why couldn't the cop turn off that sixth sense?

"I honestly don't know, Sam. But Braxton seems to be a lightning rod for both. I hope he can stay alive long enough for us to figure it out."

"Like he did with Saracen?"

Slattery threw his friend a withering glare. The agent did his job the best he knew how. He wouldn't apologize to anyone for the decisions he made. Especially when civilians stuck their nose where they shouldn't.

Further discussion of the uncomfortable subject was eliminated with the buzz of Slattery's cell phone.

"Slattery."

"Oh. Mr. Slattery. This is Tony Huang. I was expecting Sam."

"He's here in the car with me. Would you like to speak with him?"

"No, no. That's alright. I just wanted to tell you that we did find a connection between Vision One and Alameda. They own an old building on the island."

Slattery grabbed a paper bag left over from lunch and scribbled the address Huang dictated.

"Got it. We'll head over there now."

"Take the San Mateo. The Bay Bridge is a parking lot during rush hour. And give me a call if you find anything, Mr. Slattery. Or you need any help."

"Will do, Inspector. And thanks."

He flipped the phone shut and started the engine.

"What's up, Roger?" Fowler asked.

"You're getting your wish. We're going to Alameda."

Chapter 66

Braxton and Walker spent the next half-hour wandering the first floor of the building. After sticking their heads into every office and opening every seemingly discarded box, all they had discovered was how filthy an abandoned office building could be. They didn't find any evidence of a laboratory or human activity.

"Enough, Adam," Walker pleaded as they stood in the dark lobby. "We've been through these offices twice."

Braxton swung his flashlight across the cracked reception desk. "Okay. There's nothing here. But I did see people coming in today. Where were they going?"

"Downstairs?"

"But why make everyone go downstairs?"

"The building is supposed to be abandoned. If anyone accidentally came in, it would look perfectly normal–empty."

"That makes sense. The lab in Amsterdam was underground. Let's try downstairs." He headed for the elevators behind the desk.

"I doubt those are going to work, Adam."

Braxton ignored her and pushed the down button. It remained unlit. After punching at the arrow for another ten seconds, he finally swung his flashlight back to his companion. She stood defiantly in the lobby tapping her foot on the tile floor.

"Ready now?" she asked.

He grumbled under his breath and joined Walker in a search for a stairway. Behind the lobby he found an "EXIT" sign next to a heavy door. He called for her and opened the door into an empty, but not dark stairwell. Emergency power lights shown from silver boxes hung on the stairwell walls.

"Looks like somebody wants to see where they're going," Walker commented.

"Which way?" Braxton asked. He shone his light to the left, leading downward, then to the right, going up.

"Well, we said we were going down," Walker reminded him.

"Guess I'd better not ignore you this time, huh?"

The stairway only went down one floor. Braxton reached for the door, took a breath, and pulled it open.

Behind him, Walker gasped in shock. The small room they entered was nearly identical to the anteroom in the Amsterdam laboratory. This area had a desk, probably for a receptionist to meet infrequent visitors, but the pair had no doubt what was behind the second electronically-secured entrance in front of them.

Unfortunately, this time neither had the access code.

Braxton moved up to the door and peered through a small, reinforced window.

"What do you see?" Walker asked.

"Just what we expected. A floor of laboratories. You were right, Venton moved his operation here."

"Is anyone there?"

"Not that I can see. But there aren't many lights on." Braxton slapped the door with the flat of his hand. "Shit! What do we do now?"

"Well, there is still a second floor."

"What would be up there?"

"We won't know unless we go will we?"

He stared at her perfectly-serious face. He *had* to find out about Venton. Something here would explain about Amsterdam. About Megan. He knew it.

"Your logic is impeccable, Sydney. Lead on."

He followed her back up the stairway to the second floor. Entering the hallway, he swung his flashlight up and down the dark corridor. It appeared as deserted as the floor below.

"Looks empty from here," he said. "Should we check it out anyway?"

"I think so," Walker responded. "Look there." She pointed her flashlight down the hallway to the right. In the gathered dust on the wooden floor was a well-trodden path of footprints.

"Let's hope everyone is gone," Braxton whispered.

They followed the footprints down the hallway until it turned right into another corridor. Another twenty yards and the path split in two, disappearing through open doors to the left and right.

Braxton pointed to the right with his flashlight and nodded to Walker. She returned the gesture and entered the room, while Braxton turned back to the left.

He stepped into an interior office. His flashlight revealed empty, bare walls, but when he lowered the beam, the light shone on stacks of file folders standing randomly over the floor, like the skyscrapers of a bizarre cityscape. In the center of the city stood an ancient metal government-issue desk, its top equally covered in stacks of papers. A small fluorescent desk lamp sat on one corner.

Braxton carefully maneuvered his way through the piles to the desk and flipped on the switch.

"Eeeek!"

He jumped back from the desk at the scream and tripped over a mound of folders, sending him unceremoniously into a sprawl on the floor. He scrambled to his feet and ran into the room across the hall.

Walker stood motionless in the middle of a large room. Scanning his flashlight he saw five commercial vending machines hugging the bare walls. A counter with a microwave oven stood in one corner. Next to Walker was a battered table with five plastic chairs. The room was a well-stocked, and very operable, corporate cafeteria.

The only item out of place was the body hanging from an overhead pipe.

"Why?" Walker cried without turning around. "Why would Paul do it?"

Braxton walked forward and put his arm around her. She was cold and shivering. Just like in Amsterdam.

He shone his flashlight up to the bloated face above him. It was still recognizable as Paul Venton. He ran the beam of light slowly down the body, stopping at the overturned chair beneath it.

"I don't think he did, Sydney."

"What do you mean?"

"Look at the height. His shoes are a good foot above the chair seat. How did he manage that do you think?"

"Then someone killed Paul? But who?"

"I think I finally understand what Taylor meant. Megan's

murderer wasn't in Amsterdam. He wasn't even in Vision One. At least not now."

"You mean it wasn't Paul?"

"No. One thing had always bothered me. Why would Venton get involved with the militia? If his intent was blackmail, he needed to manufacture the antibiotic first. He wouldn't have destroyed the Amsterdam lab. It was someone else. Someone that didn't want the antibiotic produced. The same someone who coordinated the militia attacks."

"But who is he?"

"The only other person who knew enough about what was going on at Vision One. Benjamin Lawson."

"Dr. Lawson? But he's dead!"

"A convenient cover don't you think?" The deep male voice came out of the darkness.

Braxton turned toward the voice and was blinded by an explosion of light. When the pain had passed, his eyes focused on a short bearded man standing in the doorway. In one hand he held a bright electric spotlight. In the other, a very deadly-looking black automatic.

"Dr. Lawson, I presume?" Braxton said. "You don't look anything like your picture."

"That's the whole point, isn't it, Mr. Braxton? It really is a surprise to see you. My mercenary must be losing his touch. And Miss Marino, or should I say Walker? How nice to see you again."

"You killed Paul?" Walker asked. "Why? He was your friend."

"Paul didn't have friends. Just facilitators. All he ever cared about was power. And his ego. Why do you think his office is up here? So he didn't have to get his fingers dirty downstairs. Why did I kill him? Because he was going to ruin my plan. His scientists discovered the damn antibiotic! I couldn't let him make it."

"That's why you destroyed the Utrecht lab," Walker said.

"I never thought he would succeed. Once you two had broken in, I knew it had to be destroyed."

"Venton's second lab must have been a real surprise," Braxton commented.

"Not really. Paul was a very compulsive man. He always had a Plan B. I assumed he had another lab. It was only a matter of time until he led me to it."

"What *was* your plan, Lawson?" Braxton asked. "Why the militia ruse, the attack on the White House?"

"Oh, you connected me to the militia? Singer, my hired mercenary, was right. You two are dangerous." He walked over to a chair and set the lamp on the seat. The focus of his gun never strayed from his hostages. "They murdered my little brother in Iraq. He went there to make a difference. To contribute to his country. He wasn't a famous scientist. Wasn't a sports hero. Just a kid who wanted to be part of something. And they *killed* him."

"You mean Desert Storm?" Walker asked. "It was a war!"

"It was a sham!" Lawson yelled. "He wasn't killed by the Iraqis. He was killed by the politicians and generals. Playing around with their biological toys. When I learned Vision One was trying to develop an antibiotic for *C. Pneumoniae*, I knew what I had to do, but I needed help. And money.

"Vision One's IPO solved the second problem and I found the mercenary to deal with the first. Singer came with exceptional credentials. He had all the contacts. We created the militia conspiracy to keep the authorities away from our real target. That and to induce a little terror. Worked rather well, don't you think?"

"You were at Yale," Braxton said flatly.

"Undergrad. Heard about the hack. It always impressed me. When I mentioned it to Singer he recognized the significance immediately."

"But why the charade?" Walker asked. "Why fake your own death?"

"I had been trying to subvert Paul's efforts. Pushing the designers in the wrong direction. Erasing working files. Paul was getting suspicious. I couldn't just leave. He would expect me back here. So I had to disappear." A strange contorted smile appeared on Lawson's face. "It really wasn't all that hard. Quite exciting actually."

They had kept Lawson talking for about as long as they could. And Braxton wasn't getting any good ideas on how to get out from under that automatic. Still, there was one question he had to ask.

"Why Megan, Lawson? She loved you."

Lawson paused and a look of sadness crossed his face. "She was a very special woman, Braxton. But I couldn't afford any complications. I came back here to check out Palo Alto and Megan accidentally saw me. I tried to talk to her, explain what I was doing, but she wouldn't listen. She threatened to expose me, ruin everything I had done, everything I had planned. I didn't have a choice."

"You had a choice," Braxton spit back. "You just cared more about yourself. And your revenge. I knew Megan would never try to fight off a stranger. It had to be someone she knew. I just never figured it was you. Until now."

"And I never expected to see you two again. You really did surprise me. I was still preparing this little scene when I heard you on the stairs. I thought it was one of the researchers coming back to work."

"So now we become another part of your plan."

"Of course. Mad entrepreneur murders two intruders then kills himself in remorse." He glanced down at his watch. "If I had time I'd update Paul's suicide note, but I really have to go. Soon this lab too will be destroyed in a terrible conflagration. Over to the corner."

Lawson flicked his wrist and directed them to the far corner of the cafeteria. Then he approached the hanging body, reached into his jacket pocket and pulled out a small memory stick.

"As a cryptologist, you will appreciate the irony, Mr. Braxton. On this drive are all the formulas and the process descriptions to mass-produce the *C. Pneumoniae* antibiotic. Encrypted, of course." Lawson dropped the stick into Venton's shirt pocket. "Eventually the authorities will realize it contains the information they need. Unfortunately it will take even the incomparable NSA months to decode the content. By then my work will be done. Such exquisite justice. The very microbe they used to kill my brother will bring the leaders of the free world to their knees. Now I'm afraid it's time to complete this production."

The sound began softly, like a freight train approaching from the distance. It grew louder and louder until it filled the room with an ear-splitting roar. Braxton felt the pressure push against his chest until he could no longer get a breath.

Lawson turned toward the door and screamed "No!" just as the wall behind him erupted into flame. Braxton grabbed for Walker and yanked her under him as the windows exploded over their heads.

Once the initial shock wave had passed, Braxton poked his head up through the debris. The room was rapidly filling with hot, acrid smoke. Through the haze he saw rubble everywhere. The corridor wall had disappeared, as had Lawson.

"Sydney!" he called, over the deep rumbling of the building. "We've got to get out of here. Stay low!"

She nodded in reply, wiping dust and dirt from her face. He grabbed her hand and they ran back to where the main hallway used to be.

The hallway was even worse than the room. It was at least twenty degrees hotter and twice as dark. Spears of fire shot through the floor behind them. They tried to follow the wall, or what was left it, grabbing at the sheet metal studs left after the gypsum wallboard had disintegrated. His hands were cut and bleeding and he could see that Walker was having trouble breathing in the noxious air. They didn't have much time left.

"There!" he cried when he saw what was left of the familiar "EXIT" sign. They rushed ahead and he was about to pull open the door when Walker yanked him back.

"Wait!" she commanded. "Check the door." She placed her hand on the metal surface and pulled it back quickly. A look of resignation was etched on her face.

Braxton tried to look back in the other direction. The way was completely obscured. Fire chimney or not, the stairwell was the only way they were going to get out of this inferno. He pulled his hand up into his sweater sleeve, grabbed the door handle, and pulled.

* * *

The San Mateo Bridge hadn't been too bad, but I-880 had been bumper to bumper all the way up to Oakland. Slattery had lost his patience with Braxton's behavior, and California traffic, about twenty miles back.

He slalomed through the Posey Tube into Alameda and fish-tailed onto Canal Street. Just in time to slam on his brakes and come to a screeching stop.

"What the hell?" Fowler exclaimed.

Ahead was a jam of police cars and fire trucks. And behind them, the unmistakable red-orange glow of a major industrial fire.

"I think your friend may be in some trouble," Slattery answered.

Chapter 67

Vision One Warehouse, Alameda, California
Sunday, 5:15 p.m.

THE BLAST OF super-heated air nearly knocked them over. Braxton's face felt like it had been toasted in the Saharan sun. He managed to pull Walker through the doorway when he saw the apparition.

Lawson was standing on the second floor landing, a six foot length of twisted railing in his hand. Eyes wide with rage, his clothes singed, and flames shooting around him, he looked like the Devil guarding the Gates of Hell. Awaiting his latest inductees.

Lawson seemed to stand motionless, but the railing swung in a slow motion arc toward Braxton and his companion. If he didn't do something fast, they would surely fall into the depths of the inferno.

He shoved Walker to his right, sending her tumbling down the stairway. Then, rather than trying to escape the swinging shaft, he rushed forward, grabbing it as close to Lawson's hands as he could. The railing hit with a force that snapped back both of his wrists, but he managed to keep a grip, pulling the weapon down on top of him as he collapsed onto the landing.

Enraged that his attack had failed, Lawson leapt onto Braxton, his fists pounding at the consultant's chest, punishing his already seared lungs. Finding the railing, Lawson grabbed it and brought it down on Braxton's throat. His breath left him, and his vision constricted to tiny circles as if he were viewing his last moments through the wrong end of a pair of binoculars.

As Braxton's legs collapsed he felt something solid – the concrete block wall of the stairwell. In a last desperate effort he braced his feet against the wall, arched his back, and pushed his body upward with everything he had.

The pounding stopped and air rushed back into his starved lungs. Looking up, he saw Lawson pivot backwards over his head, do an awkward somersault, and land feet-first with a fiendish smile on his face. The grin turned to panic, however, as his momentum carried him backwards, past the now missing upper railing. With a maniacal scream, Lawson tripped over the remaining lower rail and fell head first into the flaming depths two stories below. It seemed like an eternity until the grotesque sound disappeared beneath the crackling of the fire.

Braxton collapsed back on the gritty floor, too exhausted to go on, content to let the flames finish what Benjamin Lawson could not. He had done what he had come for; extracted *his* revenge. What more was there for him?

"Adam." It was a familiar voice that broke through his dream. "Adam where are you?"

He felt someone grab at him. At first he pushed the figure away, it could only be someone else that would give him pain, but slowly the face came into focus.

"Megan?" he whispered. "Is that you?"

"Dammit, Adam," Walker yelled. "Get up. I'm not going to wait here forever for you."

"How?"

She was pulling him up. He staggered to his feet, only to have them give way under him. She persisted and he felt a surge of strength fill the voids in his muscles. There *was* something more, and he knew what he had to do.

They staggered down the stairs, hugging the sidewalls of the staircase to find their way through the black cloud. The heat and smoke became worse the lower they went. Braxton thought he had gone as far as he could when a blast of cool air shocked him back to reality. Falling through the doorway, they tumbled into the alley.

* * *

Where the hell is Fowler?

Slattery paced the pavement of Canal Street watching the Vision One building slowly disintegrate. Fowler had been with him just a minute ago, then he disappeared.

The Alameda Fire Department was unrolling hoses and making the connections that would draw the channel water up to the pumping engine and then out onto the burning structure. What looked like a random scramble of men and women was in reality a well-practiced ballet with life-saving consequences. Slattery watched with a professional curiosity as the firefighters hefted awkward hoses and spun bulky connectors. Within seconds cold bay water was streaming into the building.

As he scanned the fiery landscape, he saw a figure limping from beside the building. As it came closer he saw that it was Fowler, and he was carrying a body.

The Alameda Fire Chief had given him a walkie-talkie so they could communicate during the confusion of the fire. He pulled it from his pocket, never taking his eyes off his friend.

"I need EMTs at the northwest corner," he yelled into the device. "We've got a survivor."

The paramedics arrived with a stretcher just as Fowler crossed the fire line. Slattery saw that the body was that of a woman.

"Walker?" he shouted to Fowler as the ex-cop dropped the body onto the litter.

"I guess," Fowler replied. "I saw her staggering down the alley."

"Where's Braxton?"

Walker tried to sit up. "Back . . . inside." Her voice was barely audible.

A tall, bleached-blonde EMT eased Walker back down. He looked like an over-the-hill surfer. "You've got to take it easy," he said. "And you guys need to give us some room."

The other paramedic slipped a plastic mask over Walker's face and connected it to a small oxygen bottle. Then they began rolling their patient back to the ambulance.

Slattery stationed himself by the side of the stretcher. "Why did Braxton go back in?" He leaned forward, placing his ear as close to the mask as he could.

"Don't . . . know."

"What happened in there? Who did this?"

"Not . . . Venton . . . Ben . . . Lawson."

Slattery looked over to Fowler. He mouthed, "Ben Lawson?" Fowler shook his head.

"Was anyone else there?" Slattery pressed. "Another man?"

"Not . . . there," she replied. "Just . . . Lawson."

"But . . ."

"That's *all* sir," the paramedic said, pushing Slattery away from the gurney. "We've got to get her to the hospital." They rolled her into the ambulance, jumped inside, and slammed the doors. Slattery watched helplessly as the vehicle sped off into the night.

"Where is he, Sam?" Slattery demanded. "Why the hell did he go back in there?"

Fowler shook his head again and turned back to face the burning building.

"Agent Slattery?" The tinny voice came from his walkie-talkie.

"This is Slattery," he said into the mouthpiece.

"Captain Morales. Alameda Fire Department. I think we've found your man. Around back."

Slattery and Fowler glanced at each other and took off in a run.

* * *

The smoke was impenetrable and Braxton's eyes were teared so heavily it was like looking through a fishbowl. He felt his way up the stairway to the second floor. Parts of the roof had already collapsed and streams of frigid water fell from the night sky. When they hit the red-hot metal of the railings, geysers of steam shot in all directions. The scene was like something out of Dante.

He ripped off the sweater Walker had given him and stuck it under one of the waterfalls. After wringing it out, he wrapped it over his mouth and nose and gingerly stepped into the upstairs hallway.

Following the metal skeleton that was all that was left of the interior walls, Braxton made it down to the first turn in the corridor. He took a step around the corner, but pulled back when his shoe disappeared into the floor. A burst of flame erupted from where his foot had been, throwing him back from a now-gaping hole that opened into the depths.

He backtracked to the stairway and took the hall in the other direction, hoping there was still a solid passage to the cafeteria. He heard shouts from outside, and prayed that Walker had found someone to tend to her wounds.

As far as he could tell, there was still no one else inside the building. The fire crews knew better than to be running through a burning building. What was wrong with him? Going through this place was like navigating a gauntlet of death. If he didn't get out soon, all that would be left would be a pile of ashes.

The next turn was still passable and he continued on his circle. Three scorching corridors and one dead end later, he found himself back in the room with Venton.

The body of the entrepreneur still swung from the water pipe. Braxton reached up and pulled the drive from Venton's pocket.

It had taken only a second to get the stick. But did he still have time to escape? He couldn't go back to the stairway again. The hallways would be impassable.

He felt the heat of the fire flowing through the blown-out windows. Out to the cool night air. Did he dare try to escape that way?

It was only the second floor. And it *was* the only way out.

He yanked his sweater back over his head, pulled his hands into the sleeves, and knocked out the remaining glass. Then he grabbed the frame and crawled over the edge.

Somewhere below him was the ground and safety. The only way to get there was one step at a time. Anything else was suicide.

He dug the soles of his shoes into the joints between the bricks. Still clinging to the frame with his right hand, he reached down with his left to get another handhold. He grabbed a brick face, released his right, and repeated the movement.

With both hands clutching the rough surfaces, he slipped his feet down. A few seconds of searching and they caught. He carefully shifted his weight off his hands. The footholds were solid.

As he again reached down, he heard a loud "Crack" and looked up. The frame of the window suddenly broke free and fell toward him. He ducked his head, pressing his body as close to the wall as he could, but a corner of the heavy metal skeleton struck his shoulder. The impact broke his handholds and he tumbled backwards. He realized it was his end, but perhaps the disk in his pocket could still save Goddard and the others.

He hit the ground with a crushing thud, but it gave way under him, like when he was ten and had broken his bed playing Superman. When he finally stopped falling, he opened his eyes, but instead of his mother he saw a circle of charcoal-streaked faces. They were holding a strangely colored canvas quilt.

"I've got it," he cried as the darkness closed in. "I've got it."

Epilogue

Central Intelligence Agency, Langley, Virginia
Monday, one week later, 5:00 p.m.

"IN CONCLUSION, LET me assure you all that this administration stands ready to protect American citizens anywhere in the world, and we will never cease our pursuit of those who would attempt to usurp our hard won freedoms.

"And on a more personal note, I must regretfully report that I have accepted the resignation of Director of National Intelligence General Steven Carlson. He has decided to return to his home state of Colorado to attend to personal matters. General Carlson has served this country gallantly for over thirty-five years. I know I join all Americans in thanking him for his many contributions and wishing him well in the future."

Slattery flicked off the remote control and tossed it on his desk.

"I can't take any more of that crap about Carlson," he said to Ikedo. "But Matthews looks pretty good already, don't you think?"

"The President sure as hell knows how to deliver a speech," Ikedo replied. "I can't say I agree with everything Matthews has done, but he sure can rally the troops when he wants to."

"That's the first requirement for a politician. If he can't get the people moving, he isn't worth a damn."

"All that flowery rhetoric about justice, though. Where's the justice for what Robinson did? He's back at his old job, playing the same old games. What the hell will he do next?"

"I doubt any of them care, Manny. By decoding Lawson's disk, he saved the lives of a lot of very important people. He cut a deal, that's all. It happens all the time. You know that. But I bet internal security will keep him on a very short leash."

"Not short enough for me. I'd rather that leash was a noose. But I don't guess anyone asked my opinion did they? Anything new on Singer?"

"We're still getting leads. Mary Ellen is coordinating the domestic search. Interpol reported a possible sighting in Madrid. Complete with a cast on his right hand. But it dried up."

"If he's in Europe, Interpol should be able to find him. They've got agents all over the continent."

Slattery thought back to his days at the Farm with Singer. He knew the man would not be heard from again. Until the next assignment. "Let's hope so, Manny."

"Yeah. But hey, I hear congratulations are in order. New head of the Agency's Counter-Terrorism Center. It sounds like a real plum."

"Just another example of how no good deed goes unpunished. McLaine retired and I got the bullet. Look at these files." He swung his arm over stacks of folders covering his desk. "Beth can't believe I accepted it. Can I twist your arm to help me out again?"

Ikedo suddenly dropped his head and began shifting from one side to the other. Slattery knew something bad was about to happen.

"I'd really like to, Roger, but I applied for a new slot that just opened up. Special Liaison Agent to the FBI Counterterrorism Division. I thought it would look good on my resume to get some experience outside the Agency. Do you think I've got a chance for it?"

Slattery leaned back in his chair, propped his feet on the top of his desk, and clasped his hands behind his head. A huge grin lit up the normally somber face.

"A *chance*, Manny? I doubt you have anything to worry about."

*   *   *

On the opposite coast, another group was also watching the President address the nation.

"Well, you did it, Adam," Fowler said, setting the TV remote onto the bedside table. "I never thought you were gonna get out of that inferno."

Braxton lay back in the hospital bed, his arms and legs still bandaged from serious, but not life-threatening, first degree burns.

"There were moments I had some doubts myself, Sam. It sure was good to see your ugly face."

"He was like an angel," Walker added, giving the huge black man a big hug. "I didn't know where I was, and *you* had left me," she continued, looking back to the bed, "when this noble warrior came out of the night, took me in his arms, and led me to safety."

"Why gosh, ma'am," Fowler said with a wide grin. "Just save that speech for my wife, Sydney. I'll need the help when I finally get home. She wasn't all that thrilled when I took off in the middle of the night."

"I'd be happy to," Walker replied, "but I may need some help myself. I was already in the doghouse at DIA and this excursion to the West Coast really pissed them off. I think there's about to be a dramatic change in my military status."

"Did Wheeler say anything about your job?" Braxton asked.

The mysterious Mr. Wheeler from the Justice Department had appeared five days before, looking exactly as he had that horrific night last year at FBI Headquarters, and secured signatures from all three of them on a new National Security Confidentiality Agreement. He had saved his best threats for Braxton, but his diatribe had been cut short when the duty nurse ejected him from the hospital room after Braxton's heart rate monitor had exploded.

"Not very much. Just that I need to report to the Pentagon as soon as I'm released from the hospital. I've been milking my stay here about as long as I can."

Braxton pushed himself a little higher in the bed. "Let me give you a piece of advice, Sydney. You have knowledge a lot of people will never want to see the light of day. Things your bosses don't even know. Trust me, this is something you can use."

Walker's jaw dropped.

"Nicely, of course," Braxton added.

"Of course," Walker finally responded.

"Speaking of secrets," Braxton continued, "NSA must have cracked the formula on Lawson's zip drive. It's only been seven days and the President looked nearly normal."

"Seems so," Fowler answered. "I tried to get details out of Roger, but he hasn't been very talkative about what happened. I did hear there were problems decoding it."

"Nothing we'll ever find out about, I'm sure," Walker said. "I've been meaning to ask, Adam, is your friend Susan okay?"

Braxton shared a knowing glance with Fowler. His face flushed despite the innocence of the question.

"Susan? Yes, she's fine, thank you. A DoD doc came by and gave her the antibiotic three days ago. She sounds pretty good."

Walker smiled at him. Her forehead sported an olive drab Band-Aid, and her left hand was bandaged from minor burns, but she still looked incredibly attractive.

"You should be very proud, Adam," she said. "You found Megan's killer, and you saved all those people, including Susan. It was very brave."

"*We* did that, Sydney. I needed you and you were there."

Braxton shifted in the starchy bed, trying to find a position that didn't make his itching worse. *Why are hospital beds so damned uncomfortable?*

"Is anything wrong?" Walker asked. "Can I get you something?"

"Can you pull some strings and get me out of here? I need to get back to work. And I've had enough of doctors and hospitals for a lifetime."

* * *

They had gathered in a small coffee shop on Ludwig Strasse just outside of Darmstadt. The air was sharp and cool. A perfect background for their important discussion.

"Is good to see you again, Wilhelm," the striking blond woman said. "How is Frankfurt?"

"Worsening every day, Ingrid," replied a tall, muscular man. "Our unions have become lackeys of the new industrialists. They are destroying our Socialist State. The rights we have worked so hard to earn."

"It is the same in Kassel," Ingrid continued, sipping her *latte*. "No one remembers. They think only of their own jobs. The layoffs continue. As if we were replaceable American workers."

"Our own politicians turn their backs on us," Wilhelm added. "They give in to the French and the Spanish. Can you imagine? When have *they* ever helped us? Now this abominable Union and its false currency. What will become of us?"

"These are difficult times," a smaller, blue-eyed man said. "The people of Wiesbaden are very anxious also."

"It is those from the Middle East, Hermann," replied Wilhelm. "They come in waves. Taking our jobs, turning their backs on those of us that have built our country."

"Yes," agreed Ingrid. "They see our success. But we cannot support the world's misfits."

"But what is there to do?" Hermann asked, a bandaged hand lifting his cup.

"I don't know," replied Wilhelm. "But we must respond. The other students are ready. It is only for the right leader that they look."

"And that is you, Willy," Ingrid said. "They all know your commitment."

"As do we," Hermann added. "Perhaps I could check with some of my friends. They might have some ideas. Be able to help."

"You would do that for us?"

"Of course, Ingrid. I would see that as my contribution to the cause."

"The Cause," Wilhelm repeated. "Yes, around this name we will grow strong."

It was Hesse, and he was Hermann.

Thank you for reading *The Liberty Covenant*.
I hope you enjoyed it.

I'd really appreciate it if you would take a minute to add a review on Amazon. Referrals and reviews are the only ways for a self-published author to build a readership and compete with the big names. You can leave your review at the bottom of *The Liberty Covenant* sales page.

Get A Free Book!
Building a relationship with readers is one of the best parts of being a writer. My newsletter keeps you informed of new releases and updates to the Adam Braxton universe. And by signing up, you get *The Capital Gambit*, an exclusive prequel novella, that gives an early look at many of the characters you've come to know.

Just visit my web site at www.JackBowie.com, sign up and grab your book. And send any comments to jack@JackBowie.com.
I look forward to having you a part of my team!

Finally, if you haven't done so, check out the other Adam Braxton Thrillers:

The Saracen Incident

The Langley Profile

The Jason Betrayal

Now keep reading for an excerpt from the next Adam Braxton adventure

The Langley Profile

Chapter 1

Samar, Israel
Monday, 9:00 a.m.

TERRY JAMES DIDN'T realize today would make him famous. So far as he knew, it was just another day standing behind his video camera trying to make his subject look intelligent and not screw up.

"This is truly a historic moment for the Middle East," gushed the freshly scrubbed and painted reporter. "A moment that uniquely defines the new sense of peace and humanity in the region. Here, deep in the Negev Desert, Crown Prince Faisal of Saudi Arabia is visiting a newly remodeled school serving the education needs of a small Israeli kibbutz just thirty kilometers north of the Saudi border. The excitement of the visit is clearly visible on the faces of the dedicated teachers and their students. The visit of the Crown Prince to this unique educational facility is a sign of true progress for all nations in this long-struggling part of the globe. For World News Today, this is Caren Rodriguez from Samar, Israel."

The red light on the camera blinked off and Rodriguez dashed to the protection of their mobile van. "Christ, it's hot," she exclaimed as she threw open the door. "You'd think they'd pick friggin' better weather for these damn events." She disappeared into the air-conditioned interior.

James nodded supportively, fearing any lesser response would spawn another tirade by his new talking head. Rodriguez was attractive, of course; tall and slim with just enough chest and hips to make her a woman and not a child. Her shiny blond hair normally hung lightly around her shoulders, but with the heat, wind and blowing sand, she had taken her cameraman's recommendation to tie it back in a small bun. Her dark brown eyes and high cheekbones made his shot angles easy. She was a natural beauty and even had a few real news instincts.

But her mouth was as dirty as any he had ever heard and her temper was as hot as the chili from her home state of Texas. A prep school and Ivy League background didn't add to her humility. She was as spoiled as they came and didn't care who knew it.

The network had balked at springing for airfare to Eilat, a popular resort just half an hour to the south at the tip of the Red Sea, so he had had to endure a four hour drive through the desert from Tel Aviv. Rodriguez had done nothing the whole trip but rave on about herself in her inane Southern drawl. It was all he could do to keep from smashing her face into the dashboard.

James had managed to get along with some of the best, and the worst, reporters on the planet, but after only three weeks with Rodriguez he didn't know how much longer he could stand it.

Oh well, there's always work in video documentaries.

Surprisingly, the scene just across the tightly cordoned area of the football—well, they called it football—field *was* a historic moment. Crown Prince Faisal of Saudi Arabia was taking his message of peace and coexistence directly to the Israeli people, today in the form of a visit to an obscure Israeli kibbutz.

Samar was a small village, less than 300 inhabitants, most of whom were staunchly anti-Arab. But as he had in previous visits, the sincerity and charisma of the Crown Prince were having their effect. Already, he had been deemed the Bill Clinton of the Middle East; in his case for the former US President's personality and popularity, not his all too memorable peccadilloes. It was for the world-wide inquisitiveness of all things surrounding this new actor on the political stage, that Rodriguez had been given the assignment to cover his latest "trip of peace."

James hoped it wouldn't kill him.

* * *

Rachael Weitz gathered her students in a half-circle and waited for the arrival of the Saudi. A horde of reporters and photographers thankfully stood behind barriers about twenty meters away, chattering and clicking away. Weitz wasn't all that happy about participating in what was at best a self-aggrandizing photo op for the Crown Prince, but she had received a pleading request from Jerusalem to support the visit.

The Crown Prince, and three others, had just been announced as winners of the Nobel Peace Prize for their ground-breaking Anti-terrorism Treaty, further boosting the importance of the event. So here she was, standing in the burning sun trying to look grateful at having her well-planned class schedule completely disrupted.

Most of her students had been indifferent to the chaos of the arrangements around the event but there was one bright spot. Noam Geer was a pathetically shy boy of eleven who had moved into the area from America just a few weeks before. He and his father had decided to start a new life following the death of Geer's mother. Both were having difficulty adapting to the frontier-like lifestyle in Samar.

Geer's one love seemed to be football, which he continued to call soccer. He carried a battered ball, probably from his home in the States, stuffed into his knapsack everywhere he went. When he had heard that Faisal had been on the Saudi national soccer team in his youth, Geer had been ecstatic. Weitz had made sure he was up-front in the greeting party.

The armored Range Rover drove up the gravel road and stopped at the assigned location. Four beefy security guards jumped from the vehicle and quickly surveyed the area. Apparently not seeing any hooded militants with ammo belts and machine guns, they opened the back door and Faisal emerged in a burst of blinding white robes trimmed in gold. He was a tall and handsome man, with swarthy skin and an ebony-black beard. Weitz could almost understand the tabloids' obsession with the man.

Following the requisite introductions and flowery remarks, the Crown Prince actually made an effort to speak to the children. He shook their hands, asked their names and answered their questions. As he approached Geer, the child absolutely beamed.

"You're a famous soccer star!" Geer exclaimed.

"Hardly a star," Faisal responded with a smile. "But I did have a pretty good corner kick."

"Show me. Please!" Geer begged. "Please."

"Noam," Weitz said, putting her hands on Geer's shoulders. "The Crown Prince doesn't have time to ..."

Faisal looked around at his handlers. "But I don't see a ball anywhere," he finally replied.

"I have one," Geer shouted. He dropped his knapsack, extracted his precious football, and ran down the field.

After he had gotten about twenty meters away, he turned back and gave the ball a mighty roll toward the celebrity.

* * *

"There!" Rodriguez suddenly yelled through the window of the van. "The Crown Prince. Get that shot for background!"

James woke from his musings and grabbed his camera. Rodriguez must have been watching the proceedings from the van. In what he would later describe as the longest ten seconds of his life, he jammed the viewfinder up to his eye and scanned the field for his subject. Locating Faisal, he then zoomed in and pressed RECORD, just in time to capture the Crown Prince lining up on the rolling ball, cocking his left leg, bringing it quickly forward to its target, then disappearing in a pink cloud of smoke, sand, and shrapnel. His finger stayed frozen on the button until the explosion's percussion knocked him rudely to the gravel of the access road.

The Pulitzer Prize committee would later comment that James' footage captured the personal horror of the new face of terrorism in the same way Eddie Adams' photograph of Vietnamese General Nguyễn Ngọc Loan executing a handcuffed prisoner personified the obscenity of that war.

In the chaos following the assassination, Noam Geer, and his father, disappeared and were never located.

Chapter 2

CIA Headquarters, Langley, Virginia
Monday, 9:30 a.m.

"YES, SIR. WE will definitely prepare that ASAP."

It took all of Roger Slattery's estimable self-control to quietly place the handset in its cradle instead of smashing it down in an explosion of wire and plastic.

Slattery was a CIA lifer who had moved from field agent to division manager to his latest position: head of the CIA's Counterterrorism Center. On this journey, he had butted heads with some pretty intransigent individuals, on both sides of the black world, but the latest Director of National Intelligence was quickly rising to a unique position on Slattery's enemies list.

Morgan Dean had been in the position for over a year, taking over when the previous DNI had left under less-than-ideal circumstances. Circumstances all too familiar to Slattery.

Dean was ex-Army and ex-NSA; two black marks in Slattery's experience. Slattery had never liked Steven Carlson, the previous DNI. He had been an autocratic sonuvabitch—in other words, a typical Marine—but Slattery had never imagined the replacement could be even worse.

The current royal edict was around the CIA's report on the assassination of Crown Prince Faisal. Dean asked, or rather demanded, that Slattery prepare a comprehensive report, for Dean's eyes only, before the end of the day. Never mind that the assassination only occurred earlier that day, in Israel, under the eye of the Saudi's version of the Secret Service. Dean wanted a complete accounting of the possible assassins and an analysis of how the murder would affect the Anti-terrorism Treaty. Dean seemed more concerned about the political fallout of the death and how it affected the President than the death of the Crown Prince.

President Joseph Matthews had spent the last year personally negotiating a comprehensive treaty to eliminate, or more realistically,

significantly reduce, the funding of terrorist organizations by Iran, Iraq
and Saudi Arabia. While the threat of the jihadists was diminishing,
military action continued to be of marginal impact and very costly in
terms of political capital. Matthews' thinking was that the only way to
achieve a long-term solution was to cut off the extremists' funding
from the established Muslim states. It had taken nine months, but in
the stifling humidity of Riyadh in July, the treaty had been signed
much to the consternation of terrorists around the world.

Then last week, the Oslo Nobel Committee had named the four
as winners of the Nobel Peace Prize.

And now one of the signers, arguably the most prominent
individual in the Muslim world, was dead.

What the hell is going to happen next?

Slattery dropped his head in his hands and rubbed his throbbing
temples with his thumbs. It had already been a helluva day.

He had been awakened by an explosion of text messages at 3:15
AM. After a quick look, he got up and dressed. He padded back
over to the bed and, before leaving, kissed his wife on her forehead.
Beth opened one eye, mouthed a silent "Be careful" and promptly
went back to sleep. When they were first married, she would have
bolted upright, fully awake. It hadn't taken her long to adjust to her
husband's unorthodox schedule.

Back in Langley, Slattery had spoken with his Mossad
counterpart, Ziv Bloom, at the break of dawn. As was to be
expected, Bloom was enraged over the assassination in his country
and was scrambling to get his report completed for the Prime
Minister. As far as hard intelligence was concerned, his cupboard
was bare. Mossad had not a clue which of the Middle East actors
could be responsible. The circumstances were outlandish even for
the jihadists. The possibility of an unknown actor was even more
frightening, but Bloom had had no better explanation.

That left Slattery on his own to compose an explanation, based
completely on conjecture, that would keep Dean off his back until
they had real data.

He raised his head and noticed the digital clocks lined on the
opposite wall. Washington, London, Paris, Berlin, Riyadh, Tel Aviv,
Moscow, Tehran, Beijing, Pyongyang, Tokyo. The number of clocks
was a frightening reminder of the state of the world. Maybe he was
getting too old for all this.

As he stared blankly at the glowing numbers, their meaning suddenly broke through his daydream.

Shit! He was already late.

Slattery grabbed his coat and briefcase and headed for the elevators. He had to get to Fairfax for his *other* top priority task.

On his way out, he stopped at the desk of his new administrative assistant, Cassandra Lewis. As always, she was busy doing something on her computer.

Lewis was a pretty, fresh-scrubbed twenty-something who had rapidly worked her way up the CIA's admin ladder by her outstanding technical competence. She supposedly knew every desktop app ever developed and her ability to navigate through the CIA's maze of record systems and databases was said to be unique in the Agency. All skills that he was sure explained her placement outside his door.

The problem was her disposition. For all her abilities, she was acutely shy and seemingly insecure. She needed constant reinforcement. Skills that were not in Slattery's psychological profile. He couldn't believe she was happy in this job. It would be a race to see which of them surrendered first.

"Cassie."

She looked up from her screen. "Yes, sir?"

Slattery shook his head. None of his other admins had ever called him 'sir'." He *was* getting old.

"Tell John and Lee I need everything they have on the assassination and the House of Saud." John Carter and Lee Reaves were Slattery's lead analysts on Middle East affairs. He'd need their help if he was ever going to satisfy the DNI. "I'll be gone a couple hours. Set up a review for when I get back." He turned, but then paused and looked back. "And tell them to cancel any plans for this evening."

* * *

Colonel Henry Rockwell, U.S. Army Retired, stood at attention and stared into the cloud-draped mountains outside his office window. His silver hair was cropped close, as it had been for nearly four decades, and his gray eyes burned with the same vigor they had throughout his service to his country. Perhaps there were a few more wrinkles, and he could no longer run seven-minute miles, but he could still recognize his duty and still had the strength to execute it.

The mists of the mountains reminded him of the difficulties they had encountered making themselves known in the shadow world. You could never be sure whether the jagged peak you so carefully approached was a valuable contact, or a chimera ready to send you down a deadly fissure. He had run through every name in his address book, called in more favors than he could afford, and spent nearly all his savings, to get to this point.

Over the past year, he had secured a few minor contracts, more tests than real sanctions, but his team had performed well, satisfying his employers. Those successes had led to the current assignment: a contract that would place him at the top of the world's contract military organizations. Something that had long been his objective.

And something that would finally put his doubters to rest.

A knock broke his concentration. He reluctantly turned away from the vista and strode slowly back to his desk. Rockwell wore his standard daytime work clothes, a sharply pressed set of fatigues, carefully tailored to his five-foot-eight-inch frame. His shoulders were locked, square and broad, a characteristic that led colleagues to refer to him, at least behind his back, as Ramrod Rockwell. He sat down in his hard wooden chair, straightened the papers that were already precisely placed on the top of his desk and barked a curt "Enter."

The door to the study opened and a slim, haggard man entered the room. He was about six feet tall with dark brown hair slicked back over his head. He silently moved to a position directly in front of the desk.

William Penrose was easily underestimated, a persona he cultivated, but he was an ex-SEAL and Rockwell had seen him dispatch men twice his size with apparent ease. His nose had been broken so many times it looked like a Rocky Mountain switchback trail and sunken brown eyes exuded a simmering intensity. Smart, and not one who took prisoners, he was the perfect aide-de-camp.

"Excuse me, Colonel," Penrose began, "we have some preliminary information from Berlin."

"Continue, William," Rockwell replied quickly. He required the use of his rank but given the diverse backgrounds of his men, other military protocols were not observed.

"We have received approval to proceed, sir. The message was just decoded."

"Excellent. This is a significant milestone. Please inform the men. Everyone will receive a bonus for their contributions. Has the squad returned?"

"They are still in transit, sir. Extraction from Israel proved more difficult than we expected. Mossad reacted quite quickly."

Rockwell nodded. "Understood. As long as they are on their way. Have them report to me as soon as they arrive."

"Yes, sir."

"How are preparations for the next phase?"

"Going very well. We received the package from Germany and training is nearly complete."

Rockwell felt the satisfying surge of adrenaline. His right hand, resting lightly on the tabletop, slowly curled into a white-knuckled fist. It was time to show the world what he could accomplish.

"Gather the squad, William. Let's be sure we don't eliminate the wrong person."

* * *

Adam Braxton looked up from his laptop and gazed over the Northern Virginia countryside. He had heard the stories of the lush green pastures and the dark emerald forests of years before. He knew some of that still existed, but it was far beyond the black macadam of the access highway and Dulles airport. Now his window was filled with soaring concrete and glass office buildings and rows of picture-perfect condominiums, all housing those that ostensibly did the people's work: government employees, lobbyists and the never-ending line of consultants ready to tell anyone who will listen how to do their job.

What had been bothering him most lately was that *he* was one of those consultants. Cerberus Consulting, his company, was a boutique consulting firm specializing in Internet security. Over the past two years, he had built a solid reputation among clients in both the public and private sectors.

By all accountings, he was doing pretty well. He had a strong backlog of business. More, in fact, than he could handle. He probably should bring on some technical help, but that would mean supervision and management. Skills that he had learned were not part of his genetic makeup. So for the moment, he would go it alone.

But he felt restless. Every day seemed to be filled with writing the same reports and making the same recommendations. His father had taught him to be a problem solver. To figure things out. That's what he liked to do. Maybe that was just a child's dream.

Still, he hadn't been lied to, arrested, or shot at for over a year. That was a plus.

"Adam?"

Karen Chu's mellow voice came through the intercom and broke him out of his funk. Chu was Cerberus' first, and currently only, employee. She was, in fact, also one of the main reasons his company was still in business.

Braxton had hired Chu a month after he had abandoned Cambridge, Massachusetts and hung out his new shingle in Reston, Virginia. She had been a sharp-tongued, Gen X wife and mother who had burned out teaching math in the Fairfax County school system and had wanted to apply her considerable analytic abilities to a new profession. Chu had attacked the mess he had created like a commando, organizing every client engagement, and putting him on a strict need-to-know basis. She had learned more about the federal contracting system than any senior executive Braxton had ever known. She had been invaluable in stabilizing, and growing, his nascent security consulting business.

He had to find some way to tell her how much she was appreciated.

"Yes, Karen?" he answered into the box.

"Mr. Smith is here to see you."

Braxton paused and glanced down at his appointment card. Every morning, he found an index card on his desk, printed with his day's schedule. Sure it was a throwback to simpler days, but there was something emotionally satisfying about this simple piece of pre-computer technology.

But today's card had no entry for a Mr. Smith.

"I don't see any appointment for a Mr. Smith, Karen. What does he ..."

"It's *that* Mr. Smith," Chu replied quickly.

What kind of an answer is that? Who is she talking about?

Oh. *Him.* It had been over a year since Braxton had had any contact with his least favorite CIA agent. Roger Slattery, at least that was the name by which Braxton knew him, had single-handedly brought Braxton more problems than he could have ever imagined. And then each time brought him back from the edge of oblivion.

Maybe that's what spooks do to civilians.

He felt his heart beat a little faster. Was it fear? Or anticipation? "Show him in, Karen."

"Are you sure, Adam?"

"Yes. It's okay. I'll be careful." *Did he really believe those words?*

Mr. Smith strode into the office and offered his hand. "Adam," he said with a friendly smile.

He looked exactly as he had when Braxton had last seen him over a year ago. Heavyset, but solid, with short gray hair and gold-rimmed aviator glasses. A face that hid more stories than Braxton could imagine. He looked like a soldier forced into a business suit that he didn't want.

"Well, I certainly didn't expect to see you, Mr. Slattery," Braxton said taking his hand. "You can imagine my excitement."

"Good to see you again," Slattery replied, ignoring the barb. "I was in the area and wanted to stop by."

"Of course you were." Braxton pointed to the chair opposite his desk. "I understand congratulations are in order."

After helping to solve the Liberty Covenant conspiracy last year, Slattery had been named chief of the CIA's Counterterrorism Center. Hardly a public appointment, Braxton had heard the news from his DoD contacts.

"Thank you. I should have known you would find out. I guess no good deed goes unpunished."

Braxton nodded politely and waited. He wasn't going to make the agent's objective, whatever it was, any easier.

"Well, I guess I should get to the point," Slattery finally said. "I'd like you to do some work for us."

Braxton's heart stopped. He grabbed the edge of his desk for stability and tried to keep his breathing steady, but a tell-tale bead of sweat trickled past his temple.

"Actually, it's not for the Agency directly," Slattery continued. "You're familiar with In-Q-Tel?"

Braxton's forehead wrinkled as he tried to place the name. Then it clicked.

"The CIA's venture capital company right? You're involved?"

"Yes. In one of my weaker moments, I accepted a position on

their Board of Directors. Now I spend half my time reading investment proposals written by hotshots barely older than my son describing technologies I can't understand. It's great fun."

Slattery paused and Braxton honestly felt sorry for the spook. If there was one thing Braxton understood about him, it was that Slattery wasn't a man to sit back while events rushed past. Sitting at his desk reviewing piles of financial reports must be killing him.

"Anyway," Slattery continued without missing a beat, "we're interested in investing in a small company and need a security audit performed as part of our due diligence. I thought you might be interested."

"Why me? The CIA must have lots of contractors they can call on. To say nothing of internal resources."

"Of course. But this is an important opportunity. And honestly, I trust you. Everyone has their own agendas and I'd like this particular audit done right. Think of it as a favor for past assistance."

Braxton felt his face flush. He wanted to light into the spook, but arguing the point again wasn't going to accomplish anything. He took a deep breath instead.

"I'll let that comment pass, Slattery. I'm interested but can you tell me what kind of company I'd be dealing with? There's a rumor going around that the 'Q' in In-Q-Tel refers to James Bond's armorer. I'm not excited about working in a munitions factory."

Slattery smiled and shook his head. "Nothing like that. I can't give you a name without a non-disclosure, but it's a genetics company. Laboratory equipment and analysis software. And no one is making killer bugs this time. Still interested?"

"Sure. As long as you can pay my rates."

"Right. This is strict GSA, Adam. And don't give me any grief, I know you have a Schedule. I'll get a draft contract over this afternoon. Give it a look and get back to me. As soon as you can. We're under a bit of a tight schedule."

"Uh, sure. I can review it tonight," Braxton said.

Slattery abruptly rose and extended his hand. "Great. I really do appreciate this, Adam."

They shook hands and Slattery headed for the door.

Then he stopped and turned back. "One more thing, Adam. The company's in Boston. I thought that might pique your interest."

As the spook disappeared into the outer office, Braxton dropped back in his chair and let the spook's final comment sink in. Images flashed through his mind. Some pleasant, others not so. Boston. Dinners with Megan at their favorite restaurant in the North End. Running circuits over the Charles River bridges. And the boarded-up window in his Cambridge apartment after Paul had been murdered.

Do I have the courage to go back?

"You okay?" Chu asked appearing at the door to his office. "What did Mr. Smith want this time?"

"Nothing nefarious so far as I can tell. He wants me to do a security audit of a company."

Chu stood silently and crossed her arms over her slim body. "Are you sure you want to do that?" she finally asked.

"I think so. It's just a job this time. How much trouble could a security audit be?"

ACKNOWLEDGEMENTS

The Liberty Covenant is a work of fiction, but many of the themes are real: the militia movement in the U.S. is a major focus of the FBI, although these groups remain uncoordinated; the Clipper Chip was real, but the Gambit is my invention; *C. Pneumoniae* is an actual bacteria, only the described strain is fictional; and MIT does have a celebrated history of benign hacks, the Harvard-Yale escapade being one of the best known (you can see it live here: http://www.bostonmagazine.com/news/blog/2012/11/16/day-mit-crashed-harvard-yale/).

The story draws on the memories and experiences of many more individuals than I am able to name. My thanks to you all. Some names, facts and times have been changed to fit the storyline. All errors are mine.

Thanks to John Carter, from Vermont not Mars, for his support and high-tech insights.

Thanks to Annie Wertz for her assistance with understanding life at Yale.

A special thanks to Jim Arsenault, long-time friend and meticulous reviewer, for his spot-on comments and corrections to early drafts.

And finally, thanks to my wife Sharon, and daughters Lisa and Jennifer, for your continuing understanding and encouragement in my new journey as an author. I couldn't do it without you.

ABOUT THE AUTHOR

Jack Bowie was born and raised outside of Cleveland, Ohio, then headed to Cambridge, Massachusetts to attend MIT. After graduating, he held technical management positions in public and private sector organizations in Massachusetts, Virginia and Connecticut.

A lifelong reader of classic science fiction and espionage thrillers, Jack's writing began as a break from professional duties and grew into a passion for storytelling.

Drawing on his career as a researcher, engineer and high-tech executive, Jack's novels describe the subtle, and sometimes not so subtle, interplay of technology with personal passions and egos.

For more information on Jack, check out www.JackBowie.com, or follow him on Facebook at facebook.com/jackbowieauthor.

Made in the USA
Coppell, TX
03 April 2021

52918181R10263